IRRESISTIBLY
Undeniable

Published: Kinky Panda Publishing

Editing: Raw Book Editing

Cover Design & Formatting by Parajunkee Design

Zoey@ZoeyDerrick.com

The following is a work of fiction, events that transpire may be similar in nature to real life situation, but are portrayed fictionally here. Research has been conducted however, what you read here may not be entirely accurate.

ISBN-13: 978-0996896665

:: created in the USA :::

IRRESISTIBLY
Undeniable

ZOEY DERRICK

For All Those Who Believe In Second Chances.
And For Emily - without you - I'd still be in a funk.

OTHER BOOKS
BY ZOEY DERRICK

"IRRESISTIBLY UNDENIABLE IS truly undeniably irresistible. Dyson and Ireland broke my heart then put it back together again. Zoey Derrick definitely knows how to write a sweet, suspenseful, and sexy second chance love story that will have you laughing out loud." - USA Today Bestselling Author Emily Minton

Prologue

I remember it like it was yesterday. March 31, 2006.

It's hard to forget something that happens right after your birthday. At barely fifteen, the only things that mattered to most girls was attracting the boy of their dreams, shopping and sleep overs.

To me, what mattered most was the boy. But he wasn't just a boy. He was older than me by two years, a junior, the star football player, and my brother's best friend.

He was everything to me; the reason I got up in the morning, the thing I thought about when I went to bed at night. It was always him.

From the moment he stepped inside our little school, I knew he would be everything to me one day. Over the years, we didn't grow apart, no, we grew closer. My brother became his best friend and there was hardly a day that went by that I didn't see him, usually at my house playing with Dusty.

As I got a little older, my feelings for him grew and morphed into something different, something unexpected and something…more.

I remember how our relationship changed, but I also remember how he changed too.

When he wasn't spending time with my brother and me, he would spend it with some random girl I usually didn't know. I remember Dusty would get butt hurt because his friend would ditch him for whatever girl he was wasting his time with.

I paid attention, listening closely to Dusty's ramblings about how his best friend ditched him, but it quickly became apparent that his best friend wasn't seeing just one girl, no, he had an entire harem of them. One day or week it would be one chick, then it would be Dusty, then it would be another chick, then another and another.

The summer before my freshman year that all changed. He seemed to ditch the girls in favor of my brother and they hung out all the time, which of course, meant I was around too.

I'll never forget the day he was here, playing video games with my

brother and he was getting bored. He'd said to my brother, "Let's get out of here." I was disappointed.

I had always sat on the couch, usually pretending to read, secretly watching him. Hoping to catch a glimpse of the smile I loved or his gorgeous violet eyes. I didn't want them to leave. It had disappointed me enough that I remember fighting back tears. I don't know why, but I'd come to expect him to be here every day, and on the rare day that he wasn't, it was awful.

They'd turned off their video game and gotten up to leave.

Then the smile had come.

He had stared down at me over my book and I had looked up at him through my eyelashes. He had the most beautiful smile on his face. God, my heart had stopped in my chest. His violet eyes had sparkled in the sunlight coming through the window and I had quit breathing.

"You coming, VeeVee?"

I was so shocked that he had asked me that I sat there gaping at him like a fish. He raised an eyebrow at me; it was quite possibly the cutest thing I'd ever seen.

My brother had tried to argue with him and I remember him saying something about it not being fair to leave me alone in the house. In that moment, I felt protected, cared for even, and it made me smile.

That day started it all.

That was the day Dyson C. Richards noticed me.

That was eight months before he'd shatter my heart into a million tiny pieces.

It's become abundantly clear that I need to let this go.

That day, the day he noticed me, was four years ago today.

It was the beginning of what would become the 'summer of my life'. The only summer, really.

Being fifteen, I didn't know what I had, not until eight months later when he said all the right things, had all the right moves, and I caved.

It was the night of March 31st.

I had been barely fifteen and not in the frame of mind to make this kind of decision, but I couldn't help myself.

Despite my innocence, even I knew that Dyson was sex on legs. The girls knew it, I knew it. But Dyson and I had something special, something more than anything he'd had with any of the other girls I'd seen him with. I was the only girl, besides his mother, who had been in his life for more than five and half seconds.

I was special.

So was my innocence.

Only I didn't know it at the time.

I handed it to him without a care in the world. Desperate to feel him, and be that close to him for reasons I didn't understand at the time.

I will never forget the look in his eyes when he slid inside me the first time. His violet eyes had seemed to grow darker and his gaze had burrowed straight into my soul.

I was scared as hell, sweat had glistened over my skin, shivers from the coldness of the air and the desire I was feeling for the boy above me had racked my frame.

It had felt amazing.

It was everything to me.

I watched our relationship shift and morph in his eyes. I could feel it; every ounce of what I felt for him was poured back at me.

Then it was gone.

Shattered into jagged pieces that I would be forced to walk on for the next four years.

He left that barn after saying some devastating things to me and I had tried to tell myself it was because we'd connected, I knew it, and he knew

it.

I didn't know what I was going to say to him the next day. Talking to Dyson was nearly impossible to do because he always managed to muddle my brain. He'd had an uncanny ability to make my mind go blank. But I was determined.

I had marched the three blocks to his house. My determination was only sidetracked by the fear of what I would find when I got there. Both emotions rolled through me like waves in the ocean, bringing with it a fight or flight decision.

As I drew closer to his house, something wasn't right. Something wasn't- my heart dropped to my toes as it hit me. Everything that I'd noticed and dismissed in the couple weeks leading up to this came crashing down on me. His absence from school and my house. Dusty's piss poor attitude about everything, and even the way my mom behaved, but no one had bothered to tell me. The house had stood there empty.

For the second time in less than twenty-four hours, my already broken heart was crushed.

He was gone.

He didn't say good-bye.

He never even told me he was leaving.

Happy fucking April Fools' to me.

I've held on to this for way too long. Four years too long.

I'm back, standing in front of the house that held so much promise that April morning. I was going to tell him everything, but I never got the chance.

I never got to give him a piece of my mind and most importantly, I never got to say good-bye.

I never told anyone what happened in the barn that night.

I went through it all, all the stages of grief. First, denial. I was convinced he would show up at school. That he'd just moved across town, that he wasn't gone. After about four days of him not showing up, I got angry as hell. That was the longest phase. I was mad at my mother. She

was friends with his mom, how could she not tell me they were moving? I was furious with my brother. He'd argued that Dyson swore he was going to tell me himself, that's why he was here alone that day. I didn't believe him.

I had tried to convince my brother to let me talk to him, but he refused, denied even knowing where he was or how to reach him.

That's when the depression finally set in. I didn't eat hardly at all, I barely got through school, though my grades never slipped, and I guess I've been living in that depressed little bubble for the last four years.

I knew somewhere, deep down in my gut, that he would come back for me.

After Dusty graduated – Dyson had too – I thought maybe he'd show up back in Joplin, but he didn't. Dusty had made remarks the last couple of years about missing his friend or bitching that everyone in school seemed to have it out for Dyson. He'd rumble on about how it was unfair the way they were treating Dyson. Just because he'd moved away, people needed someone to blame, but I think most of the girls in our school just needed someone to hate. Dyson was a player, but every girl seemed to think they were in love with him. I was no different. Then the summer ended, Dusty went off to college in Chicago, leaving me to finish high school. Alone.

When I graduated from high school a month ago, I'd hoped he would show up, like Dusty did, and surprise me, but he didn't.

And now, I stand here in front of what was his house. Twirling the rock in my hand. Consumed with the memories of the man I loved, the man I desperately wanted to talk to, the man who would never come home again.

It was an acceptance I was unwilling to face, but I had no choice.

The rock in my hand grew heavier by the minute. It was the last thing connecting me to him. It was the sister to the rock I'd given him on his first day of school in Joplin.

"He's never coming back," I said through tears. "You don't know

where he is or what he's doing, but obviously, you aren't part of that plan." The pep talk I gave myself worked. The tears streamed down my face as my new reality washed over me and I threw the rock at his house. It pinged off the door. That rock was my heart that rock represented everything about the man I loved and it landed on the steps, where it would stay, forever.

Prologue Two

"She's dead," I say into the phone. It's taken me a week to be able to make this call. All the fucking red tape I've had to crawl through and I don't even know how this is going to go down with him. Either he's going to accept this or it's going to backfire in my face. Fuck that, it's going to backfire. I've been keeping something from my wife's best friend for far too long. She deserves better and I'll be god dammed if this is going to destroy her again like it did the last time.

"Who? You're going to have to be more specific here, man?"

"Lauren."

"What? How?" The shock in his voice surprises me, I hadn't expected that.

It takes me a moment to gather my wits before explaining further. "Drunk driver, it was an accident."

"Are we sure it wasn't something else?"

"Positive." I've read and re-read the police report and rehearsed my lines in my head so many fucking times I'm numb to any feeling regarding it. The weight I feel lifting off of my shoulders makes me grateful to finally pass the burden. Keeping this from my wife is fucking killing me. She knows something is up, but I keep having to pacify her with, "it's work related, can't disclose," but I tell her everything and this is becoming impossible anymore.

"Does she know?"

"Now *you're* going to have to be more specific. Does Lauren's daughter know that she's dead? Yes. Does Lauren's daughter know that her father is alive and well? No. She's about to turn twenty-five, but with the death of her mother; I've already had to send it. Given the circumstances, I don't see her reaching out to me anytime soon."

"And the other one?"

Good god, this is 2012 all over again. I shake my head. Fuck me. This is not going to go well at all. "How many more times am I going to have to do this?" I snap at the voice on the phone.

"None, this is it." For once he actually sounds sincere. Though I would know if there were more secrets because I'd be the keeper of the keys.

"Fuck, are you sure because I can't take it anymore and you're going to completely destroy her all over again. You realize this, right?"

The voice coming over the phone sounds pained. "They're telling me this is almost done, that I'll be able to come out of hiding soon."

"I fucking hope so because goddammit, I did not fucking sign up for this and you know it."

"I never expected you to have to clean up my dirty work. You already know that. And you've been well-compensated for doing so, have you not?"

"Sometimes money doesn't buy everything."

"But it can silence those who need it the most."

Then line goes dead and I close the burner phone. I'm not so sure the money is worth any of this. The headache alone is going to kill me. I pinch the bridge of my nose. The headache I prayed was going to go away when I had this conversation rages on.

Chapter One

IRELAND – AGE 24

Fight Song (Acoustic) - Rachel Platten

"Vy," I hear the gentle voice before the knock comes. The gentle rap of knuckles against my door makes me jump before the knob turns. "Vy, come on, you're gonna be late."

I don't acknowledge my slightly pushy, sometimes obnoxious roommate, Becca. I don't need to. She's going to barge her way inside no matter what I do. That's just who she is and that person is who I'm most thankful for this last week.

"What are you doing sitting in here?" she asks with genuine concern in her voice.

"I just need a minute." *To compose myself.* My voice is sad.

She sits down on the bed next to me before wrapping her arm around my shoulders, pulling me into her side. If I wasn't so worried about the three-hour job I just did on my make-up, I might have started to cry again. I managed to keep it in check while I was attempting to conceal the hollowness in my cheeks and eyes. I don't need to go ruining it now.

"I'm not trying to sound bitchy or pushy, but you've got to go. They're being overly generous with this when they don't have to be."

I sigh. She's right, like always. "I don't know if I can do this," I tell her, but I can't meet her eyes. I know what I will see there and I can't look at her and still hold it together.

"Now you *are* being ridiculous. It's only an interview," she says in a way that makes her sound like my mother. I want to cry.

"But it's *thee* interview," I retort. The nerves that I'd managed to tamp down when I came to sit on my bed come roaring back. My leg starts to bounce. A nervous habit I've had since I was a kid.

She laughs at me a little then says, "It is, and you're going to kick some major corporate big-wig balls. Now come on, let's get you freshened up and on your way." She stands, then grabs my hands and pulls me up. My sadness is too much for her happy-go-lucky self and she finds the right

words to kick me into action, only it's not the kind of action I needed to hear. "You know she'd kick your ass right now if she saw you like this."

Her voice is so matter of fact that I give her a humorless laugh. "Well, she can't, so…" The thought trails off and her eyes instantly water. "Don't, dammit, don't start," I scold, but it's too late. I feel the first wet, hot tear slide down my cheek.

Seven days ago, my world fell apart.

The one person who knew me better than I knew myself is gone.

Three days ago, I buried my mother.

I stand in front of the mirror in my bathroom, taking in my hollowed cheeks, my lifeless stare and the fiery red hair that surrounds my face in tight spiral curls. As if being blessed with naturally curly hair wasn't a curse by itself, the natural fire engine red color is enough to make a girl stand out in a crowd. I prefer to hold up the wall.

I did the best I could to hide my sadness behind a few layers of makeup, but it's really no use. I look like complete and total shit and I'm going to blow the one, well, technically second, chance I've got at my dream job.

I slowly close my eyes, pull in a deep, cleansing breath and silently count to ten. By the time I'm there, I'm ready to open my eyes again, but before I do, I turn, so I don't catch myself in the mirror. It works and I head out of the bathroom. I grab my bag off the hallway credenza and head straight for the front door. I don't stop to look for Becca. I've managed to compose myself, but if I see her red-rimmed, freshly cried out eyes, it's going to unravel me once more. I need to get out of here before I let that happen.

"Knock 'em dead, sista," Becca hollers as I walk out. Shutting the door behind me makes me feel like I'm locking myself out of my own little safe haven.

I walk the half a block to the train station. It's unseasonably warm

for an early February day in Phoenix, but I don't mind. I'm leaving with plenty of time to get downtown. This will give me plenty of time to cool off before my interview, plus compose myself enough to walk into the reception area of Wellington Ad Management for the second time. Most people would be glad to get a second interview and I truly wish that were the case here. Instead, it is my first official interview and unfortunately, my second impression on those who may or may not wish to hire me. Reese, a dear friend of mine, had informed me that last week was Wellington's last week of interviews, yet somehow they're making an exception for me. I can't help wondering if they're placating me because of what happened the last time I was there.

The train is packed, which is odd considering it's early afternoon and I'm heading downtown, not uptown. I manage to find a rear-facing seat in the first car, which is good, it will put me closer to my favorite coffee shop when I get off the train.

I went to school a few blocks away from one of Wellington's head offices. A company like Wellington belongs in New York, or Los Angeles, but instead it has made its home here in Phoenix. Ever since we had 'career day' at Arizona State University, I've wanted to work for Wellington Ad Management. Their client list is extensive and ever growing, which is exactly what I want in a career. If you can put Wellington Ad Management on your resume, you're doing something right. Not to mention the wide variety of advancement opportunities they have available. Needless to say, if I somehow manage to impress them enough to offer me a job, they could pay me a dollar per hour and I would still say yes.

I use the knowledge as fuel for my interview. I have nothing to lose because I have everything to gain.

During my college education, I had to spend time interning as part of my degree so I spent three summers working for Stauffer, Inc., which is another advertising company here in Phoenix. I loved working for them, despite their much smaller client base; it afforded me a great learning opportunity and a wonderful stepping stone into Wellington or any other company for that matter. Kerrigan, my old boss at Stauffer,

offered me a job in their midst, but I told her I had to try first for a job at Wellington. Thank god she was my friend, most people would have told me to take a hike after that. Not Kerrigan, she's known for years that working for Wellington is where my heart truly lies. Her respect for that is what got me last week's interview.

A shiver rocks through me at the memory of last Tuesday. Fighting the tears, I take another deep breath and focus my attention on some notes I'd made before last week's interview about Wellington, some of their clients – the publicly available ones – and the history of the company. I wanted to sound smart and well-researched without sounding pompous. I'm not sure I can do that anymore.

The train comes to a screeching halt as the overhead voice informs me that this is my stop. I quickly toss my notepad into my purse and stand up. I'm just a shade too soon and I get tossed back into my seat when I can't hold my balance. With embarrassment flooding my cheeks, I bashfully look around. Relief washes over me when I realize no one seems to be paying attention. Or if they are, they've hidden it well.

Now that I've gathered my composure, and the train has stopped completely, I stand up again, this time on more solid ground before hopping down the two steps to the floor of the train. I dart through the doors just as they start to close.

That was close.

Though the next stop isn't all that far down the road and I have some time, I don't have *that* much time.

I adjust my skirt, making sure I'm not flashing any bits that shouldn't be seen, and check my blouse, before I run a hand through my crazy curls and I pull the ear buds from my ears – tossing them into my bag for the ride home. Looking around and straightening up, I find my favorite Starbucks and head for the entrance.

Once inside, I order my comfort drink- white chocolate mocha, extra shot, with whip and extra hot. Despite the low ninety-degree temperature outside, I need the caffeine boost to get me through what's coming.

With my coffee cup in hand, my confidence starts to return.

Reminding myself that this is what I've been studying and preparing for over the last six years while pursuing my Master's degree in Business Administration & Marketing.

I need this job.

I need this distraction from the hollow shell my life has become.

Reaching the building, I look up. It's no New York City sky rise, but in Phoenix you can see it from most anywhere. I reach for the door with my free hand as someone exits. He's a dickwad and walks away without holding it open for me. "Jerkoff," I grumble under my breath and reach for the door again. *What the hell is it with banker types? They've got to be the biggest asshats on the planet.*

The building Wellington Ad Management is located in the same building as one of the big five banks. I had to double check the address last time to make sure I was in the right spot because when I step into the lobby, the bank's branding is everywhere.

I found the directory last time after some confusion. There is a security desk in the middle of the wide lower level, but they don't seem to do much other than watch the monitors. The directory had listed the bank, then the various floors that housed different departments, then there were still a few floors left over. Wellington occupied twenty-two through twenty-four and another company, *Tigress*, occupied the top five floors.

Tigress? What an odd name for a company.

Thinking about Tigress and where my thoughts had gone after seeing the name, the memories of last week flood back in with a vengeance. I shake my head, not now and not again. I'm not about to let what happened last week affect what happens today. I simply can't do that to myself. There is too much at stake right now.

I need a job and I desperately want it to be this one.

Today I will dig down deep, down past all the pain, the hurt, and the nausea I feel at being back in this very building, and pull on my big girl panties to do what needs to be done to land this job.

I breathe in deep.

My chest tightens.

God, I miss her.

Without meaning to, my thoughts drift toward my mother. With little warning I am caught up in the last time I saw her here in Phoenix. She'd come down for my graduation and spent a week here with me and Becca. I showed her around town, we laughed and had a good time. That was six months ago.

I can't stop thinking about her gorgeous smile, the way she looked at me with such love and devotion. She was an amazing woman. She put up with all my wild, harebrained ideas and the things I wanted to do with my life, but most importantly, she never let me fall.

The phone call she made a week ago, wishing me all the luck in the world at my interview was the last time I would hear her voice. She'd called just before she left work for the day. She was so sure of the job interview going my way that I had two dozen white and purple roses waiting on my kitchen counter when I returned to the apartment. They wilted and died before I had a chance to read the card.

My thoughts have me completely distracted when I walk around the corner to the elevator area of the building.

Without warning I slam my coffee-holding hand into a hard, muscle-clad, delicious smelling body. Slow motion takes over as I watch my coffee become a lost cause at the moment of impact. My hand instinctively tightens around it, squeezing it hard and popping off the lid, sending coffee flying everywhere. All over my hand, my outfit, the floor, my shoes- but also all over the man I collided with.

"What the ever lovin' fuck, lady?"

The voice sends an unwanted thrill through me, unlike anything I've ever felt before. Instead of feeling a chill of pissed off, I get the warmth of lust spreading through my body. My nipples pucker and a flood of embarrassment races visibly to my cheeks.

Survival instincts kick in and I should argue with him that I was

walking on the right hand side of the hallway, where normal people walk, but that's lost the moment the pain in my hand registers as it shoots up my arm. It takes only a moment to realize that the coffee was scalding hot and is now splashed all over my hand. I drop the cup completely, sending more coffee flying on me and him. "Ow, ow, oww," I groan.

I want to shake my hand, shake off the coffee sitting there, but the last thing I need is more coffee flying everywhere.

I've made enough of a mess.

"This is a three-thousand dollar suit." His voice is hard, ice-cold, hateful.

My heart sinks, my eyes go wide and panic quickly overtakes the pain in my hand. He's going to make me pay for it, I just fucking know it. Despite the fact that he rounded the corner and slammed into me, I get the impression this is going to be all my fault.

"I'm sorry, I…" My eyes trail a path up his chest to meet his eyes. They're angry and not looking at me at all. No, they are looking through me as if I don't exist. As if I'm nothing more than an inconvenience to his day. There is something oddly familiar about the violet hue, but I can't even begin to think about where I know them from because I'm too shaken up over the coffee being spilled everywhere.

In fact, I don't do anything but stand there, dumbstruck.

Unsure of what to do, how to make it better, I blurt, "I'll pay for the suit." *What the fuck is wrong with me?* I can barely afford my rent, and that's a quarter of what his suit is worth.

The tears I'd been fighting all day well up in my eyes. My hand burns, my outfit is a complete and total mess and I've just ruined this man's three thousand-dollar suit.

"Excuse me," I stammer while holding back the sob that's ready to rip from my throat. I head for the bathroom, a place to hide and a safe haven to calm down.

I'm so distracted that I nearly walk into the men's restroom at first, but I find the right door and step in. A moment of relief rolls through me

when I realize no one is inside. I debate for a minute about locking the door before deciding against it when I see that the handicap stall has a sink and mirror in it. Thank god.

I lock the makeshift door behind me and head straight for the sink. I toss my purse on the edge of the counter as I do everything I can to will the tears from my eyes.

It doesn't work and I watch as the mirror turns blurry, and I come completely unglued.

This is a huge mistake. I shouldn't be here. I'm not ready for this. I can't even make it to the elevator without completely falling apart. *How am I supposed to make it through the most important interview of my life?*

DYSON
Blue Ain't Your Color - Keith Urban

My eyes follow her as she makes her way to the bathroom; she's a complete and total mess over some spilled coffee. *Because you snapped at her, asshole.* The visual of her bouncing red curls brings back visions of a girl I once knew. A girl I would give anything to see again.

"Mr. Cole, are you all right?" I roll my eyes in irritation at the security guard interrupting my visual of her walking away. Of course the idiot would come after me rather than the girl who burned her hand. Fucking prick, and here I thought I was the asshole. I just shake my head.

"I'm fine," I grumble as I pull my eyes away from the redheaded *tigress* who just stomped off. "I'm not sure if she is or not." I gesture in the direction of the bathroom. He looks toward the bathroom and then shrugs it off. I was severely irritated before and now I'm bordering on irate at the moron security guard. I make a note of his name, Effrin, and vow to have words with his supervisor about his ability to handle a situation like this. Just because I own half the fucking building doesn't give him the right to ignore what really matters. My eyes drift to the

bathroom again before I brush the coffee droplets off my suit as best I can and Effrin hands me a towel.

"Oh for fuck's sake," I snap as I snatch the towel out of his hand. Before I realize what I'm doing, I'm headed toward the restroom. "Get your supervisor down here, now," I growl.

It's rather unfortunate that she noticed she was headed for the wrong bathroom because going into the women's restroom was hardly on my list of things to do today. I smile at the idea of her going into the men's restroom and how I would have loved to rib her about it. *What the fuck is wrong with you? This chick just poured hot coffee all over you and you want to pick on her?* I snort at my own thoughts.

I carefully push open the door, unsure of what I'm going to find on the other side of it. I don't know if there is anyone else in here and it's one thing to barge in on her, she did just dump coffee all over me, but to have someone else in here would just... I shudder. It only takes me a minute to realize that there isn't anyone in here but her when I'm met with sniffles and a sob of emotion.

I really don't fucking need this right now.

I glance at my watch. I'm already running late, at best, I'll be ten minutes behind, *fuck*. I war with whether or not this is worth it and I nearly turn to walk out of the room, I don't need this right now. I'm already fucking late and now I have to change my goddamn clothes. That's when I hear her gentle yet scolding voice. "Get it together, Vy, come on, you got this." I hear her sniffle a few more times. *Vy? Who calls themselves Vy? And why in the hell is that ringing alarm bells in my head?*

I stop the thought in its tracks. I've already imagined it enough for today. My daily dose has been delivered and I know that I can't go down that path again, *ever*. I shake my head, shaking away the thoughts I have no business having and a place I can't venture. Besides, she's in Missouri, not in Phoenix fucking Arizona. Dammit, the thoughts won't stop. She's probably married to someone who doesn't deserve her– I growl internally at the thought and I don't finish it.

"Here," I say, though my voice comes out as more asshole than the

gesture suggests. Thinking about Ireland has me even more irritated than I was over the whole coffee incident.

I hear her gasp. I've startled her and she squeaks out what sounds more like a hiccup than a scream. Then the chaos erupts as I hear something slam against tile floor and then I hear the bouncing of various items as they hit the bathroom floor. "Mother fucker," she growls. Ahh, so the hair matches the attitude. She's truly a tigress. *Stop it.* The whole thing is just comical and I can't stop the laughter that bubbles up from somewhere deep down inside.

"I have a towel for you." I raise it up over the top of the stall door. "Might help you clean up."

"What's the point? I'm completely ruined as it is." I hear a smack and for some strange reason I imagine her smacking her hand over her mouth and it brings a wicked grin to my lips.

"I'm pretty sure your boss will understand. Take some time, get cleaned up."

She gives me a humorless laugh as she takes the towel from me. "I'm pretty sure I've already gotten one pass, I don't think they'll give me another." Her cryptic statement makes me curious as to whether or not she's always this discombobulated. Poor thing. I hear a sound, then the water comes on and then I hear the sound again. She must be trying to wash off the coffee from her top. Something rolls into my foot and I look down. It's a tube of chapstick and I can see the red label has two small cherries on it. Just like…*Stop it, Cole, she's not who you want her to be, so forget it.*

"It's not gonna come out," I tell her, more as a distraction to where my thoughts are threatening to wander to.

"Thanks." The sarcasm that drips off her statement is potent enough to make me shake my head. "Are you gonna stand there all day?"

I smile at the tiger behind the door and walk out of the bathroom, giving her some much needed privacy.

There's a new security guard standing around, supervising the other

idiots trying to clean up the coffee mess on the floor. I snap my fingers. "You." I point to the newcomer. "Your fucking security guards are idiots." The guy looks at me with a petrified expression, good. "When someone spills something, it's a good idea to pay attention to the lady instead of me. Do I make myself clear?"

"Yes, Mr. Cole. I assure you it won't happen again," the supervisor states. "Is there anything we can do?" He takes in my coffee speckled suit.

I glare at him. "It's a bit late for that, don't you think?" He nods. The security guard who handed me the towel looks at me then. "Send her up to my office when she's done in there."

"Yes, Mr. Cole."

I go to the elevator, thinking about the blazing, tear-filled green eyes of the tiger in the restroom. I fucking made her cry. *Jesus, I'm an asshole.* I shake my head and swipe my card, calling the elevator to me quickly and I step in. Once inside I insert the card again and I'm whisked to my floor at the top of the building.

In the hallway, I call over to my receptionist, Andy, "Cancel my meeting."

"Yes, sir." His response is quick and I'm not met with the usual argument I've come to expect from him. This meeting was important and he knows it, but I will never make it. I have to deal with the *tigress* from downstairs.

Why in the hell did I tell him to send her up?

So you can get one more look at her to satisfy your fucking ego, maybe make her feel more like shit than she obviously already does? Or is it because you're hoping against hope that she just might be the woman you've been pining after for more than a decade?

I step into my office and close the door, running my hand through my hair in frustration before throwing the switch that turns the clear glass of my office opaque. I walk toward the bathroom, shedding my jacket and shirt along the way. It's nearly impossible to ignore the raging hard-on between my legs. The moment I looked into her eyes, I was a complete

and total mess. There is something electrifying about those bright green eyes of hers and it made me hard the moment our eyes met. I was so thrown off by the fact that simply gazing into someone's eyes could get me hard that I acted like an asshole.

I shed my pants, reluctantly pulling on a new pair. It wouldn't take but a second to relieve myself of the strain in my pants, but I don't have time. Not if she's coming up here.

Thank god I keep a couple spare suits in the office. This, however, is the first time I've ever had to change because of having coffee spilled on me. The thought makes me smile a little.

I get myself straight once again and as soon as I come out of the bathroom, my desk phone beeps as Andy is trying to reach me. I walk over quickly and I'm suddenly nervous. She's here. Shit, I never told Andy she was coming up. *You're an idiot.*

"Yeah," I snap when I press the button.

"Mr. Wellington needs to see you, right away."

Fuck. "Did he say what for?"

"No, sir, and it sounded urgent so I didn't press him too much."

"I have someone coming to my office. Security should be bringing her up shortly. I'll see Mr. Wellington after."

"Yes, sir."

I hired Andy more than a year ago. After a string of god-awful assistants, I realized the women from the agency were nothing more than useless bimbos who couldn't handle my mood swings. They either ended up in tears and getting fired or they quit on their own. I needed someone with a tougher skin and Andy fit that bill. He's done a damn good job since he started and he's not afraid to stand up to me when I'm being a douche.

My phone chimes again. Good, she's finally here.

"Send her in," I say into the phone.

Andy hesitates briefly. I notice he does that from time to time when he

thinks he's delivering bad news. "Uh, she's not here. Security called up to let you know that she refused to come up."

"Why would she do that?"

"Apparently she has an appointment at Wellington."

I sit up straighter in my chair. "Thanks, let Mr. Wellington know I'm on my way down."

What in the world was she doing at Wellington's office? Shelly finished up the interviews last week and I highly doubt she's a client. *Yeah, because that wasn't asshole-ish.*

I let the thought evaporate as I don yet another jacket. This one is more charcoal grey compared to the lighter one I had on earlier. Had I worn this one in the first place it wouldn't have been an issue and I could have still made my damn meeting. Irritation flares briefly. Not only have I missed my meeting and had a three-thousand dollar suit splattered with coffee, I've spent the last twenty minutes doing nothing but drumming my fingers on my desk waiting for her to come up here and now I'm running down to Wellington's office on the off-chance that I see her again.

The desire to see her again is nearly overwhelming as I flip the switch on my office glass once again, brightening the room so people know I'm not here.

I stop at Andy's desk before I go to the elevator, confirming the rescheduled meeting. For some reason I'm stalling and I don't understand why.

I rap my knuckles on the top of his desk and head to the elevator. The longer I have to wait, the more impatient I become. I want to see her, but there is a part of me that hopes I don't. I don't need these ridiculous distractions.

My cock throbs again at the idea of seeing her again. *Fuck.*

Finally, the elevator arrives and I step inside, press for Wellington's floor. I fidget with my tie, run a hand through my hair using the brass covered walls as a mirror until the doors open.

I suck in a deep breath and step out.

Turning, I see her standing at the receptionist's desk. She hasn't made it very far. Her fiery red hair is on full display. Her perfectly bubbly, little ass is on display in the black pencil skirt she's wearing. I notice then that she has something around her ankle. I smirk, *tigress has a tattoo.*

Chapter Two

IRELAND
Titanium - David Guetta w/ Sia

I look like complete and total shit. Despite every effort I made in the bathroom downstairs, I still couldn't get out all the coffee spots. If I'm honest with myself, the asshole-suit was looking much worse for wear than I was when it was all said and done with, but I still look like hell.

The more fucked up this day gets, the more I wish I would have cancelled this fucking interview when I had the chance. It was completely ridiculous of me to think that I would be in any shape to do this so soon after getting back from Missouri yesterday. But they'd been insistent that despite what happened last week, I deserved a chance to come in and sit down with them. I know that in order to land this job I am going to have to be spot-on, but just looking at my clothes says that I'm a complete and total mess already.

I somehow managed to get rid of all the spots on my legs and shoes and I was able to wash out the spots on my skirt, at least the ones I could see. But my shirt is a total mess. This is what I get for wearing white and drinking tan colored coffee. If it had been black, I may have had better luck, but no, I have to have all the sugary sweet shit in there too. Thank god for detergent pens that remove stains from clothing, and a hand dryer that I could use to at least attempt drying off the wet spots, otherwise I would be in worse shape than I am right at this moment.

My irritation is at an all-time high when I walk into the reception area of Wellington Ad Management. Despite all my efforts and the counting exercises I did, nothing is working. It doesn't help that every time I close my eyes all I see are those eyes, those deep blue-violet eyes that seemed to look right through me. And the perfectly sculpted jaw, the stubble that lined it. I suppress a sigh as I approach the receptionist's desk. She greets me with a smile and I somehow find the courage and my voice.

I give her my name and tell her I have an appointment with Michelle Iverson and she promptly calls back to her as she holds her finger up, indicating for me to wait.

My early arrival proved pivotal in what happened downstairs. It gave me the time I needed to truly do the best I could with what I had to work with. By the time I was satisfied, I got upstairs with just a few minutes to spare. Still early enough to look punctual, but late enough to not look overly desperate.

Maybe there's a reason I ran into the *dickwad* downstairs. Spare me from sitting here for far longer than I should have to. I smile a little at that idea. Finding some good in the crazy that has been my day so far.

I start to hope, just a little, that this might actually pan out better than I thought. Giving me a small morsel of hope that I might land my dream job?

A week ago when I arrived at Wellington, I was sitting in this very waiting room when my phone buzzed in my purse. I pulled it out and looked at the unknown Missouri number. I get calls from all over all the time, so I did my best to ignore it. But something was nagging me in the back of my head that I needed to answer it. I nearly missed the call because I stared at it for so long before glancing down the hallway to make sure no one was coming before I hit the green button. Within a few beats, my world started tilting on an axis I didn't need. It was the local Joplin area hospital telling me that my mother had been in an accident and that she had been brought into the emergency room via ambulance. The woman on the phone said that I should come to the hospital quickly. I still have a Missouri number, but I let her know that I was in Phoenix and I wouldn't be able to arrive for a few hours. When we hung up, I took a deep breath, trying to refocus. I could do my interview and then head straight to the airport, right?

Wrong. Less than five minutes later, my phone buzzed again and it was my brother. Again glancing down the hall to make sure I had some time to answer and seeing no one, I answered it. I'd told my brother that the hospital had already called. He told me there was more. My world went into free fall at that point because I don't remember what happened after that. I just know that it was all kinds of awful and somehow I was let out of my interview with a promise to reschedule.

I shiver, banishing the thoughts from my mind as best I can when the elevator behind me dings and I know, though I have no clue how, that it's *him*. The hair on the back of my neck stands at attention and my body starts to hum the closer he gets to me. At the same time, the receptionist hangs up the phone and turns to the new visitor.

"Hello Mr. Cole, Mr. Wellington is expecting you."

Cole?

Violet eyes?

There's no way.

It's impossible.

His last name was Richards. But his middle name started with...what was it? A C. That's it, but what was his middle name and why would he use his middle name as a last name?

I turn, my conscious wins out over better judgment in an attempt to get a better look at the man I'd dumped my coffee all over. To find something about him that isn't the man from my past. But before I can get a look at him, he manages to turn down the hall before I see his face again.

He changed his suit. *Fucker.*

He's gone from a light grey to a dark grey one and he walks with a cocky confidence that belongs in a three thousand dollar suit, but the hair, the eyes, neither one of them matches the façade he is trying like hell to pull off. Then again, if you can afford that kind of a suit, it doesn't much matter what the man inside him looks like. The suit alone screams money and power. *And sex.* What the hell is wrong with me? His hair is longer than one would expect from a businessman, falling past his ears and he reminds me of someone in a surfing video or at a skate park – if he were seventeen – and nowhere near a corporate office. The light brown locks are straight yet disheveled in a way that makes him sexier than he should be.

"Ms. McKidd?" I turn toward the voice to see a well-dressed, statuesque blonde standing to the right of the reception desk. She's

wearing a pantsuit that makes me jealous. I wish I could pull off something like that as well as she does.

I'm not short by any means, but I certainly don't have the slender body to pull off the look.

I push back, hoping to find some confidence between here and the inevitable handshake that's about to happen. "Ms. Iverson?" I ask.

She smiles. "Call me Shelly." She extends her hand to me and I take it. I do my best to ignore the pain her grip causes me. While I was in the bathroom, I did what I could to inspect my hand in the awful light of the handicap stall and it didn't look horrible and I didn't see any blisters, but it still hurts.

Somewhere in the middle of our handshake I pull together my confidence. I'd trained for this, over and over again with Kerrigan and my friend Reese, hoping like hell I could master an interview as important as this one. I breathe in deep and put a smile on my face. "Okay, Shelly." My smile grows a little wider. "I cannot thank you enough for allowing me to reschedule," I tell her, my comfort level rising slightly as I do.

"It was my pleasure. Did everything turn out all right?" she asks as she ushers me down the hallway.

I don't really know how to answer that. I gently shake my head and say, "Under the circumstances, it was..." I don't bother to finish. The look in her eyes portrays her understanding and I let it go.

"Then I'm deeply sorry for your loss."

The line has been said to me a thousand times over the last week, but for some reason this one feels different. There is a quiet apology in her voice that I respect. She was here when I'd gotten that second phone call. I swallow. "Thank you," I manage to choke out while keeping my tears in check as I follow her toward the conference room. "I also need to apologize."

"For?" She turns to me and her eyes roam up and down. Great.

"Someone ran into me downstairs. I was carrying a cup of coffee and-"

"No apology necessary," She gives me a sad smile that doesn't reach her eyes and I'm not entirely convinced it's not needed, but I let it go. No use in pointing it out again.

She leads me into a conference room where there are two other people sitting at the massive, cherry wood table. Shelly introduces me and I shake both their hands. Again, ignoring the pain as best I can. It doesn't hurt so much as long as someone isn't touching it.

The next hour flies by in a daze and a flurry of questions coming at me from all three people sitting across from me. I do my best to answer them all and I think I impress them in some areas and maybe not so much in others.

Shelly was kind enough to point out that I'd previously applied for their internship program, three times, but what that had to do with anything was beyond me. I simply explained it had been my desire to come to work for Wellington and I thought the internship would be a great place to start. I'll never admit it to them, but I'm glad I was able to intern at Stauffer because it turned out to be a better choice and fit for me. Especially if I get the job here today.

The interview is winding down. They're discussing among themselves whether or not they have any further questions for me when the door behind me opens. Curiosity burns but I realize we're probably taking up someone else's room time. However, my interviewers don't seem too surprised and they all stand, I follow them in a show of respect.

"Mr. Wellington, Mr. Cole, what a surprise," Shelly says and the name I hoped I wouldn't be hearing again jolts me into looking up and I freeze.

He works for Wellington. He'd come off the elevator before, he could have worked anywhere in the building but why would he be in this room during my interview if he didn't work for them.

My heart sinks.

I've officially succeeded in making myself look like a complete and total ass in front of someone I'm going to be working with. What are the odds?

"This is quite possibly the longest interview I've ever seen you

conduct, Michelle." The voice isn't the one from downstairs and I turn to acknowledge Mr. Wellington, doing my damnedest to ignore the suit behind him but he is a force in the room. You simply cannot ignore him.

I take a cue I should show some initiative by introducing myself. "It's a pleasure to meet you, Mr. Wellington, I'm Ireland McKidd." I extend my hand to him and he takes it gently. I'd almost wager a guess he knows about what happened downstairs; either that or he has a weak handshake. I'll stick with the latter of the two.

The man who came into the conference room with Mr. Wellington takes a step back, putting him closer to the wall and farther from me. His eyes flare as if someone has a chokehold on him. I find some courage somewhere inside of me to show him some level of professional respect, despite our meeting downstairs, by extending my hand. His eyes move down to it and I know he sees the redness when his eyes soften briefly, but then the man in the dark grey suit starts glaring at me.

Trying my best to ignore the dark grey suit in the corner, I turn my focus toward Mr. Wellington. I cannot, for the life of me, figure out why he'd be freaked out by my name.

"The pleasure is mine," Mr. Wellington says with an appraising look and a warm smile. *Oh god, the coffee. Fuck! He makes no mention of it when he asks me his own form of an interview question.* "Would you mind filling me in on why you want to work for me?" I smile at the middle-aged man. He's not unattractive by any means, but definitely been rode hard and hung up wet.

"Certainly," I state with a smile and I lapse back into the sales pitch I'd given Shelly and the two, now silent, gentleman in the room. Making a few alterations as I go along, hoping to avoid having it sound scripted.

My eyes are focused on Mr. Wellington, Shelly and the other two gentlemen in the room in an attempt to avoid the cocky asshat in the corner glaring at me. He is throwing daggers in my direction and the more I ignore him, the harder his stare becomes.

When I'm done, Mr. Wellington asks a few more questions of his own. Ones not previously asked, and Shelly jots down notes, or the

questions, I'm not sure which. Then he launches into a couple of rapid fire marketing questions, slogans mostly and I'm able to rattle off the company or product they're associated with until finally he throws one at me that I don't recognize, but I scrunch my nose at it.

"You don't like that one?"

I shake my head. "Personally, no. Professionally, it works, depending on the product."

"Let's just say it's a new communication device that will revolutionize the way we communicate," the suit in the corner chimes in. The scowl hasn't left his brow but at least I feel confident that he's not throwing daggers at me anymore, for the moment.

"What else does the company do?"

"A little of this, some of that," the suit says vaguely, not wanting to provide me with too much information, which I completely understand. I'm being put on the spot and my heart races with excitement for the first time in more than a week. This is what I live for.

I cock my head at him. "Are you under patent? Ready to go to market? Where does the product stand?"

He smirks. "It's light years ahead of anything else out there right now." The cocky-asshat showing his colors, again. His superiority complex is palpable and I do my best to ignore the animosity rolling off him. I can't begin to imagine what it is he's claiming to have in his portfolio, but whatever it is must be good if it is granting him this overly cocky attitude about it.

"Infinite possibilities, today," I rattle off and a few eyes bulge in my direction, including the suit.

"That's it," Mr. Wellington exclaims with so much enthusiasm he makes me jump, forcing my eyes away from the dark blonde, blue-violet eyed god. "Hot damn!" He claps and looks directly at me. "You're hired, Ms. McKidd."

The look the man in the suit throws my way tells me otherwise, but I do my best to ignore him.

"Michelle, whatever it is you need to do, get it done and get her in here. She's young, fresh and I'm excited to see what she can do when she's given the entire portfolio to consider before coming up with a new strategy."

"Yes, sir," Shelly replies and she smiles at me. "Congratulations, Ms. McKidd." This time, the smile reaches her eyes. And I too find my smile.

DYSON
Vice - Miranda Lambert

"It's a pleasure to meet you, Mr. Wellington, I'm Ireland McKidd."

Fuck my goddamn life.

I glare at her. I'm unwilling to accept the fact that the person I was hoping she was, truly is the woman I want her to be.

It's fucking her! God, nearly ten years have done her good. She looks stunning. *Stop it, Dyson.* Of all the places on this green earth she could land, she has to throw coffee on me and waltz her way right back into my life. *Fuck, fuck, fuck.*

The only way this is going to go any better is if she doesn't know who I am. I can only hope at this point she hasn't put two and two together. This will make this so much easier. Who the fuck am I kidding? For the last seven years, I've been looking for her.

There is no denying the fact that I need her to know. I want her to know so bad I can't stop glaring at her. Willing her to know. I'd imagined this day so many times in my head, but in my head she knew me immediately, and in my head, she spewed hatred at me and stormed off. At least that's what I thought I would need to hear, because then, maybe, I could get over her and move on with my life. It wasn't for a lack of effort, but karma has been a real bitch to me these last ten years. This way I can know she's pissed off at me, and I can have a real reason to be mad at her over the superficial one I've made up in my head.

God, she's so fucking gorgeous.

She's not the lost, little fifteen-year old girl I left on a pile of hay on a barn floor nearly ten years ago. She's a woman, a beautiful woman. She changed, she's grown, she's lost so much weight and she's still the woman of my dreams.

I'm so unbelievably fucked.

I try and settle into the corner, hoping to catch some of what she's saying as she explains to Wellington why she wants to work here. She graduated from ASU. I internally shake my head. She's been around the goddamn corner for how long now? Three years? While she does her best to convince Wellington of her worthwhile employment, I contemplate the steps I need to take to ensure she doesn't work here. I don't need the constant distraction of knowing she's right downstairs, especially if she never figures out who I am. For some reason I need her to come to that conclusion on her own. She may not figure out who I am, but I have no intention of telling her myself. If I allow Wellington to put her in close proximity to me on a daily basis, there is no doubt in my mind she will figure me out.

I watch her carefully. There is a passion in her eyes as she speaks about Wellington Ad Management, about her school background and her internships at Stauffer over the last three summers. That passion she exudes is the biggest turn on and my already aching cock throbs, straining relentlessly against my pants. Watching her talk, listening to her voice- sweet torture. She has a sexy little rasp to her voice that makes her sound like the best fucking phone sex operator in the world and she's nearly got me coming in my pants. Jesus, I could get off just listening to her talk.

Wellington puts her through her paces and she doesn't falter in the slightest. She's good. Damn good. Suddenly her working at Wellington isn't so much about having her so close and yet so far away. Her working for him makes it so she can't work for me. The more I listen to her, the more I realize Wellington might not be the place for her. I think she may be better suited upstairs. It would be fitting after all.

I listen more intently as he gets to the slogan he'd hit me with in his office. That's what he wanted me for when he called Andy. He wanted to go over it, run it by me and I absolutely hated it, but his delivery told me he was pretty put off by it too. His office has had more than a month to come up with a slogan and a marketing plan and the truth is, Wellington's people are old, tired and highly unimaginative and that doesn't work for me.

She shakes her head. "Personally, no. Professionally, it could work, depending on the product."

Wellington opens his mouth to speak and I stave him off. "Let's just say it's a new communication device that will revolutionize the way we communicate."

I watch her intently. I can almost hear the wheels turning in her head as she thinks through what I've said. I didn't exactly make it easy for her. "What else does the company do?" she asks.

"A little of this, a little of that." I don't want to give her any more information. I want to see if she's as good as I'm afraid she is.

She cocks her head at me, exposing a neck I desperately want to run my tongue along, and asks me directly. Her eyes bore into mine as if she's trying to find my secrets. She is unaffected by my smirk. "Are you under patent? Ready to go to market? Where does the product stand?"

"It's light years ahead of anything else out there right now."

It takes her all of ten seconds to say something that will alter everything I know about the woman standing in front of me. "Infinite possibilities, today."

My eyes bug out of my head and Wellington erupts in laughter and excitement. She just did in thirty seconds what Wellington's entire team couldn't come up with in thirty days. I can't say I blame him when he hires her on the spot.

I, on the other hand, decide that whatever Wellington will pay her, I will offer her triple just to keep her closer to me.

Chapter Three

IRELAND

Never Say Never - Tristan Prettyman

What the hell just happened in there?

I walk out of the conference room and wait for Shelly to join me.

I can't believe it; I've landed my dream job.

The smile on my face no doubt stretches from ear to ear.

I walk a couple steps past the door, my hand still on the handle when I hear, "You can't hire her." It's the suit's voice that reaches my ears.

"On the contrary, she just saved your company and didn't even think twice about it," Mr. Wellington's voice fires back.

"Just because she spouted three words doesn't mean she's worthy of a full-time job…" The voice continues but it's muffled as I let the door close behind me. My heart sinks. *What the hell did I ever do to him?*

Wouldn't that be the icing on the cake to an already shit week? Some fucker, who I don't even know, forces me out of my job before I've even started it?

When I introduced myself to Mr. Wellington, I'd seen the flare of recognition in his eyes when I said my name, but I can't for the life of me imagine where it is he's met me before. Sure, those blue-violet eyes are a little too familiar, but the notion that it could be him is just too absurd to consider. They moved to Atlanta all those years ago. Why on earth would he be in Phoenix? *Probably for the same reason you're here, something new.* My subconscious is meddling again.

The door opens again, the voices continue arguing about something, but I can't quite make it out before the door closes and Shelly strides over to me. "Don't worry about them. Mr. Cole has no real ground here."

"He doesn't work here?" I ask in disbelief.

She smiles. "No, he's a client of Wellington, though that's putting it mildly."

The flood of relief that washes through me is almost tangible. So he

has no power over whether or not Wellington hires me? Sure, he can argue left and right and Wellington can certainly give into him if he's a large client, but if he's only a client, what ground does he have?

The sense of relief spills over when I realize I don't have to work with the bastard in a suit who's done nothing but treat me like a lowlife pariah since I ran into him downstairs. "Thank god," I mutter.

"You know him?" Shelly asks me. Something in my reaction has her curious. I shake my head, unsure if I want to go into the details of why I'm relieved I won't have to work for him. "Well, he seems to know you." She gives me a quizzical look.

"If he is referring to our run-in downstairs, then sure, he knows me. He's the reason I'm a mess." I gesture toward my torso and my blouse.

"Oh," she says in surprised understanding. "Why doesn't that surprise me?"

"What do you mean by that?" I ask her.

"Mr. Cole isn't exactly the kindest person when it comes to people who are unlike him." There is a bit of disdain in her voice and I wonder why that is but I can't fathom a guess without assuming it's some sort of jealousy on her part. He's drop dead gorgeous. Just the kind of man who remains aloof and out of reach for anyone who doesn't have the bank account to match. I find my senses and nod my head as she leads me back toward the reception area. I refuse to look at the seating area, afraid my high of getting a new job will be overshadowed by what happened last week.

Shelly leads me to the front desk. I check out a little, thinking about the suit in the conference room, and don't pay much attention to what Shelly and the receptionist are discussing until she turns to me. "Cara from Human Resources will be meeting with you. She'll be right out. Why don't you take a seat," Shelly says, ushering me toward the chairs. "We will get all your paperwork done and then set you up with some tests."

I squint at her in confusion. "What kind of tests?"

She chuckles. "Background check, drug test, things like that. Once we have all that stuff back, we can get you started."

"How long does that usually take?" I ask. I don't want to sound desperate, but I need this job to start sooner than I'd planned. Having to rush off to Missouri at the last minute has left my finances in shambles and if I can't start in the next couple weeks, I'm going to have to find a part-time job to keep myself afloat. We don't need to go into the fact that my mother left all her money, life insurance and the insurance payout for the car to my brother in her will. I was left with a cryptic note on the outside of an envelope that says, 'All will be taken care of shortly', like I'm supposed to know what that means.

"Depends on how fast you can get the test done, but assuming your background is clear and you're not a drug user, we should have them in about a week or so. HR will go over your salary, and give you some material to read up on before you start. We'll set a date once we're ready. Probably two, maybe three, weeks, tops."

"Sounds great." I extend my hand to her again, this time it doesn't hurt quite so bad when she takes it. The last thing I need right now is a trip to the emergency room because of a prickweed.

Shelly leaves me in reception and I pull out my phone while I wait.

I start to text my mother to let her know I got the job, but I stop myself. The reminder that no one is there anymore sends a single tear down my cheek.

I text my friend Reese instead. He's the reason I have this interview in the first place, not to mention Kerrigan will be happy to know all her hard work with me has paid off.

Got the job. Starting soon. Squishy kisses! xx

Reese: Congrats, baby girl, you deserve a slice of happy. K says well done. Dinner soon?

Ireland: Call me soon. I need some time.

Reese: Still on for Lee at Blu?

Ireland: Definitely.

Next I text Becca:

Got the job! Details soon.

Becca: YES!!! We're celebrating tonight.

Arguing with Becca through text is like throwing spitballs at the wall and so not worth the mess afterward, but I'm not going out. Sure, I may have gotten a new job, my dream job even, but going out and celebrating is the absolute last thing on my mind right now. All I really want is a big ass glass of wine, my most comfortable sweatpants and my Kindle. Another tear slides down my cheek before I can stop it. Thankfully I can still see my phone clearly so I know a meltdown isn't on the way.

I was hoping the high of getting a new job would overshadow the sadness I feel, and it did, until I remembered that I don't have anyone else to tell besides Becca and Reese.

I swipe away the tears as the hair on the back of my neck prickles once again and I look up in time to see the asshole-suit walking toward me. His eyes are scrutinizing me like I'm some sort of enigma.

I turn away from him by burying my face in my phone and hiding the fact I was crying. This man has seen too much of my vulnerable side since I met him downstairs and I can't give him anymore. A set of shoes that probably cost more than my entire bedroom come into view.

"You got a new job, hardly a reason to cry." He tries to sound sweet but instead it comes out sarcastic and cocky.

My eyes dart to his and that all too familiar violet shade in his eyes sends butterflies flying around my stomach. "If you had it your way, I wouldn't have a job," I snap at him.

His eyes flare and then they dart down the hall and back to me as he realizes I overheard part of their conversation.

"No, most definitely not." His voice is full of anger.

My whole body vibrates with my own frustration at him. I cannot fathom a reason why he thinks I don't deserve a job. There are all kinds of things rolling around my tongue to spout at him, but we're interrupted by a soft, female voice. "Ms. McKidd?"

The interruption breaks our eye contact and in a huff he turns and walks to the elevator and presses the up button. The only thing above Wellington is Tigress. *So that's where you belong, isn't it?* I find my legs, toss my phone back in my bag and follow the petite woman down the hallway he'd disappeared down earlier.

I spend over an hour with Cara from HR going over some rules, signing papers, including a NDA (non-disclosure agreement) pertaining to clients and working projects. I knew this was coming. Marketing firms are held in the strictest of confidence by their clients and anonymity is the highest priority.

When it was all said and done with, she handed me a folder with copies of everything I've signed, plus a bunch of other materials pertaining to employment guidelines and the rules of the office. Somewhere in that folder is my official offer letter. I haven't even looked at it yet; it's tucked inside an envelope.

For an entry level position, I'll be surprised if I'm making twenty-five grand a year. But, like my internships, it's completely worth it. I'll get a second job if I have to.

I manage to escape the office and the building without coming in contact with Mr. Stubborn-Ass-Expensive Suit Wearing-Prickhead. Thank god for the little things.

I hopped on the next train and headed home.

Becca wasn't home when I got there, thank god.

I don't need the comments about how messed up I look. Despite getting the job, Becca is usually only good for pointing out my screw-ups. Like the fact that I have coffee splattered all over me.

Stepping inside my apartment, I freeze, dropping my bag to the

ground for the second time today.

My eyes have got to be playing tricks on me or I've walked into some sort of twilight zone. Sitting on the kitchen island that separates the kitchen from the living room is a crystal vase filled with white and purple roses, just like the ones that were here a week ago when I'd come home to pack for Missouri.

My heart freezes in my chest, tightening, making it nearly impossible to breathe. I put my hands on my knees in an attempt to tamp down the rising panic attack, but my stomach rolls and I dart for the kitchen sink. Unleashing nothing more than dry heaves because I honestly can't remember the last time I ate.

The front door opens, then closes. "Vy, what's wrong?"

How can she possibly be clueless about what's wrong? I point to the roses on the counter.

"What about them?" Is she really that clueless?

"Where did they come from?" I snap.

"They were delivered about an hour ago. What is wrong with you?" Her eyes narrow at me.

I scowl back at her. "Do you not remember what was on the counter a week ago?"

She gives me a puzzled look, then it dawns on her. She looks at the roses, stares at them might be a better description, as if she's joined me in my little moment of déjà vu. "They can't be from her?" she says as a question, as if she can't possibly believe it herself. I watch as she starts sifting through the flowers looking for the card. When she finds it, she plucks it off the stick and hands it to me.

I shake my head. "I haven't opened last week's. What makes you think I can open that one?"

Tears are now streaming down my face, the panic rises once again. I feel the unwelcome snap everyone seemed to think was coming for me. Somehow I managed to hold it together for the last week or so- stepping in and planning the funeral, taking care of all the arrangements and

leading the effort of trying to go through mom's things. It wasn't until we got to the will reading that we learned the house was free and clear and it was being left to Dusty – my brother – and me. Though that was the only thing I got in the will besides a stupid letter. But I feel it, it's building inside of me and it's about to come pouring out of me like nothing I've ever felt before. My chest tightens as Becca opens the card.

Her eyes scrunch up, scrutinizing the card in a way that makes me wonder if it's really that bad. I watch as she flips it over, then unfolds it. She's looking at the receipt printed on the back, and then she finally hands me the card. I snatch it from her hand in irritation and my eyes land on the foreign script of the florist who prepared the bouquet.

Congratulations on your new job, sweetheart. I am so very proud of you. *– Love, Mom.*

Before I even finished reading the card, tears are dripping on it, blurring the letters and soaking the card.

"How?" I choke before Becca scoops me up into her arms and I unleash a flood of tears. Screaming and sobbing in a way I never knew my body was capable of.

I've finally snapped.

Chapter four

DYSON
Wish You Were Here - Pink Floyd

Ireland McKidd...

I tap my fingers against my laptop keyboard waiting for Google to do the whole search engine thing.

I left that conference room with a new determination to find more information about Ireland McKidd, in an effort to prove she's not the fifteen-year old girl from Joplin, Missouri. But the longer I looked at her sitting in that chair, her eyes and features obviously tear-stained, the more I realized the twenty-something woman in Phoenix, Arizona was in pain.

Between that meeting and now, I've stupidly tried to convince myself she's not the same girl. It's just a coincidence.

I roll my eyes at my own stupidity. *Who am I kidding?* There is no way. Who names a red-headed, mostly Scottish blooded, all-American girl, Ireland? Lauren McKidd, that's who.

I really need some more information on her and I know where to find it, but that folder has been locked away for a long time, no need to dig it out now. The truth is I don't want to go into that folder and find out that the woman who ran into me today is not my Ireland.

The information finally loads and a heavy weight lands on my heart.

The green-eyed tigress is *my* Ireland.

It's a completely futile effort, trying to convince myself otherwise because I knew, deep down, in the darkest, coldest corners of my soul, that it was her the moment I looked into her eyes. The first time I saw those scared green eyes staring at me, she stirred something inside of me that died ten years ago when I walked out of that barn.

The word Asshole flashes in my mind as I scroll through the most recent search results. I scroll past the initial before my eyes land on Arizona State's website listing fall graduates and her name is highlighted

in the preview box.

I scroll back up, letting my heart crack for the woman who was in Wellington's office today.

The Joplin Globe is the first result to pop up.

I click the link.

Local Joplin Woman Killed by Drunk Driver
Joplin, Missouri

On Tuesday, while on her way home from work, Lauren Vyolet McKidd was killed in a head-on collision by an oncoming vehicle. The vehicle was being driven by Alex Miller, of Joplin. Miller survived with only minor cuts and bruises but the impact of his vehicle killed Lauren...

I don't need to read anymore.

I hit the back button, then I see Lauren's obituary printed in the same paper and I read through it until I get to the end where it states that Lauren is survived by her son, Dusty (April) and their unborn child of Chicago, and her daughter Ireland of Phoenix. I can't read anymore. I close the browser.

No wonder she was such a mess today. Jesus.

Something cracks inside me. Something happens that I haven't felt in a very long time. Dusty was my best friend. We were inseparable. We'd do everything together, which always meant Ireland tagged along with us. It was inevitable what happened between us ten years ago. What I never expected was what I would feel when it was over.

She was a freshman and I was a junior.

She was an innocent girl and I was a dickhead with a cock and an itch to be scratched and she certainly did that for me but at an expense far greater than she deserved.

I pick up my phone and scroll through my contacts, pulling up my mother's name.

She answers after a few rings.

"Dyson, what's wrong?" I look at the clock and it's nearly seven here in Phoenix, which means it's nearly nine in Atlanta and for my mother, it's late.

"Sorry, mom, I didn't think when I called."

She yawns on the other end of the line. "It's okay, what's up?"

"Don't worry about it, sorry I called so late," I tell her but she stops me before I can hang up.

"It's alright, what's going on?"

"Did you know about Lauren?"

I hear her sigh into the phone. "I did."

"Why didn't you tell me?" My voice is much harsher than I intended it to be.

"I didn't know I had to," she snaps. I deserved that.

"I'm sorry, I just… do you know anything about Ireland?" I ask before I can stop myself.

"I just know she moved to Phoenix to go to ASU after high school graduation. I remember Lauren emailing me something about her graduation from ASU, but I don't remember when that was."

"I didn't know you and Lauren were talking again." It comes out more statement than question.

"I wouldn't call it talking, exactly. I found her on that social media website, thing," I can't stop the smile that spreads across my lips at my mother's description. "We messaged back and forth, became friends, but it was never anything like what it was before we moved." She pauses a moment. "Come to think of it, I remember her posting something a few months back about Ireland's graduation and Lauren leaving to visit her daughter. Then it was followed up with something about Ireland staying to find a job."

I pinch the bridge of my nose in frustration and anger. Not at anyone but myself. Ireland is going through something no child should have to go through so young. She has no one to turn to besides her brother and maybe some friends. But I doubt any of them really knew Lauren or could sympathize with her. And here I was treating her like complete and total shit. When I saw her crying in the lobby, I should have known something wasn't right, but I was too stubborn to see it.

After a beat, I ask my mother, "Did you go?"

"To the funeral?" she clarifies.

"Yes."

"No, I didn't. I didn't feel it was my place to go. I haven't seen either of the kids since they were teenagers."

"Lauren was your friend, I'm sure they would have understood," I tell her.

I hear her quiet sob on the other end of the line. "I know," she sniffs, "But we'd grown so far apart…" She doesn't say much else beyond that in regards to Lauren or Ireland and my heart cracks a little over the sadness in my mother's voice.

If she's this shaken up about Lauren, I can only begin to imagine how Ireland feels right now.

"Thanks, mom."

She yawns again. "Anytime, you doing okay?"

"Always," I tell her and we end our phone call.

I put my glasses on and decide I need some more information. I call Shelly on her cell phone. My curiosity is getting the better of me.

She answers on the second ring. "Dyson, you finally decided to take me up on my dinner invitation?"

I snort into the phone. "No. But I need some more information from you."

"Dinner first." She tries to negotiate with me and I'm not having it. I'm not in the mood.

"You finished your interviews last week. Why were you interviewing her today?"

I hear her resolve on the phone, changing our conversation from pleasure to business is enough for her to drop the persistent dinner invitation she keeps throwing at me. She's not my type and I don't date women, period, especially if they work for me. I prefer to fuck 'em and leave 'em. No strings, less complications and none of the morning after mess.

"I did," she answers my question but offers no further information.

"Then why were you interviewing her today?"

"I think that's kind of a personal question, Dyson. Maybe you should ask her yourself."

I snort. "No, you can tell me."

I hear her sigh into the phone. "She showed up for her interview, on time, early in fact, and she was waiting in reception when she received a phone call from someone. I don't know for sure who the first phone call came from but then she got a second one and was then on the floor in a total daze. Elle rushed over and took the phone from her. Someone named Dusty, I think, was on the phone." I let out a slow, painful breath as she finishes, "Her mother had been in an accident. She didn't make it."

"Thank you," I tell her.

"She overheard you after she left the conference room today."

I hang my head. "I didn't mean for her to overhear it."

"Then maybe you shouldn't have been spouting a bunch of bullshit," she snaps back at me. I'm not hearing it, not from her or anyone else, and especially not tonight. "Give her a chance, would ya? If she doesn't work, you know Wellington will fire her. But she's had it rough enough this last week, she certainly didn't need to overhear your hatred for her, just because *you* ran into her and got coffee spilled all over one of your precious suits."

You're way off base here, sweetheart. "Tell me something. If Wellington hadn't walked into that interview and hired her on the spot,

would you have chosen her over all your other candidates?" I try to keep my question and my tone professional. I don't need anyone catching on to the fact that this girl is tearing me up inside. Especially someone like Shelly who is notorious for latching on to the slightest hint of something she can use against someone.

"Yes." She doesn't hesitate. "She's highly ambitious, but unafraid to start at the bottom. Kerrigan at Stauffer gave her a glowing recommendation. When I'd asked Kerrigan about why they hadn't hired her on after her internship, she said they offered her a position a few days before her mother died. Under the circumstances, they're waiting for her acceptance or rejection."

"So there is a chance that she won't take Wellington's offer?"

Shelly snorts a laugh into the phone. "Hardly. She'd be dumb to turn down this job, unless money is unimportant to her."

I already know that's not true.

There is a long, awkward pause before I hear Shelly sigh again. "One more thing, Dyson."

"What?" I toss my glasses onto my desk and pinch the bridge of my nose again.

"Apologize to her."

"For what?" I snap.

"For slamming into her downstairs."

"Is that what she told you?" I argue.

"Yes, but don't deny it. You were in such a damn hurry you clipped the corner and slammed right into her. You owe her an apology, and a new blouse," she tacks on with a chuckle before she discontinues our call.

Witch.

I won't admit it, but she's more right than she realizes. I owe her far more than an apology for slamming into her in the lobby today. I owe her for walking out on her ten years ago.

IRELAND
Wish You Were Here - Avril Lavigne

After more than an hour of sobbing uncontrollably in Becca's arms, I finally manage to calm down. Becca stuck by me the whole time, playing with my hair, hugging and holding me. She knew it was coming. I'm pretty sure everyone did. Sure, I've cried the last week and I've cried a lot, but nothing at all like this. I cried until the tears ran out.

Needing some answers, I asked Becca about what was on the card other than what was written by the florist. She said it was just the date the order was placed. She said it was ordered last week Tuesday, the same day mom died, and probably at the same time she ordered my good luck flowers. I can't help but wonder what Dusty knows about this so I find my phone and call him. I scroll through, looking for his number and once I find it, I hit the little phone icon.

I'm still a little jumpy from my crying binge and each time it rings in my ear, I jump.

"Ireland, what's wrong?" Dusty answers the phone.

"She sent me roses." My voice is shaky and uncertain.

"What do you mean?" he asks.

"Mom, she sent me roses."

I hear my brother take a deep breath on the other side of the phone. Dusty was the only person I could truly cling to this last week. We'd never been close, but for some reason, I needed him. "Did you know about these?" I ask, and although I'm not sure why, something in his sigh tells me he does.

"I honestly forgot all about it."

"What do you mean?" I ask, desperate for an answer to why my mother was sending me roses from her grave.

"Last week, I talked to her on Monday. She said she was going to order you flowers for your interview the next day. She said she planned on ordering a second set to be delivered this week, but that she planned on changing the card and delivery date depending on when you heard about the job. She must have set the date for today."

I had my answer. It was typical of mom to do things like this. Dusty and I talked for a couple more minutes after that. Mom was always a planner. Though it didn't take away the haunted feeling I had about them arriving, I found comfort in them as well. She'd planned ahead one final time.

When we were cleaning out her house in Joplin, we found cards already signed, sealed and labeled in a box. They all had a date where the stamp would go when it was time to send them out. There were birthday cards, Easter, fun little Halloween ones, Christmas Cards and so many others. They weren't just for me and Dusty, but for her friends and what little family she had. There were also some for Dusty's unborn child. He and his wife April are expecting their first child in four or five weeks. I brought home my cards. I didn't open them and I put them in a basket on my desk in my room. I have hope that on those days I will be able to open them and smile at the memory of my mother.

We all fell apart the day we realized Lauren McKidd, the lover of all children, would never meet her first grandbaby. And then we cried for Dusty's unborn daughter because she'd never know what a wonderful person our mom was. My anger toward my mother didn't build until after we buried her and we sat in that stale office while some lawyer none of us knew read off our mother's final wishes.

Dusty and I hung up after promising that he'd call when April was in labor. I'd told him I wanted to try and come up, but I was going to have to see how the new job was going. He congratulated me on getting the job and wished me luck with starting it. That was pretty typical Dusty and while I had hoped the death of our mom might bring us closer together, I don't know if I can truly see that happening.

After I got off of the phone with Dusty, I got the lecture from Becca

about how I looked, but I didn't bother explaining to her what happened, just that I'd spilled coffee all over myself when I accidentally dropped the cup. I was thankful the red blotches on my hand had diminished significantly so to her, my story held true.

She did her best to convince me to go to our favorite bar, Blu Phoenix, but I told her I wasn't up to it. She argued, telling me I needed to celebrate the fact I got my dream job. She didn't seem to understand why I didn't want to celebrate that accomplishment. I've noticed little things like this with Becca since graduation. She gets upset at me over the littlest things, like not wanting to go out. She ended up going out, but came back a little while later, having changed her mind and I promised her a rain check for another night, when random roses from my mother didn't show up.

After reading the first card and talking to Dusty, I decided to open the card from the first roses.

Knock 'em Dead. – Love, Mom.

Instead of tears, I smiled. The message was simple, but every bit of who my mother was.

I curled in bed around nine with a glass of wine, my Kindle and the packet of paperwork HR had given me before leaving the office. I prop up my pillows in the way that makes me most comfortable so I can finish the book I'd started this morning about a stuck-up suit. Not at all like Mr. Cole. Nope, exactly like Mr. Cole.

Before that, I open up the folder with all my shiny new Wellington Ad Management paperwork and start leafing through it.

There's several papers clipped together with a note on top. "These will need to be signed on your first day."

I flip through the paperwork and its various things like computer assignment items, a cell phone agreement, and other standard hiring

paperwork. I find it rather odd that I'm receiving all this stuff as an entry level position but I shrug it off until I come across my offer letter. Tearing it open I read through it.

It has my name and all the legal mumbo jumbo about my job and then my eyes land on my title.

Marketing Team III

From all my research of Wellington I should have been a marketing assistant, not actually on the team. Which is where I want to be, eventually, but I expected to have to work my way onto the team, now I'm going to have to work extra hard to stay on the team.

My eyes keep reading through the letter, stuff about when benefits will be available, what kind of vacation time I get and then my eyes land on my salary and I scream.

Becca comes running into my room. "What's wrong?"

Then she catches on to the fact that I'm beaming, laughing and ready to jump up and down. I haven't felt this happy since Reese called me about my interview.

"Look!" I toss the paper at her while I lay back and smack my feet against the bed squealing with excitement.

"What am I..."

"Keep reading," I tell her. I'm suddenly glad I didn't look in the office and more importantly, I wish I would have looked when I got home. This would have changed my mind about going out. *Maybe.*

"Oh my god. Ireland, is this... seriously?"

I smile wide at her, taking the paper from her and standing up, tossing the paper behind me. "Yes," I tell her and we spend the next few minutes bouncing and dancing around my room.

My measly estimate of a twenty-five grand salary just tripled.

Chapter five

IRELAND
Go Ahead and Break My Heart - Blake Shelton & Gwen Stefani

After Becca and I celebrated, I was wired. The emotional ups and downs of the day culminated into something good, something happy. I needed happy in my life. Getting my dream job with a desirable salary was exactly what I need to start putting the pieces of my life back together. Until I read that letter, I had no idea my dream job would become more than just a place to spend my days.

I drank several glasses of wine to help settle me down, but I still stayed up way too late finishing my book. The humor I'd missed in the first quarter of the book thanks to my mood really shined through. It was two in the morning when I fell asleep happy for the first time in more than a week.

I woke up to the sun shining in my room around eight-thirty with nothing to do for the day, so I lounged around until my phone rings at nine-thirty. It's the lab company with an opening in the next two hours. Wow, that was really fast. I'm thankful I now have something to do, at least this morning, because I could feel the walls closing in on me again and I don't want to go back there. Not now anyway.

Becca hasn't left for work yet. Good, I need her car. Public transit in Phoenix is plentiful, however, getting somewhere quickly isn't an easy feat and I need her car or I will miss my window.

"I need your car," I tell her as I walk out of my room dressed in jeans, a t-shirt and my hair pulled up into a beanie; I don't want to deal with it today.

"What for?" she asks with narrowed eyes. I often borrow her car but with more warning than this.

"I have to go take a drug test. I have two hours to get there and I don't have time on the bus."

"You'll have to take me to work," she tells me.

"No problem."

"You know, making all that money, you can buy yourself a new car."

I smirk at her. "What for? I have yours and the train."

She shakes her head. She can't seem to understand why I enjoy taking the train and public transportation, and sometimes I don't understand it either, but it's just easier this way. Sometimes I think I just use it as an excuse to stay close to home. On the nights we go out, she drives. I usually end up driving myself home in her car because she ends up finding someone to go home with, or I have to take her home.

With about fifteen minutes to spare, I manage to drop Becca off at work, get to the lab, fill out the paperwork, pee in the damn cup and sign the paperwork for the testing. I asked the nurse how long before the results would be available. She said by Thursday or Friday. I smiled at that, maybe I can start next week.

As I'm walking out to the car, I start thinking about the drug test. Drugs are not my thing, never have been. It's been more than ten years since…the summer I turned fourteen. My brother, his friend, the dirt road that led to the pond. Violet eyes, gorgeous, the love of my life.

Reality slices through me like the blades of a knife.

I started my freshman year thinking that the best summer of my life was coming to a close. I was just about to turn fifteen and instead of spending that summer with my girlfriends – not that I had any to spend time with – I spent the entire summer hanging out with my brother Dusty, and his best friend.

That summer we smoked, we drank, we got into loads of trouble – usually for missing curfew – and we'd run all over town. That was the same summer my brother's best friend finally seemed to notice me.

It had started small with winks and flirty fun – more so than usual – and it eventually led to full on flirting, then hugging, touching, kissing and finally first and second base.

I wasn't ready to go all the way. Hell, I was only fourteen at the time. He was sixteen. We never actually dated, just hung out. When we were together he was always hugging on me, kissing me, and hanging on me

like I was his reason for breathing.

On the rare day that I didn't see him, or the days Dusty and I were grounded, were like an endless night. Then the next day he would show up with this megawatt smile and send butterflies crashing through my stomach, my heart would beat a little faster and sometimes I would even break out in a cold sweat from looking him up and down.

The feelings I had for him were undeniable.

Despite the two-year age difference, I fell in love with him the first time I laid eyes on him in elementary school. His gorgeous violet eyes seemed to see right into the very depths of my soul.

I wanted him.

He wanted me.

It was an irresistible attraction that never faded.

I was the little girl; he was the sexy older guy.

He was my brother's best friend.

His name was Dyson Cole Richards.

He must be using his middle name as his last name. There is no denying it. No matter how hard I want to, Mr. Cole is the Dyson Richards of my childhood.

"What's wrong with you?" Becca demands when I walk into the Dunkin' Donuts where she works part-time and I hand over her keys.

"Don't worry about it," I tell her. She gives me a very skeptical look. "I'm fine, promise." I kiss her on the cheek, put her keys in her hand. "I'll see you tonight."

"Uh, okay, but you're telling me what the hell is wrong with you when I get there. You look like you've seen a ghost."

"Ha. Ha." I sass. The irony of her statement isn't lost on me in the slightest. To Becca, I'm sure it looks like I'm sad about my mother, but she hasn't the first clue. I leave the store, thankful for the small line that will keep her from running after me.

My 'not so little' revelation has me off kilter, on edge and paranoia has me looking behind me, thinking he's watching me because my skin keeps prickling with an awareness of something or someone else.

Up until yesterday, I hadn't seen Dyson since the first and last night he was between my legs.

Little did I know, at the time, he'd planned the whole thing all along.

He knew what was going to happen the next day but I was completely clueless. Either I didn't want to see it, or no one bothered to tell me. In hindsight, Dusty had been acting pretty strange for about a week before it happened. Whenever I tried to go out with him and Dyson, he'd yell at me and tell me to stay home. I'd just turned fifteen and was well aware of Dyson's penchant for different girls, but it never occurred to me they wanted me out of the way. Once school had started, Dusty and Dyson did their thing. I often saw Dyson after school, but mostly on the weekends, but like everything else, he'd changed. Or rather, I thought he'd changed. No, Dyson was just doing what Dyson did before that summer and me.

I was in love with the most popular boy in school and behind closed doors he acted as though he was in love with me too. He was a little too excited to keep his distance from me in school. But he'd known how to keep me at bay with my own decision about drawing unwanted attention to myself. At the end of the day, when reality dawned and he left, I knew he was just keeping me as the 'side chick'.

I was cool with the whole thing because I'd had a hard enough time fitting in. Between the four walls of our tiny ass high school dating Dyson would have brought me popularity, but it would have been the wrong kind. High school girls are catty bitches and these girls were no different. Dyson and I would have become the laughing stock of the school and neither one of us needed or wanted that.

At the time, it worked for us, or I thought it did. Again, hindsight is always twenty-twenty, right?

He spent school days ignoring me and a couple nights a week trying to convince me I was ready to take our relationship to the next level. I wasn't ready and each time I turned him down, he'd try harder the

next time. It became impossible to resist because Dyson was just that irresistible.

For nearly ten years I've thought about why I decided that night was *thee* night to give in and after those ten years, I've yet to come up with an answer. At least a logical one. But it happened. I handed him my virginity on a silver fucking platter because I was naïve enough to believe Dyson Richards loved me. I believed the sweet words he spoke to me were the truth, I had every reason to doubt his sincerity but yet when I looked into his eyes, the world fell away.

I believed him when he said we would be together forever.

As I step on the train to head home, I'm transported back to the barn that warm March night.

I can remember, like it was yesterday, the prickles of hay poking into my backside. The well-used smell of the barn and the hay so close to my nose.

Dyson's violet eyes staring down at me, boring into my soul and capturing everything I have to give him as he slipped himself in and out of my body.

"Say my name," he breathed.

"Dyson."

"Love you, VeeVee," he whispered as he thrust inside me.

"Say it again," I begged.

"Love you, baby."

I'll never forget those words. They consumed me in that moment and tortured me for years to come. When he was done, he pulled out of me and pulled up his pants, leaving me on the hay. He said, *"About fucking time you put out."*

His words were like daggers cutting every inch of me; my entire being was shattered in that instant. The hammer came down when he walked out of the barn and I never saw him again. His family had already packed

up their house and they left early the next morning.

I never saw him again after that.

Until yesterday, in an unlikely place, in an impossible situation. I know with every fiber of my being that the man who works for Tigress is the man who still holds the shattered pieces of my broken heart.

A honk brings me back to the present and a new tremble washes over me at the memory of what Dyson did to me that night.

What the hell am I supposed to do now?

I spent the rest of Wednesday wallowing in the fact that Dyson Richards – well, Dyson Cole, now, is going to be upstairs from me every day I'm at work. When I was done drowning myself in my own self-pity, I did everything I could to tamp down the old feelings that threatened to return. Trying, in vein, to stifle the hope blossoming that maybe, just maybe, there was still something between us.

Yes, he hurt me in a way that no human being should ever be hurt, but he also helped me in a way he has no idea about. I was destroyed for months, years even, after his words and actions, but in the end, he's helped me build up a wall around my heart that no one has come close to penetrating. A wall no one has been able to knock down, yet.

Unfortunately for me, he's the kink in my armor.

I find a mountain of busy work to do around the apartment. Becca and I only moved in a week before everything went to hell in a hand basket. Our apartment is still littered with boxes needing to be unpacked. Mostly common room things, like the nonessential kitchen stuff. We haven't done much cooking since we moved in. I kept myself busy unpacking and organizing the contents throughout our apartment, though I leave Becca's stuff alone. I manage to completely unpack and decorate my room. It is all I could do to keep my mind off the anxiety I felt every time I thought about Wellington calling me, or that by working in the same building seeing Dyson again is inevitable.

By Friday afternoon, I'm going stir crazy. I text Becca, hoping she's free because I need to get out of the house. I tell her I'll take her up on

that rain check and she's more than happy to oblige. As we walk into my favorite bar, Blu Phoenix, I vow to wash away all thoughts of new jobs and old loves.

DYSON
I'm On Fire - AWOLNATION

Somehow I managed to convince myself that going out was a good idea. It's an awful idea. I have way too much work to do to be sitting inside a bar. But it was becoming impossible to ignore the old hungers inside me. Things I haven't felt in a long time came bubbling to the surface and I couldn't tamp them down anymore. I need to find a way to rid old *and* new Ireland from my system and this is the only way I know how. Find someone who is wholly and completely unlike her.

Finding a willing woman is easy, especially when you exude confidence and have the air of money, which I have both of in spades. I have the good looks and killer smile that leaves women eating out of the palm of my hand.

Yes, I'm that cocky. Why shouldn't I be?

I've had females throwing themselves at me since I was eleven years old. I snort at the memory of a bouncy redheaded seven year old who grew into a woman capable of giving me fuck-me eyes at the age of fifteen. When we met, she was nine. It was my first day at a brand new school, in a brand new town my mother moved me to after divorcing my father. I was pissed off. I had to leave my friends in Chicago, and they were the only source of normal in my life because at home everything always imploded. Top it off with the fact I had no choice but to start over again. At eleven years old, that's hard to do. My anger subsided when a little girl with a head full of crazy, curly red hair came bounding up to me with the biggest toothless smile on her adorable face. It was like watching an angel appear out of nowhere. That day she smiled at me like I was a breath of fresh air and handed me something, a silly little rock

that looked like a tiger's eye. The same rock that sits in my pocket still.

The memory of the gorgeous, fiery redhead named Ireland makes my cock twitch and pushes me further into finding something to wipe her from my mind. The feeling is only temporary, but at this point, I will take what I can get. Anyone who isn't a tenacious redhead with eyes like a tiger will do.

I'm sitting in a dark corner near the inside bar of the club I'm in. The music is bumping some crazy techno dance shit that's drowning out the band playing on the back patio for those who want away from the live music. I look over my bottle of beer and spot a tall blonde with stick straight hair as she walks into the bar. I look her up and down, small tits, next to no ass, and from here her eyes are dark, brown maybe. She's definitely no Ireland with her curves, ample tits and fine ass. The blonde is a spitting image of every woman I've had on my cock for the last eight, nine years. When you're the star football player in high school, all the cheerleader types want you; you're the epitome of everything they hope to accomplish during school. The blonde tonight is exactly what I'm looking for to take my mind off her. The tall, skinny, bony type is not my cup of tea. Ireland's curves were the first thing, once I discovered what the thing dangling between my legs was good for, that attracted me to her. She was exactly the opposite of everyone who threw themselves at me and I found myself drawn to her. Maybe *that's* what drew me to her in the beginning – she never threw herself at me. No, I had to fucking work for that one.

I watch the blonde, taking my time, finding the right moment to strike. She's walking around the bar, talking to a couple of people, saying hi and laughing. I can hear her laugh over the sound of the music and it makes me cringe. She's going to be one of those. It's obvious she's a regular here and I start to rethink my choice. I like the fish out of water types because when I walk away in the middle of the night, I haven't ruined their favorite bar.

I continue to watch the blonde as she makes her way toward the back door and the live band. I'd been so focused on comparing everything about her that is not Ireland I managed to block out everything else

around her. She steps outside the door then turns back, talking to someone and I look to where she's looking. Stepping out from behind a group of guys is not someone I wanted to see tonight.

My living hell on legs is talking back to the blonde.

So much for drowning out all thoughts of Ireland with a leggy blonde and a hell of a lot of alcohol.

IRELAND
Sweet Home Alabama - Lynyrd Skynyrd

The main building of Blu Phoenix isn't all that big. It's longer than it is wide, and while it's big enough to manage a smaller summer crowd, it's prime season now. The cooler 'winter' months. Summer in Phoenix is brutal and I'm sure all bars suffer during those few months. Hell, lots of businesses suffer because no one wants to be out in one hundred ten degree heat. Let alone drinking in it.

Inside and to the left of the door is a small stage and a wooden dance floor that is littered with tables on nights like tonight when there's a live band playing on the much larger back patio stage. The inside bar is all the way to the right of the door. Far enough away from the stage that you can put some distance between the speakers and a place to sit and drink during live performance nights. When the interior is void of live music, the bulk of the tables are spread out throughout the interior and then there are several out back as well. Across from the main entrance are the back wall and the doors to the fenced in patio area. The previous owner actually had a mechanical bull area set up back here and that was the source of entertainment for the country bar it once was. The new owners took out the pit and put in a ton of concrete, a sandpit for the 'on the beach' feel and a huge dance floor around it. It's early February and the weather is perfect for a party on the patio.

Tonight there is a local band playing and they're pretty good. I'd recognized the name when I checked the bar's website, but I've never

heard them play live before. When we first started coming here about a year ago, we figured out that checking the online schedule was important. There are often private parties taking place inside the bar and when you've got plans to hang out with your friends, you're crushed when you show up and are turned away at the door. We've been turned away enough to double check before showing up.

Becca and I step up to the outside bar and grab two rounds each. We find our favorite table empty and we snag it. We're close to the bar, but it provides the best view of the band and stage. The dance floor is right in front of us to, giving us the perfect vantage point for people watching. What else are you going to do in a bar besides pick up guys, which is more Becca's thing than mine?

Becca is very attractive. She's a leggy blonde, super skinny, small chested, with green-brown eyes. She's gorgeous if you want the truth of it, and men always seem to flock to her, which suits her just fine.

Tonight is no exception and it takes all of twenty minutes before Becca is off dancing with some cute guy and I sip my second Jack and coke while dancing in my chair to the music being played by the band. They have a female lead singer and she's pretty damn good. Her blonde hair and punk rock style reminds me of Gwen Stefani, and I really start to get into the song, then before I know it, it's over.

The next song they start to play has very familiar guitar chords that the crowd automatically recognizes. Who wouldn't know this song? The familiar chords of Lynyrd Skynyrd's "Sweet Home Alabama" start to fill the air and my blood runs cold.

I'd been doing everything I could to rid my mind of all things Dyson, but my mind quickly flashes back to ten years ago, the summer before Dyson moved away. Dusty, Dyson and me hanging out. I remember it like it was yesterday, the smells, the warm summer night, not at all unlike tonight. That was the night Dyson Cole finally seemed to really notice me. It was also the night he 'asked me out'. Ironically, I didn't say yes right away. Dyson was my brother's friend. I didn't know how my brother would feel and I didn't want to become one of the girls Dyson talked about behind their backs.

We'd been friends for years, compliments of his friendship with my brother, but I also had a front row seat to his courting of girls around town. I watched him take girls into private bathrooms, barns and wherever else he could manage to get them alone. I was too young to understand what was happening behind those doors, but that didn't mean it wasn't making me jealous.

With his penchant for women came his whining and complaining to my brother with each and every one. He'd bitch about how they were too clingy or they kept calling him afterwards and how much it drove him crazy. He wanted to do his thing and be done. It didn't matter what my brother told him, or how many times he tried to talk him out of his ways, he still kept doing it. I remember feeling so jealous of all those girls. They had the attention of the enigma that was Dyson Richards. But then I would feel angry toward him for how he talked about them behind their backs to my brother. He never seemed to like any of them and I don't know that I ever heard the same name twice. I never really understood why he did it, but I could understand why the girls clung to him, Dyson could tell a woman anything she wanted to hear just so he could get between her legs.

For me it was different. Yeah, we all say that, but he did things with me I'd never seen him do with anyone else. Sure, I never went to school dances, parties held by the popular crowd, or hung out after the football games – that would mean I actually had to go to one of them. But I never saw him hit on a girl, or at least not the way he did with me. The girls did all the hitting. It seemed like any girl who paid Dyson attention, got his attention in return. Except for me. I never purposefully tried to give Dyson attention and I think that was part of the challenge. And maybe even part of the reason he said what he said when he was done with me. He'd reached his goal, no matter the cost, and he was satisfied with the result.

There was always a constant flow of girls hanging on him at school. He was, after all, the star receiver for our football team. He could have any girl he wanted and here he was hitting on me? He always seemed to throw up little signs that showed me, in his own way, I was different

from the other girls. But at some point I came to wonder if the attention he was lavishing on me was for the sake of saving face with my brother. I always felt different, special even. It took him that whole summer to convince me he wanted me; the plus-sized, bright red-haired, green-eyed freshman to be.

Turns out, all he wanted was one more notch in his belt.

Chapter Six

IRELAND
So What - P!nk

"Where'd you go?" Becca asks as she returns to the table and "Sweet Home Alabama" comes to a close. I shake my head. "You've been awfully spacey these last few days. You alright?"

"Yup." I hop off my stool. "Just peachy. Want another?" I lift my empty cups. Two down, a whole lot more to go.

"Definitely." She polishes off her second piña colada, hands me her empty cups, and I head toward the bar. I purposefully ignore the guy she brought back to the table because she's ignoring his attempts at trying to lick her face off.

I didn't tell Becca what was on my mind because the Dyson is a story from my past that I've never shared with anyone. It's too embarrassing for me. Given the circumstances and looking back on it over the years, I was an idiot for thinking someone like Dyson could really be interested in someone like me. Well, the me I was then. Who I am now wards men off without even trying. Becca asked me once if I was a lesbian and I'd scoffed at the idea at the time. But it kind of made sense she would think that. I'm not the girly girl type like she is. I like my jeans, my Chucks and my bad t-shirts, plus she's seen me talking to guys, maybe even flirting with them, but I never got the butterflies. *Unlike when you're looking at Dyson.* That little voice inside my head is doing all she can to remind me of the one person I really need to forget. *Ten years, girlfriend… ten damn years and you ain't forgotten him yet.*

My mind wanders back to that time while I wait for our drinks to be made.

Dyson leaving town caused uproar in the school with the girls. Aside from leaving the football team high and dry, he left his bevy of bimbos behind too. It didn't take long for me to deduce that there was hardly a girl in our school he hadn't successfully managed to charm into bed. That's when I became nothing but a number, another notch, another scratch in his long list of girls he screwed. My self-esteem plummeted to

the bottom of the barrel. But somewhere in my lowest point I found the strength I needed with me to do something about it.

After he ran out on all of us, really, I was determined to win him back, prove I was the girl he was meant to be with. It was stupid of me to think I was something more than a girl he screwed as he passed through town. But the idea gave me motivation and I started running, eating healthy and by the time I graduated high school, I was a total knock-out rocking a size eight versus the size eighteen I was when he left me naked, scared, hurt and alone in the barn.

By the time I reached knock-out status, we'd all lost touch with Dyson. Even my mother and his mom didn't talk anymore.

That's when things really started to fly. I graduated high school and realized I needed to find it in myself to let him go. I did the best I could before my life brought me here to Phoenix. When I stepped on campus, I was a new woman. Self-confidence, good looks and a newfound decision driving me forward. It was a whirlwind of new friends, new school, career choices and busting my ass for my diploma. Coming to Arizona was the fresh start I needed, and coupled with the pact I'd made with myself that summer to forget Dyson altogether, it worked. Dyson's name never left my lips, but he never wandered far from my mind.

On lonely nights when my friends were out partying and I'd done something responsible, like picked studying over drinking, or when I would crawl into bed after a party left me wanting more, I thought about him. It was hard not to. I imagined running into him again, then I'd think about all the things I would say to him if I ever saw him again.

Eventually the hope of seeing him, finding him, faded. Though I never actually went looking for him, I kept hoping fate would intervene and I would run into him. It finally did, but is it too late? Now I have my chance, but with the events of the last couple weeks, I hardly have the strength to consider what it is I will say to him if I'm ever given the chance.

While I'm standing there, consumed with whether or not I should give Dyson a piece of my mind, I ignore everything else around me. I

love coming here and over the years I've becoming a little more outgoing, meeting guys, talking to them, flirting with them and even dancing with them on occasion, but the reality is, I never go home with any of them and I never give out my phone number. I usually pacify them by ditching them completely, or giving out fake digits.

As the bartender finally slides my drinks over to me, I decide that all things Dyson need to be wiped from my mind before I return to the table. I need to have a good, stress free, enjoyable night. I can do this.

"Here, darlin'."

"How much?" I ask.

"Already paid for."

"What?" I ask, my eyebrows knitting together and she points to her left, my right, and I follow her finger. I reach her intended target just in time to see Dyson Cole turn away from the bar and my heart sinks into my stomach. So much for leaving him out of the rest of my evening.

I quickly ponder my options and the way I see it, I have three choices to choose from.

First, ignore him completely. Be a total bitch and not thank him for the drinks. This is the total cop-out option in my opinion. I know this isn't much of an option because it will spoil my night no matter what. If I attempt to avoid him altogether, I know I'll still be looking for him, watching for him everywhere I go, everything I do. In the end he'd get his own little bit of satisfaction out of it. He wins, no matter what. I might as well go home and save myself the trouble. Then I'll wear myself ragged wondering what would've happened if I'd chosen one of the other options, because I'm masochistic that way.

Would this option lead him to assume I know who he is? If I avoid him altogether, he could easily make that assumption and I might never get to say my piece, or rather scream it at him at the top of my lungs.

Second choice, I can be nice, sweet and thank him for the drinks. Play the innocent card like I don't know who he is. *Would he confess? Or would he leave me guessing?* I guess there is potential for the opposite.

What if he were to pursue me again, not realizing I know who he is, or I pretend like I don't know who he is? Would it be different this time? Not likely, I already know who he is. Then again, no, he knows exactly who I am. He's had the pleasure of actually hearing my full name. His reaction in that conference room says it all.

He seduced me once. I have no doubt he could do it again.

Or three – which is my favorite, let the cat out of the bag. Make sure he knows I know exactly who he is. Give him a piece of my mind that's been brewing for nearly ten years. Finally give in to what it is I've wanted to say to him. Why on earth can't I find it in myself to be angry with him anymore?

The second choice is the one that's more appealing. Thank him, be kind to him and in the end he won't know I know who he is and I manage to save face with someone I'm going to be working with. I grab our drinks off the counter and head to our table. The pondering of my options has forced me to lose track of him and I don't really want to look like an idiot wandering around the bar trying to find someone I don't even know is still here. For all I know, he bought the drinks and walked out the door. "Yeah right," I snort. I couldn't be that lucky.

This is such a bad idea.

I should have gone after him but Becca spots me and smiles before I can change course. The guy she'd been dancing with earlier has disappeared. How unfortunate for her.

"What happened to that guy?" I ask as I hand over her drink.

"Meh, he was cute, but kinda brainless."

I snort. "Since when does that stop you?"

She sips her drink but smiles at me around the straw. "It doesn't." She sets her drink down.

"You wanna dance?" she asks me as the band switches over to a new song.

I hesitate then I hear the song they're playing and I smile, "alright." I say with a little bit more enthusiasm than I feel. But I can't help

wondering if he's actually watching me and small part of me hopes that he is.

Becca and I hit the dance floor and line up.

The band has been playing a mix of country and rock songs and even some rock-country and this one is one of my favorites to dance to. We hit the dance floor and line up with the rest of the crowd. Mostly girls, but a few guys are there too and we start dancing to *Footloose*.

I get so into the song that Dyson completely slips my mind until the hair on the back of my neck stands up and I smile to myself, but refuse to look around for him. I will not give him the satisfaction.

When the song comes to an end, I'm sweating and I want another drink. The band kicks over to a song I don't recognize, probably one of their own, and I tell Becca I'm going get more drinks. "Get me one?" she smiles but keeps dancing to the new song.

I nod and head back to the bar.

I order our refills and this time I pay for them myself. Thank god. Maybe he left once he realized I had no intention of talking to him tonight.

I grab our drinks and return to our table, which, surprisingly, hasn't been taken. I slide up to the high top table and set down our drinks. I start to look around, not admitting to myself that I'm really looking for Dyson. When the song changes again, I expect Becca to come back to the table for her drink. Especially once I realize it's a slower song. Not Becca's speed when it comes to clubs and dancing. Sure, she'll dance with guys but she prefers the sexier version of dancing. Usually using men as stripper poles.

I don't see her and I shrug it off. The slow songs are always good for clearing out the dance floor. Girls run to the bathrooms, guys run to the bar for more alcohol. This song is no exception when the line between me and the dance floor starts to part ways. That's when my eyes land on the man I was inadvertently looking for. He's dancing with someone, but I can't tell who or even what she looks like, but there are definitely arms wrapped around him. My blood runs cold. He's either that short-minded

or he's playing me. When I finally get an eyeful of the blonde woman he's dancing with, I know he's fucking playing me.

Son-of-a-bitch.

Why, in all my infinite wisdom, did I not consider he was here with someone? Or that he wouldn't pick up someone else? God, I'm an idiot. Then they turn again, and as if it was previously coordinated, someone blocks my line of sight. I stand on the rung of my chair, hoping for a much better look at whoever he has in his arms.

That's when I see her.

Fire burns through my veins. Anger unleashes inside of me like nothing I've ever felt before.

Either this son-of-a-bitch has no clue who I am, or he doesn't give a shit because he's dancing with a leggy blonde, better known as my fucking roommate.

I sit down, weighing my options.

Leave.

Stay.

Ignore it…no, I know I can't do that because I know Becca *too* well.

I shudder at the thought of Dyson sleeping with my roommate. *Better fucking not.*

The idea of Becca bedding Dyson, and certainly never the other way around because that's the kind of control freak Becca is when it comes to men. Her rules, her terms, nothing less. She will drive men to the point of madness to get what she wants. I've seen it too many fucking times.

With that knowledge, I slam back my brand new Jack and coke and grab Becca's untouched piña colada off the table and I walk toward the dance floor.

I squeeze my way past a few people then I have an unobstructed view of him. My clear view gives me a solid eyeful of Becca giving him her best impression of a slut, which I know is Becca speak for 'take me home'. I can't hear their conversation but she is starting to rub all over him.

Why do men think that's attractive? She looks like a desperate whore.

The jealousy burning hot and heavy in my veins drives my anger up a notch. If he truly has no clue who I am, then fuck him, I'll make sure he knows exactly who I am. If he does know who I am and he's been watching me tonight, then he knows we've been hanging out and he can go fuck himself.

Despite the ten years since our last encounter, my anger toward him has softened. Maybe it's because I tried like hell to move on, tried to be the bigger person? Understood there was no way in hell that I would ever see him again? I don't know the answer to that question for sure, but I do know watching him interact with her, looking as fucking sexy as he does, sends butterflies to my stomach. Though I can't tell if they're the flutters of desire or the burning rage building in my veins.

Despite his casual appearance, Dyson is the epitome of money and sex. It pours from his body in waves and any woman, even Becca, would be crazy to miss it. Despite my self-imposed celibacy, I can feel it. He's wearing a pair of black jeans that are snug at the hips and flare slightly toward the bottom. I can see he's wearing black boots, but on top he is wearing a black dress shirt. The sleeves are rolled up to his elbows and it's unbuttoned enough to see a grey undershirt peeking out. The shirt is much tighter than most men I've seen wear, but why shouldn't it be? It completely outlines all his muscles and I imagine there's at least a six pack under his shirt and then that sexy V leading into his jeans.

Looking at him, really looking at him, and realizing he's the Dyson Richards who broke my heart so many years ago gives me a new perspective on my choices. How dare he look so fucking good?

Karma isn't quite the bitch I'd always hoped she was.

I straighten my shoulders. The alcohol I slammed burns my stomach and warms me up enough for my confidence to rise higher with each step I take.

I watch as he turns, putting his back to me and I see him try and push Becca off of him. It's not aggressive or even rude, but I get the impression that whatever he was trying to accomplish tonight isn't working for him.

Either that or he saw me coming and he's trying to find a way to save face with me. *Fucker.*

He turns back around, just in time to see me standing a couple feet in front of him. Tonight I was going for casual dressy. I'm wearing well-worn jeans, flared at the cuff, my black peep-toe pumps that make my five-seven frame just a shade taller. With the jeans, I'm rocking one of my favorite tops that hangs off one shoulder. It's grey, but the tank top and bra underneath are both lime green. My hair, despite my better judgment, is pulled up and back at the sides and flowing down my back.

I watch him closely and see a brief flare of panic in his eyes as he looks from me to Becca and back again. Becca looks at me in an inviting, come join us, kind of look. She's oblivious and as much as I want to be angry with her, I have no reason to be. She has no idea she's dancing with the love of my life.

I can see decision in his eyes as he throws me a Dyson original megawatt smile. The kind that would have had my panties combusting under different circumstances. I smile sweetly at him. My anger falters slightly.

I search for diplomacy. Playing up the innocent, I have no idea who you are card first.

"Thank you for the drinks, it wasn't necessary," I tell him and Becca raises an eyebrow at me. I never told her the first round I'd grabbed wasn't paid for by me.

His panty melting smile morphs into one that's more genuine. The act causes little crinkles to form in the corners of his eyes. The look is not lost on me and my body hums with a need I didn't know I had buried deep down.

"You're welcome. The least I could do." His voice has a deep timber to it, not at all like it was the last time I really listened to it in the barn. He's grown up a lot, which is why I didn't recognize him when I first saw him. Losing more than eighty pounds and ditching the nerd look is what threw him off, at least in the lobby. No doubt by the time I left that conference room, he knew. Though a small part of me wonders if

he realized it before his compassionate side got the better of him in the bathroom.

"Come here often?" I ask him, making small talk. Further attempting to play up the idea I have no idea who he is.

He shakes his head. "First time, you?"

"All the time." His smile falters a bit. Like he senses something is up.

"So what brought you here tonight?" I ask. Making small talk is getting old and I'm wishing like hell I had another Jack and coke to drink.

"Just a random invite from a neighbor."

"Oh," I say with some surprise, "are you enjoying yourself?" I let my eyes narrow a little, letting the frustration inside of me get the better of my facial expression.

He shrugs. "Yeah, are you?"

I smile sweetly at him. Becca is obviously confused by our exchange. She keeps looking between Dyson and me, back and forth, like she's trying to figure out what the hell is going on.

He's actually being sweet but the idle chit-chat is getting old.

I try to answer Becca's unspoken question before she voices it aloud. I need to ask him something that would explain why it is I seem to know Dyson because I know that's what she's thinking. That combined with something along the lines of 'why didn't you tell me you know a hot as fuck guy'.

I decide to try and work toward my third option. "So tell me, Mr. Cole, why don't you want me working at Wellington?"

Becca catches on to the conversation quickly and kind of backs away. There is an edge to my voice that only comes out when I'm pissed off and she knows it.

"I just don't think you're right for the job," Dyson answers.

Well played, asshole. "So tell me something?" He nods. "Will what I'm about to do cost me the job you obviously don't want me to have?"

"What are you…"

I toss Becca's piña colada on him before he can finish, nailing him in the face and chest.

"What the fuck, Ireland?" Becca shouts as she attempts to wipe away the part of her drink that got on her.

A hysterical bubble forms in my throat.

"That's for not wanting me to have a decent job," I snap at him and his dumbstruck expression.

Then I walk up to him, place my hands on his shoulders, playing sweet as I lean up to whisper into his ear. "And this," I bring my knee up into his groin and I hear his grunt of pain as I make full contact with his man-parts, "motherfucker, is for leaving me on a pile of hay ten years ago."

"Shit," he grunts.

I smile, release his shoulders and walk away from him, leaving Becca standing there with a completely dumbfounded expression on her face.

"Where are you going?" Becca asks me as I'm walking away.

I put my hand up, indicating that I don't want to be followed. "I'll take a cab."

The crowd parts for me as I walk toward the door of the bar. I can feel Dyson's eyes burrowing holes into the back of my head as I walk away from him. Leaning against the door inside is a good friend of mine. "I'm sorry," I mouth and he smirks at me. I approach him and whisper, "Play along for me?"

"What are you-" I press my lips to his and kiss him. He stiffens, but I know the moment the actor in him kicks in because he kisses me back, wrapping his arms around me and holding me to him. There is no heat, no passion, nothing between us. I pull back from the kiss.

"Tell Cami I'm sorry and I'll explain later." I wink at him and walk away. I catch Cami's dumbstruck expression and I mouth, "I'm sorry," with pleading eyes and she starts laughing and shaking her head. No

doubt she's already heard about what happened on the patio.

No one stops me, some girls actually cheer for me, though I'm not sure if it's because I kneed Dyson in the balls or because I kissed the ever gorgeous Tristan Michaels, and he kissed me back.

I make it two steps from the door and the safety of outside the bar when the son of a bitch grabs my arm, spinning me around to face him. His touch is an electric shock straight to my heart. It reminds me of everything he'd said to me ten years ago on that nasty hay covered floor. It felt so raw and real and now with his hand on me, it solidifies I wasn't crazy for thinking he meant all those things, or maybe I'm still fucking nuts.

"Veevee, stop." His voice is soft. Almost condescendingly so.

I turn toward him and get in his face. "You lost the right to call me Veevee the day you walked out of that barn. Now, let. Me. Go." My anger burns hotter now than it did when I kneed him.

I need to get through the door. Then I can get out of here before I do something that will get me booted from the bar. Getting outside and flagging down one of the waiting cabs is my goal and when I clear the outside door, a sense of relief washes over me.

I start to lift my hand to call attention to one of the cabs, but it's stopped.

"I'll take you home." I close my eyes. This is one battle he will not win.

"Like hell you will," I snap. "Where's your friend?" I ask sarcastically.

"Where's yours?" His tone is almost humorous. I glare at him. "You shouldn't run around kissing married men. Their wives might get the wrong impression."

I scoff at him. Fuck, he knew. All along, he fucking knew. That's why he's not mad at me for kissing someone else. I shake my head and turn again to leave, he stops me.

"You shouldn't go home by yourself." His tone is softer but no less demanding.

Where the hell is this Mister protective act coming from?

"I'm perfectly capable of finding my own way home, fuck you very much." No need to tack on the fact I don't want him knowing where I live.

"We need to talk." His voice is softer, less arrogant and more defeated.

"I'm not sure what we have to talk about, Mr. Cole. I've said everything I needed to say."

He sighs. "That doesn't mean I've had a chance to say my piece, to explain myself."

I turn on him; he steps back slightly as if he thinks I'm going to hit him again. His hands are up in surrender but I don't let the gesture get to me. I can't let it bother me because I need to say all the words, get them out of the way. "You've had ten fucking years to make your peace and you've not done that or even made an attempt to, so why in the hell would I give you the time to do it now?" My voice betrays me, by the end, the fight I felt deflates within me and he sees it.

Seeing his chance, he steps in closer, bringing his hands to my face, holding my cheeks. "Because until now, I couldn't do this." He pulls on me slightly, tilting my face up to his. I've stopped breathing altogether. I'm excited, nervous, anxious, pissed off, you name it, anything, but when he slants his lips over mine, that's it. I freeze. The gentle stroke of his tongue along my lips and the nudge of his thumbs on my cheeks is his way of coaxing me to relax and open for him.

I do.

My mind slips into a deep fog of need and desire as my body gives into him. I breathe out and open my mouth. His tongue darts in along my own and I can truly taste him. He tastes of beer and something distinctively Dyson Cole. It's a flavor I've been craving like a sober alcoholic craves alcohol and until it's on my tongue, I didn't realize I needed it so bad.

I moan into his mouth and he pulls me closer, moving one of his hands from my cheek to the small of my back. Our bodies press against

each other, his erection prominent against my belly, and desire explodes.

The fog in my brain grows thicker until he pulls back slightly, giving me a chance for fresh, un-Dyson-tainted air and the haze in my brain clears.

I pull back from him. His eyes are a blazing violet haze and he blinks slowly.

"Goodnight, Mr. Cole."

"Say my name," he tells me.

I shake my head. "I'm sorry, I don't know your name." I won't give him the satisfaction.

I turn out of his hold and raise my hand, walking away from him. The cabbies all noticed me come out so it takes a heartbeat for one to pull up right in front of me. I open the door as soon as it comes to a stop.

Don't look at him.

Don't look…

Don't do it, Ireland, do not give him the satisfaction.

DYSON
I Know You - Skylar Grey

Look at me.

Come on, Veevee, look at me.

Dammit, look.

It doesn't seem to matter how hard I will her to look at me, she doesn't seem to do it. She opens the door to the cab that pulled in front of her the moment she raised her hand. She turns slightly, *come on, look at me.* She turns a little farther in my direction, hanging on to the door with her right hand as she's about to slide inside and disappear.

I smile wide when the bright green of her eyes meet mine.

She pulls her hand away from the door and flips me off before sitting down inside and slamming the door shut.

I burst out laughing.

That's my *tigress.*

I watch as she pulls away and out of the parking lot before I go back inside. I need to calm down before I drive. Right now, I am ready to go knocking down her door and if I leave now, that's exactly where I will end up.

I walk back inside the bar and I see Tristan talking to Cami. They're both laughing, so obviously there isn't any jealousy between the two of them. Good thing, I'd hate to see a kiss based on rage and an insane need to piss me off ruin a good thing.

I stroll up to the bar and take one of the stools. It's pretty quiet inside since the band is playing outside. "What can I get you darlin'?" Cami asks me from behind the bar.

"Are you mad at him?" I ask.

She snorts a laugh. "I've known Ireland a long time. I saw what she did to you, so obviously you did something to piss her off and kissing my husband was exactly what she felt she needed to do in order to get back at you. Tell me, Dyson, did it work?"

I laugh. "No, I knew what she was doing. I used her friend to get her to pay attention to me, and that was her way of getting back at me."

She shakes her head in exasperation. "Good, then what will it be? Besides a towel." She takes in my wet shirt. Raising an eyebrow she asks, "Maybe an icepack?"

I smirk at Cami. My balls are fucking killing me, but that doesn't mean I don't have a raging hard-on from putting my lips on Ireland's once again. Jesus, that was a fucking mistake. I'm having a hard enough time keeping her off my mind, and now I have the perfect physical feeling go right along with my own delusions of getting my VeeVee back.

"No icepack, no towel, just a Sam's," I tell her and she reaches into the cooler to pull one up for me. She pops the cap and then sets it on the bar

in front of me, but she doesn't let it go when I reach for it.

"That girl has been through hell the last couple weeks. I don't know why she threw that drink on you or better yet, why she clipped you in your nuts, but I do know whatever you did to her, she certainly didn't deserve it."

"Shouldn't you be at home with that little boy of yours?"

"Do you and Tristan conspire against me?" she questions, but she's got a playful little smirk, much like Ireland. The idea has me looking a little closer at Cami and there is something similar in her eyes when compared to Ireland. I've never seen it before now, or maybe my mind is fucking with me. Or it's the adrenaline from being kneed in the balls. "No, we most definitely do not."

"Good, and one of my girls called in sick. I mean it, Dyson, don't fuck with her. She's a good girl." With that, she walks away, helping another customer at the end of the bar. I turn away from her and I can see Tristan standing in the doorway, watching over things. He gives me a raised eyebrow. I'm sure he's curious too, but I raise my bottle to him by way of a salute and slam it back.

The little firecracker is right. Ireland did not deserve what I did to her, but I don't think Cami realizes the apology I need to make isn't for tonight, but something I did nearly a decade ago. There's a lot of built up rage inside that little tigress and if giving me a knee to balls is the worst pain she'll dish out to me when I deserve so much more, I'll take it.

I stand to leave and nearly slam into the blonde I was dancing with earlier.

"There you are," she says, her voice a wanton purr.

"I'm sorry," I narrow my eyes at her. What is she doing?

"S'okay. I knew I'd find you."

"I'm sorry, I'm leaving."

"Nooo, don't go."

I roll my eyes and catch a glimpse of Tristan watching us. Though I

don't need a babysitter, I definitely don't need a drunk hanging on me. "Sorry, on my way out."

"But we had a good time."

I lean down, "No, sweetheart, you had a good time."

"We did, didn't we?"

I shake my head. This isn't going to go very well at all. "No, you're drunk, I'm going home. Maybe you should do the same."

"Okay." She wraps her arms around me.

I pry her off me, my eyes finding Tristan, pleading with him to help me. He just shrugs. Fuck.

"No," I say a little more sternly.

"Becca," a female shouts behind me, it has to be Cami.

"Yeah?" She pulls away from me, but her arms don't let go She searches for the source of who called her name.

"Leave him alone," Cami calls.

"But we were just leaving." She gives Cami a 'don't fuck with me smile'. Even I'm a little taken aback by it.

"No, he's leaving, you're staying." I look over my shoulder and Cami sets down one of their signature blue plastic cups and like a moth to a flame, Becca releases me and stumbles over to it, climbing on the bar stool and picking it up. Cami's eyes meet mine and she gestures toward the door.

I mouth a silent 'thank you' and she smiles before returning her attention to Becca and I turn to leave. Tristan walks up beside me. "It's just coconut juice," he tells me. "Becca's a regular in here. We know the drill." He follows me toward the door.

"Why don't you guys lighten up her drink load?"

He snorts. "We do, usually. If she orders, all the bartenders know to go light on the alcohol, but as you've probably guessed, she's a gorgeous girl and there are a lot of drinks purchased for her."

"Why even let her in at all?"

"Because she's brought us a lot of business, including Vy." He smiles and leaves me standing there. I turn back to see Becca nursing that blue cup like it's a lifeline and I realize that girl has some serious issues. But Tristan wasn't kidding, she's got guys lining up to talk to her. I was one of them a short time ago. She is absolutely gorgeous, but good looks and crazy go hand in hand. I do gorgeous, not crazy.

Chapter Seven

IRELAND

Peter Pan - Kelsea Ballerini

The entire cab ride home is complete torture.

All I can think about is that fucking kiss.

Jesus, *what the hell am I supposed to do with that?*

I cannot believe I caved with him so easily. I can't possibly see how I can come back from that. How can I go back to hating him, being mad at him or even ignoring him after something like that? I let him consume me, heart, body and soul, if only for the briefest of moments. Now that I've crossed that line, even though I didn't mean to, how am I supposed to go back to being oblivious to him?

His scent, his touch, his lips, his tongue, his taste…my head swims.

Getting home, that's the goal. Get home, get the clothes off, take a shower, wipe his scent off me and forget it ever happened.

Who the fuck am I kidding?

God, his erection between us. There is no denying that kissing me had him hard. Despite the attempt, I know damn well his hard-on between us had nothing to do with Becca and everything to do with me. Even after I kneed him, he was still hard.

Maybe after all these years he still wants me.

Or he wants to see if he can bed you one more time for shits and giggles.

My subconscious is a real bitch sometimes.

I brush my teeth, twice. I still taste him on my tongue.

I shower, throw my clothes in the washer. I still smell him.

My body hums with a need unlike anything I've ever felt before.

What am I going to do?

I can't give into him, not like this. I need answers to all my questions. I have to know what happened that night. I can't possibly give into him again, not until I have my answers. Those answers hold the key to

unlocking a languishing, dark part of me and if I don't get those answers, how can I possibly trust him again? How can I possibly find it in my heart to forgive him? Can I get those answers and walk away from him? Satisfied that what happened between us wasn't in vain? Or will those answers shatter the walls around my heart? Break free from the loss I feel because of him? I don't know, yet.

What I do know is Dyson Cole has a hard-on for me.

I put forth extra effort to get to bed and get the lights turned off before Becca comes home. I'm hoping that if she thinks I'm either not home or I'm sleeping, she'll leave me alone about what happened tonight. I listen to her talking to someone and the panic rises from my stomach. Jesus, she better not have brought him home with her. I will never forgive her for that. Or Dyson for that matter.

Fuck, my curiosity gets the better of me and I climb out of bed and carefully open my door so I don't make any noise that will alert her to the fact I'm home and awake. The guy she's with finally says something and relief floods through me. It's most definitely not Dyson's voice. I can't stop my annoyed eye roll. He better be fucking gorgeous because that voice is obnoxious as fuck. I may not date guys, but even I have higher standards than that.

I quietly close my door. Once I'm satisfied they didn't hear me, I crawl back into bed.

I don't understand how she does it, but Becca has always been able to sleep with men she doesn't know. Usually on the first date, usually drunk, and usually someone whose name she doesn't remember in the morning. I've never understood how she can do that, but it's obvious she and I are wired differently. For me, sex and love are synonymous. But then again, my one partner hardly makes me an expert, especially considering he left me after telling me it was about time he got between my legs. At least I know to prepare myself for morning. She's a bitch. Between the hangover she'll no doubt have and the typical Becca style walk of shame, she's a bear.

Becca is predicable in a way that means one of two things is going

to happen. One, she'll be pissed because the dude fucks her and leaves without spending the night. Or two, she'll be pissed because they're not leaving in the morning. In a way, I get it, but at the same time, make up your fucking mind, would you? This is how she's been as long as I've known her.

I make her sound like a complete and total slut and that's not true. She's not a 'different guy every night' kind of girl, just a 'different guy every time I go out' kind of girl. She goes out because she's horny, wants to get laid or get drunk. All of which lead to her getting drunk and laid. Sometimes not in that order.

I was delighted when we moved out of the dorms and into an apartment during our junior year, at least then I didn't have to sleep with headphones on and facing the wall when she brought men home with her. She had her own room.

Thinking about Becca and her bevy of men brings my thoughts back to my lack of men and right back to Dyson. My lips still prickle from his kiss, his taste lingers on my tongue and his scent is still in my nose. God, I will never be rid of him.

Until I looked at him and saw that panty melting smile on his face, walking away wasn't that hard to do. He was still the prick in the barn, but that look, it said everything that words couldn't. His erection between the two of us said even more. He still wants me.

The wetness between my legs tells me that he's not the only one.

Flicking him off was on instinct. A survival tactic. I didn't want him to think he'd won already and when he busted up laughing, I knew it didn't work. *Fucker.*

Trying to get Dyson off my mind, I return to the new book I started earlier. This one is a sweeter romance, but if it didn't tell the story of me and Dyson, I might not have been so interested in it. Then again, books like these always have a happily ever after and right now? That isn't in the cards for me and Dyson. *How could I possibly take him back after what he did to me?*

I doze off before my brain becomes too muddled with the idea of

finding it within myself to forgive him just yet.

"What the hell happened to you last night?"

I jump three feet into the air when Becca barges into my room, the door slamming against the wall. "I was sleeping, wench," I groan, not ready to wake up.

"It's damn near noon." She bounces onto my bed, sending me off the bed slightly then back down. I grab the covers and pull them over my head.

"Good. I didn't want to see your boy toy from last night." She doesn't say anything. "What was his name?"

She doesn't answer and I peek under my covers to look at her, and she shrugs. Her eyes are sad. "You know you shouldn't do this to yourself," I admonish her.

"I know, but you ditched me and…" she sighs, "I don't know. It just kind of happened."

I snort. "Blu is twenty-five minutes from here, it doesn't just happen."

"Speaking of which, I have to go get my car."

I roll my eyes are her. "You let him drive you home?"

She laughs. "Sure, I was pretty tipsy anyway." She pulls the comforter down farther, effectively forcing me to look at her. "What the hell got into you last night?"

"I don't want to talk about it." Because talking about it means I have to tell her everything and I don't want to do that. Not in the slightest.

"Spill it, woman."

"The dude was being a dick to me earlier in the night. I figured I should save you from yourself. I threw your drink on him and took my

knee to his balls for other reasons." I give her a pointed look, as if I was trying to protect her from another douche and she seems pacified, for now.

She bursts out laughing. "What about your drink? Why'd you have to waste mine?"

I laugh with her. She would totally point out it was her drink and not mine. "I needed the liquid courage, so I slammed mine. Yours was collateral damage."

We banter back and forth for a while before we're interrupted when the door buzzer goes off. "I'll get it." She bounds off toward the front door and I climb my way out of bed assuming it's Mr. One Night Stand forgetting something.

I go to the bathroom and debate on taking a shower again. Last night I did what I could to remove him from my nose, but failed. I need to wash my hair and take a real shower.

I strip out of my clothes and I'm standing there naked waiting for the water to warm up when Becca barges in. I roll my eyes at her because closed doors don't stop her, at least when it comes to me. I only closed the door all the way because I thought it was her one-night boyfriend at the door.

"Apparently Mr. Piña Colada likes having drinks tossed on him."

"What the hell are you talking about?" There is no way Dyson knows where I live, *is there?*

I grab my robe from behind the door and turn the water off. She's given me the impression Dyson is standing there waiting for me and panic rises as I take in my barely-there robe. It leaves nothing to the imagination.

When I walk around the corner into the kitchen, I'm not prepared for what I see. I'd expected Dyson, not a huge bouquet of yellow roses sitting on the counter next to my mother's.

"Open it, open it." Becca jumps up and down.

"No." I walk back toward my bathroom. I need a shower and some

fucking coffee if I'm going to have to deal with Dyson Cole today.

"You can't ignore them forever," she yells at me as I close the bathroom door.

"Watch me," I mumble to myself. Sliding the robe from my shoulders, the silkiness of the fabric sends goosebumps down my arms and my nipples harden. "Dammit," I grumble as the visual of Dyson kissing me last night plays through my mind. The feel of his erection against my stomach, the need and desire I felt burns hot in my veins.

I lock the door and climb into the shower.

I've always been well-endowed in the chest. Even after losing all that weight in high school, the one thing that never went away were my tits. Though their double D size makes tits a loose representation of the term. No, they are boobs. Big, voluptuous boobs. With equally large nipples atop them. If there is one thing I am thankful for with my body it's that I have porn star quality tits without surgery to achieve them.

The curves of my chest are matched by the curves of my hips and the bubble of an ass I have to go along with everything else. I thought for sure losing all that weight would tone them down, but running and exercising only made them more pronounced.

Thinking about my body reminds me it's been more than two weeks since I've gone to the gym. I shrug it off. I'll get there, eventually.

While in the shower it takes every ounce of strength I have not to slide my fingers through my sex, and find the release I so desperately seem to need. I don't know why I stop myself, but I do.

Once I'm out of the shower, Becca pounces all over me to open the damn card. Finally, once I've got my hair pulled back into a pony tail, my favorite Nirvana t-shirt on with a pair of jeans, I go into the kitchen to make myself some coffee. Becca managed to disappear and I look at the clock, it's just after one. "You working today?" I shout toward her room.

"Unfortunately," she replies.

Thank god, I don't need her prying further about the card. I reach for it, hoping like hell I can read it and throw it away before she comes back out.

Just as I'm about to lift the flap of the envelope, she comes out of her room. "About time."

"Why didn't you just open it and look yourself?" I ask her. "You're not exactly the 'keep your nose out of other people's business' type."

She blushes bright red.

"I fucking knew it. So, Miss Snoopy Pants, what does it say?"

She scrunches up her nose. "I have no idea. It didn't make any sense to me."

I cock my head at her and pull the card from the envelope. There is no name on the card, just one simple line:

Say my name.

Bastard. "Huh," I huff and shake my head.

"Care to explain?" Becca asks me.

"Nope." Not in the slightest.

"You're no fucking fun. I tell you everything."

I glare at her. "And some things are far too embarrassing to say out loud," I snap at her.

"You have nothing to be embarrassed about. Look at you, you're fucking gorgeous."

I snort. "I didn't always look like this."

It's her turn to give me a quizzical look. "You've looked like this as long as I've known you."

"Come on," I tell her and head for my room. I haven't bothered to open my yearbook in years. It got to be too painful to look at.

After Dyson left town, we'd already taken the school photos that would appear in the yearbook so I made mom get me one just so I could have one more photo of him. Though I didn't tell her that. In fact, I never told her about what happened between Dyson and me. She just knew

whenever Dusty mentioned Dyson's name, I'd leave the room.

I open up the yearbook and flip to my freshmen class. It was small, only fifty-six people in it, so it isn't hard to find me.

"Holy shit." She looks from the picture to me and back a few times. "There is no way that's you," she tells me in disbelief.

"Oh, it is." I pull out a picture I'd stuck inside the book. It was the picture that was my daily motivation for a long time. It's a full body shot, with clothes on, I had mom take for me so I had a visual of what I used to be and I show it to Becca.

"Well, look at you, I would have never guessed."

I laugh, "Where in the hell did you think the hips and ass came from?"

Becca laughs, "I would have never guessed. You eat anything and you don't think twice about it."

"Yeah, but I also spend way too much time in the gym burning it off."

Becca had to leave for work after our talk and I stand in the kitchen staring at the damn yellow roses Dyson sent me. I concoct a plan sure to make him crazy.

DYSON
Damn I Wish I Was Your Lover - Sophie B. Hawkins

The rest of the weekend passes in a blur. I was busy dealing with some issues in New York. I need to get up there and take care of them before they get too far out of hand, but I'm avoiding it like the plague it is and I couldn't figure out why until this morning. I'm holding out, waiting for Shelly to tell me when she's starting. Then I can make my plans so that I'm back before she starts working downstairs.

It's nearly ten on Monday morning and, I'm up to my elbows in spreadsheets, numbers, statistics and a few branding ideas for our new

product line and I have a meeting in forty minutes. I'm trying to get through some of this shit before the meeting.

The clock on my desk chimes, indicating it's ten and the door to my office swings open. The glass is clear so I have no problem seeing Andy walking in. But what he's carrying has me thrown for a loop.

"What the hell is that?" I ask as I get a better look at the narrow black vase in his hand and the single black rose sitting in it. It looks half dead.

"This was delivered about five minutes ago with the express direction to wait until ten to bring them in," Andy says as he sets it on my desk and I reach for the card, shoo-ing him out of my office so I can open it in peace.

What I see on the card has me laughing out loud.

Asshat.

No sender necessary. I know exactly where these came from. My laughter draws Andy's attention and I'm sure I look like I've lost my mind. Who knows, maybe I have. This girl makes me fucking bat shit crazy.

I contemplate my own plan. If this is going where I think it's going, I'm going to fight back.

I place an order for her own bouquet of roses with my own little reply back to her.

Let the war of the roses begin.

IRELAND

The door buzzer goes off. I catch the time on the microwave before opening the door. It's eleven o'clock on Monday morning. As I reach the door, my heart starts pounding in my chest. He obviously knows where I

live. What's going to stop him from showing up here? Fuck, I don't need him here, not right now, not until, at the very least, my little game is over.

I open the door and standing on the other side is a rather short gal holding up a vase with a single white rose inside the crystal clear container.

I thank her for the delivery, she turns to leave and I close the door, bringing the rose to my nose and I smell its fragrance. I smile and pluck the card off the stick. I set the vase on the counter and I open the card.

Say. My. Name.

"Never."

DYSON

My meeting lasted longer than I'd expected so it's just after noon when I return to my office. Walking inside I see two more vases sitting on my desk next to the first one Andy brought in and I chuckle to myself.

I walk over to my desk and pull the card out of the one closest to the first vase. The rose is in better shape than the first one, but not a whole lot better.

I open the card:

Prickweed.

What the hell does that even mean? It still makes me laugh.

I open the next one. This one is attached to a slightly lighter black rose, but it is just a bud, not the fully opened bloom like the first two. Hmm, wonder if the florist is running out of dead black roses.

Cocky Bastard.

I'm glad I caught on to her game earlier in the day because I'd already planned one to be delivered at noon, then one and so on. I want to be angry with her, between the drink and kneeing me in the nuts, then leaving me standing there in front of the bar, but I can't find it in me to do anything beyond smiling.

One o'clock rolls around and Andy strolls in, this time he's holding a vase with two roses of the same color as the last ones and he is shaking his head.

"I'm beginning to wonder who you pissed off, boss."

I laugh, "No one, at least not that I know of."

"Or not yet." He smirks and sets down the vase on my desk and I pluck the card from the stand and open it.

Stuck-up Three Thousand Dollar Suit Wearing Pencil Dick.

"Oh sweetheart, it's far from a pencil." I snicker as I add the card to the growing pile and move the new vase to the credenza along my wall.

I go back to work, but I eagerly await the chime for the next hour to roll around and what exactly Ms. Tigress has in store for me next.

IRELAND

I knew he'd caught on to my game when each hour more deliveries showed up at my door.

The next bouquet of a half dozen yellow rose showed up at noon. The card simply said:

Say. My. Name.

The next one came at one, this one a bouquet of pink roses and it said:

I can make you scream my name.

The one after that was a dozen purple roses at two o'clock which said:

And it won't be in anger either.

I knew exactly what he was implying because this little game of ours was turning me on like nobody's business.

The last delivery came at three. Two dozen long-stemmed red roses with a card that nearly had me reaching for my vibrator:

It will be while my mouth is buried in that sweet pussy of yours.

DYSON

Four o'clock rolls around and Andy dutifully brings me my next delivery. This time instead of black roses, he's carrying a bouquet of a dozen white ones. A show of surrender?

My eyes wander back to my credenza and the array of black sitting on top of it. I shake my head remembering the two o'clock card that said,

Manwhore.

That was followed up by the three o'clock card:

Arrogant Fuckwad.

So the white roses are a surprise. I deserve to be called every one of these things, in fact, I probably deserved far worse, but I'm not ready to give up trying to get her to say my name. Each of the cards I'd sent got a little sweeter and little sexier, a little more poignant. But make no mistake, I mean every word.

Andy leaves my office after setting them down and I find the card quickly, pulling it off the stick and flipping it over. There is only one word written on the card. It's the only word I've wanted to see all day.

Dyson.

She did it, she said my fucking name. Okay, fine, she wrote it, but none the less, she said it and I am smiling from ear to ear when Shelly walks into my office.

Chapter Eight

DYSON
Down - Jason Walker

"Well, that's certainly a different sight to see," she teases as she takes in my huge smile. "Uh… who sends someone black roses?" she asks, taking in the sight on the credenza of the black roses Ireland has sent me today.

"Someone you've severely pissed off," I tell her while putting the card on the stack with the others and I move the roses to the side of my desk where they can stay. I'll have Andy dispose of the black ones later.

She snorts a laugh. "Well, obviously you didn't piss them off that much if they're sending you roses."

"Hardly. Now, what can I do for you?"

"I just came up to let you know that Ireland will be getting a phone call in the next hour. Her tests came back fine and we're going to start her on Monday. Are you going to throw a hissy fit about her being hired?"

"Yes," I state simply.

"Care to explain why?"

"Not really." No need to let her in on the fact that once Ireland becomes a Wellington employee, the fraternization policy goes into effect and she can no longer date me. At least if she wants to keep her job. I curse internally, but even that's not going to stop me. I've had a taste and I need more.

"On second thought, no. Hire her. If she doesn't work out, you'll fire her and life can go on as it was."

She glares at me. "You've got something up your sleeve when it comes to this girl, don't you?"

I put my hands up in surrender. "I have no idea what you're talking about."

"Bullshit, Dyson, I've known you for a long time, and you never give in this easily."

She calls my bluff, but I don't back down. Let Ireland start her job, I'll continue to meddle with her anyway I want to and eventually Wellington will have no choice but to fire her for violating the no fraternization policy. It's a win, win. I get the girl to work for me and the girl I've dreamed about for more than ten years.

"Whatever, but I will tell you Wellington is quite fond of her already and he barely knows her." I can't stop the growl that escapes but she doesn't seem to notice. "I think it is going to take a lot more than whatever you have up your sleeve to get her fired." She tosses a file on my desk. "There's the information you wanted."

I don't need to tell her I already figured it out. I asked for it under the guise of wanting Tigress to run its own background check. Though she'd glared at me about it, she didn't argue. It would have been strange if I hadn't done the same with every employee of Wellington that works on Tigress related items.

"Thank you," I tell her but I don't pick up the folder. "Anything else?"

She places her hands on my desk and leans forward, showing off a little bit of cleavage in the process, not that she has much to show off in the first place. "Dinner, tonight?"

I suppress my annoyance and simply shake my head. "Not tonight, not ever."

Her hopeful face falls and she straightens up. "You'll regret it."

No, sweetheart, I regret ever giving you the impression I wanted dinner with you. "Hardly," I state and with that she strolls out of my office. There is an extra sway in her hips as she does, trying in vain to show me something she truly doesn't have to show off.

The image of Ireland's ass as it walked away from me last night is something burned in my brain and no one will ever compare to her.

IRELAND
Walk Into This Room - Edward Kowalczyk
And Neneh Cherry

Five o'clock rolls around and two things happen at once. My cell phone starts to ring and the door buzzes. On my way to the door, I grab my phone and look at the number. It's a downtown number and I panic briefly thinking it's Dyson calling me. I almost ignore it, but then I think about Wellington and slide to answer it.

"Hello?" I say with some hesitation, bracing myself in case it's him on the other end of the line.

"Ireland, hi, this is Cara from Wellington Ad Management." The HR rep. Disappointment slides through me that it's not Dyson.

"Hi Cara," I say as I walk toward the door and the next delivery from Mister stuck-up, good for nothing but making me crazy, Cole. "It's great to hear from you. I hope you have good news for me?" I ask.

"I do. Everything in your background came back clean." Duh. "And your drug screening is perfect. I'm calling to see if you can start next week Monday?"

My mouth falls open as the person at the door bypasses the buzzer and the knock comes through the door. "So soon?"

"Is that a problem?"

"No, no, not at all." I open the door and I'd expected to see the delivery gal that has been delivering my flowers all day, but instead I am met with another two or maybe three dozen long-stemmed red roses and Dyson 'fucking' Cole.

I fight the urge to slam the door in his face, but he sees I'm on the phone and steps into my apartment. *Fucker.*

"Next Monday would be wonderful, Cara, I just have one quick

question."

"Anything?"

I watch Dyson out of the corner of my eye as I ask the question that's been bugging me for almost a week. "The amount of pay, on my offer letter, that isn't a misprint, is it?" I ask.

"I can double check, but is it too low? I can talk to Shelly about…"

"No. *Jesus*, more money? My eyes flare wide in surprise and I ignore Dyson. "Not at all, but it is way more than I was expecting, so I just wanted to make sure."

She laughs on the other end of the phone and Dyson is staring at me with his eyebrows raised. "Nope, it's accurate, I assure you."

"Okay then," I say with a smile, though I turn away from Dyson.

Cara goes over a couple things about dress code. *Fuck, I need to go shopping.* Then she tells me to be at the security desk at seven-thirty Monday morning. They will set me up with a security badge and I'm supposed to bring the remaining paperwork with me. Meanwhile, Dickhead is making himself comfortable on my couch, looking around my apartment like he's trying to gauge something I'm not grasping or he's just trying to get a read on me. My frantic attempts at ignoring all thoughts of Dyson and my mother have left the apartment absolutely spotless.

Finally, after another minute or so Cara and I end our call. I lock my phone and say, "What the fuck are you doing here?"

He smirks at me. "I figured I owed you your last bouquet of roses from my hands." He stands and stalks toward me in a way that makes my panties melt. "And, I wanted to hear you say my name in person."

"This couldn't have waited until Monday?" I scowl at him.

He shakes his head. "After the torture you've put me through all day with the name calling, I thought you owed me something."

"I owe you nothing, Mr. Cole." I tack his name on at the end just to watch his eyes flare in frustration.

Jesus, he's fucking gorgeous. He's ditched the tie to his suit, the jacket too. He's wearing a fitted charcoal grey dress shirt, open at the top, still tucked into his dress slacks and his sleeves are rolled up to his elbows.

"On the contrary, tigress, you owe me a chance to explain myself."

Tigress? Where...

I take a step back from him, trying to ruffle my way through the thoughts roaming in my head. "How many women have you called tigress?" I ask in almost a whisper.

"None but you," he says with a cocky confidence that shouldn't surprise me in the least.

"Then why is your company called Tigress?" I ask, but the voice that comes out is barely audible to my ears.

"Why do you think?" he asks with an insulted look, as if I should know the answer to his question.

I take another step back and he stops stalking toward me. I bump into the kitchen island currently holding all the roses he's sent me and the ones that my mother sent last week. The force rattles the vases and it draws his attention to the array. When he gets to the white and purple ones from my mother he narrows his eyes. "Do you have a boyfriend?"

"What? No. Why..." The shock I feel at his question is surprising. Why would he think I have a boyfriend? I follow his line of sight to the roses and my shoulders slump, my fight leaves me. "They're from my mother," I breathe out.

I have no idea why Dyson seeing the roses is making me emotional. Maybe it's the prospect of having to tell him that my mother is dead. She was a second mother to Dyson the way his mother was to my brother, and even to me, growing up. Both of them were single moms, both working hard to keep roofs over our heads and food in our bellies.

I've managed to make it through the entire weekend without shedding a single tear even with looking at the roses on the counter and I'll be dammed if I'm going to start now. Not in front of him. "Dammit," I breathe, willing the tears in my eyes to stop.

"I'm really sorry to hear about your mother, Ireland." His voice is

softer than I've ever heard from him and it's my undoing. His quiet sympathy is too much.

"I think you should go," I whisper.

"What did I say?" His voice is hurt. He's hurt, dammit, why do I care?

"Nothing, just please…" The tears I was fighting unleash down my cheeks and I can't stop them. The next thing I know, Dyson has his arms wrapped tightly around me and he's holding my head to his chest. It's the most comforting place I've ever been in in my entire life. Even my mother's arms don't compare to this.

Surrounded by his warmth and gentle caresses, I cry softly. Soaking his shirt. Realizing I'm ruining yet another article of clothing he's wearing, I try in vain to push him away.

He won't let go, he simply holds me tighter. His cheek comes to rest on top of my head as his thumb rubs small circles on my back and his other hand strokes through my hair.

I'm bawling over the loss of my mother and yet his touch is turning me on in ways I never knew existed and it's making him irresistible. Once again, I'm lost in his touch, in his quiet compassion, and the scent that is sweet and spicy, and all Dyson.

DYSON
When We Were Young - Adele

"Make me forget." Her voice is soft, barely above a whisper. "Please, take it away." Her sobs come harder, but I get what she's implying. "Just for a little while? Please," she begs me and I don't know that I have the strength to do this for her, to her. She deserves so much better than this.

I pull back, looking into her red eyes and I see that she's completely serious. "Ireland, I…"

"Please," she interrupts me. "I need…" she sniffs, "I need to be numb for a while."

I take her cheeks in my hands, wiping away her tears with my thumbs as I hold her face up toward mine. What happens next surprises me. I don't know how I do it, but the next thing I know, my lips are crashing into hers.

I watch as the emotion starts to fade, her tears start to dry up and she closes her eyes. Her body melts perfectly into mine and that zing of awareness sparks things deep down inside me that I haven't felt in nearly ten years, not since the last time I held her in my arms. The heat radiating off her is an intoxicating feeling, making my head swim with lust and her desperation makes it impossible to ignore what she's asking of me. I can't say no to her. She is undeniable.

Her lips against mine are soft, warm, and just like they were last night, stiff and tense from the fear or anxiety, which, I'm not sure.

I give her a teasing flick of my tongue against her lips and rub my thumbs along her cheeks, hoping to coax her to open for me once again. I'm silently begging for her permission, granting me access inside so I can give her what she wants and what I desperately need. Until her lips met mine a moment ago, I didn't realize how much I needed another taste since Friday night. Friday's kiss reminded me of everything I've been missing in my life. This kiss is no different. Kissing her once was hard enough to deal with; this one is going to wreck me in ways I'll never recover from.

Her gently moan as she lets my tongue inside her mouth is like unlocking a caged tiger. Lust and desire explode through my body, my cock grows impossibly stiffer, twitching as it becomes hard as steel, straining against my pants, searching for the place he wants to be most. Buried inside her delectable pussy. Fuck.

This girl is going to be the death of me. I know she's not going anywhere so I release her cheeks and let my hands slide down to her neck and then her shoulders, still holding her to me, but giving her some space. I need to know this is what she really wants from me. I need her to take the lead because I'm dancing on the edge about to pass a point of no return.

Her tongue curls around mine and her breathing slows more. She presses harder into me. Her hands take hold of my sides, pulling me closer to her. There's no space between us and I feel the softness of her curves mold against my body.

Unable to breathe anymore, I pull back from the kiss. "My control is hanging by a thread," I breathe against her lips. "If you keep going, I won't be able to stop." My lips move against hers as I speak and I watch her shiver.

"Don't stop," she moans back.

"Where's your room?" I ask and she pushes on me gently, coaxing me backwards. Her hands go to the bottom of my shirt and she starts pulling it out of my pants. I don't stop her. She needs this. I need this. We need this to happen. At the end, she will either tell me to fuck off, getting her revenge for my harsh words all those years ago, or she will draw me in closer, pull me into the world that is Ireland, a world that once I'm inside, I will never be able to leave again.

This is my chance to prove to her I have no intention of letting that night be the last time we're together. I have to prove to her that what I did wasn't real. This is the first step to that. Take her to bed, let her forget, let her be numb, and then prove to her I'm not going anywhere, not without her. Not unless she forces me away from her.

I was trying to protect her all those years ago. I didn't want to hurt her and I did what a dumb ass seventeen year old kid who had just witnessed his soul crashing with another human being would do. I freaked the fuck out.

No matter how hard I tried to say I was protecting her, it wasn't for her, it was for me. It was easier for me and for no one else. The attraction sparking between us is starting to pick away at the resolve I'd found years ago. It was a kid's way of looking at the world. Now with her body pressing against mine, her hands unbuttoning my shirt, I know that wasn't the case. If that were true, my heart wouldn't be pounding in my chest from fear of the unknown. For the first time in my life, I'm afraid to hand over the power to hurt me to a girl I destroyed when she was only

fifteen years old. If anyone can hurt me, it's her and only her. Sleeping with her in that barn had been a mistake. Not the kind that I would take back, just the kind I wish I could do-over, a chance to do it right.

She starts unbuttoning my shirt as we round a corner and the hallway darkens the deeper into the space we go. She's managed three of four buttons but she's never taken her eyes off of me. "Why?" she breathes.

"Why what, tigress?"

I expect her to ask about the barn, thinking that she's reading my mind, but she doesn't. Instead, after a moment of hesitation she asks me, "Why don't you want me at Wellington?"

Not a question I want to answer because I don't want it to sway her decision to go to work for them. I need her that close to me. I realized that when Shelly left my office. I have to have her that close to me. I need her to give me the chance to right the wrongs of our past, together.

"Because if you're at Wellington, I can't do this." I reach for the hem of her t-shirt and start to pull it over her head. She lets go of my shirt with one of two buttons left to go and raises her hands above her head. I free her of the band t-shirt she's wearing and I'm met with a soft pink, sheer bra that gives me the most perfect shot of her taught nipples. "Fuck," I groan and her hands are back on my shirt, quickly freeing me of those last two buttons.

She reaches up, pushing the shirt down my shoulders until it catches on my elbows, restraining me. I chuckle and she smiles at me. I drop her shirt and move to help her. When I take over the shirt duty, her hands are quickly all over my chest. They're soft and warm and I feel her fingers tug on my nipple rings.

I hiss through my teeth and my cock pulses in the confines of my pants.

"Not something I expected out of you," she breathes then leans in and runs her burning hot tongue over one, then the other. I groan, but bring my hand to tug slightly on her belly button ring.

"Oh, I'm full of surprises, and so are you," I tell her with no indication

of what's left to be revealed the more she undresses me.

I place my hands on her hips and let them roam up her sides until I reach the swell of her breasts. She was always well-endowed in that department and despite the weight loss, she managed to retain them. "Fucking gorgeous," I whisper to her as I run my thumbs over each of her nipples. She moans and I watch her eyes roll up in her head at the pleasure I'm giving her.

"Tell me, tigress?" I say as I press my forehead against hers. She nods for me to continue. "How did you get to be so fucking perfect?"

She snorts, "I'm far from perfect."

"You've always been perfect to me," I tell her before I can stop myself.

I see her eyes flare slightly, but it quickly disappears. It's almost like a light bulb goes off but doesn't stay lit for very long. She's thinking about something but she doesn't give me a chance to ponder it further when her hands move to the waistband of my slacks and she runs her fingers between them and my hips. "Less talking, more doing." She smiles at me. It's a full, genuine smile that makes her look years younger, reminds me of when we were kids.

"Tell me what you want." I breathe, my lips brushing against hers.

"I want to scream your name while your face is buried between my legs." I watch the blush spread across her face. Just like when we were in the barn.

I smile despite the fact I get the feeling she's pretty new to what's happening between us. Her own lust is driving her actions.

I slide my hands around to her back and finding her bra clasp, my eyes seek permission from her and she nods. With the flick of my fingers, I undo the clasp before sliding my hands up and over her shoulders, bringing her bra straps with me as I go, pulling them down her arms. Maintaining contact with her skin leaves little goose pimples in the wake of my touch and her nipples grow harder as the covering falls away. Her mouth falls slack, her eyes close once again and she's standing before me completely topless.

She has the most amazing tits I've ever seen. Plump and full. Her nipples are a dark rose color that makes me want to suck them into my mouth.

As I pull her bra from her body and toss it on the floor, I turn her so she's between me and the bed. I don't bother looking around her room, I don't care, I just need her. I need to taste her, to feel her. "Lie down," I tell her, and she smiles and does as I ask.

She slides into the middle of the bed and I climb on top of her, rubbing my nose gently against hers and I kiss her again, this time harder, more desperate. Throwing everything I feel for her into the kiss. My free hand slides up her stomach to cup her breast and she moans into my mouth.

The thread hanging on to my control snaps. I need her so bad.

I roll her nipple between my thumb and forefinger and she arches her back, deepening the kiss. I put one knee between her legs, and she spreads them for me, giving me access to her. When she moans at the contact of my thigh against her denim covered sex, I kiss her harder, swallowing her pleasure.

I pull back from the kiss, needing air and desperate to taste her flesh. I kiss along her jaw, down her neck until I find that sweet hollow between her neck and shoulder where I lick and tease gently. She moves her head to the side, giving me more access and I kiss along her shoulder, down toward the nipple I just had in my hand and I find it, sucking it deeply into my mouth and she writhes again.

Her hand slides into my hair, holding me to her so tight I can barely breathe. I'll take it.

I nibble on her nipple between my teeth and she cries out before I back off and lick at it gently.

"I can't take it anymore, please, I need you," she mewls.

"Say it first."

Her eyes come to mine in a lust filled haze. "Please." I roll her nipple between my fingers again. "Please, god, Dyson," she cries out and a very

satisfied smile spreads across my face.

"I knew I'd get you to say it."

"Dyson," she says softly. "Dyson," a little louder. "Please Dyson, I can't take it anymore."

"What, baby? What do you want?"

"You, help me forget, please."

"Aw baby, I can't help you forget anything."

"Then make it go away, just for a little while, please?" she begs me and I can't say no.

But I have to as I realize my big mistake letting things get this far. "I don't have a condom." I didn't show up here with the intention of taking her to bed. No, I'd planned on taking her to dinner.

I watch as she pulls her bottom lip between her teeth in contemplation. "I'm on birth control," she breathes and that makes me smile.

"But I owe it to you to at least get tested first," I tell her. I watch realization come to light in her eyes. "You should too," I tell her and she sits up, pushing me off her and she climbs from the bed. "Where are you going?"

"I don't need to get tested, Dyson. I'm clean."

"So then why are you running away? What the hell did I say?"

"How many women, Dyson?"

I sigh. "Enough. I always glove up."

She pulls her t-shirt back over her head. "I think you should go."

"What the hell, Ireland? What, it's okay that you've been with other men, but not okay that I've been with-" Something in her expression makes me stop and cringe. "You've never been with anyone but me, have you?" I ask her.

She simply shakes her head.

IRELAND
Walk of Shame - P!nk

I can't find my voice to answer his question because embarrassment floods through my veins. I didn't expect him to wait around for me, but why, when faced with the fact I've slept with no one but him, since him, am I suddenly so embarrassed? His confession was what I needed to give me the moment of clarity I was desperate for. I was already warring with myself about whether or not this was a good idea and now I know it really wasn't. I didn't want to give myself a chance to think about it, a chance to back out. I know that sleeping with him means the same as it did when I was fifteen and I'm so scared of what will happen if we do cross that line again, especially before I'm really ready to go there again.

College guys hated the virgin and I wasn't one, but yet I couldn't bring myself to put out. Some of the guys I tried dating joked that I didn't get a good enough experience to decide whether or not I enjoyed sex. The first time is always awkward, but that's just it, mine wasn't. Mine was, and still is, everything to me.

His face portrays a look of complete and total shock at my admission. "Why?" he breathes.

"I don't know." That's the truth, I don't honestly know.

"You mean no one's ever tried?" The flare in his eyes and the raising of his brows portrays his skepticism.

"No, they have, I just…" I wrap my arms around my stomach, fighting to hold on to any shred of dignity I have left and not wanting to go too far into detail with him about why I couldn't bring myself to sleep with anyone else. "It just never felt right."

He stays quiet for a moment before he adjusts himself on the bed, moving to sit at the end of it. "Would you believe me if I told you the same thing?"

I snort, "Hardly."

"I'm serious, Ireland."

"I find that hard to believe, Dyson." His lips twitch, playing at a smile when I say his name again, but he keeps himself in check. I can tell he's fighting to stay on subject and for some unnamed reason I like that.

"It's true. Whether you want to believe it or not. It's very true. It was true even before our night in the barn."

I hold my hand up in a 'don't go there' gesture.

"Vee…" he stops himself and I regret telling him he lost the right to use the nickname he gave me all those years ago. When I was a kid, I hated being called Ireland. Kids made fun of me because I was named after a country. They had enough to poke fun at when it came to my weight. Having the name Ireland gave them the fuel to tell me I was as big as the country I was named after. They were really harsh. So I started going by Vyolet, my middle name, and that got shortened to Vy and it stuck. "Ireland, we need to go there. We need to talk about it," he tells me.

"I'm not ready to hear it," I tell him.

"Don't you think after ten years, it's time we buried the elephant that stands between us?" he asks, genuine concern in his eyes. "If we don't talk about it, I won't get the chance to tell you how sorry I am for what I did to you, why I did it to you, and most of all, beg you to forgive me."

I take a deep breath – he's telling me what I want to hear. He's doing it again because he wants to get laid. *Then why did he stop it because he didn't have a condom?* My sub-conscious is really a bitch sometimes, I know she's right but this is easier. "I really think you should go," I tell him, but there is a part of me, a very large part, that doesn't want him to go.

I'm surprised when he stands up and starts looking around for something. His shirt. He finds it in the doorway of my room and he disappears. Once he's out of my line of sight, my knees wobble.

I hear the bathroom door click closed.

The tears he managed to eradicate with his wonderfully soft lips threaten to return. Only this time they are not tears for my mother, but

tears for me. Tears I've been holding in for a very, very long time. Each one of them has Dyson's name stamped on it.

I manage to pull myself together just in time to hear the bathroom door open again and he comes back into the room. He's standing there, looking sexy as fuck in his dress shirt, tucked in, the sleeves still rolled up and this look of complete and total devastation in his eyes. "I'm sorry," I breathe out.

He comes to me and grabs ahold of my arms and unfurls them from my body, wrapping them around his. I place my cheek against his chest and he holds me close. "I made a promise to myself the night I walked out of the barn." His voice is soft and the vibrations in his chest tickle my ear. "That one day, I would make it up to you. That one day, I would explain everything to you and let you decide for yourself where I stand in your life." I hear him pull in a deep breath. "I never gave you that choice and I would really like the chance to do that."

"I need time, Dyson."

He pulls back and studies me. "How much time?"

I shrug. "I don't honestly know. I spent the last eight or so years accepting the fact you were never coming back and now, here you are. I need time to wrap my brain around that and I haven't been able to. Memories of you are filled with memories of my mother and…I just need time."

He gives me a small, sad smile. "I've got time, baby girl." He pulls something from his pocket and hands it to me. "This has my number, my email address and my home address on it. The ball is in your court, Ireland."

I nod and take the card from between his fingers. He leans down and kisses the top of my head before he leaves my room.

The loss of him walking out is nearly unbearable and I have to brace myself against the wall so I don't fall over. I hear the click of the apartment door as he leaves and I crumble to the floor. Crumble into a million tiny pieces. Again.

Sometime between Dyson leaving and Becca returning home, I found my feet with the prospect of being able to come apart in the comfort of my own bed. I cried myself to sleep with the scent of Dyson all over me. For the first time in eight years, the recurring dream of the man who opened the doors to the world for me has a face. His face is of the one and only Dyson Cole.

I didn't hear Becca come home last night and she didn't wake me up the next morning before work. It felt strange, given the display of roses on the kitchen island. But knowing Captain Snoopy Pants, she read the cards anyway. Eventually she'll put two and two together on her own. Despite still having not told her about Dyson, she's not stupid.

I do my best to ignore the memories of last night and my dream by focusing on the fact I'm starting work on Monday and I need new clothes to accommodate my new office position within Wellington Ad Management. The idea of shopping sends a chill through me. I hate clothes.

After I manage to make myself a pot of coffee among all the roses in the kitchen, I go back into my room and grab my four-year old, busted laptop and open it. I need to figure out a few things so I know what kind of money I will have for clothes shopping.

Flying back to Missouri and burying mom really wiped out my savings. Dusty isn't entirely broke, but he's got more going on with his money than I do. Things like a wife, and the baby she's expecting. I felt obligated to at least pay for half of everything, despite his objections. At the time I didn't realize what kind of impact it was going to have on my financial status. I knew my mother had life insurance, and I knew, because of the accident, there would be a lawsuit, but what I didn't expect was my mother leaving everything to my brother. With the exception of the house, Dusty got everything. I got a letter I still haven't opened. On the outside of the letter it said that 'all will be taken care of soon'. I have no idea what this means and I'm not ready to open the letter to find out.

Dusty wasn't happy about it, but he also didn't make any attempt to pay me back for my portion of the expenses. I thought that was the least

he could do. Somewhere between Missouri and returning to Phoenix, I decided it didn't matter. Under the circumstances, it's easier to be mad at my mother, than it is to be upset with Dusty – he's all I have left.

I open up the folder with the Wellington information in it and I'm thankful I saw a pay schedule in there. I pull it out and go to work on a budget that will get me through until my first payday at Wellington.

When I'm done, I send a text to Reese. He is, after all, the reason I got this job interview.

Ireland: Background & Drug Test passed – starting on Monday.

Reese: Good for you, baby girl. We need to celebrate.

I smile at the text. Unlike Becca, Reese is respectful of my time. He often lets me come to him when I'm ready. Right now he knows that despite the brand new job, I'm hurting and he will wait until I'm ready.

Ireland: concert this weekend?

Reese: You got it baby girl. Kerri says Gratz!

Ireland: Tell her thanx. Bring her this weekend? I miss you guys.

Reese: We miss you too. I'll talk to her. Smooches.

Ireland: back at you.

Reese's personality in text is rather dull. The man is a machine of activity, always. I swear he has ADHD and can't physically sit still, but then again, he's naturally happy all the damn time and if I were that happy, I wouldn't sit still either.

I text Becca next. The whole point of this damn budget was to figure out if I can afford new office attire.

Got the job, officially. Start Monday. I need new clothes for work. Shopping? When's your next day off?

Becca: Are u gonna talk about all those roses?

Vy: Nope, I'm sure you read the cards.

Becca: Off tomorrow and go in late Thursday.

Vy: Thank you Becca-boo.

Becca: Yeah! Yeah! Love your face.

I smile at her last text. I know Becca is giving me distance and space since my mom died, which is why I know she's not pressing me about Dyson, or in her case – Mystery Man. But eventually I am going to have to explain everything to her.

What nearly happened between the two of us yesterday was too much and it's getting to be too much to hold in anymore and I need to talk to someone. Or maybe I need someone to smack me upside the head.

I walk into the kitchen, living room, dining room area of our apartment. It's extremely open, with the island separating the kitchen from the living room, and I walk over to the last bouquet Dyson brought me and I find the card. It's obvious the nosey roommate found her way to it because it's front and center. I pluck it off the stand and open it, pulling the card from the inside and this note is handwritten in the same script on the card he gave me last night.

No matter the time or the distance, when the time is right, I'll be waiting.

This card came with the roses so how would he even know what would happen between us last night? The truth is, he already knew. He knew I was going to need time and my heart swells a little more at that idea. The idea he's willing to give me some time.

By mid-afternoon Tuesday, I'm going stir crazy again in the apartment, but I have nothing else to do. The kitchen is cleaned up, I

have food in the crockpot for dinner tonight, I moved around some roses, combined some and even though I cried doing it, I set mom's roses to dry upside down in my closet. I want to be able to keep them as long as possible and that seemed like the best plan.

Unable to resist any longer, with no more busy-work to do, I pull out my phone and find Dyson's card.

Ireland: Why Tigress?

That's all I text him and I wait for his response. It comes quickly in the form of bouncing dots and I wait, and wait, for what seems like forever before I finally get a reply.

Dyson: Have dinner with me, tonight?

I roll my eyes.

Ireland: too soon, need some answers first.

Dyson: Some answers are better explained in person. Dinner?

Ireland: Lunch, Thursday?

Dyson: Can't wait that long to see you. Tomorrow, lunch?

Ireland: Can't, plans.

For some strange reason I can picture him glowering at the phone as I counter everything he says with a new term.

Dyson: Feisty tigress today aren't we?

I smile.

Ireland: Always.

Dyson: Fine, Thursday, Noon, meet me in the lobby.

I shake my head despite the fact he can't see me.

Dyson: Before you argue, we're not going to eat downtown. It will be faster if I drive us.

Ireland: Where are we going?

Dyson: Fajitas

I smile wider. Fajitas is one of the rare dishes I loved that his mother made when we were kids. I don't know what it was but she had a true knack for it and it always seemed to bring us closer together. My mom would join us on those nights and they were some of the best nights I can remember as a kid.

Ireland: Noon, Thursday, Lobby – see you then.

Dyson: Ireland?

Ireland: Yes?

Dyson: thank you.

I stow my phone but don't get the shit eating' grin off my face before Becca walks in the door. I watch as she breathes in deep. "You made chili?" she asks, slightly confused. Chili is something I make for comfort food. Thankfully it's cooler outside today, at least that was the excuse for making it, but she sees right through me.

I smile wide at her hopeful expression and give her the four words she so desperately wants to hear. "We need to talk."

"Kill A Word" - Eric Church

Dyson: What are you wearing?

I roll my eyes at my phone while I'm standing in the middle of a dressing room in Saks Fifth Avenue's Off 5th store at the outlet mall where Becca and I are shopping. Finding a moment of courage, I respond to him.

Ireland: Nothing at the moment...

Let that one sink in, Mr. Cocky-Stuck-Up-Three-Piece-Wearing-Suit.

Becca and I talked over dinner last night. I confessed to her what happened when I was fifteen and then explained to her how I ran into him again; spilling coffee on him. Then I launched into what happened Friday night at Blu and finally why all the roses.

She couldn't understand why I couldn't just forgive him and move on. She seemed to think it would be easy and there is definitely a reason behind why she thinks that, but she won't elaborate on it. I didn't expect her to. She's not one for talking and I came to accept that about her a very long time ago.

Though one thing she said was quite poignant and it's stuck with me all night and into this morning.

"You can't live life in the past. If he is so obviously what you want and he wants you, then somehow you need to find a way to forgive him."

That's exactly what I'm trying to do, but I still need answers before I can do that. I need to understand where his mind has been these last ten years.

Dyson: I'm coming over.

I laugh out loud as I type my reply.

Ireland: Lucky for me, I'm not home.
Dyson: Where are you?
Ireland: Shopping
Dyson: Fine, but I want proof.

I laugh again. "What are you laughing at?" Becca says from the other side of the door. She's been irritable all day and I don't understand why. She loves shopping and she especially loves any chance she gets to doll me up. Hence why we're here and not at a hand-me-down shop, which is where I like to buy a lot of my clothes. They're cheaper and more my style.

I sober a little. "Him."

"Him, who?"

I roll my eyes again as I look in the mirror. Hmm, I wonder.

I open the camera feature on my phone. "Dyson," I tell her as I hold the phone up to snap a picture for him. I have no idea where I've gotten so brave all of a sudden. I've never even so much as let another man see my tits before. Why am I so willing to send him a picture of me, in a bra and panties, in a dressing room?

Instead of snapping a picture of myself directly, I'm able to angle the camera just enough to capture all the clothes on the hooks and the curve of my nearly naked hip and I hit send before I chicken out.

I set my phone down and start trying on clothes, but it only takes a second for Dyson's reply to chime on my phone. Embarrassed by my brazenness, I ignore it and try on a couple of outfits before it chimes again and I can't take it anymore.

I look at my phone:

Dyson: What I wouldn't give to have those hips in my hands right now.

I feel my cheeks warm as the blush spreads. His lack of filter when it comes to me and my body is something I'm not used to from anyone. Becca and Dyson are the only two people, besides my brother, who know I wasn't always this skinny. But I'm surprised by the confidence or maybe the desire I feed off of him knowing that a simple little picture means more to him because it's me and my body. It makes me smile. All it takes is a tiny glimpse of my nakedness and his filter breaks. It makes me giggle with happiness to know that I'm doing that to him.

I read his other text:

Dyson: What are you shopping for?

I reply to him, ignoring the hip comment altogether because honestly, I don't know how to handle that much forwardness.

Ireland: Work clothes. I'm pretty sure Wellington frowns upon band t-shirts, chucks and jeans.

Dyson's reply is quicker than I expected it to be

Dyson: you looked fabulous when you came for your interview.

Ireland: so you did actually notice me?

Dyson: Of course I did. It wasn't until you said your name that I knew I was looking at YOU.

Ireland: well that answers one question.

Dyson: I know I knew you from somewhere, but Ireland, you're a gorgeous woman. I'd be a fool not to notice.

I blush again and set my phone back down, trying to focus on the shopping task at hand. I can't possibly get this done fast enough. I hate shopping.

I'm finally done with the second load of clothes we carried into the fitting room and I'm settling on six different outfits. I try not to get too crazy about the price tags because I really need the clothes. I'd had to dress up when I worked a Stauffer, but those were summer clothes and this is still winter-spring in Phoenix, so sleeveless dress shirts and short, flowy skirts won't work for a couple more months. With this stuff and what I already have, I should be able to make it a couple weeks without having to wear the same thing twice until I get my first paycheck and then I can do this all over again. I make a mental note of the stuff I really liked so when I have to come back, I know where to start and save myself an assload of time and headache shopping.

Becca and I plan to have lunch at Fired Pie when we're done here and she said she needs to run into a couple different stores. She drove, so I'm cool to hang out with her and do whatever.

I'm about to pull my jeans back on when there's a knock on my door. "Yeah?"

"Try these on," Becca says from the other side of the door.

"I already have enough clothes," I argue.

She flips whatever she has in her hand over the top of the dressing room door. "These aren't for work."

"Oh." I squeak as I look at what she flung over the door. "What exactly do I need these for?" I take them from her and hold them up. She's handed me a bunch of bra and panty sets that match perfectly to each other, unlike all the other stuff I have at home which is color coordinated but hardly matching.

"The big D," she says and she laughs out loud. I don't catch on to her little joke and I crack open the door.

"What's so funny?" I whisper.

She blinks at me. "Dyson…dick…the big D?" I still don't get it and she leans into me. "You really only ever slept with one man your whole freakin' life?"

I sigh. "So? What's wrong with that?"

She shrugs and starts to walk away. I pull her by the arm and drag her into the dressing room with me. "Let me go," she argues and tries to pull away from me.

"No," I whisper. "I spilled my beans, now it's your turn. Why? Why do you throw yourself at men the way you do?"

She takes a deep breath. "I don't expect you to understand."

"Why? Because I'm more or less a virgin?"

She stares at me before answering, "No, because I'm pretty sure you've never had to grow up around what I had to, let alone, understand." She stands up but turns on me again. "I'm not the one who's spent the last ten years pining over a man who left me naked in a barn." Her words sting and I let her go as she storms out of the dressing room, leaving the door wide open and me staring blankly at her.

God, she seriously has a point. Without even meaning to do it, I've done exactly what it is she says. I can't deny that. I never looked at another man the way I look at Dyson. Sure, I made friends, that was easy, but anytime something got close to being more than that, I shoved them away. Whether I was conscious of the choice I was making or not. God dammit.

Becca is seriously obnoxious and sometimes demanding when it comes to what's going on with me. I have a light bulb moment in the middle of the dressing room as it dawns on me that Becca has never once been forthcoming with me about her past, about her boyfriends, about… anything. This isn't about me at all. This has everything to do with the mask she's chosen to hide behind. Getting the juicy details of my life

makes her feel better, makes her feel like she can keep hiding behind her own walls.

Not bothering to look at the bras she brought me, I toss them on the pile of 'yes' clothes and throw my jeans, shoes and t-shirt back on. Ready to put everything back if it means I have to go chasing after her. She's my ride and I can't even begin to guess how long it will take me to get home on the bus from here.

One of the sales ladies stops me, asking if I found everything okay. I look at her then my pile of clothes in my arms. "Is there any way you can hold this for me?"

"Sure, we can hold it 'til close of business."

"Perfect," I tell her and we walk to the counter where she takes everything in my hands and puts my name on a card. While she does that, I'm looking around the store for Becca but I don't see her.

I reach for my phone and call her. That's when I hear 'Crazy Bitch' playing and I follow the sound. She obviously doesn't get it turned off before I'm able to find her and I hang up. That's when I find her phone and no Becca.

"Fucking wonderful."

I leave the store in search of her and end up in the parking lot where we parked the car and it's gone.

"Mother fucker. I'm gonna fucking kill her."

I scroll through my phone, looking for the cab service I like to use and call them. I let them know where I am and find out how much it will be. When she tells me the price, I tell her to forget it. I'll find the bus and take it home.

My phone chimes with a text.

Dyson: Any luck?

I debate on not answering him. Sure, I found a shit ton of clothes

I like but what's the point when you've pissed off your best friend and she's left you high and dry at a mall a good two hours away from your apartment by bus – at least.

Ireland: Clothes – yes. Becca – not so much.

Dyson: Who's Becca?

Ireland: My pain-in-the-ass roommate – the one you were dancing with the other night – who just left me in the middle of the outlet mall with no way home but the bus.

I put my phone back in my bag and go sit on one of the chairs outside the store. Frustrated and unsure of what to do. A part of me hopes Becca will come to her senses and come back to get me. Another part of me tells me to just start walking toward the bus stop. Another part of me tells me to go inside and pay for my clothes, but then I war with carrying all that shit home. It's going to be at least two if not more bags and I don't want that kind of hassle. Then again, if I ditch the clothes, I can afford the cab ride home.

I reach for my phone in my bag. I didn't hear it go off with Dyson's text.

Dyson: Stay where you are, I'm coming to get you.

Ireland: Be my white knight?

Dyson: Always.

Ireland: you don't even know where I am.

Dyson: Stay there.

Fuck me. I shouldn't have said anything. I was okay with seeing him tomorrow, but not today. I'm definitely not ready and with the mood Becca's put me in, it's going to be all kinds of awful and he doesn't

deserve my ire over my roommate.

I go to stand and call the cab company back to have them come and get me when he steps in front of me with his shiny shoes, dress pants cuffed with a slight flare, pressed with the perfect crease in the front. I can't stop the slow, lazy gaze up his body. I know it's him because the hairs on the back of my neck are at attention. When I come to the slight bulge in his trousers, I lick my lips and he groans. I smirk.

He's not wearing a jacket, but he has a matching vest on and I feel my pussy heat up. My breathing hitches and I take in the slow sexy view of Dyson Cole wearing a white dress shirt under his vest, his tie is undone and the top two buttons of his shirt are unhooked. I'm pretty sure his sleeves are rolled up and his hair is falling into his face.

He raises an eyebrow at me. "Enjoying the view."

I lick my lips again and he lifts me off of the chair. "You keep that up and I'll bend you over right here, right now."

My breathing hitches and my jaw goes slack. A part of me wants to argue with him that he wouldn't, but the look in his eyes says he wouldn't hesitate in a heartbeat.

"Now, where's your stuff?"

I try and pull in a deep breath, to pull myself back together, but I am assaulted with the scent that is Dyson and Dyson alone and the fog gets foggier. "I put it back," I manage.

"Why would you do that?" He steps back, giving me a little bit of space to clear my head, thank god.

"Because I can't afford those and a cab ride home." Realization dawns on me. "You got here really freakin' fast."

His eyes are riddled with guilt, "I saw the logo of the store in your picture." He runs an unsteady hand through his hair. "I was on my way to surprise you."

"Oh," I breathe. I should be pissed he was stalking me, but instead I'm a little thrilled. I didn't realize how much I wanted to see him until he was standing in front of me.

He steps closer to me, grabbing my hips and pulling me to him. "Oh? Is that all you can say?"

"I…uh… yup, oh is all I got."

He chuckles. His eyes crinkle in the corners and I can't help smiling at him. "Come on, let's go get your clothes."

"No, really, Dyson, it's alright."

Thinking about the fact that buying clothes means I couldn't really afford a cab ride home has me thinking just because I can afford rent, I can't really afford much else. I should have gone to Walmart or something.

"What's wrong?" he asks me.

"Nothing," I tell him. "Can you take me home?"

He gives me a sad smile, but nods his head. "Come on, baby girl, let's go." He slides his fingers between mine as he pulls me along to the parking lot.

Chapter Ten

DYSON
Words - Skylar Grey

It takes everything I have not to take Ireland back in the store and buy everything she picked out, but I know it's not what she wants or needs me to do for her. She obviously feels bad enough about not being able to afford clothes and a taxi ride; I don't need to rub my wealth in her face too.

I lead her to my car, so much for not rubbing my wealth in her face. I should have brought the Nissan. I watch her carefully as her jaw drops. She's taking in the sleek, shiny and new, deep blue metallic Tesla model S she's about to climb into. I'm about to have this girl in my car for the first time and my nerves spike with the knowledge as I hold open the door for her. I haven't been this close to her with nothing more to do than talk in so long. Road head certainly isn't her style. I smirk at the thought of one day, maybe.

Hesitantly, she slides inside.

I bite my tongue from saying something cheeky like, 'you look good in my car' as I close the door and walk around to the driver's side and slide behind the wheel.

"This car is gorgeous," she says with wonder and excitement as she takes in the interior. Her excitement is contagious and it makes me feel like a giddy school boy again.

"Can you drive?" I ask her.

"I can, I have my license. I just don't."

"Mind if I ask why?" My curiosity to know more about the adult version of Ireland is going to get me into some serious trouble if I keep this up. The question is simple and innocent, but I know if she starts talking, I'll keep asking her questions.

She shrugs her shoulders. "Cheaper, I guess. I live half a block from the light rail. I can get anywhere I need to go within a few minutes, and cars are expensive to own."

I press the ignition to start the car and watch her wide-eyed expression as the car starts with very little noise. It's hard to tell the car is running but I slowly back out of the parking spot and head toward the highway.

"You do realize I live in the other direction, right?" she says with a smirk.

"I do, but this car is fully charged and ready to put some miles on the tires," I tell her and turn onto the highway, going north instead of south which is the really long way around.

She giggles as I punch the pedal and the car goes flying up the ramp. "Wow," she says in amazement. "I had no idea electric cars could go this fast."

I just smile and drive while glancing at her wide-eyed expression every few seconds. It gives me a thrill to know something as simple as a car can cheer her up.

"Do you want to talk about what happened with your roommate?" I ask, curious to know what on earth she could have done to make her roommate leave her at the mall.

"Which time?"

I give her a raised eyebrow before returning my gaze to the road. "Today," I tell her and I see her grin.

"Not really, actually, I'm not even sure what I did." She sighs and settles into the seat. She looks out the front windshield at the road as she continues talking. "Becca isn't exactly the most forthcoming person. She has no problem making you crazy begging for information, but when you want it from her, forget it."

"I know a few people like that." I look very poignantly at her.

Her head turns toward me and then back to the front. "She said some things that were very hurtful to me, and no, Mr. Pushy-Pants, I'm not going to tell you what it was. Last night I really opened up to her for the first time since I've met her."

"About?"

"You," she whispers and my head snaps to her and back to the road.

"Why me?"

"Well, why not you? First, the day I figured out who you were I completely ignored her. Didn't talk to her or even want to tell her anything at all. Second would be the night at the bar. I'm pretty sure she's still pissed at me – though I think it has more to do with whatever happened between the two of you." She pauses but I don't comment on what I did in the bar or what happened after she left. I get the impression Ireland doesn't know the details of what happened between her roommate and me. Though what Becca did is no excuse, I didn't exactly give her any other impression because I was determined to spark something inside Ireland and I certainly did that. I was ignorant to the idea of her already knowing who I was. .

"Will it help if I apologize?" I ask.

"I have no idea why you would be apologizing."

"Because I did it on purpose."

"You…" she huffs, folding her arms over her chest as she pouts. It's quite possibly the cutest thing I've ever seen.

I smile. "I did it on purpose, but the thought never occurred to me that you had already figured me out. When *did* you figure it out exactly?"

She unfurls her arms and starts fidgeting with her hands. "The day after the interview. I'd gotten called for my drug test and it got me thinking about the last time I smoked pot." She pauses, turning to look out the passenger side window. "It was the summer before you left." Her voice is soft, small, and pained. It's hard to believe after all these years, what I did to her still hurts her. Then again, it still hurts me. It's made worse by the fact it continues to bother her. "That's when I put two and two together. All the things clicked into place and I sort of checked out for the rest of the day."

"I knew it was you the moment you introduced yourself to Wellington," I tell her softly. "I didn't want to believe it could be you."

She looks at me, her eyes are full of emotion and I can't look at her

anymore. She doesn't say anything so I keep talking, "I knew there was something familiar in your eyes, your hair, but I couldn't believe it was really you. The last name threw me for a loop. It took me until the next day to remember your middle name. Why do you use your middle name?"

The question I hoped she wouldn't ask me comes to light. "Because it sounds better than Richards," I say, omitting the details of why, when I lived in Joplin, my last name was Richards and not my real last name, which is Cole. I don't have a middle name.

"I have to agree with that." She gives me a small smile before turning to look out the window as we drive past Bell Avenue and the Arrowhead area.

"So, if you knew it was me, why'd you try and sabotage my interview? Tell Wellington he couldn't hire me?"

I sigh. "I never wanted to tell you why," I tell her honestly. "But if you go to work for Wellington, there is a strict no-fraternization policy between Wellington and their clients. You'd lose your job because Wellington can't survive without me as their top client."

"That's awfully presumptive of you," she tells me and I can't help but smile.

"You're in my car, are you not?"

"I'd be on a bus if you hadn't stalked me to the outlet mall. How'd you know I was at that one?"

I laugh. "Because it's the closest one to your house."

"And to yours," she tells me. So she did look over my card and not just my phone number.

"So tell me, is there a reason you didn't want to get your clothes?" I decide we need to change the subject a little bit, it's too heavy and I don't want to continue down the path this conversation is going, not yet. I'd much rather be able to look into her eyes and tell her everything versus being distracted by the road.

Her eyes meet mine briefly before I have to look back at the road. "Yes,

but I don't want to talk about that either," she tells me.

"That seems to be a common trend with you." I smirk. "Any particular reason why?" *Stop pushing her, dumbass, let her tell you on her own.*

"Why I don't want to tell you?" I look at her and nod. "Because I don't know what good it would do to tell you."

"It would let me know what's going on in that pretty little head of yours," I tell her as I look to her quickly then back to the road. I need her to know she can talk to me.

She snorts a laugh. "Because if I tell you, you're going to feel like you need to fix it."

"If it's within my power to do so, I will," I admit. "But I can understand why you wouldn't want to. If I promise I won't try and fix it, will you tell me?"

She laughs again. "No, because I know better than to trust you to stick to your word." She slaps her hand over her mouth and her cheeks turn pink.

She's right, of course. I haven't exactly been the picture of honesty and promise keeping. "I'm not that boy anymore," I proclaim.

Her hand comes away from her mouth. "I know, I'm sorry, I shouldn't have said that." She takes a deep breath. "With mom dying and having to run back to Missouri so fast, the funeral and moving into the new apartment, my savings is depleted pretty bad," She admits with a good bit of reluctance and I can understand why. "I didn't expect any of that stuff to happen and I truly wasn't prepared for it and now I have to wait to start at Wellington and get paid. I just, I thought I could afford to go shopping, but I really can't. What if something happens with my job and I lose it, I have nothing to fall back on. Rent's due, Becca is being a bitch and…" she stops ranting with a sigh, "I'm sorry, you don't need to hear all this."

"On the contrary, I think I do." I smile at her. "This is the most you've said to me since I saw you last week and I truly appreciate your candor."

"You promise you're not going to try and fix it?"

"No," I tell her. "I told you if it is something within my means to fix, I will do it. This is within my power to fix. Will you let me fix it?"

I'm giving her a choice- she can either let me fix it with her help, or she can let me fix it without it. There are plenty of things I can do without her permission to fix her problem, so the choice is hers.

"It's not up to you to fix my life." Her snarky tone has returned and with it, my tigress.

"I'm not trying to fix your life, Ireland. I'm simply trying to help you out of a tough situation."

"By, what? Throwing money at me? Which you obviously have more than enough of. What makes you think I want your money?" Instead of fighting with her while driving, I pull off at the next exit and take a right, finding the parking lot of a gas station and I pull into it. Putting the car in park, I turn to her.

"No, I am not trying to throw money at you, but I can make sure you can go back and get those clothes you say you need. The Ireland I know isn't fond of clothes shopping." She scrunches up her nose. "I can see that hasn't changed." She rolls her eyes at me and I smile. "Had Becca not run out on you, you would have bought all those clothes, am I right?"

She nods and shares. "I thought I had it all figured out, until I hung up from the cab company when I realized what it was going to cost to get me home. I realized that I couldn't do both and keep on eating for the next three weeks. Then I realized if I couldn't afford to pay for clothes and a taxi, that I couldn't afford to live for the next three weeks until I get paid." The tigress has settled down some. I lean in and caress her cheek.

"Thank you," I tell her, rather than irritate her again.

"For what?" she asks with narrowed eyes.

"For being honest and open with me."

She turns her head, pressing her lips to my palm and she smiles. "So does that mean you'll drop it?"

I smile and pull my hand away, throwing the car into reverse and I back out. "Nope."

IRELAND
"Say Something" - A Great Big World

I want to be furious with him about the whole clothes thing, but I can't find it in me. Something in the back of my mind tells me he plans on rectifying the situation whether I want him to or not. Dyson Cole is a man who goes after what he wants; he's also a man unwilling to give up so easily. He showed up at an outlet mall to see me because he knew I needed rescuing before I knew I needed to be saved. *The insufferable jerk.*

"What if Becca hadn't stranded me at the mall? What would you have done when you got there?"

He laughs, "I have no idea. I thought maybe I'd take you out for lunch."

"We have a lunch date tomorrow," I remind him.

"Why don't we push it up to today?" he asks me.

I give him a skeptical look. "Why?"

"Your plans have obviously changed and as much as I want to drag this out a little longer, I can't wait until tomorrow," he says as he turns onto Interstate 17 headed south. This is one way to get to my apartment but it's also the same road to get to Fajitas. My stomach growls. "And you're starving." He smirks at me.

"I need to get Becca's phone back to the apartment before she reports it missing or stolen." Yup, because that excuse totally works. Uh huh, brilliant I am.

He shrugs. "She left you in the middle of the mall, and left her phone. She can suffer a little longer without it."

I shake my head, and roll my eyes. "You're impossible," I tell him and he laughs.

"Sometimes, but you're in my car, at my mercy, and I'm going to get

some lunch. You can either sit in the car and wait for me, or you can come in and protest by not eating, either way I have your undivided attention. Or you can pull on your big girl panties and enjoy lunch with me today?"

"Are those my only options?"

He chuckles, "Yup, because the closest bus stop to Fajitas is about half a mile away." He has a smirk on his face that screams, 'gotcha'.

Fucker.

I cross my arms over my chest, pretending to sulk at him and huff a little. He sees right through my façade and laughs a little harder. I don't know what on earth prompts me to do it, exactly, but I put my hand in his. He instantly sobers, his eyes wandering from the road to our joint hands. His eyes slide back up to the road and he brings the back of my hand to his lips and he kisses it. That little zing flies between us and the air in the car grows thick with something I can't put a name to. Appreciation, apprehension, desire, I don't know, but it's so dense it would take a machete to chop through it.

I lean back in my seat, turning toward him, with our hands intertwined between us and watch him drive. It's obvious he feels it too because he doesn't say anything until we're pulling into the parking lot. "Ever been here before?" he asks me.

I nod. "It's one of my favorite places to eat when I need some space. It reminds me of home," I tell him.

"Mine too."

He climbs out of the car. "Stay there," he warns as he closes his door.

Before I can think too much about why he wants me to stay in the car, he's at my door opening it for me. As I climb out, I look at him in his half suit and think about my jeans, t-shirt and Converse shoes. I suddenly wish I'd been wearing something more elegant than I am. "You know this kind of chivalry is better served to a woman in a dress," I tease him.

"No, it's best when the woman is as beautiful as you are." His voice is so smooth and without any type of hesitation. Oddly enough, I get

the impression he's never been this way toward anyone else. My cheeks heat from his comment. The back of his knuckles stroke gently down my cheek. "I like making you blush," he teases and I blush an even brighter shade of red.

He chuckles and takes my hand, before ushering me inside. It's early afternoon but post lunch rush, so there are only a few people in the restaurant. We're seated immediately. He orders a beer, and I cannot resist a margarita from this place so I order one. I roll my eyes when the woman cards me and not him, he laughs.

After she returns with our drinks, he puts his elbows on the table and steeples his fingers under his chin. It's a highly effective power move. "I believe you have some questions for me?" he asks me. My mind goes blank and I stare at him like he's grown six heads. His power is palpable and his posture sends a thrill through me. Think what he's capable of with that kind of power.

Finally, after gazing longer than should be legal into his blue-violet eyes, I breathe out, "Tigress?" As if I just asked a lengthy question.

He smirks before replying, "Why do you think I named my company, Tigress?"

I chuckle, finding the fog in my brain clearing as he pulls his arms down and relaxes. "Honestly? I have no clue."

He smiles wider, "I'm looking at it."

It takes a minute for his statement to register in my mind. 'I'm looking at it'. "Me?" I point to my chest with my thumb. "You named your company after me?" I can't even begin to stifle the shock I feel as the words leave my mouth.

His smile settles, but doesn't leave his lips. "It was all I could think of when I started the company. I couldn't get you out of my mind even then." He winks at me. "Feisty, yet strong, sensitive yet powerful, quick and reliable and most importantly- fierce. That's what I was going for when I wanted to brand my company. You're all of those things and that's what I was thinking of when I was naming my company. You were my feisty, fierce tiger." His eyes actually sparkle at that. Or it's really good

lighting at the right moment.

I let his words sink in while he takes a sip of his beer and I contemplate my next question, or rather, build up the courage to ask it. "When?" That's all I manage.

"Just over four years ago."

He looks into my eyes as he says this and my mouth falls open in shock. I don't know what to say to him, but he doesn't make me say anything, he simply continues with something I never thought I'd hear him say. "I said what I said that night, in the barn, because I needed you to hate me. I hoped it would be easier- my leaving, if you hated me for what I said. It ate me up inside every single day." He pulls another long drink from his beer. My mouth closes but I feel like I need it open so that I can breathe better. "It turns out that the idea of you hating me was harder on me than I'd realized it would be before I did it."

"Why?" I manage.

He gives me a sad smile. "Because I realized I was being forced to walk away from the love of my life."

DYSON

Little Did You Know - Alex and Sierra

"Why are you telling me this?" Tears fill her eyes as she questions me. "Why now? Why not back then?"

I have the answer for that, but I don't know if she wants to hear it. If she's ready to hear it. That's when the waiter arrives, distracting us with food as she lays out the spread of sizzling meat, toppings and containers of tortilla shells. While the server does this, I observe Ireland closely, looking for any indication of her willingness or even her readiness to hear what I have to say. She polishes off her margarita and orders another one from the server. Her eyes are avoiding me and I realize if this is to go anywhere from here, I have to be honest with her. If I hold back on this part of who I am or why I am this way, she'll never learn to trust me.

The server leaves and I reach across the table to stroke the back of her hand gently. I need the contact for some strange reason. I need to know this isn't a dream and touching her grounds me. She's really sitting in front of me. Her eyes meet mine and I can't look away from her.

Lost in the depth of her vibrant green eyes, everything I felt that night plays through my mind. Bringing that night back to me with a vengeance.

"It started as a challenge," I breathe and her eyes widen. "No one put me up to it or anything like that. But when I came over that afternoon, I was determined…" I pause, taking a sip of my beer and steadying my nerves. Suddenly the current flowing between us shifts and I feel the now all-too-familiar spark flying between us like the filament of a light bulb. I take a deep breath. "I started out with the intention of 'getting it out of my system'." I scrub my hand through my hair realizing that this truth is it. She will either stay or she will run like hell. I have to find it in me to be okay with option two and her running like hell. She should run, hard and fast, because this line is about to be crossed and once I do, there is no going back for me. I can only protect myself from this one more time. I've said the words so many times in my head, in the mirror, while talking to myself, but the result was never there, never one I could gauge

for myself because I don't know what she's going to do.

I look at her, pleading with her, begging her not to run. "Please, Dyson." God, I love it when she says my name. "I need to know. No matter what the truth is, I need to hear it." Her green eyes plead with me, begging me to tell her my truths.

"You're undeniable." My resolve settles over me. Willing to accept either outcome, no matter what it is, I swallow the rest of my beer and the server returns with her new margarita. We haven't even touched our food. "Eat," I tell her.

She shakes her head. "I can't, not until you tell me the truth."

I lean forward, getting as close to her as I can manage with the table between us. "What if the truth sends you running for the hills?"

She pulls her eyes away from me, looking down and bringing both her hands into her lap as she contemplates what to say next. Losing the eye contact makes me uneasy and I start to fidget with my shirt collar, a nervous habit I've had since playing football. I would always grab the collar of my jersey and my shoulder pads as I watch the game from the sidelines.

"In ten years, I've concocted every possible scenario as to why you left me that night. I'm pretty sure the truth can't possibly be any worse than what my mind has managed to make up." Her voice is soft, pained.

"Look at me, VeeVee." My nickname forces her eyes to me, but I don't see hatred or panic in them, I see the same look of devotion I saw in her eyes when I looked down at her the moment I broke through her virginity, so trusting, honest and loving. She handed me her heart and soul through her eyes that night and I trampled all of it like it was a useless object. I was seventeen years old, blissfully unaware of the priceless gift she was bestowing on me that night. "Because the minute I slipped inside of you," I whisper. "I knew I loved you more than life itself."

She gasps and sits up, her eyes wide in shock, confused. Desperate to wipe the look of hurt off her face, I continue, "When I showed up at your house, I had every intention of telling you I was leaving, that I was

moving the next day. I'd made Dusty promise he wouldn't tell you on the pretense that I wanted to do it myself." I take a deep breath. "When I got to your house, you looked…" I struggle to find the right word to describe her that day. "Like an angel. Your hair was down and particularly unruly that day." I smile at the memory of her when she opened the door. "You had on that silly t-shirt you'd bought at the State Fair the summer before and the cutest pair of pajama pants ever. I remember they were pink with little red and white hearts on them." The memory consumes me. "You were watching that ridiculous movie."

"How to Lose a Guy in 10 Days," she mumbles.

"In hindsight, that movie isn't so bad," I tease her a little, fighting to break the tension.

She smiles back, but it's not entirely the smile I love and I realize it's because I'm dodging the answers she desperately needs. "We sat on the couch and you snuggled right into me like old times." I see our waitress pass and I raise my beer bottle, indicating I need another one and she nods. "When you settled in to watch the movie, I couldn't keep my eyes off you. I realized then you weren't like all the other girls I'd dated," no need to rehash the obvious, "you always did what you wanted, what came naturally to you and that day was no different."

The waitress appears with my beer and asks, "How's everything?" She takes in our untouched plates, confused.

"We're fine," Ireland cuts in. The sound of her voice brings me back to the present.

The waitress nods and walks off, I pull on my beer, sucking down half the bottle, needing the liquid courage to continue my story.

"I realized I'd been delaying as long as I could. Having you in my arms, knowing I was leaving the next day. Realizing there was a good chance I might never see you again, it broke my heart." I lean forward, bringing my elbows up on the table, looking at her, but looking through her, past her, as I watch the memories play in my head for the millionth time. "I needed to be close to you the only way I knew how. But what I didn't realize when I'd gotten you into the barn, was just how beautiful

you really are." I watch her blush at the compliment, but I don't stop, "I realized in that moment I couldn't leave you. That leaving you was going to kill me and I couldn't stop myself from proving to you that everything we'd been flirting with since we were kids was truly real. That I fell in love with the girl when I was just eleven years old." I reach my hand into my pocket and I pull something from it. I rub my thumb along the now smooth and almost shiny surface and it brings me a calming comfort like it did my first day at a new school.

"Give me you hand," I tell her and she doesn't hesitate, I take it with my free hand.

"The day she gave me this." I gently place the well-worn rock in her hand and her eyes fly to mine, then to the rock and back to mine. Oddly enough, the rock was everything Ireland was then, and is now. "I remember looking at the rock and thinking of a tiger's eye when I did. I was eleven, I was a boy and it was a rock, but I never let it go," I tell her, my voice full of all the emotion I've suppressed for more than fifteen years, since the day I met a girl with fiery red hair and a personality to match.

Her eyes well with tears as she takes the rock from my hands. I can't for the life of me imagine what's going through that pretty little head of hers as she stares at the rock in her hand. I desperately need to finish the story, finish telling her everything before I lose my nerve. I take comfort in watching her thumb rub over the same surface I've used to find my balance for sixteen plus years.

"When we finished, the horny teenager went away and I panicked because I realized the girl I was head over heels in love with was going to be left behind. That I had no choice and that I could no longer leave her. When we were together you poured everything out through your eyes, your love, your heart, your soul. I felt like my soul had found the one thing it was missing to complete me. Everything you gave me that day was precious and a gift that should have been cherished and no matter how my head processed everything in those moments, it all lead to the inevitable truth that I had to leave." I pause and take a deep, steadying breath. "It was too much for my seventeen year old brain to handle in the

moment. So I told you what I thought you would need to hear. I thought you would be angry with me for taking advantage of you, but I figured you'd chalk it up to experience and move on with your life and I would find a way to move on with mine." I shake my head back and forth, closing my eyes. "But I was wrong. No matter how hard I tried, you were never far from my mind. I quit talking to your brother because I couldn't take having you so close and yet so far away at the same time. He told me, one day, that you absolutely hated me and he couldn't understand what I had done to make you feel that way. I couldn't tell him. He knew my taste in girls and I was selfish enough to believe he wouldn't want to be my friend anymore if he knew. Then it got to a point where I could no longer keep it from him, and so I stopped talking to him." I sigh, "I needed you to move on with your life, forget about me, because I didn't deserve to be forgiven, only forgotten."

Her tear filled eyes meet mine. Her voice is barely above a whisper. "That's just it, Dyson; I was so sure of what I felt for you that I couldn't believe you truly felt that way. That you honestly thought of me as another notch in your bedpost." She wipes a tear from her cheek. "It wasn't until I ran to your house the next day that I realized you were gone, your mom was gone, and your house was empty. I never got the chance to prove you wrong, prove to you that what I saw in your eyes that night was real, and it was raw and it was everything to me. Never being able to do that broke me, Dyson."

Her words are like a knife to my heart. A knife I didn't see coming and all the pain of ten years missing my girl slices through me like hot shards of jagged glass in my veins.

IRELAND
Feel Again - One Republic

I watch as unbearable pain washes over Dyson's face as I tell him that finding his house empty completely broke me. It's probably the truest

statement I've ever made. Seeing that pain is worse than anything he could have ever done to me. It's the worst feeling in the world watching my words completely shatter him. I want nothing more than to comfort it away for him, but I can't bring myself to do it.

Ten years' worth of unbearable pain, a shattered heart, wall building, hatred and resentment, all consume me and all I want to do is run out of this restaurant and never see him again. I have my answers, but getting those answers means my heart is shattered all over again. It never fully mended in the first place, but it was breathing, it was trying to live because I needed it to, but now, now it's broken and barely beating.

Our waitress returns, snapping him out of his trance. "No, but can we get some boxes, please?" he asks her, his eyes never leaving mine. The kaleidoscope of unshed tears fills my vision and he knows. I can see it in his eyes. He's scared. He knows I'm going to run away. He knows that I can't handle this and that hurts almost as bad as when he told me it was about time I put out. No, this is worse. This is way worse than seeing his old house empty the next day.

The waitress returns quickly with several boxes and some foil. I mindlessly watch Dyson scoop the meat and veggies, then box up the condiments and finally wrap up our tortillas. The sight of the food makes my stomach roll. I swallow back the bile and the words that will shatter him completely. The truth is I can't do this. I don't know if I ever could. Knowing now, that there was so much more between us than I could have fathomed at fifteen years old is just…it's too much.

When he's done, he throws a hundred dollar bill on the table then he stands up, surprising me by holding out his hand for me to take. "Come on, angel, let's get you home." His voice is as pained as I feel. Automatic response and motion brings me to my feet. I feel listless, torn and empty. I can't stop myself from taking his hand in mine. The all-too-familiar spark igniting between us once again as we leave the restaurant.

He leads me to his car with tears still dripping down my cheeks. I wipe them away with my free hand as best I can, hoping he's not paying much attention as he opens the door for me. *Keep it together, Ireland.*

Just a few more minutes until you get home then you can fall to pieces. I'm losing him all over again. He's slipping through my fingers and I have the power to stop it, but I don't know how, I don't know if he wants me to stop it. Why isn't he stopping it? Why is he just taking me home? Why isn't he fighting for this?

I slide into the seat and he places the bagged tower of food boxes between my legs before closing my door and walking around to his side of the car and folding himself inside, he starts the car. Our close proximity, his cologne, a scent that screams Dyson, fills the air around us and my head begins to fog. *Stop this, Ireland, stop this from being the end. You have that power.*

If I had been able to hate him all those years ago, would this be easier? Would we even be here now? The truth is I don't know because I was angry with him all those years ago, sure. That was easy, eventually. But I never hated him. A part of me knew he'd done it to protect himself, maybe even to protect me. He wanted to give me the chance to move on with my life because he couldn't be there for me anymore, but in truth, I never wanted him to let me go.

Dyson says nothing as he drives toward my apartment and neither do I. I can't find my voice or find a way through the fog of everything roaming in my brain to form a coherent question or statement. I can't find anything to do or say to right the ship, to bring him back to me, to bring us back together and stop this from sinking beyond repairable.

I need Dyson like I need air.

His pained expression when I told him he broke me is a look I will never forget. It will be forever engrained in my mind just as he realized his own self-preservation that night was more important than what I was going to go through. I know he cared about how it would impact me because that pain was real, raw and it was reopening old wounds in both of us. Despite trying to protect me and save himself, in the end, we both ended up broken and alone.

The answers he gave me today prove I wasn't crazy then and I'm not crazy now. He really did love me back then. The pain in his eyes today

tells me he still does. But what happens when he needs to leave again? When he needs to walk away again? What then? I'm already broken into a million tiny pieces because the part of my heart I'd let him expose inside me was full of hope we could be again. I am a fool for thinking we were reigniting that old spark again.

He takes the fastest way back to my apartment. I don't blame him. I'm pretty sure he was running a million different scenarios in his head about getting away from me as fast as possible or if he could drop me off somewhere to catch my own ride back home.

He pulls into the parking lot of my complex and parks in Becca's empty space before he turns to me. "You deserve the world, Ireland, and you deserve it from someone who can give you everything." His whispered words break the deafening silence in the car. "You deserve to be happy, VeeVee."

I set his rock on the center console between us and his eyes go to it. I didn't realize until now I was rubbing it between my fingers. For the first time in more than six years, I miss its twin. The one I half-ass threw against his house before leaving for college. The tears come harder, faster now. I can't look at him. How do I tell him the only thing that will make me happy again is having him in my life? Being able to finally find out what this spark, this irresistible attraction and undeniable draw are between us.

I open my mouth to say something.

Then I close it, open it again, and close it again. I suck in a shattered breath. "Good-bye, Dyson." I barely manage to get the words out. My hand goes to the door handle and pushes it open. I climb from the car and go running up to my apartment. I can't look back, I can't…

He hasn't moved. His car still sits in the same spot, but I can't see him. He's not running after me.

With shaky hands I unlock the door.

Open it.

Turn.

One last look at his car as it drives away.

It's like being in that barn all over again. I shut the door and fall to pieces against it as my soul shatters in to a million little pieces right next to my heart.

Chapter Twelve

IRELAND
Sound of Your Heart (Workout Mix) - Shawn Hook
Don't You Remember - Adele

I couldn't sleep.

Every time I closed my eyes, I saw the pain in Dyson's face, but it wasn't the grown up version. No, it was a lost, scared seventeen year old version of him. If it wasn't an image of the pain he was feeling, then it was those violet eyes as they looked down at me as our bodies came together in the most intimate way possible. The love that transferred between us that night was so crystal clear. I realize I was never a fool for believing what we had between us was real. It is real. Even now. It is everything I know now to be true. It's what I've been fighting for all these years. Why I held on to hope that maybe, one day, we would be together again. And now? Now I know he was doing what he could to protect me at the same time as he was trying to protect himself. It was easier for him to survive if he thought I was mad at him, that I hated him or even that it didn't mean to me what it felt like for him.

I don't know at what point I managed to make my feet move to my bedroom. I did a half-ass attempt at putting on pajamas but I ended up in nothing more than a tank-top and panties. Thank god Becca never came in when she got home around three in the morning. I guess my note was enough for her to know I was home so she never bothered to check to see. I don't need her bullshit. I left her phone on the kitchen island with a note I wrote in the heat of being hurt by Dyson and being angry at her for stranding me at the mall. I needed an outlet and someone to blame. If she hadn't left me in the mall, Dyson would have never rescued me and I would be blissfully unaware of the pain I would feel during lunch today instead of yesterday.

A lunch that would never happen.

When morning dawned, I was exhausted and managed to close my eyes long enough to doze off for a little while.

My phone buzzing is what wakes me up. I catch a glimpse of the time and panic briefly about being late for my lunch date, only to remember

there wasn't going to be a lunch date anymore.

I don't know why I thought there would be after what happened yesterday, but I think it was that little blossom of hope that allowed me to fall asleep in the first place. I look at my phone and the tiny pieces of my heart I'd managed to put back together in the wee hours of the morning fall off their foundation.

Dyson: *I am leaving for NY this morning.*

My heart hurts.

I don't get to dwell on the pain in my chest when I hear a lot of noise coming from the living room of our apartment. I jump out of bed, grab my robe off the back of the door and throw it on as I walk down the hallway toward the kitchen.

I see Becca in the kitchen and realize she's picking up one of the vases of flowers left on the island from the other day. I put most of them into one vase where I could and even brought a bouquet into my room, but apparently she's still having issues. "Will you fucking clean this shit up?" she snaps at me.

"Fuck you," I growl at her. "It's my apartment too."

"Then fucking take them to your room because I'm tired of fucking looking at 'em."

Becca's words hurt so much more than they did yesterday. I don't know if it's because I'm completely shattered already or if it's because the friendship I thought I had with her is disappearing. "Go to hell," I snap.

Her eyes meet mine and her nostrils flare as she takes in my totally fucked up state of affairs. "How the hell did you get home?"

"What the fuck does it matter to you? You obviously didn't care enough to come back for me." My anger flares hotter than it should over what happened yesterday between us and unfortunately I have Dyson to blame for that.

"You look like shit."

I roll my eyes. "Thank you, Captain Fucking Obvious. It's nice how you can only ever seem to point out my fucking faults so you can hide from your own. I'm over it, Becca. I'm not fucking perfect, so stop putting me on that pedestal so you can feel better about yourself. I don't know what your fucking deal is because you won't take the time to talk to me, to tell me. Then maybe I would better understand. Whatever it is that you're going through, or have been going through, you either need to talk about it or get the fuck over it. I'm done. You left me in the middle of a goddamn mall because you couldn't take the fact I did to you exactly what you do to me every day. Stop trying to force me to tell you my shit so I don't ask you about yours and don't fucking tell me I look like shit again, because honestly, you look like a slut." I turn to go back toward my room, leaving Becca in my wake staring at me. Passing the bathroom, I decide to redirect my plans and step inside the door, closing it and locking it. I need a shower, I need-…the front door slams shut as Becca leaves.

"Ugh!" I cry out in frustration.

First my mother dying, then Dyson pops back up into my life, Becca leaves me in the middle of nowhere, then Dyson and his truths and now Becca, again.

The last three weeks have been complete and total shit and I'm over it all.

I step into the shower with a newfound determination. I'm tired of being railroaded by people who are supposed to be my friends and I'm done being the fucking doormat everyone steps on or over on their way to something else, something bigger or better.

I turn the water on as hot as I can stand it in an attempt to scrub it all away. All of the anger, frustration and irritation at the turns my life is taking. I scrub the hell out of my body. After I'm red and blotchy from the scrubbing and hot water, I realize the water's not hot enough, my washcloth not abrasive enough, to scrub away the shitstorm my life has turned into. As the water runs cold, I realize no matter how hard I try to

piece myself back together, I feel so completely broken all over again.

I climb out of the shower, shivering. I feel numb.

I go through the motions of drying off, drying my hair, getting dressed, finishing dying my hair, gathering my clothes for the washer, and cleaning up the kitchen. The smell of roses becomes an overwhelming reminder that I can't handle anymore bullshit so I throw them all away, but not before plucking each card from each vase and stowing them in my room.

I clean the apartment, and I mean, really clean the apartment, from top to bottom. Blissfully lost in the numbness as I move from room to room. Cleaning as I go. Changing laundry when necessary, putting away clothes and the list goes on and on.

When I finish cleaning every surface, I get into my workout clothes. I'm already gross and sweaty, might as well make the best of it. I run to the train station, my iPod hooked on my arm along with my membership card, driver's license, my debit card, and my train pass, with music blasting in my ears. My water bottle in my hand. While on the train for the two stops it takes to get me to the gym, I stretch my arms, stretch out my legs, do the best I can to get myself warm, not wanting to waste time. I need to feel the burn in my legs and when I finally get there, I run, and I run and I run until my legs are on fire and my lungs feel like they're going to burst in my chest. To cool down, I climb on the elliptical machine. When I'm finally done, it feels like it's been forever. I feel deliciously worn out when I stroll back to the train station.

Feeling the burn is a welcome enjoyment, overrides the numbness I feel. I like that it makes me feel alive.

The entire time I was running, I couldn't take my mind off Becca and her bullshit. Fuck her. God, I thought Dyson was a dick, but Becca is winning that war hands down. It isn't until I am pacing on the platform of the train stop that I realize the burn in my body has finally pulled out all the heartache I feel when it comes to my mother, and now my best friend. Becca is going to take a lot of work to repair, if we're repairable. Blowing off a little pissed off steam is good for anyone once in a while

and maybe that's what I needed since I haven't been to the gym since before going to Missouri.

When I get home, I am greeted by no Becca and the smell of a clean as fuck apartment and my own sweaty mess of a body. Knowing I need to cool down before hopping in the shower, I go to the fridge for a bottle of chocolate milk and pull the seal off, downing it. My body temperature slowly cools down. When the milk is gone, I reach for a glass from the cupboard and pour myself a glass of cold water from the fridge, tossing my water bottle in the dishwasher.

I'm standing in the kitchen, trying to decide what to make for dinner, though I'm not at all hungry, when the door buzzer sounds. Hope fills me until I remember his text from this morning. He's in New York. That gives me a new determination as I reach for the door knob. Maybe I'll get lucky and it'll be Reese. I open it quickly and stand there dumbstruck as three men are standing outside my door.

"I have a delivery for Ireland?" There is a hint of a Scottish accent in the man's voice and it makes me smile, remembering what little I can of my mother's accent from when I was a little kid. As I got older her accent faded, except there were always a few words that made me giggle. Even thinking about them now puts a smile on my face. It's nice to finally smile at a memory of my mother.

"That's me," I tell him. He smiles at me as I push open the door. He steps back and the two men behind him come into the apartment. They're both holding bags in their hands. I raise an eyebrow at the guy with the accent and he just smirks at me.

They walk in with their bags and they both go straight to the dining room table that sits between the kitchen island and the living room. They put the bags there and I look more closely at them. The store logo on the side of one makes my blood run cold. *That son-of-a-bitch.*

From the doorway, holding open the door, I watch the two men who stepped into my apartment, they're both dressed like they belong on a security detail and not delivering bags of clothes. I wonder if these men work for Dyson, but I don't ask. One of the two men turns from the table

and he has a bag in his hand that I can't make out the logo on. I don't recognize it. He starts pulling out what look like food containers and the other man joins him in setting up plates, silverware and then a bottle of wine and a single wine glass. What in the world? One opens the bottle of wine and then the other opens another white bag with a silver apple on it. I narrow my eyes and watch as he pulls something out. It's a huge box and I can't quite tell what he's doing until he's done and sitting on a keyboard stand is a freakin' iPad. I shake my head.

My temper starts to rise as I realize what's going on. Though the iPad is a true mystery, Dyson and his determined ways have found a way to take control once again. I haven't even talked to him in twenty-four hours and these guys show up.

I pull in a deep breath, breathing through my nose in an attempt to calm down, when the smell of the food hits me and my stomach growls.

Just as fast as the men entered my apartment, they're gone. "Good evening, Ms. McKidd." the Scottish ones says as he leaves my doorway with the other two men and I nod. Unsure of what to say. What the hell am I supposed to do next?

I close the door and stand there for a moment looking at the four bags on the table, plus one smaller one with the Apple logo on it. Before I know it, my legs are pulling me toward the table. Looking at the bags, there's a Fifth Avenue logo on display and I peer inside.

"You son of..." A strange ringing noise catches my attention but it's not my phone. It's coming from the counter behind me and I spin around.

I see a still image of Dyson's face appear on the screen as it keeps ringing. I walk over to it, "fuck me," it's an iPad Pro. I'm just staring at it like it's going to bite me, but the ringing persists. The dumbstruck expression doesn't leave my face when it stops and in true Dyson predictability, it immediately starts ringing again.

Hesitantly I reach for the green button and press it.

It takes a moment but then his face, live and in living color, is on the screen. "Hi gorgeous." He gives me a panty melting smile that sets my

insides on fire.

It's like I've walked into the twilight zone. "Do you have multiple personality disorder? Or a twin I don't know about, because the last time I saw you, you didn't say a word to me," I snap toward the device.

He sighs. "I wanted to give you a chance to take in everything I said to you yesterday. I had planned on giving you until I got back to Phoenix, but I couldn't wait." His voice is still his, just with a mechanical edge to it compliments of the machine between us. "I had to cancel our lunch plans, so I made dinner ones."

His voice is so hopeful and despite the fact that my stomach is roaring I tell him, "I already ate." My snarky tone gives me away.

"Bullshit." He calls my bluff and I move into the camera's line of sight. My image is reflected back in a small window in the corner of the screen and I look like hell. "Jesus, what's wrong?"

I shake my head. "Nothing, I just got back from the gym."

He shakes his head at me. "You look like you haven't slept in days."

"There is that too," I mutter.

"Eat with me?" He ignores my statement about not sleeping and points to the food in front of me.

"The last time we tried this, it didn't go so well," I remind him.

"I've decided that no matter what, I need to try and do this right," Dyson shares with a sad look on his face. "No matter what it takes."

"So you're buying me clothes? Dyson, that's not the way to make up for what's happened between us yesterday or ten years ago."

"Sit," he says more as an order and for some unknown reason, desire courses through my system as I follow his request. His face lights up with a smile.

"The clothes have nothing to do with making this up to you. The clothes are because I'm trying to help you out the only way you'll let me." His voice is somber as he talks. "I want to do so much more for you, Ireland, but…" he trails off, pausing briefly, "I don't want to scare you

away again." He points downward again. "Eat."

I shake my head but the smell of the fettuccini alfredo is too much on my empty stomach and I open the wrapped silverware as he smiles at me again. I know I can put an end to this by simply pressing the red little button on the screen, but I can't seem to do that. There is a gentle plea in his eyes that I can't ignore.

He doesn't say anything for a minute, then he lifts a glass. I pour myself a glass of the wine the guys opened before leaving and I hold it up to him. I giggle.

"I love that sound." His smile is something else, not just the panty melting one he gives me, but it lights up his eyes in a way I've never seen before, even through a video screen.

"This is so corny," I giggle again.

He laughs with me, "I wish we could have done this in person, but I…" he pauses for a moment, "I was hoping to lighten things up between us. Yesterday, things…" I watch as he gets flustered, running his hand through his hair before scrubbing his fingers along the growth on his chin.

"Thank you." The words are out before I can let him finish. I don't want to rehash what happened at the end of our 'meal' yesterday. As the words slip past my lips, I realize I mean them more than I originally thought.

He cocks an eyebrow at me. "For?"

"Telling me. I know it might not seem like it, but…" I pause, flustered to find my words, "I didn't mean to cause you pain." I feel a tear slide down my cheek.

"Oh, sweetheart, is that what you think?"

"I know it is. I saw your face yesterday. I, god, this is going to sound so crazy, but I never want to see that look on your face ever, it nearly broke me again, Dyson."

"I never meant to break you, VeeVee. What I did all those years ago was selfish. I see that now."

I think about his words, about what he said yesterday and I look into his hope filled eyes in the video screen. "I forgive you," I tell him softly.

"Truly?" His face is lit up with an overwhelming excitement.

I beam at him. "Always."

"Damn it," he growls.

"What?" I ask.

He looks into the camera lens and deadpans, "I'm fucking hard as a rock and you're twenty-five hundred miles away."

I blush beat red, so red I can see it in the video playback of my camera and it makes me blush even more. I try and cover up the camera. "Oh no, you don't," he growls at me through the screen.

I laugh and drop my hand. "When will you be home?"

He sighs, "I'm not sure. Probably not until Monday sometime or Tuesday."

"Damn it. That's a really long time," I grumble.

"Come to New York?"

I hesitate. "I can't afford that, Dyson."

He holds up a finger, pulls something from his pocket, his cell, and presses a couple buttons. "Hi, yes, I need a first class ticket, Phoenix to JFK...as soon as possible...no, one way."

"Dyson, I start my new job on Monday," I squeal.

He gives me a smirk that tells me I'm not going to win this argument no matter how hard I try. He looks at his watch. "What time does it land?" Silence while he listens to whoever is on the line. "Perfect, yes, book it. Ireland McKidd, nope, her information is on file..." that causes an eyebrow to raise, "Yup, thank you." He hangs up the phone and looks at me. "We're going to have to cut this dinner short."

I stare at him, completely and totally dumbstruck. "Why?" I continue to stare blankly at the screen.

"Your flight leaves in," he looks at his watch, "four hours."

"Shit, Dyson, I need to pack, I…" Fuck me. "I have to go to work Monday morning."

He gives me a knowing smirk. "I'll have you home in time for your first day."

"I still have to deal with Becca."

"Fuck her, come on, VeeVee." His pleading voice matches his eyes. "I can't wait till Monday night. Please," he begs me.

I'm running out of excuses. "I have to go pack. What airline?" I ask so I know where I have to go.

"American. Terminal four. Oh, and VeeVee?"

"Yeah?"

"Pack lightly. You won't be needing clothes."

"Dyson Cole, I can't…" I blush as red as a cherry into the camera again.

"You can, and you will." Something in his voice tells me not to argue with him. "Go, pack. Text me when you're on the train."

I sigh, shaking my head. I've never done anything so spontaneous in my entire life and here I am, having a video call with the man of my dreams and I'm about to get on a plane to New York *fucking* City. "Fine," I squeal, giddiness consuming me and I can't help it.

He smiles wide at me again, my body heats at the hooded look in his eyes. "And VeeVee?"

"What, you crazy fool?"

He throws his head back in laughter at my term then he grows serious for a moment. "I can't wait for you to forgive me in person."

I shake my head with the craziest smirk on my face as I hit the red button on the iPad.

A moment later, my cell chimes with a text, it's Dyson.

Bring your new iPad with you. The box for it is in the bag. I put a few

things on there you might enjoy. ;-)

Ireland: You're one crazy ass fool.

Dyson: Only for you.

My heart starts pounding in my chest at his text and I spring into action. I gulp down the wine in my glass and throw a few bites in my mouth. I haven't eaten all day and god only knows when I'm going to get something to eat again.

I grab all the bags off the dining room table, pulling the iPad with me as I head into my room. I plug in both my phone and the iPad before I leave. I may need the distraction on the plane.

In a little over an hour, I'm showered, my hair pulled up into a messy bun and ready to be stuffed into my beanie. I don't have time to do anything with my crazy ass curls, and I'm going to leave the house with wet hair. It's chilly outside. The Indian summer we seemed to be having has passed and the temps have dropped dramatically. Which reminds me of New York, it's still winter there.

After tracking down the heaviest coat I own, and putting it on top of my suitcase, I'm as packed as I'm going to get given the amount of time I've had. I have to get moving if I'm going to make it on this damn flight. I shake my head at what he's done but I can't help feeling excited and yet a little nervous.

After what almost happened the other night, I don't know if there will be any way to slow him down from seducing me once I'm in New York. Then a thought occurs to me. I don't want him to slow down. This is fucking insane. I don't even know him, not really, and here I am running off to New York City to spend the weekend with him? What is wrong with me? *Hormones.* My subconscious finally rears her head but rather than talk sense into me, she's telling me I'm an idiot for still standing there.

"Gah!" I groan.

I reach into the Apple bag on the counter, the iPad box isn't the only thing in there and I pull out a pair of vibrant red Beats headphones. I shake my head. It's too damn much. But I can't help opening the box. They're gorgeous. I throw my backup battery I use for my phone and all my charging cables into the old make-up bag I use to hold my cables and I throw everything into my travel bag. I look around the room, making sure I'm not leaving anything necessary as I close the case on the iPad and slip it into my bag. Grabbing my phone, I stop at the island. *Shit.*

I scarf down a few more bites of the dinner Dyson had sent over for me before cleaning up the dishes and corking the wine and placing it in the fridge. I scribble a note for Becca and I leave it on the island.

B –

Gone away for the weekend, be back sometime Sunday.

We need to talk.

Call me.

-V

I grab my keys from the counter, turn out the lights and leave the apartment with my roller bag behind me and my tote slung over my shoulder. All my fun new toys are inside as I walk the half a block to the train station.

I'm in luck when it arrives just a few minutes after I arrive on the platform.

I send a text to Dyson.

On the train, you crazy ass fool.

Dyson: Get here, faster.

Ireland: I can't make the train move faster or the plane for that matter. Patience grasshopper.

I imagine his chuckle at the expression. It's an oldie, but a good one that I used to use on him all the time.

Dyson: I've been waiting ten years, my patience has run out.

I smile wide at the screen as the train trudges toward downtown Phoenix and Sky Harbor airport.

Chapter Thirteen

IRELAND

Leaving On A Jet Plane - Caroline Pennell

The whole time I've been sitting here on the train, I've been grinning like a Cheshire cat. I put my old headphones in my ears. I didn't want to show off the new ones Dyson got me and I keep my iPod in my purse. Occupational hazard of riding the train for too long. Especially at night.

We passed through downtown and I only had a couple more stops before the airport when my phone buzzes.

Becca: Where are you going?

Ireland: New York.

Becca: What the hell is in New York?

Ireland: Dyson. He's flying me out there for the weekend.

Becca: I guess we really do need to talk.

Ireland: When I get home, k?

Becca: K. Don't get dead.

I roll my eyes at my friend. That's her usual retort when it comes to me doing something she doesn't necessarily agree with and I can't help wondering what her problem is or has been since we were at Blu last week Friday. Jesus, I can't believe how much things have changed in less than a week and I haven't even begun to see where in the hell this might be going with Dyson.

Before I can dwell on it, the Sky Harbor stop arrives and I climb from the train, checking my watch. I have a little over an hour before my flight. I take the escalator to the skyway toward the tram that will take me to the airport terminal.

Once I step into the airport, I'm thankful I have just under an hour left before my flight. I panic briefly when I see there's a line for boarding

passes, but then I remember there are kiosks upstairs where I can check-in and print my pass because I don't have bags to check.

The airport is shutting down for the night, the shops are closing up and there are not very many people milling about. Thankfully, the line through security is short.

After I got on the train, Dyson texted me my confirmation number and I punch it into the kiosk and go through the steps until my boarding pass spits out of the slot and I walk to the security line only to see more people in line than I'd originally thought. My heart sinks. I'm gonna miss my flight.

I walk to the nearest TSA Agent and I show him my boarding pass and he directs me to a line along the window and I'm confused. "First class," he states simply.

Holy shit.

I'd heard Dyson say it, but I never expected I would be able to dodge the line. No wonder he booked this flight. He knew I would make it, no matter what.

I walk tentatively down the line toward the TSA checkpoint, feeling like a line dodger, pretending to be someone I'm not. As I go I pull my wallet from my purse and grab my ID as I wait for my turn. There is only one other person in front of me and no one standing at the belts to put their bags on. I smile. He'd inadvertently thought of everything without even trying.

I hand the guy my boarding pass and ID, he does his thing, making sure I'm legit, gives me a once over. No doubt the Chucks, the 69 Bottles t-shirt, jeans and beanie have him all sorts of confused. Before I know it, I'm through security headed to my gate.

Ireland: You're spoiling me with this.

Dyson: Always. Are you through security?

Ireland: Yup, almost to the gate.

Dyson: Good, I can't wait to kiss you.

Ireland: Is that all you want to do? Just kiss me?

Dyson: Oh no princess, my tongue is going to lavish your entire body.

His text sends a tingle of heat down my spine that pools in my core. Fuck, this is going to be a long flight. I can't stop smiling at my phone like an idiot until I nearly collide with someone. Apologizing, I walk around them and head toward a seat to wait for my boarding.

I pull out the new iPad and click the button. The background image is of a bouquet of white roses that appear to be sitting on a desk. Until I see the card propped up against the vase, I didn't realize it was the roses I sent him during our little war of roses on Monday. It makes me smile. Looking past the background I smile wider when I see he's added a few apps to the iPad for me, the Kindle App for one. "How'd he know?" I mutter to no one. I open it up and I realize I have internet access. There are bars in the corner indicating I have a wireless signal. I shake my head, but sign into my Amazon account and I have access to all the books on my cloud. I go searching for the one I've been reading about an ex-Navy Seal and his long lost love. I hadn't known that's what it was about until I started reading, but I got hooked and haven't been able to stop. I remember Dyson mentioned something about putting things on here for me and I scroll through different apps until I get to the movies app.

The huge grin I already had on my face grows impossibly larger as I see one of the movies he downloaded for me. How to Lose a Guy in Ten Days. I shake my head, but that's when I note the mail icon. There's a little red number 1 on it. Impatience wins out and I press it. The mail program opens and there is only one email account, "Tigress." I click on it and see an email from Dyson addressed to me.

"Good Evening, ladies and gentleman, welcome to flight…." The announcer goes on talking about starting the boarding process and I stow the iPad. I'll read it when I get on the plane.

I stow my suitcase overhead and tuck my purse under the seat in front of me after taking out my headphones and iPad and I pull my phone from my pocket.

There are only two other passengers in first class with me and I put my headphones on, ignoring the boarding passengers as I plug the headphones into the iPad and I go to the music app, forgetting that I don't have my music on here. I smile like an idiot when I see there is a ton of different music on here and then I notice a playlist labeled 'Dyson' and I click on it. I smile when I realize the songs on here are a lot of the ones we always seemed to be listening to as we were kids. But then I notice some newer ones and I realize he's given me a taste of Dyson, then and now, and it makes me even giddier. I feel like I did as a girl in high school- struck stupid by the idea of a new friend or even a new boyfriend. Though Dyson has been the only one, it reminds me of that time.

I press the random option and let the playlist play. The first song to pop-up is Uncle Kracker's 'Follow Me' and I grin to myself as it starts to play. God, that song. I sing quietly along with the song as I start to read Dyson's email to me.

My Dearest VeeVee,

Thank you.

Those words hardly begin to express what I'm feeling right now. Your forgiveness means everything to me. I always dreamed about the day I would finally manage to find you after all these years. A million and one scenarios played through my mind about what I would say and how I would handle things, but I didn't know until I saw you how much you still affected me and every idea I'd had over the years flew out the window.

I need to apologize for my behavior in the lobby that day, the day of your interview. My actions were uncalled for and I should never have snapped at you the way I did. I could go deeper into why it is I was so upset that day, but it had nothing to do with you or the coffee and you got the brunt of that anger when you truly didn't deserve it. Even if you weren't

you, I would still feel this way, so please know I mean it.

Second, I need to apologize again for yesterday. You were right, I was hurt, but I wasn't hurt by you. I was crushed because my attempt at doing the right thing did no good for anyone. Not me, not you, and certainly not your brother. I didn't want to leave Joplin. I was happy there, but I was only seventeen and I didn't have much of a choice. All of my attempts to convince my mom to let me stay were thwarted. I even tried to convince her that your mother would let me move in to finish out high school. I think at some point even Lauren suggested just that, but my mother wasn't having it, so to Atlanta I went, without you.

After I graduated high school and turned eighteen, I wanted to go back, to find you, to win you back. I tried so many times, but I could never make it all the way to J-Town. I lost my nerve. I was so afraid I'd really hurt you, that I'd never be able to win you back and I couldn't handle the idea of never holding you in my arms again.

As the years went on, I was afraid to go back because I was afraid of what I would find when I got there. I was afraid I would find you'd moved on with your life. That you'd be married, with a family, or simply had gotten over what it was that we had. I know now that wasn't the case and I want to do everything I can to make it up to you.

That's what made me realize I had to make something of myself before I could even attempt to find you. I know it sounds so cliché, but it's true.

*There is much more to this story, but the whole point of this email is to say that I need you in my life. No matter what. I can understand if you don't want to be **with** me, but I beg you to please let me into your life. Even if it is for nothing more than for friendship. I watched you walk into your apartment yesterday and the idea of losing you again destroyed me. VeeVee, I need you.*

Always Yours,

Dyson

I read the email twice before killing the Wi-Fi signal and texting Dyson, letting him know I was on my way. His reply was quick and three little words.

I.Can't.Wait.

Once we are airborne, I reread the email three more times, taking in everything he said to me, even though it was written, it is the most open and honest he's ever been with me and it tears at my heartstrings.

If I ever wondered whether or not I could let Dyson back into my life, the heartache of the last twenty-four hours is proof I don't have much of a choice. Without him, I will either fall apart completely or become the skinniest, cleanest woman on the planet.

While we flew through the night, I compose my own email to him.

When I am done, and satisfied with it, I connect to the plane's internet and send the email. I want him to have it before I land, so he will know what is in my heart and on my mind as I fly across the country to him. I wrote the email with the sounds of Dyson's playlist in my ears.

DYSON
"Learning To Live Again" - Garth Brooks

I've been pacing around my penthouse for too long and the sound of the silence is making me insane. I thought for sure once she was airborne I would have settled down some but she's been on the plane for a little over three hours already, and I'm still pacing.

Why am I so fucking nervous? I don't understand it. I've never had a problem with women, ever.

But this is her. This is *my* VeeVee.

My phone chimes with the new tone I set after setting up the email

account I used to email Ireland. I don't do much with personal emails and I didn't want her emails going through work. Truthfully, I don't want them to get lost in the constant flow of emails coming into my inbox. I want hers to be front and center, always.

I grab my phone and click on the email program to find the email. For the first time in about three hours, I sit down, then I read her words to me.

Thank you, Dyson.

I am sitting here in what can only be described as the biggest airplane seat I've ever had, checking out all the goodies you've left for me on this iPad, which by the way, is way too much. On top of the headphones, which are amazing too. Add to that the clothes you so obviously went back and purchased after yesterday. I feel like I'm going to be thanking you forever. So I guess I'll just say this…

I can't believe I'm coming to New York.

I've never been to the Big Apple before.

There's a first for everything, I think before I continue reading her words.

You say that you need to make something of yourself, why? I can't believe I ever gave you the impression you weren't what I wanted or you weren't good enough for me. Though I think we both had the same feeling because after you left, I fought hard to lose weight, get in shape and be someone worthy of your attention. So I guess in the end, we're both a little guilty of thinking neither one of us were good for each other.

God, I loved her exactly the way she was. That's the reason I always found women who were the exact opposite of her. Always. Blondes, skinny as rails, straight hair, no glasses, anything that wouldn't remind me of Ireland.

I never imagined seeing you again, though like you, I had a million and one things that I would say to you when and if it finally happened, but instead, I kicked you in the nuts. Though I am sorry I did it, I won't deny the sense of gratification I got out of it. If you hadn't been dancing with my roommate at the time, I might not have gone to such extremes.

That's my tigress.

Don't get me wrong, I won't hesitate to do it again when you're being an asshat, prickweed, manwhore, stuck-up-cocky-bastard, or three thousand dollar suit wearing pencil dick, or any combination of the above.

I let out a long roar of laughter as I remember her roses. "I would expect nothing less out of you, sweetheart," I say aloud to no one.

In the end, Dyson, I have no idea where all of this is going to go, where this is going to lead, and I am scared to death of giving you even the tiniest piece of me. I don't want to feel that way, but I know if I don't give into this, I will regret it for the rest of my life. In the end, and what's most important, I have no idea how to do this, so please, be patient with me.

Your VeeVee

The smile on my face won't leave, no matter how hard I try to make it.

My fingers twitch with the desire to reply to her. Obviously she's taking advantage of the airplane's onboard Wi-Fi, but I want her to rest. I can't promise she'll get any once she's here.

Her parting lines make me think about the precious gift of trust she's offering me and I don't know how to handle that. How do I prove to her I'm not going to run, not ever again?

Time.

The voice in my head tells me, *you have to give her time. You can't expect her to trust you so fast. You have to give her the chance to trust you, prove to her that you're worthy of all that she's trying to give you, despite the fact you don't deserve it.*

I check my watch for the thousandth time. Less than two hours. It's approaching five in the morning in New York, and I look out the window, seeing a few flurries flying between the buildings and the steam rising out the of the vent shafts of the buildings that surround mine. I should have told her to pack a jacket. Shit, does she even own a jacket?

I call Byron.

"Yes, boss," his deep timber comes through the phone.

"We need to go to JFK in about forty-five."

"Yes, sir, I'll have the car ready."

"I want the limo."

"You got it. Anything else, sir?"

"How cold is it outside?"

"Right now, around seventeen, but it's supposed to warm above freezing today."

"Thanks, I'm picking up a weekend guest." I know he's not going to ask questions, I pay him not to, but I hate the fact this is a familiar discussion. Dread washes over me at the idea that Ireland has, for some unknown reason, remained celibate and I've been, well, to use her word, a manwhore. "I'll need to go into the airport and I don't know if she's going to have a jacket."

"No problem, I'll get Kensington."

"Thank you," I say and end the call.

Looking at my watch again I curse, "Dammit." It's only been three minutes since the last time I looked.

I stalk off toward my bedroom and an ice cold shower.

Chapter fourteen

IRELAND

Dangerous Woman - Ariana Grande

My ears pop, waking me from my fitful sleep on the plane.

The flight attendant comes over the intercom telling us they'll be making another pass through the cabin to clean up, yada yada… I zone out, fighting to calm my nerves. I hate landings.

"Would you like some orange juice?" the first class attendant asks me.

"Please," I tell her then I straighten myself out. The iPad is off because the movie ran out at some point while I was sleeping and I click on it. The Wi-Fi is still connected and I check for an email from Dyson. Disappointment slides through me when I see he didn't respond to my email. Then I feel like an idiot. New York is two hours ahead of Phoenix. When I got on that plane, it was nearly two in the morning his time. *Smile, Vy, you're about to see him.*

I flip over to the music icon and start up his playlist and that's when Ed Sheeran's voice comes through and Lego House plays as the flight attendant brings me a glass of orange juice and I drink half of it before setting it on the tray.

The attendant comes back a few minutes later and takes my cup and I pull my iPad off the tray and stick it in the seat beside me so I can keep listening to Dyson's playlist. Another song comes on I don't recognize so I hit the button to pull it up, Elliot Moss – 'Slip'.

We continue to descend and I open the shade of the window to see the city of New York below me. It's breathtaking to see it. There are piles of white on top of buildings; some look like a fresh dusting happened overnight. The lights on buildings still twinkle bright but the sun is fighting to make an appearance through the grey clouds. The traffic below is picking up as the Friday morning rush hour begins to take shape.

God, what I wouldn't give to live in a city like this.

The constant hustle and bustle of everyday life. The people coming

and going. I can only imagine the air of excitement in a city like this. I haven't even touched down and I'm already falling in love with New York.

The ground starts to get closer and I sit back in my seat, a little straighter, a little stiffer. I hate this.

Breathe, Vy, I tell myself.

Though I'm not entirely sure if it is the descent that has me wound up tight. Once these wheels hit the ground, it's only a matter of minutes before I can see him again. My heart starts pounding and the desire I've been suppressing since the plane's doors closed comes raging back. My mouth falls slack as the memory of Dyson's mouth on mine sends a new thrill through me. *I'm in so much trouble.*

Finally, the wheels hit the runway and I breathe for the first time in I don't know how long as the breaks engage and the plane starts to slow.

Then my breathing picks up for a whole other reason.

Dyson.

It feels like it takes forever to reach the gate and then for the doors to open. There are only three of us in the first class cabin so I have my bags before I double check to make sure I don't leave anything behind and I turn on my phone.

It only takes a minute for it to connect and adjust to the time in New York. Then another second for a text to chime through. It's Dyson.

Waiting for you in baggage.

I smile and text him back,

I didn't check a bag.

His reply is instant.

Follow the signs to baggage, I'm waiting. Hurry.

I giggle.

I'm trying, tell them to open the damn doors.
Dyson: On it.
Ireland: Too late, on my way.
Dyson: Thank god, RUN!

My heart is racing in my chest, but not from running, more from his sheer excitement at seeing me and I'm equally as excited to see him and I shouldn't feel this way. I have no idea what's going to happen and I'm scared shitless.

I keep trudging through the airport. *Jesus, this place is huge.*

I see what I'm after- the turn off into the baggage claim area, and my heart speeds up as a huge, panty melting smile greets me and I nearly drop my bags because I want to run to him.

Fuck it.

Pulling my carry-on behind me, I sprint toward him and drop it as I leap into his arms.

"God, I missed you," he breathes before he slants his lips against mine and the world falls away. Nothing matters but him. Nothing but his lips on mine. He flicks his tongue against my lips, coaxing me to open for him as he places his hand on the back of my head, holding me to him and I slide my tongue along his as I moan.

The taste of Dyson Cole is enough to ignite every nerve ending in my body. He doesn't slow our kiss despite both of us breathing heavily and I don't want him to stop, but he pulls back, then kisses me again, then

pulls back, then again. I start laughing. "Hi to you too," I say completely breathless.

"Come on, gorgeous."

He sets me down then leans down to grab my roller bag.

He stops abruptly. "Do you have a jacket?"

I smile and nod. "It's in there." I lean down to get it out and our hands meet on the zipper. That quickly becoming familiar, spark ignites. I pull my hand back, unsure what to make of it, he continues with the zipper and I pull my jacket out.

"Here." He takes my bag from my shoulder and I slip my jacket on. "Is that all you have?" he asks me.

"I live in Phoenix, remember?"

He chuckles softly. "The car's out front." He hands me back my purse and I sling it over my shoulder and he switches hands with my suitcase so he can slide his fingers between mine. I look at our hands intertwined as we walk toward the door. "You feel it too, don't you?" he inquires.

I blush a little and nod, unsure of what to say. I took a chance on him and slept with him ten years ago and he left me. Now, I've flown across the country to a strange place and I have no idea what's about to happen. I'm both scared and nervous, but somewhere, at thirty-thousand feet, I realized I'm scared of everything. I've lived my life being scared of being hurt because I had nothing else to compare it to. I let myself be scared of falling in love with someone who wasn't Dyson, someone who would hurt me worse than anything he did. But on that airplane, I realized I need to take the risk. Take a chance, and if this weekend is the only weekend I'll ever get with him again, I'll take it.

I look up and smile as we walk through the last door and out into the freezing New York air.

I suck in a deep breath. "Fuck me," I shiver.

He laughs. "Welcome to New York at the beginning of February." His laugh fades into a smile as he ushers me toward a waiting, sleek black limousine.

"Ms. McKidd, Mr. Cole." I look at the hulk of a man who opens the door. He's just as tall, if not a few inches taller than Dyson is, and Dyson is fit – there is no mistaking that, but this guy is huge.

"Ireland, Byron, Byron, Ireland."

"Pleasure to meet you, Ms. McKidd."

I smile at him in greeting. Despite the tough, gruff exterior, his voice is sweet, genuine. "Call me Ireland, or Vy." I extend my hand and he takes it gently in his. There is a stark contrast between his olive skin tone and my red-haired, pale complexion, but it makes me smile.

"Hop in," Dyson says behind me and I smile again at Byron before I climb into the limo and slide over so Dyson can climb in too.

"He's huge," I whisper to Dyson when the door closes.

Dyson laughs, "That he is. But he's the best man I know when it comes to security."

I smile knowing Dyson has someone looking after him. I don't fully understand the extent of Dyson's wallet, and I don't care, but I would imagine there are a lot of things he needs protection from.

It's all a bit overwhelming.

Dyson's warm hand comes to my cheek and I press into his warmth. "You're freezing." As if on cue, I shiver.

"I'm alright. It's just a big contrast to Phoenix." I smile at him and raise my head when he pulls his palm away.

His eyes are wide and, excited and yet I can sense he, like me, is a little nervous. "I'm going to have to leave you to your own devices for a little while today." His voice is concerned. "If I'd been a little more reasonable about you coming here, I would have flown you out this morning instead."

I put my finger to his lips, silencing him. "I'm a big girl, Dyson. I can take care of myself for a while." I try to hide the disappointment in my voice, but I don't think I was successful.

"Come here," he says as he pats his lap. I raise an eyebrow at him.

"You're too far away, princess. Come here." I smirk at the nickname. Reminds me of when we were kids.

"You use to call me that when you were mad at me." I look at him with narrowed eyes.

"No, I was never mad at you. I thought you were acting like a snotty little princess." I laugh as I settle on his lap and he wraps his arms around me. Wrapped in his warmth, I settle my head on his shoulder.

He pulls the beanie from my head to find a mess of curly red hair. Then he finds the clip that's holding it all in place and my hair falls down my back and he buries his head in my neck, inhaling deeply. "Strawberries," he breathes as he slowly shakes his head back and forth. "Little did I know you really are a princess."

"I think you're bias," I tell him with a smirk.

"I think you're right." I hear the humor in his voice as he pulls his head out of my hair.

The electricity that hasn't stopped burning since I jumped into his arms ignites again and his hand comes to my chin, lifting it up so he can look me in the eye. The eye contact fades the moment he presses his lips to mine. I close my eyes, savoring his warmth, his touch, his scent. There is something about the way he smells that makes my head fog over with desire. His tongue slides in along my own and I don't care that we're driving through New York on our way to wherever. There's just us.

My heart speeds up in my chest, my breathing wavers and my desire for the man I'm kissing grows hotter, more desperate. I need so much more of him than what he's giving me right how. I pull back from the kiss, desperate for air. His breathing matches my own and I can't help the smile that spreads as I look at him. I can feel the warmth in my cheeks as he takes in my expression with gentle eyes. They're soft with an air of mischievousness playing at the corners of his lips.

"God, VeeVee, you're so fucking gorgeous." He tucks a stray strand of hair behind my ear and he shifts beneath me.

"Am I hurting you?" I ask as I'm about to climb off him.

His hands wrap around me, holding me to him. "Not at all. It's just…" I feel it then when he twitches against my thigh.

"We could do something about that, you know?" I look around the limo, or rather what I can see of it, and there's plenty of room.

His eyes become hooded and full of the same desire I'm already feeling between my legs and my breathing hitches again. I lean in to kiss him again and he stills me. I fight the feeling of rejection that's threatening to consume me by closing my eyes.

His hand comes off my thigh and presses to my cheek gently. "Look at me, Ireland." His voice is stern, but yet his tone is soft and I open my eyes. "I owe you better than a limo our first time." His eyes are gentle. "You deserve better than that. The first time I took your virginity in a barn, the second time I nearly took you because you begged me to, but my reasons were more selfish than that." A small tear escapes my right eye, and he swipes it away with the pad of his thumb. I have no idea why I'm crying, maybe it's the remnants of the rejection I felt at first, I don't know, but he doesn't comment on it. "The next time I bury myself inside of you, it will be on a bed, the right way."

My chin quivers at his statement because the look in his eyes says all the things his voice is not.

"Besides, we don't have too much further to go before we're at the penthouse."

"Penthouse?" I choke.

He smiles wide at me then, not the panty melter I enjoy so much, but one that crinkles the corners of his eyes. "I started my business in New York. My home is technically here."

"Oh," is all I can manage as the reality of him not living in Phoenix settles over me.

He catches on to my change in mood quickly. He removes his hand from my cheek and places it back on my thigh. "What's that look for?" he asks.

"I thought you lived in Phoenix."

He smiles again. "I do." Relief washes over me. "But I spend almost as much time in New York as I do in Phoenix, so rather than get rid of my house here, I've kept it. It makes it easier to come here. Sometimes I have to stay for a month or so."

"That's not making me feel much better."

His smile turns sad. "That makes two of us." He leans his forehead against mine. "Why do you think I flew you out here this morning? I couldn't stand spending three days away from you."

Starting to feel a bit uncomfortable sitting on his lap like this, I shift, his eyes grow wide and I smile as I adjust so that I'm straddling his legs and he growls at me, nipping at my lips with his teeth. "So not helping, tigress."

I give him my best sexy smirk, and flick my hips.

The next thing I know, I'm on my back and Dyson is on top of me. "Oh," I squeak as he presses himself against me. His hand brushes the hair from my forehead and he plays with one of the curls. "Bed," he groans.

His hand slides up my thigh, caressing me with gentle strokes. "Do you promise to take me to bed?"

"Every fucking night."

I lean up to kiss him, but miss and end up with his chin instead. I give him a gentle kiss and whine.

"What do you want, Ireland?"

I moan my frustration as he keeps his lips just out of reach.

"Tell me, princess."

"Your lips," I beg.

He looks down at me, smirking. "Oh really, how bad?" he asks as he presses his hips against mine and I can feel his erection pressing against my sex.

I moan and throw my head back as the action sends a sharp spark of pleasure through my body and the next thing I know he's kissing along

my jaw, down my neck, pulling my jacket out of the way so he can find more skin and I turn my head, allowing him the access he so desperately seems to want.

"Five minutes," a voice interrupts us and I jump.

Dyson chuckles, "Don't worry, he can't see us."

He pulls back from me and grabs my hand to pull me up. "You don't fight fair," I grumble and he laughs.

"I never said I would fight fair, princess."

I huff and fold my arms over my chest in a mock pout and he moves his face in front of mine. He nips at my bottom lip, grabbing it gently and pulling it sweetly and I can feel the heat rising in my veins. The limo is suddenly too warm.

Before I can get any more worked up, he backs off. "You're going to be the death of me." He sits back against the bench seat, but he takes my hand in his and gently kisses each of my knuckles. Until he stops at the ring on my pointer finger.

Recognition lights his eyes. "You still have this?" he asks and I smile at him. Looking between his eyes and the ring, they're almost the same color. "What's purple mean again?"

"Crazy as fuck," I laugh.

He smirks at me. "Why would you be crazy as fuck, Ireland?"

"Because you make me crazy."

His smirk turns into a salacious grin. "How so?"

"Oh, I don't know, Mister Spontaneous?" I laugh. "Among other reasons."

The car comes to a stop and one of the doors open up front but Dyson doesn't pull back, he's still looking at the mood ring on my finger. Though it used to reside on my ring finger, it doesn't fit there anymore, it's too big, so I moved it to my pointer finger. I don't wear it every day, but knowing I was coming here, I was hoping he'd remember it. "It's my rock," I whisper.

He gives me a goofy grin. "I can't believe it still works."

The door behind Dyson opens and I catch a glimpse of Byron before Dyson slides out and offers me his hand, thank god, because if I had to breath him in any longer, I was going to rip off all my clothes and demand he take me right then and there.

I slide out. There are a few snowflakes floating down from the grey sky overhead and I can see steam coming up out of a couple sewer grates and I shiver. "Come on, let's get you inside."

Chapter fifteen

DYSON
Be Still - The Fray

God, I had no idea I had that much willpower in me.

Ireland's close proximity, the way she jumped into my arms, the way she smells, fuck, I can't believe I made it out of that limo without taking her right there. The desire to prove to her this isn't just some one-night-stand was too hot to ignore.

I meant what I said. I've never done anything right by her and I owe it to her to do this the right way. Though the right way would probably be actually courting her, getting to know her, but I have no idea how to even begin to do that. Let alone figure out how to keep my dick in my pants.

I escort her into my building. It's not the tallest building around, but at twenty-two stories, it's still quite tall. I live on the Upper West Side of Manhattan, and I live here because I can afford to. Definitely not for the neighbors. If I'd known what I was going to be getting into when it came to them, I would have chosen a tiny studio in Midtown over this place.

Regardless, the penthouse has an amazing view that makes the nosey, stuck up neighbors worth it. I watch Ireland carefully as I take her to the elevators. The lobby is quite upscale, decorated in whites and gold and there is probably more money in this lobby than she's ever seen in her lifetime. If I wanted to avoid throwing my wealth at her, I should have taken her to a hotel, but the idea of something so impersonal when it comes to her makes me feel like a dirty asshole.

The elevator arrives. "Wait, where's my suitcase?"

I assure her, "Byron will bring it up after parking the car."

"You own the limo?"

I give her a quizzical look. "Yes," I answer with some hesitation.

"Jesus, how much money do you have?" I watch with a smirk on my face as she slaps her hand over her mouth.

I kiss her forehead, the sexual intensity in the elevator ignites again and I watch as she drops her hand and her mouth falls slack. "You really

want to know?" I ask her.

"No."

"That's quite definitive there, tigress."

"It's none of my business, Dyson," she says, a hint of anger in her voice, but her eyes betray her curiosity. "Besides, it doesn't matter to me if you have five dollars in your wallet or five million." Her terse tone tells me she's serious and I start to rethink our distance these last ten years. This of course makes me feel more like a prick than I already do.

Changing the wayward thoughts, I ask her, "Are you going to freak out on me when I show you my apartment?"

"Probably."

The look on her face is too serious and I laugh, "Good to know."

The elevator dings, indicating our arrival on the top floor. The doors slide open into the foyer. There is only one door, my door.

"My housekeeper was going to prepare breakfast for us. Are you hungry?"

"Famished," she says without a comment about my housekeeper. At this point, I should probably just rip off the band-aid, that way there are no surprises later on.

I enter the code into the door. She watches me carefully. "Seriously?" She looks at me, a little confused with a whole lot of skepticism.

"Best day of the year."

"That's my birthday," she mutters in shock.

"It is." I smile at her and push the door open.

"How long has it been your code?" She raises an eyebrow at me.

"Since the day the door was installed."

"When was that?"

I laugh, "You really want to know?"

"I don't know, do I?"

"I bought the house on March twenty-ninth." She gasps. "Three years ago, the door was installed the next day."

"Dammit, Dyson." She turns on me, "Why?"

"What what, VeeVee?"

"Why didn't you come find me?"

I push her up against the hallway wall and bring our bodies together. "I tried."

"It couldn't have been that hard. Mom's phone number never changed."

"I didn't want you to find out I was looking for you. I was afraid if you knew I was coming, you'd run away from me before I could find you." I brush a stray curl out of her face and I smile at her. "Besides, if I had come to find you, what would you have done?"

"Probably exactly what I did at the bar the other night."

I can't help but laugh. "That still hurts, by the way."

"I'm sorry."

I chuckle a little, "I'm not."

"You really are a crazy ass fool."

"*Your* crazy ass fool," I counter and bring my lips to hers. I kiss her gently, and despite my attempt to keep it platonic, I fail as she gently drops her purse on the ground before wrapping her arms around my neck, holding me to her, and pressing her body against mine.

She pulls back and makes eye contact. "There's a bed in here somewhere, right?"

"Ah, my feisty tigress, yes, there are several actually, but…" I reluctantly look at my watch, it's quarter after eight, "I don't have enough time to fully savor your body the way it deserves." Her breathing grows ragged at the idea of me savoring her. I grin. "Come on, tour, then breakfast."

She sighs but reluctantly comes along.

IRELAND
Gonna Make You Love Me - Ryan Adams

Dyson's penthouse apartment is… overwhelming. There really is no other description for it.

The ceiling is at least twenty feet high in the main living area, which is divided into two parts by a free standing gas fireplace. On one side is the living room or my idea of one anyway. There is a couch, coffee table and a couple of chairs facing a large flat screen that has to be at least sixty-five inches. Underneath it is a very sleek, very discreet entertainment center.

On the other side of the fireplace is a rather informal looking dining room with a bar height table and bar stool type chairs, that's where our place is set for our breakfast. Which smells divine. Beyond that table is a doorway to a much more formal dining area. To the left of that is a kitchen that looks state of the art but he takes the way of the hallway near the big television so I don't get a good look. Down the hallway are two bedrooms that are probably as big as, if not bigger than, my whole apartment back in Phoenix.

Both rooms have king size beds and a simple décor. Beyond those two bedrooms are two more doors. One is locked with another keypad entry. He points out that it's his office, but doesn't open the door. The other portal is an entryway into the entertainment room. There is another television, more well-used furniture, including a sectional couch and a couple of oversized chairs. Behind the couch is a pool table, and on the walls are old beer signs you'd find in bars or pubs down on the streets of New York. Beyond the pool table, like much of the penthouse, is one huge floor to ceiling window.

In front of the window a ridiculously comfortable looking chair I could see myself reading in for hours with the bustling New York streets below to look at. Though the people are tiny from up here, you can see

them moving around each other and in and out of traffic as they make their way to their destinations. The idea of making myself comfortable in that chair reading brings a slice of fear about this being our only weekend. Will this be the only time I'm ever in this apartment? I don't like that idea at all and I try, in vain, to squash it before it blossoms into something worse. That fear is replaced when the vision from the airplane comes back to me. The view from up here reminds me of how much it made me want to live in New York. Watching from the window now is no exception.

"Penny for your thoughts?" Dyson asks as I look out the window.

"I was just thinking about how much I think I would enjoy living in New York."

I see his reflection as he steps closer to me, a huge smile spread across his face. "We could always make that happen."

I look at his reflection in the window. "I'm about to start a new job in Phoenix, I couldn't possibly…"

"I just meant that if you wanted it bad enough, I'm confident we could get you transferred here."

"I know, I just…I guess I just need a change of pace," I sigh.

"Explain, please?"

I cross my arms over my chest. "Working at Wellington scares me."

"Why?"

I turn around to look at him, searching for how best to explain this. "I haven't exactly had the most positive experiences when it comes to Wellington. First, getting the phone call about…" I don't finish, he knows and I don't need to, "Then, no offense, but our confrontation in the lobby, followed by you arguing with Wellington about not hiring me, add to that the fact you still don't want me working for him."

"No, I don't. But my reasoning is purely selfish."

"How so?"

He reaches for my hand and I give it to him. "Because of two

reasons. One, I didn't know how I would be able to do my job with you downstairs. Even if you hadn't figured out who I am, it would have killed me to have you right downstairs and…I guess I didn't think you'd find it in that pretty mind of yours to forgive me." He gives me a small smile. "The second reason is because if you did figure it out or if I somehow managed to rekindle what we had all those year ago, you working for Wellington poses an issue."

"The no fraternization rule."

 "Exactly, though if Wellington wants to keep my business, he wouldn't fire you." He pauses as if he's pondering something, then he sighs. "And I guess there are really three reasons. Though I hadn't been there for the entire interview, I realized, listening to you talking to them, that you have a real knack for business and marketing. At the time, the reason I argued with him was because I wanted you to come work for me."

"Dyson, please don't take this the wrong way, but I need to be able to work on my own. I need to be able to prove myself. I don't want you becoming my white knight when it comes to my job. I've gone to school and worked my ass off for six years to work at Wellington. I won't let you or anyone else stand in my way."

He smiles wider at me before declaring, "That's the tigress I know."

"Promise me," I say and he raises an eyebrow in question. "That if I lose my job at Wellington, because of whatever reasons, you'll stay out of it?"

He nods his head reluctantly. "I will stay out of it, I promise."

"Thank you." I return his smile.

"Come on, there's some more to see."

He tugs on my hand and pulls me back down the hallway toward the living room and that's when I see someone in the kitchen, but he doesn't take me in there, instead he leads me up the spiral staircase that leads to the second floor and down a small hallway to a single door. "The Master suite," he says as if it is almost a dirty word and the Cheshire grin on his

face tells me his mind is in the same place mine is as he opens the door.

Stepping inside the massive room is… Wow," I tell him. Directly opposite the door is a huge picture window that extends floor to ceiling and wall to wall. The view is… "Wow," I breathe again.

There aren't any buildings between his and the river below. "That's the Hudson, across from it is New Jersey," he explains.

"It's gorgeous from up here." I smile and then turn toward him. On the wall – to the right of the door – is a massive four poster bed. No canopy, but its iron frame is gorgeous nonetheless. There are night stands on each side, and a large, gorgeous picture hanging above the bed.

The picture is in black and white, and along the bottom are silhouetted flowers painted from one side to the other, the flowers continue deeper into the picture where there is a silhouette of a girl, with curly hair. My eyes go from it to Dyson and back again.

"I commissioned it a couple years ago."

"Dyson, it's…I don't even know what to say." Here I thought I'd had a hard time getting over the fact I felt like I was still in love with a man I was likely to never see again, but the little things that keep popping up prove I was never far from his mind either.

He comes up behind me and wraps his arms around me, kissing the top of my head. "One more room, then food." My stomach growls at the thought of food and he leads me into the ensuite bathroom.

"Jesus, you could swim in that thing," I giggle when I take in the sight of the massive bathtub sitting center stage in the room. To the left is a dual sink vanity, one side has what is obviously his stuff, the other is… "What's all that?" I ask him, pointing to the other side.

"I didn't know what kind of toiletries you would pack, so I had someone run and grab them this morning."

"How'd you-" I stop myself, remembering the other night when he'd gone into my bathroom to get dressed again after…I shake my head and smile. "Is there anything you don't think of?"

"Of course, I'm far from perfect." I turn around and wrap my arms

around his neck, pulling his head down to mine and I kiss him. It was meant to be chaste but he takes it up a notch and before I know it, my breathing is ragged, my heart is racing and that desire that had cooled before burns hotter and brighter.

"Food," he growls as he leads me out of the bathroom. That's when I notice the matching chair to the one downstairs with my suitcase sitting next to it. I smile as he leads me downstairs to the table and to the wonderful smelling breakfast his housekeeper made for us.

Chapter Sixteen

DYSON
First Love - Adele

Leaving Ireland alone in my penthouse is quite possibly the worst feeling in the world. What was I thinking, bringing here all the way to New York? I was thinking with my dick, that's what.

I'd introduced her to Kathy, my housekeeper before we sat down to eat. As much as I didn't want our time together to end this morning, I have to go. I don't have a choice. This meeting is really important and it's the whole reason I'm here and not back in Phoenix.

Byron opens the door to the Escalade parked on the street in front of my building and I slide inside and do everything in my power to wipe my mind of the fact *my* tigress is up in my apartment, waiting for me to come home. I can't take the distraction today. I've been putting off coming to New York until I knew when Ireland was starting her job. For some reason I needed to be there when she started. I didn't understand it and now that I'm in New York, I'm going to miss her first day anyway.

If I hadn't gotten the call I did on Wednesday, after going shopping for Ireland's things, I wouldn't have been able to wait until Monday or until she was done processing everything I'd told her. I knew staying in Phoenix was going to be trouble for me and for her. Then I end up bringing her here anyway. At least I don't have to sit in my condo less than a block away wondering what she's doing or if she's going to call me.

It brings me a sense of calm knowing she's here, she's in my apartment and she's safe. Now to get this shit over with so I can go back to her.

IRELAND
Ride - Chase Rice

A whirlwind of things hits me all at once after Dyson leaves. The adrenaline rush of coming to New York and seeing Dyson, the desire Dyson ignites inside me, and pure exhaustion consumes me the moment

he walks out the door. As much as I hated to have him leave, the kiss he left me with still has my lips prickling with a desperate need to kiss him again.

Kathy, Dyson's housekeeper, is sweet. Maybe in her early to mid-forties and her sweetness comes from the motherly way she handles things. It makes me think of my mother and my heart aches.

It's all too much.

I need something to clear my mind before the thoughts of my mother consume me in a ball of tears on the floor and I make a move to help Kathy clean up. But she's humming along to a tune in her head and looks perfectly content to be doing what she's doing so I don't interrupt her.

I make my feet move forward and allow them to carry me up the stairs and into Dyson's bedroom. Bedroom is an understatement; this room is at least the size of my whole apartment, if not two of them. His decorations are simple and yet very Dyson.

I find my bags and pull my new iPad from my purse, then go rummaging through my suitcase for a change of clothes and head into the bathroom. I decided during breakfast I would take some time in the massive tub and relax while I wait for him to return to me.

I set my iPad up on the counter, away from the tub and all things water related, and start up his playlist again. I put it on random and let it roll through the songs. I'm surprised when the music comes out louder than I'd thought it would, but… I look around the bathroom. It's not blaringly loud, but it's louder than my iPad should be producing and I reach for the button to turn it down. The sound lowers but it pops up and says Bluetooth.

Shit…

I walk out of the bathroom, leaving my iPad on the counter and I don't hear anything, so I go into the hallway which overlooks the living area below and I don't hear anything there either, not even Kathy.

I shrug and go back into the bathroom. Must just be in that room. Odd. I shrug it off and adjust the volume to something comfortable,

regardless of what song plays, it shouldn't blast me with noise.

I go to the tub and sitting near the faucet are some balls, about the size of a softball. I pick one up and realize it's wrapped in plastic and I turn it until I find the label.

"Oh," I squeak when I read the label. I've heard about these things, but I've never seen them before. There are several in a basket and I grab one of the light purple ones and see that it's a lavender-chamomile combo. I turn the faucet on, find a good temperature and I push the plug down, letting it fill. I'm about to stand up when I see something flicker. It's built into the tub, it's a screen. I chuckle glancing at it and realize it's got all kinds of options. One is quick fill and I can't stop myself from hitting that button. The room fills with noise and I look into the tub to see several of what I thought were whirlpool jets start to spout water, filling the tub.

I stick my hand in it, checking the temp, it's a little colder than I like but I decide to check the screen before messing with the faucet. I smile when I push a couple buttons to bump up the temp and after a few heartbeats, I check the bigger faucet and it's warmed up more. Good.

I leave the bathroom just as a song I love comes on the iPad and Birdy's voice fills the room with her soulful voice singing Skinny Love. I smile. I'm about to pull my shirt off when I remember this room is completely surrounded by light from the outside. "Hmm."

I wonder if his room is as tech savvy as his bathtub is and I start looking for blinds or something along the windows but I don't see anything. Shit. I don't even know why I came out here to change in the first place. I can do that in the bathroom. I turn and something catches my attention, a series of switches along the small hallway from the door in the bedroom and I walk over to it. Of course, nothing is labeled, but there is a knob of sorts and I turn it. Immediately the room starts to darken and I keep turning it until the room is nearly pitch black. "Well, that's nice," I smirk and flip one of the other switches that doesn't seem to do anything, then I try another and then finally one last one and a soft light illuminates near the bed.

Satisfied, I pull my shirt over my head, then reach up between my tits and unhook my bra, pulling it off. I push my pants down and I am suddenly overcome with the fact I am naked in Dyson Cole's bedroom. The desire I'd managed to suppress during breakfast comes back and I tremble. My nipples harden and my sex heats.

The idea of Dyson, here, with me, naked, is almost too much to bear but a chime from the bathroom brings me out of my sex fueled fantasy and I drop my clothes in my suitcase and head into the bathroom.

My cheeks heat when I see the text from Dyson.

It's killing me that you're in my apartment and I'm stuck here. Tell me, princess, what are you doing?

I smile wide. This is so not going to help, but I can't resist the opportunity to mess with him, even if it just a little tease.

DYSON

Concentrating is my middle name. I can do this…I can… my phone vibrates and I pick it up.

Ireland: Wishing you were here.

Then 'Ireland sent a photo', is displays on my screen and I pull it back from the table, shielding it so only I can see it.

Big fucking mistake.

My cock swells to the size of Texas and I have to hold back the rush of air I need to release. My eyes grow hooded as I take in the picture that's been sent to me.

She's standing, with her back to the mirror, the bathtub in the background; she's standing in front of my mirror. But who gives a fuck about that. Her back is to the mirror, her left arm across the front of her body, her phone over her right shoulder. She's completely naked. Her right hand is cupping her left breast, and her hair is cascading down her back into a point just before it disappears below the counter. Giving me the perfect view of her gorgeous curves. My eyes finally make it up to hers in the picture and she's giving me a hooded look. I can't see all of her face, but it's enough to practically having me coming right here and now.

I finally manage to pull my head out of my ass when someone says something, not toward me, but just enough to pull me back to the reality of the conference room I'm sitting in conducting business.

I let my fingers fly over the keyboard as I text her back a reply. A mischievous grin on my lips as I do.

IRELAND
I Want Crazy - Hunter Hayes

My phone chimes.

I don't know what the hell came over me to send him that picture, but I am so fucking horny, and I want him to feel as miserable as I do. If only for a minute, I pray that the picture affected him, made him waiver in his confidence, just for a moment.

I look at my phone and I smile in victory.

I almost came in my pants, in the middle of a conference room,

surrounded by fifteen different people, including my lawyer.

I smile wider than I thought was possible. I grab a couple towels and move to the bathtub. I put one towel on the side of the tub and my phone on top of it, the other I drape over the side.

The tub stopped filling shortly after I shot the picture. I am pretty impressed with my bathroom mirror selfie skills. I grab the bath bomb I'd chosen and I drop it into the tub and I watch as it immediately starts to fizz up to the surface. Looking at the control screen again, listening to the sounds of one of my all-time favorite songs by Bonnie Raitt called Lover's Will, I see a whirlpool option with various settings, I set them to low and listen as the water kicks up just a notch and I smile, climbing into the warm water.

The fizz of the bomb tickles my legs as I walk past it to sit on the other side and I lower myself in just as my phone chimes again.

I pick it up, grateful my hands aren't wet yet.

Dyson: how's my tub?

I smile and lower myself to sit on the low bench and stretch out a little.

The whirl of the water and the bath bomb is enough to blur the water so I snap another picture, this time of my legs, under the water, stretched out.

I send it to him with a caption that says, 'almost perfect'.

His reply is almost instant.

Dyson: you're fucking killing me here, tigress... y almost?

DYSON

We're wrapping up our meeting. It's gone well, despite my distractions with Ireland back in my apartment. She hadn't replied to my last question before we started wrapping up and I stowed my phone. I didn't know how long this meeting was going to last and I have some things I need to do in the office, but I don't know that much is going to get done knowing she's home, naked, in my bathtub.

I feel my phone vibrate but I'm talking to the owner of a company Tigress needs to bring into the fold and I ignore it until a more appropriate time.

Normally, I'm not one to fuck around on my phone during a meeting and it's making me off kilter, but I realize I'm not the only one checking their phones, iPads or tablets. I guess this is the market of business anymore. A market we're desperate to tap into as soon as possible.

I pull my phone from my pocket, grinning like an idiot as I look at it. Then my face falls when I see a name that doesn't belong to Ireland and it's a name I never wanted to see again. I remove it from my lock screen and go back to my conversation.

The name on my screen sends my blood to boil and my cock softens like someone poured ice water on him. *Fuck.*

Chapter Seventeen

DYSON
Already Home - A Great Big World

I am headed back to my office when my phone buzzes again. I pull it from my pocket and my melancholy mood disappears immediately.

Ireland: Because you're not here.

I reply back to her,

I'm almost done.
Ireland: Good, hurry.

I'm smiling like a loon, staring at my phone as I step into my office and movement catches my eye. I snap my head up. A pair of dark brown eyes stares back at me. She looks slightly frazzled, which is actually a strange comfort to me.

"What the fuck are you doing here, Jill?"

She smiles, tries to smooth herself out, checks her hair with her hand and then steps toward me. I put my hands up and lock my phone at the same time.

"I came to ask you about tomorrow night?"

"What about it, Jill?" I say her name with complete and total disdain.

She fidgets. She knows she's not wanted here and I'm pissed the receptionist let her come back to my office.

"Are we still going together?"

I scowl at her. "Jill, we were never going together. I don't know what put that in your head, but we are never going anywhere, ever again, together."

"I'm sorry," she whines. "I…I thought we could work this out."

I roll my eyes. "We have nothing to work out, Jill. It was one night, a long time ago."

"But it wasn't just one night and you know it."

My heart hurts. "I don't know that for sure, and neither do you. So why," I shake my head, closing my eyes, "why do you keep bringing it up?"

"Because it was real, it was us."

"Jill, enough. Stop calling, stop texting me, and stop showing up at my office. We had a one-night stand that meant nothing to me." I watch my words slice through her and I have no compassion for her whatsoever. What she did to me was completely inexcusable and I know the truth, despite what she wants me to think.

"There's someone else?" She scrutinizes my face.

"What the fuck, Jill?" She steps closer to me and I back up toward the door. I don't want her getting her hands on me because every time she does, she gets crazier than she already is.

"There is, isn't there?"

"Whether there is or not is none of your fucking business. Now leave, before I call security and have them escort you out."

"You wouldn't," she challenges.

I square my shoulders. "Then I'll have them call the cops and have you arrested for trespassing." I side step, clearing the way for her to make her exit without coming close to me.

"We had something really special, you and I. Why can't you see that?"

I step toward her, and I whisper, "The only thing special about you, Jillian, is that you think you're deserving of my money." She sucks in a breath. I'd known what she was immediately when she approached me eight months ago. She's a gold digging bitch. What followed a few weeks later made me shake my head in shame, not for me, but definitely for her. She's so desperate to get her claws into some rich son of a bitch that she did something no self-respecting woman would do. The anger roars

its head again. "Get out, now." I growl in her ear. "Do not come back here, do not call me, do not try to contact me, ever again," I snap and she jumps, scurrying away from me and out the door as fast as she can.

I hear her fake as fuck sob as she passes by my assistant's desk. "Call security, make sure Ms. Polis leaves this building." I hear her sob again, only further down the hall. I'm not exactly being quiet about my request. "She is never permitted in this building again. Should she come here, she is to be handed over to the police for trespassing."

"Yes, sir," the blonde at the desk tells me as she picks up the phone.

I don't even know the girl's name. She hasn't been here that long and this is only the second time she's encountered me. She's an executive assistant, but she's more of an assistant to my management than she is to me since I'm not in New York much. Andy, my assistant in Phoenix, lives and works in Phoenix, but when I have to make the inevitable move back to New York, he's coming with me. I don't care what it will cost to make him do it, it will happen.

Jill's ignored text then her showing up in my office unannounced and uninvited really did a number on my Ireland buzz and I need to return my focus to Ireland. I debate on whether or not I need to tell Ireland about the bullshit Jill pulled, but I can't see a real reason to tell her. No matter the logic in my mind, I can't seem to find a good enough reason to bring it up.

Once I make that decision, I bury myself in paperwork. I talk to my COO about some things, and we discuss the meeting we had today.

The next thing I know, it's nearly four in the afternoon and after looking at the clock, I can't stop thinking about Ireland back in my apartment.

I managed to remove Jill from my mind with work and now all I can think about is getting home.

After wrapping up at the office, Byron manages New York City rush hour with efficiency and gets me home in record time.

Walking into the apartment I smell something cooking, it smells wonderful. I go into the kitchen and see Kathy cleaning up. "Good evening, sir." I purse my lips. No matter how often I tell her to not call me 'sir', she refuses. She's a good fifteen years older than I am and it seems weird.

"Kathy, everything alright today?"

She turns and smiles wide. "Perfect. I went ahead and made lasagna for dinner. You just need to pull it out. There is garlic bread in the warming oven and salad ready in the fridge."

"You're too kind." I smile at her.

"She's a gorgeous girl. Very sweet."

I smile wider. "I know," I tell her despite myself.

"Good, then I will be off. Will you be here Monday?"

"I will, leaving sometime Monday afternoon."

"Okay, keep me posted," Kathy says as she finishes what she's doing. She's my full-time housekeeper and I pay her as such, despite the part time stays here in New York. When I'd told her I was going to Phoenix indefinitely she panicked, thinking I was going to let her go. I explained that wouldn't be the case and she was all too excited since it meant she could spend more time with her granddaughter.

I don't know why but the idea of coming home to Ireland in my kitchen sounds much more appealing than having Kathy around. It warms my heart and I give her a warm smile. "She upstairs?"

She shakes her head and points down the hall toward the game room.

"She went in there a couple hours ago." She chuckles, "After she got done freaking out about her iPad following her from room to room over the Bluetooth."

I laugh softly, "I didn't even think to tell her about that."

"I explained it to her because I thought the poor girl was going to lose her mind."

"I appreciate that, thank you." I turn toward the living room and wave a farewell to Kathy as I go in search of my girl.

The closer I get to the game room, the louder her music becomes. JonnySwim's 'Pay Dearly' is playing and I wonder if she's listening to my playlist. When I walk around the corner into the room, I see she's curled up in the chair near the window. The room has grown quite dark, but the table lamp near her is on.

She's sound asleep and my heart skips a beat watching her slow, steady breathing.

She's so peaceful. She looks younger than her years. I can still see the sweet fifteen year old girl I once knew. The song ends and the piano chords of Jason Walk's 'Down' starts to play and I'm convinced now that she's listening to my playlist and it makes me smile. I go to the wall controls and lower the volume a little. Her music's not loud, but I am going to wake her up and I don't know how this is going to go.

I turn back and she's stirred a little, but she's still sleeping. She's shifted, giving me some room on the chair to sit next to her. A part of me is bummed she's wearing clothes, but after being gone longer than I wanted to be, I didn't truly expect her to be naked.

I sit down on the chair and she stirs. She leans into me and I wrap my arms around her and adjust myself so she's more on top of me, snuggled in my arms.

I can't help taking a deep breath, pulling in the scent that is very sweetly Ireland. Her hair smells like fresh strawberries. I absently start playing her hair. It's so soft, and I love how it curls around my fingers as I gently run my fingers through it.

"You're home?"

I smile and put my lips to the top of her head, ignoring the fact she said home and my heart jumped in my chest. "I'm sorry it took so long."

"S'okay," she yawns. "I didn't mean to fall asleep."

I smile and kiss the top of her head again, I can't stop myself. I need to touch her, kiss her and make sure that she's truly real. "I'm glad you did. You were dead on your feet this morning."

She snorts, "That's because someone demanded I fly through the night."

"And you're complaining?" I tease.

She shifts in my lap and I pray my erection remains unnoticed. She looks at me and her eyes are still heavy from sleep but I can tell she's waking up. "Not one single bit." She smiles at me and I lean in a little closer. For some reason I feel the need to seek her permission and it's a strange novelty to me.

She meets me halfway and I crush my lips to hers. The hand I had in her hair tightens and I pull her close to me, as close as I can get her isn't close enough, and she whimpers in my mouth.

I seize my chance and slide my tongue in along hers and she responds quickly as she squirms on my lap. She manages to turn herself so she's straddling my legs and her hands come to the sides of my neck and she pulls me into her I still can't seem to reach the closeness that my body needs.

Her breathing changes. She's pulling me in harder, begging for something deeper. We're both desperate for it. Our breathing is ragged but she won't pull her lips away from me. She needs this as much as I do. Her hands slide down my shoulders until she finds my tie. One of her hands winds around it, holding on to it for dear life as she moans into my mouth. She flicks her hips against me and then I'm the one groaning.

I break our kiss and she puts her forehead against mine as we both fight to catch our breath.

Somewhere in the distance an alarm goes off.

She slowly blinks at me. "Wow," she breathes.

I chuckle, "My thoughts exactly."

"What's that noise?" she asks, though I can tell by her tone she really doesn't want to ask that question because she doesn't want it to be what it is.

"That would be dinner."

"Oh," she smiles and pushes her lips against mine again in a chaste kiss. "That's an amazing way to wake up, Mr. Cole."

I smile back at her. This is the way I want to wake her up every day, but I have to keep myself in check, we're not fifteen and seventeen anymore. I can't assume that's what she'd want. And I'm determined to take this as slow as possible. I need to make sure that she's truly forgiven me.

"Are you hungry?" I ask her.

"Famished."

"We can't have that now, can we?"

She giggles, "No, I suppose not." She moves to stand up and I hold her to me, I don't want her to get up just yet. "That alarm is really annoying," she says through her giggles.

I press my lips to hers, this time it's not so chaste but it's softer, sweeter. My desire hasn't cooled from when she assaulted me moments ago. "Food," I murmur against her lips and she smiles as she stands up.

I take her hand in mine and grab her iPad off the table and bring it with us. I'd set up all the Bluetooth information on it before sending it to her. The information here is the same as in Phoenix so bringing her here wasn't preconceived. I never expected her to forgive me so fast.

I lead her down the hallway and I hear her pull in a deep breath. "Smells wonderful." She beams at me.

"Oh no, this is Kathy's cooking," I chuckle. "Though I *can* cook, she made this one tonight."

She laughs, "I would have been really disappointed if you'd been home

long enough to make lasagna and you didn't wake me up to watch."

"Well, then I guess I'll have to make it for you sometime," I tell her, planting a seed of hope, just to see how she handles it.

She looks up at me with excitement in her eyes. "I'd like that very much."

I squeeze her hand and lead her into the kitchen and put her on a bar stool to watch.

I take my vest off, followed by the tie and I roll up my sleeves, getting comfortable. She watches me with rapt attention. I give her a wink and she blushes because I caught her watching me. "Don't you want to change out of that?" Her voice holds a small hint of humor in it, but I immediately understand what she's picturing. Spaghetti sauce and an expensive suit.

"I will before we sit down."

She nods and I turn the timer off on the oven. It did its automatic thing of switching to a keep warm setting so I pull the bread out first, then the salad. "Do you like wine?" I ask her.

"White. I don't like reds."

"Do you want to pick one out?"

She winkles up her nose and shakes her head. "I haven't a clue about wine," she says as I pull the salad from the fridge and place it between us. I reach my hand out to her. She hesitates only for a moment, trying to figure out what I'm doing, but she takes my hand and climbs off the stool. "Where are we going?" she asks.

I open a door leading to a controlled temperature room and my wine cellar. I hold the door open for her and show her inside.

IRELAND

18th Floor Balcony - Blue October

I could listen to Dyson talk about wine all damn day. The man has a knack for it, which seems a bit odd. I'd pictured him more as a beer or bourbon drinker. Though I did notice several bottles of alcohol, he kept my attention on the wine.

He took the time to ask me what kind I liked and I told him. He smiled and knew right where to go when he was done with his little lesson. I took note of the fact there were at least two hundred bottles. Not all wine, there was definitely some champagne and hard alcohol, but it was all arranged by type and year. The bottle he chose has some dust on it, so I can tell he's had it for a while. He wipes the bottle clean and leads me back to the kitchen. He pops the cork and sets the bottle on the counter while he goes about setting our places in the kitchen. I like sitting here, reminds me of last night, though I was there and he was here, but still.

When he'd taken his vest off, undid his tie and rolled up his sleeves, I didn't think I was gonna be able to keep my hands to myself. The desire burning through me has me desperate to kiss him again.

The man is truly sex on legs.

The expression brings me back to the day I'd decided to move on with my life. No matter how many times I'd repeated the mantra over and over again, I don't think I ever truly believed it. I wanted to, I convinced myself I didn't want him anymore, but the truth was I never stopped wanting him.

Sure, I dated in college, but I avoided high school dating altogether, I wasn't ready for that. I'd always held out hope Dyson would return to me in Joplin as soon as he could. Though he never said he would, I wanted that hope.

"Can I ask you something?" I ask as I watch him pull the lasagna from the oven.

"Anything, always," he says, but I guess my expression has him a little

uneasy.

"Why, after you graduated, did you not come back to Joplin?"

He sets the pan down on the rack he'd set out, but he doesn't answer me right away. He just stares at me for a moment. "How shall I put this?"

"The truth," I tell him.

He gives me a small smile. "Always the truth, Ireland. Just not sure how to explain it."

"Try?" I ask, but it comes out more of a whisper, like I'm begging.

"I didn't know how." Our eyes lock. "I didn't know what to say if I did come back. I mean, sure, Dusty and I were still friends at that point, but…" He pauses and breaks our eye contact to grab something from the fridge and he comes back with a bowl of something and some dressing for the salads.

Seeming to be satisfied with everything, he reaches for the bottle of wine and grabs the glasses he'd set out. He pours a little into my glass and hands it to me. "You ever taste tested wine before?"

I nod and smile at him, despite the fact he's dodging my question.

I bring the glass toward me and I swirl it around. He's watching me intently as I watch the glass, then I bring it to my nose for a whiff and it smells sweet, which is how I like my wine. Then I taste it. It's like fireworks in my mouth and I hold it there for a moment before swallowing. "Wow," I breathe.

His eyes darken. The sparks start flying between us, the desire I'm feeling explodes and I squirm in my seat. Realizing the effect he's having on me, he looks away and I smile on the inside knowing he's equally as affected as I am.

"Back to your question," he says after a beat and I can't help but truly smile at the fact he doesn't actually dodge the question. "There were a few reasons. Dusty was one. We'd started to grow apart. I didn't know what he'd think of me being back in town." He fills my glass, then his before continuing. "The other was the fact I'd changed a lot after leaving Joplin. I went from being the most popular kid in school to being a

nobody and I didn't take to that very well. Though for my senior year, I managed to make the varsity team, but I was no longer a starter. It gave me a little credit in school, but not that much." He sits down next to me but he doesn't take his eyes off me and I like that he's looking at me while he talks. We just won't talk about what his looking at me is doing to my body. "I was depressed, if you want the truth of it."

"Always the truth, Dyson."

He gives me a sexy little smirk. "I love it when you say my name."

"Dyson," I lean toward him, "Dyson," a little closer, "Dyson," I breathe and his lips claim mine again. His kiss is passionate, full of longing and I shiver as need explodes. "Let's forget dinner," I grumble as he pulls away again.

"Eat, you're going to need the energy," he teases.

"Oh really, and why is that, Mr. Cole?"

He gives me the most salacious look that nearly knocks me off the stool I'm sitting on. He knows exactly what he's done when he gives me one of his panty-melting smiles. "Keep that up, Ms. McKidd, and you won't eat for the rest of the weekend." His voice is strong, determined, with a tiny hint of humor and I gape at him.

He chuckles but hands me the bread basket and I pull a slice from it. He takes one of his own and I am met with a sense of normalcy I never expected to feel. Sitting here, with him, about to enjoy an unhurried meal feels right. It feels normal.

I pull a hunk off the bread as he hands me the salad bowl, but I shake my head. "This smells too delicious. I'd hate to fill up on salad, since I'm going to need my energy and all." I wink at him and put down the bread but slide the small piece into my mouth.

I feel his mood shift right back to sparks igniting again and I have no idea how we're going to make it through this meal without tearing each other's clothes off. I try to ignore him and take a sip of the wine. The taste is divine and a compliment to the garlic bread I've eaten.

He breaks his gaze and follows suit, starting with his salad. I smile.

Looking at his body I could have guessed he'd fill up on that over the carb heavy meal in front of him. He surprises me when he returns back to my question. "I was depressed, but I… god, this is going to sound so stupid…"

"It's okay, please, just tell me."

"I was afraid I'd lost my charm."

I squint at him. "What do you mean?"

"I was afraid I was no longer the person I was when we'd…" he clears his throat, clearly uncomfortable with the direction of the conversation, "I'd changed, and I know you'd changed and…" he pauses again, staring at his food, "I was afraid I'd find you with someone else."

I blink at him. I don't know what to say to that.

"Dusty never said anything, but then Dusty never talked to me about you. But that was my fault too."

"How so?" I ask him.

He snorts humorlessly. "I'd told Dusty I didn't want to talk about you. I didn't want to hear it."

I shake my head and fight the inevitable eye roll I feel coming on.

"I was eighteen, VeeVee; please don't hold that against me."

I look at him, square in the eye. "I was still in love with you, I couldn't even think about dating anyone else. There was…" I stop myself. I don't want to tell him this part.

"There was what, Ireland?"

I sigh and set my fork down. I pick up my napkin and I wring it a little, needing to focus on something. My leg starts to bounce. He reaches over and stops it. His touch is gentle and warm and the butterflies flutter around again in my belly. "After you left, people hated you. When the team didn't make it past the first round of the state tournament, they blamed you for leaving. Instead of being someone they would have cheered, they smeared your name everywhere. Dusty did what he could to try and change their minds, but I often wondered if he started to

blame you too."

"He never said anything," he says, the shock evident.

"I would imagine not. They wanted someone to blame and you weren't there so they chose to pick on you. Which is why I was afraid to date anyone at school." His eyebrows knit together in confusion. "God, this is so stupid," I mutter, looking at my hands. "I didn't want to have to tell anyone what we did. I was…well, I wasn't a virgin anymore and guys always seemed to ask that question. I never understood why, but they did and I knew the inevitable follow-up question would be, 'who have you slept with' and I wasn't socially smart enough to make-up someone."

"Were you embarrassed?"

"Yes, no, I don't know. Dyson, they made it sound like you were the biggest prick to walk the halls of JPH. I was a sophomore, I… it was stupid." I take a deep breath, I'm fighting tears of embarrassment and I try to smooth things over a little by telling him what came next. "After homecoming that year, I realized they were just bitter. I understood the disdain they all seemed to feel for you was superficial and because the football team sucked. You were an easy excuse. I quickly learned it didn't matter to me what they thought of you. I didn't regret what happened that night, well, up until you…" My voice trails off. I don't need to remind him of what he said to me that night.

His hand comes to my cheek, and I lean into his touch. It calms me in a way I know I'll never understand.

"I was sixteen," I breathe as if that explains everything.

"So was that the only reason you didn't…" He doesn't finish the question, he doesn't have to.

"I tried, like, really tried. But I waited until I got to ASU and found my footing there. I made new friends, went to parties, that kind of stuff. I'd made a pact with myself after graduation and for the first couple of years, it worked."

"What was the pact?" he asks, releasing me and we both turn to our food. I suddenly feel very full and I realize I've eaten nearly all of my dinner. Huh?

"I let you go," I admit.

He stops breathing, doesn't say anything, and when I can't stand the silence between us any longer I break it. "I was leaving, starting fresh. It was two years since you graduated, almost as long since Dusty had heard from you. I… I stood in front of your house and promised I wasn't going to think about you anymore."

"Huh, how'd that work out for you?"

"I'm still single, aren't I?"

"Touché." He smiles at me. "You said you tried?"

"I did. I dated a few guys, mostly toward the end of my sophomore year in college and through my junior year. I was determined to find someone who could make me feel at least half as good as you did. But it never happened. I never made it past first base with most of them. Then they'd dump me because I wouldn't put out or whatever." I pause needing a second to collect my thoughts. "I saw someone, on campus, toward the end of my junior year that reminded me of you. Well, you when you were seventeen. I had no idea what I was looking for in an adult version."

I rake my eyes up and down his body, taking in as much as I can through his suit pants and shirt. He smirks knowingly at me.

I sigh. "When I saw him, all I could do was think about you, think about the fact I'd missed my chance to find you. Or that maybe I'd run into the guy again because I really did believe it was you. But when I did find him on campus again, he wasn't anything like you." I crinkle my nose. "I'm pretty sure he was gay."

Dyson chuckles. "That, Ms. McKidd, I most definitely am not."

"I know. Reese is totally gay though."

"You became friends?"

"Yup, he's the reason I got the interview at Wellington."

He leans over to me then kisses my temple before standing up and grabbing our plates. "Remind me to thank Reese someday."

"What for?" I ask in mock horror.

"Two things, one, for being gay and for not being like me, and two, for getting you that interview."

I smile wide at the idea of introducing Dyson to Reese, though I don't picture them being fast friends, I think they would both like each other. "I like the sound of that," he says suddenly. "But what are you laughing about?"

"Oh, I didn't realize…I was thinking about you and Reese meeting. I hope you're not put off by forward men."

He laughs at that one. "Thanks for the warning. I'll make sure to have you wrapped around me so he knows to back off."

I can't help but laugh at both the visual and then the idea of him meeting Reese and doing what he can to throw Reese off any idea he may get in his head about Dyson being available.

DYSON
Pillow Talk - Zayn

"So now you're happy I'm going to be working downstairs from you?" she asks me and I knew she would ask that question again. We've already discussed it before, but I get the impression she's seeking approval from me.

"I am." I give her a playful smile. "My reasons, originally, were very selfish, but my reasons now," I laugh, "are still selfish."

She gives me a quizzical look. "Why, because you can keep me close?"

I put my hands up in surrender. "Guilty as charged, Ms. McKidd." She shakes her head in annoyance with me. "Do you not want to be that close?" The words tumble out before I can stop them. Anxiety slices through me as I wait for her answer. This could go either way and I am afraid it will not go the way I want it to.

She looks at me, confusion and a little bit of fear in her eyes, and I lower my hands. "What are we doing here, Dyson?"

I pull in a breath and it feels like it takes years to fill up my lungs. I close my eyes, my brain cycling through different answers to this question, a million dollar one at that. This answer will either bring her into my arms or send her packing. Either way, I need her to decide for herself and not for any reason other than that. "Honestly, Ireland, I don't know." Fear takes over her features and I continue quickly, "But only because I don't have a crystal ball." She relaxes a little bit, but there's still tension in her shoulders. "I'm not who I was ten years ago, you're not the same as you were then either. I know somewhere in that pretty little head of yours you're worried I am." She doesn't nod or acknowledge my statement, which means I've hit the nail on the head. "What I do know is I am determined to prove that to you, no matter what the cost."

"Buying me clothes and toys isn't exactly the way to do that, Dyson."

My lips twitch with a smile. My feisty, little tiger is coming out to play. "I told you, if it was in my power to fix it, I would."

"The iPad and expensive headphones, the pencil, that wasn't part of fixing the problem."

Now my lips pull into a full on smile. "No, it wasn't. That was me doing something nice for you." I step closer to her. She doesn't flinch or try to move away, her eyes lock onto mine. "That was my way of making up for missed birthdays, something to make you smile. Something to remind you of me." By the time I'm done with my little speech, I'm standing directly in front of her and she wraps her arms around me. I sag in relief. The iPad was overkill, but my words speak truth because that's what I was thinking when I stood in front of them at the store.

I'd seen her phone and the deplorable looking laptop sitting on her desk in her room and I thought she could use something nice, especially considering the new job she was getting ready to start.

I wrap my arms around her, holding her to me for a moment before I reach for her chin and lift her eyes to mine. They're full of emotion, a small pool of unshed tears in the corners, ready to spill over. "You

deserved something nice and I could give that to you." I give her a reassuring smile.

"Kiss me," she whispers.

"Say my name."

The tears in her eyes disappear down her cheeks when she lights up. "Hmm, I seem to have forgotten. Maybe I need a reminder?" she teases.

I raise an eyebrow at her before bending down and bringing our lips only a hair's breadth away from each other. "Say," I brush my lips feather light against hers, "my," I breathe, and then I lick along her bottom lip with the tip of my tongue. She shudders beneath me and her eyes narrow as the desire ignites in her veins. Her breathing hitches. "Name," I finish.

"Dyson," she whines and I capture her lips with my own. She opens to me immediately and I pull my hand away from her chin, confident she's not going anywhere. I slide my tongue along hers, but pull back briefly.

"Say it again," I tell her softly.

"Dyson," she moans.

Her desperation builds, my cock twitches in my pants and my mind goes blank the moment I capture her lips again. I pull back to tell her, "I fucking love it when you say my name."

"Dyson," she moans, this time more desperate and her hands fist in my shirt on my back, pulling me closer to her. "Please," she begs.

Shivers rock my entire body. I can't decide which one is more intense, her saying my name or begging for more. They're equally intoxicating and her close proximity has me losing my fucking mind. I reach for the sides of her shirt. I ask for permission with my eyes and she gives me a slight nod. I smile and pull her shirt up. She releases me and gives me the access I need to lift it over her head.

I have to take a step back to appreciate the full view. "Fuck," I groan when I see the red, lace bra she's wearing.

Hanging on to her shirt with one hand, I hold out my other hand to her. Again, asking for her permission before her hand intertwines with

mine and I lead her toward the stairs and my bedroom.

I need her, now, more than anything, more than life and breath. I can't hold back anymore.

I lead her up the stairs and into my bedroom, kicking the door closed as I turn on her, pressing her against the wall, holding her there with my body. Her breathing is erratic when I look at her. Her eyes are wild with excitement and maybe even a little fear. I'm going to try and do this without scaring the hell out of her. I brush my knuckles gently along her cheek and she leans into my touch. I drop her shirt on the floor and gently take her face been my hands. Her eyes flutter closed as she relaxes into my touch. "All you have to do is tell me to stop, and I will."

Her eyes open, they're hooded, her desire evident. Kissing Ireland is something else altogether, each time more amazing than the last; I can only imagine being buried inside of her. "Don't stop," she breathes and that's all the permission I need as I slant my lips over hers. She moans into my mouth, her already jagged breathing skips a few more beats along with my heart when her tongue slides in along my own and I'm fighting everything to not rip off her clothes and slam into her right here.

I pull us away from the wall. She comes willingly with me and I lead her farther into the bedroom until I bump her up against my bed. The contact is enough to pull her, unwillingly, away from my lips. "This is how I should have done this the first time," I say and reach for the buttons on my shirt.

Her soft hands replace mine and she starts to undress me. I reach for the button on her jeans and flick my wrist, unbuttoning them in a beat and her breathing shows every reaction her face can't. She tries to concentrate on the buttons on my shirt, but I can feel her fingers trembling against my chest and I move to help her.

I pull the shirt from my pants and unbutton the cuffs. By the time I'm done, so is she and her hands slide up my naked chest to my shoulders as she pushes my shirt off me and it falls to the floor. Her hands are on my biceps and her touch is obliterating any sense of control I had a moment ago. I lean down and find her lips again. She takes mine with as much

fervor as I'm giving her and it makes my cock jump.

I pull back slightly and start kissing my way from her lips to her jaw as I wrap my hands around her body, pressing them together. Feeling her nearly naked skin against me sends a thrill through me.

My newfound position gives me the ability to reach behind and unclasp her bra. She shudders as the straps loosen and fall down her arms. I help the bra to fall away completely before I lower myself to kiss her shoulder, then farther down her chest as I make my way to my knees before her.

Her hand slides into my hair, guiding me to one nipple, then the other before she releases me and frees herself from her bra. "Don't stop," she moans again and I suck one taut pebble into my mouth. She trembles with desire beneath me. Her hand returns to my hair and she guides me to the other one and I lick, nibble and suck it into my mouth, pulling on it hard before releasing it with an audible pop.

I continue lower, kissing, licking and biting gentle nips down her stomach until I reach the fly of her jeans and I lower the zipper with my teeth. She giggles above me, but it's an erotic giggle and one I hope to hear again.

With her jeans undone, she hooks her thumbs inside and pushes them down her thighs. I'm met with a pair of matching red panties. I lean in, breathing hotly across her sex and her legs wobble. Then I dart my tongue over her soft, hot center and she moans. "Lie down for me," I tell her and she complies, pulling herself up on the bed and I pull her jeans from her legs, freeing her.

When they're gone, I slide my hands up her legs toward her hips to free her of the gorgeous panties she's wearing. She lifts her hips just enough to give me access. Her panties are stripped away and I'm met with the most beautiful pussy I've ever seen.

There is a small patch of bright red curls just above her slit and the rest is bare. "Fucking gorgeous." I stand up, desperate for no barriers between us and I slide my pants down, bringing my boxer briefs with them and freeing my cock. Her eyes nearly pop out of her head. I give her

a salacious smirk and she swallows hard. "Not a pencil," I remind her of the card and her insult.

She swallows hard again. "No, definitely not." Her tongue darts out and slides across her lips as she takes in the full package. I move slightly and her gaze moves from my cock to my thigh and she gasps before sitting up. Jesus, she's gonna kill me.

Chapter Nineteen

IRELAND
Beneath Your Beautiful - Labirinth

When Dyson's pants fell away, I instantly regretted the 'pencil dick' card I'd sent him. Definitely no pencil there, but I was quickly distracted by something on his leg. His thigh, to be exact. I couldn't see the entire thing, but I could see black, orange and red striping. The red was a close match to the color of my hair.

I sit up and reach for his thigh, hoping to get him to turn. I look at him and beg sweetly, "Please." He turns slightly, giving me a better look at what's on his thigh.

Staring back at me are a pair of emerald green eyes, eyes that look a lot like my own, set in the most beautiful face of a tiger I've ever seen in my entire life. I urge him to turn farther. The tiger is perched on a tree branch and the branch is attached to a tree of sorts. The tiger is angled down toward his knee and there is a tail that disappears behind the trunk. I urge him to turn more, and this time he turns all the way around, giving me a full view as he does.

The tiger's tail trails around his leg and ends near the inside of his knee. "Dyson, that…wow, I don't even…"

"You like it?"

I search his eyes for an explanation to his hesitation. "No, Dyson, I love it."

I watch as relief washes over him and he relaxes. I hadn't noticed him stiffen up until he was sagging with relief. "Thank god," he breathes.

"Why would you think…" Realization dawns on me in that moment. The tiger, Tigress, my nickname, the emerald green eyes.

"I told you, I never forgot about you. I knew if I couldn't have you, I needed something to hold close to me."

Tears well in my eyes at his words. I feel so overwhelmed.

Before I know it, Dyson has his arms around me and he's pulling me from the bed. We're both completely naked and I'm completely falling

apart. Anger, frustration, confusion, lust, desire, all mix for one hell of a reality cocktail in my head and in my heart. It's nearly too much to handle and he's going to watch me completely unravel in his arms.

Embarrassment floods through me and I try to pull away from him, but he holds me tightly against his chest before scooping me up in his arms and sitting down on the bed. I'm back in his lap and without even meaning to, I snuggle into him. The tears refuse to quit.

Through heavy tears, I try and tell him something but I'm not sure he catches it because he brushes the hair from my face and forces my chin up to look at him. "I'm never going to get this right," I mumble to him.

He chuckles, "What are you talking about, princess?"

"We get naked and I start crying," I grumble and fight his fingers to lower my gaze from his, but he's not having it.

"I should have warned you."

"About what?" My tears are starting to subside a little and my breathing is less hysterical.

"My tattoo."

"Oh," I say before wiping tears from my cheeks. He seems satisfied I'm not going to hide from him anymore so he releases my chin, but moves his hand over to my shoulder where he gently brushes his fingers along my skin, moving my hair from it. "I'm glad you didn't," I tell him and it's true.

"Why is that?"

"Because I think it would have taken away the impact of it." I smile a little at the words. "I mean it, I really do love it. It's just..." I shake my head as if I'm a damn Yahtzee cup and I can change the outcome of my thoughts once they're tossed around a little bit. "You have all this stuff, these things that remind you every day of me. I tried to do everything I could to not be reminded of you and I still thought about you every day. I really was trying to move on and to see that you've held on to it, held on to the past, it-" I pull in a deep breath and finish, "It's overwhelming." I try and smile but I fail and that makes him smile at me.

He brings his hand up to my face where he taps my nose with his finger. "I don't mean to overwhelm you, but with the exception of the tattoo, nothing has been deliberate," he tells me. "When I got asked to pick a code for the door, I picked the first date that came to mind."

"My birthday?"

He nods. "The rock? That's been in my pocket every day since you gave it to me. That was the same day I met you, met your brother, and truly found a place where I belonged. It became my good luck charm. I always had it with me, try-outs, games, the night in the barn, the first day at a new school, the first day of college, the day I started my business, all of it. It became a part of me and if I didn't have it in my pocket, I stressed about where I'd left it."

"I threw the other one away." His eyes widen in shock. "I thought that...I thought I was bad luck. I'd given it to a boy who I thought was the most beautiful thing I'd ever seen in my life, then I kept it with me, always."

He chuckles. "I remember seeing it in your pencil box once."

My eyes snap to his. "Really?"

His chuckles settle a little. "Really."

"We'd grown close, until you went to a new school and I was left at the old one, without my friends. Though you still hung out at the house, you were different, you'd changed," I share and pull my eyes away from his. "I'd hear stories from Dusty, though he never actually told them to me. I overheard you guys talking all the time, then you weren't around as much. It broke my heart."

I hear his sharp intake of breath as the reality of what I'm telling him washes over him, I can't stop now. "Then that summer, before I started my freshman year, you changed back. You started to notice me again. You dragged me everywhere, despite Dusty's objections. I was one of the crowd, you know? Then we got to high school." My nerves take over as I ramble. I wish I could pace the room, but I'm more afraid of standing up because I'm completely naked. At least this way I can hide most of it. The memories consume me as I share them with him. "You changed again.

You acknowledged me, but we weren't friends. I fought to tell myself it had more to do with high school etiquette. You were a junior; I was a freshman, so I let it go. Then I'd see you with some girl and it would crush me all over again. But then you'd show up at the house like nothing was different between us." The memory overtakes me. I'm remembering that night at the end of March so long ago. "Then I hadn't seen you for a few days, you hadn't been in school or hanging around with Dusty, and he was moody and pissy. No one ever told me what was going on. I denied it for so long, but all the signs were there. I was just too dense to see them for what they were. I was so confused about you. I didn't know what to do, or what I was doing wrong. Then you were at my door, and I was home alone. We watched that movie together and then…" I don't need to finish the rest of the story. He knows where it's going. But the memory of Dyson being inside of me sends a new wave of desire through me. I am desperate to feel that again, to feel that connected to someone. Especially him.

He buries his head in my hair. He takes a few deep breaths to settle himself. I need to finish what I started to say, so I take a deep breath too and find a calm place inside me and hold on to it for added encouragement. "I fell in love with you the day I gave you that rock," I confess and immediately I want to run away from him. The admission is almost too much for me to handle and the tears come back when his arms wrap tighter around me.

"And now?" he breathes against my neck.

"Now? I'm scared shitless," I whisper.

From somewhere deep down inside of me, I don't know where she's been buried all these years, but the feisty Ireland roars to the surface. She's tired of being alone, tired of being the shy quiet girl and she takes over my body. I try to stand, but he holds me tight. "Please, don't run." His voice is pained.

"I have no intention of running, Dyson," I tell him, my confidence returning from somewhere, from that little person inside of me who died the day he left me. He reluctantly lets me up and I reposition myself to straddle him. My hot, wet sex brushes along his cock and he jumps.

I flick my hips against him and his eyes take on the sexiest look. My mouth falls slack.

I continue to slide my sex up and down his cock. The sensations make my body come alive, and my nerves hyper sensitive. I reach between us, wrapping my fingers around his shaft and I lift myself, pressing the head of his cock against my clit and moving it back and forth. The pleasure rises higher with each passing second.

I'm not that innocent. Well, Dyson Cole Richards is the only man who's ever been inside of me, but I'm no stranger to orgasms. I've given myself enough over the years and I know I'm getting closer than I ever thought I would this fast. The need to have him inside of me is almost unbearable.

I know he feels it too when he slams his lips against mine and his cock finds the entrance to my body where he belongs, where I desperately need him to be and I lower myself onto him. He's stretching me in ways I've never felt before. He strips away his kiss and demands, "Ireland, stop."

I freeze, my eyes pleading with him. "Why?" I breathe. Rejection tries to take hold.

"I'm not wearing a…"

"I know," I tell him and claim his lips once again as I slide farther on top of him. I push him back on the bed as I slide farther down his cock. He wraps his arms around me, holding me to him. My hair creates a curtain around us, blocking out the rest of the world as his mouth claims mine. His cock claims me once more, taking me higher with each thrust and flick of my hips.

My orgasm explodes around me and I press down on him, holding him in place, but doing everything I can to grind my way through my orgasm. He pulls his mouth away, his features displaying his desperation to hold back. "I'm...fuck, Ireland." His eyes meet mine and my insides quiver around him again, clamping and releasing his cock as I slide up and then slam myself back down.

His arms squeeze around me as I feel warmth flood my insides and he cries out my name as he explodes inside of me.

Chapter Twenty

IRELAND
Lay Me Down - Sam Smith

Slowly our breathing returns to normal. I'm sprawled on top of him with a light sheen of sweat drying across my skin. He's still hard inside me and my sex clenches around him. He groans and flips me onto my back. He brushes my hair out of my face, his eyes bore into my soul and I'm instantly fifteen, back in the barn. His eyes darken as he reads my body language, despite my attempts to hide it.

"I'm not going anywhere," he reassures. His voice is soft, barely above a whisper and his hips push into me to emphasize his words. My eyes roll up into my head as pleasure ignites in my veins again. "I will be here, as long as you want me here."

Reality comes back into focus when he doesn't move again. I push the hair out of his eyes, tucking it behind his ear, it doesn't stay and he smiles. We don't need to say anything to each other. Everything is right there in our eyes. I'm scared shitless, he knows it because I told him as such. The slight tremble in my body is another telling sign. "It's my turn." He thrusts into me again and the fireworks ignite. My orgasm builds from a slow simmer to a boil as he pulls out to the tip and he slips back in. He doesn't stop and my sex clenches around his, milking him. The skin to skin contact is heady and while I have little to compare it to, I don't know that I could ever stand a barrier between us. "Is this okay?" he asks, unsure of himself.

"Perfect." I wink, giving him a little playfulness while still trying to hide the nerves threatening to consume me.

His pace increases and he adjusts himself. He uses his thighs to raise me up higher, pushes in deeper and that feeling of closeness consumes me. I wrap my arms around his neck, holding him to me, and he lowers his head to suck a nipple into his mouth and I moan. My head lulls back, my eyes roll up, my body comes alive as he pushes deeper before pulling back out and sliding back in.

"Dyson," I mewl.

"Tell me, princess."

"Faster," I groan and he doesn't hesitate to increase his pace. My body is desperate for him. My pussy tightens around him, trying to hold tight and never let go.

His thrusts are matched with bursts of grunts and labored breathing, his eyes never leave mine. He releases my nipple and kisses up my body until he finds my lips and he claims them. I whimper and wrap my legs around his waist, using my heels to encourage him to go faster. He smiles against my lips, but reclaims them quickly. Breathing has become impossible for us both.

All the pain of ten years washes away in heartbeat. It's me, it's him, it's us. It's everything I've longed for since I was nine years old and he's proving to me this is what he needs with me. The overwhelming emotion pouring off him causes my head to pull back, my eyes to close, my body to lock up, my toes curl and then my orgasm rockets around him.

I feel so much for him as he lets go, emptying inside of me, that tears of unbelievable happiness spill out. I'm no longer capable of holding them back anymore.

DYSON
I Think I'm In Love - Kat Dahlia

It's never, not even at seventeen, felt like this. I never knew it could feel like this. Letting go and showing Ireland what she means to me was easier than I ever imagined it could be. She felt it too; at least I hope that's the reason for her tears. "Talk to me, VeeVee."

She sniffs, but opens her eyes and meets my inquisitive stare. She's fighting back more tears and through them she says, "I don't know what to say, Dyson. I really don't." She takes a shuttering breath. "I have no words for what I'm feeling right now."

I press my lips to hers and let myself fall out of her. My cock is still semi-hard and I don't want to push her too far into something else at this point, but I could do this with her all night. I press my forehead to hers and tell her, "You don't have to say anything. I understand."

She lets out a sigh of relief and I give her a gentle smile.

Words between us aren't necessary. Everything she's feeling, I'm feeling too. It's intense, it's...euphoric and in a way cathartic. Ten years of pent up anger, frustration and wanting has been washed away. Leaving us both exposed and raw. A weight on my shoulders I hadn't realized was there is gone. She's everything I remember and so much more. She's everything I've held onto for all this time. I pull back to look at her. "Shower with me?" I ask her. It doesn't take much thought because she nods quickly and I sit up, pulling her with me.

"Whoa," she laughs, "too fast." She sits on the side of the bed and I sit next to her. I brush the back of my hand down her arm because I can't stop touching her. Afraid she's going to disappear at any minute. Afraid this fantasy is going to end and I'm going to wake up alone.

"Better?" I ask.

"Much." She smiles and stands up, grabbing my hand and leading me into the bathroom. Her sexy ass body sways sweetly as she goes and I am already hard again.

This girl is going to be the death of me.

Once inside the bathroom, she releases my hand and goes to the sink I'd put her stuff on. She digs through a little bag and pulls out something that looks...I don't even know, but I watch as she gathers her gorgeous hair and twists it around, bringing it up and clipping her hair into a claw looking thing. I smile at her in the mirror. "I don't want it to get wet again," she shares. "It's a pain in the ass to dry." Her green eyes are brighter than normal as she turns to me. There's still a faint flush to her skin from what we did in the bedroom. She's absolutely stunning.

"I definitely prefer it down," I tease her.

"Me too," she winks and walks toward me. I can't help brushing a few

of the shorter strands behind her ear. Any excuse to touch her. Keep her real and alive in my mind. Drag out this dream for as long as possible. "I thought you wanted to shower?" she teases and I pull myself out of my thoughts about dreams coming true and smile. I reach into the glass enclosure and fire it up.

Once the water warms up, I lead her inside and she waits for me against the wall. The shower is big enough for a party to fit inside, and I don't like the distance between us. "Come here."

She shivers and comes under the spray with me. I let most of it hit me so her hair can stay dry, but she doesn't seem to care when our bodies press together. "Jesus," she mumbles.

"What?" I ask.

"Will this feeling ever go away?" Her voice is soft, but serious.

"Do you really want it to?"

She laughs aloud and I smile. "No, I don't, but I'll be dammed if I can keep my head when you're near me."

I lift her chin and gently kiss her lips. "You're not the only one, princess."

She kisses me again, and just as it heats up she slinks back and reaches for something. What is she doing? Curiosity is getting the better of me as I watch her pour my body wash into her palm and she lathers it up between her hands. "Come here." She uses my words against me and I step closer to her. She meets me halfway and starts to slide her soap covered hands up my chest, over my shoulders, down my arms, across my stomach.

Her innocence shows through and it makes me blush a little when she avoids the erection standing between us. I kind of like it, but the need for her I've been trying to suppress ignites again, and my breathing hitches.

"Turn around." Her tone is terse, but effective.

"Ahh, there's my tigress," I tease but I do as she says. Her hands slide up my back from my butt to my shoulders and back down again. Her hands are warm, comforting. She pulls her hands away and I think she's

done, but then I hear a bottle squeeze and after a beat her hands are back and she grabs my ass. "Yup, she's back."

She giggles behind me and then her hands are on my thigh and working their way down to my knee and my calf. She's massaging as she goes and I start to relax. I remember she used to give me backrubs when we'd sit and watch movies. Feeling her firm hands makes me miss them for the first time.

She moves to my other leg, repeating the process, and I notice she takes special care when she gets to my tattoo. "How long have you had this?" Her voice is soft, reverent of the artwork.

"Um, three years ago. It was a present to myself when I made my first million."

Her hands still. "A million dollars," she chokes and I chuckle, turning around and kneeling before her. The soap on my body makes it a little weird and I get thrown off balance briefly.

"Are you alright?" I ask. "You're really pale."

"I'm always pale." She gives me a sideways look, showing her claws.

"Paler than normal." My voice sounds like I'm trying to deliver a bad joke and she gives a small snort of laughter.

"I didn't think that was possible." Her eyes lock on mine. "But seriously? A million?"

"My first million."

"How many more have you made?"

"This conversation might be better had while clothed and out of the shower," I tell her and she nods. She suddenly looks melancholy. "What's wrong?" I ask as I step under the spray and clean off the soap. I reach for my shampoo before lathering it into my hair, my eyes haven't left hers.

"I just..." she shakes her head.

"You promised me honesty."

"I know, I just, that's a lot of money, Dyson." Her voice is sad and I rush to finish up. I want to figure out what's bothering her before it has a

chance to take root and bother her more than it should.

"It's only money, VeeVee." I hope the nickname softens her a little and it does.

"I know, but…" she pauses, breaking our eye contact, "I can't imagine it."

"You weren't exactly poor growing up."

"No, but my mom worked her ass off," she defends, sadness still coloring her tone and I don't know if it's the money talk or bringing up her mother. I finish with my shower and turn off the water. I wrap her up in a towel before grabbing another one and wrapping it around myself.

I put my hands on her shoulders, working to dry her off, and she smiles at me. It doesn't quite reach into her eyes, but she looks better by the time I'm done drying her off. She adjusts the towel around her and I dry myself quickly before returning the towel to my waist.

"Before we have this discussion, I'd like to know if there's anything you'd like to do while you're here, in New York, I mean." I felt the need to clarify that. I don't want her to think her trip here only includes sleeping in my bed all weekend, because it doesn't, not if she wants to go out.

She shrugs. "Honestly, I hadn't even thought about it." She smiles. "But do we have to go out? It's freezing out there."

I snort, "Touché."

"I've never been here. I guess I thought when I came here I'd plan it all out. Fill each day with something to do, but…" she pauses and I lead her out of the bathroom, "I haven't planned anything, including being here."

"Well, I'd like to think you'll be back here again."

"When it's warmer, though," she clarifies with a smirk before going to her suitcase.

"So tonight?" I ask, prompting her to decide if there is something she wants to do. I don't want to lock her in my ivory tower if she'd rather be out clubbing somewhere.

"I think I saw a few movies in your collection."

I can't stop the huge smile that spreads across my face. "I'd like that, very much." I wrap my arms around her. "Why don't you slip into something comfortable, and we can curl up in bed and watch movies."

"Uh, Dyson?"

"What, love?"

I watch as a wave of emotion plays out in her eyes at my new term for her. I honestly didn't even think about it, it just spilled out, but, fuck it – if the shoe fits.

"You don't have a television in here?" It comes out as a question and I walk to the panel near the door and press a few buttons. The windows were already dark; she obviously figured those out earlier, so I lower the television from the ceiling. It folds flush against it and the backing is the same as the ceiling so it blends in completely. "Holy shit," She laughs as she watches it. "If I'd known that, I would've stayed in bed."

I chuckle, "Well, now you know."

She drops her towel and I hiss through my teeth at her brazenness and the fact she's got the perfect fucking body and it's naked in front of me. "Get dressed before I put the TV back up and we don't watch any movies tonight." My tone is a little harsh, and I sound like a sex crazed teenager. She looks at me in challenge and gives me a full frontal shot of her body. "Fuck," I hiss.

Then she reaches up and pulls the clip from her hair, setting it free to cascade over her back and shoulders. It's long enough to hide her breasts from view but the fiery red patch at the junction of her thighs stands out against her pale, gorgeous skin and I have to brace myself against the wall before I fall over.

"If this is a dream, for the love of all things holy, never, ever let me wake up," I whisper.

Her eyes twinkle with humor. "You're bias."

I straighten a little. The tigress wants to challenge me, does she? "Hardly, Ms. McKidd."

She snorts, "Prove it."

With the flick of my wrist, I drop my towel. My cock is hard as fucking stone and I grab it in my hand, stroking it up and down. Her eyes widen and that innocent blush returns to her cheeks, making her hotter than ever. I expected her to turn away from me, but she's staring at me, her mouth agape with shock as I stalk toward her, stroking my cock. The pleasure is incredible knowing where I get to bury him. "What do you say, Ms. McKidd, is this proof enough?"

She snorts, "You were hard in the shower."

"You were naked in the shower."

"We'd just had sex."

Oh, I love this fucking game. "Then he should have been soft, spent. Not primed and ready for round three." I wiggle my eyebrows at her and she moves her hair behind her shoulders. God, I want her to touch herself, but I'm afraid that's going to go too far. I'm going to come any fucking second just looking at her. "You're a damn goddess, you know that?"

Her cheeks redden further and she pulls her eyes from mine, breaking the contact and effectively ending our little game.

Chapter Twenty-One

IRELAND
Setting The World On Fire - Kenny Chesney ft. P!nk

Dyson's hand comes to my cheek and he slides his knuckles gently toward my neck, and over my left breast. I shiver and my nipples harden. His fingers continue until they rake over the pebbled nub. He grabs it gently with his knuckles and tugs. The pleasure that ignites in my body sends my sex pulsing and clenching, grabbing onto nothing and there's an ache there. I flinch a little.

"You're sore," he says softly and he pulls his hand away from his cock and he lifts my chin. I don't know how he's managed to do it, but his eyes lack the lust that was there a moment ago. "Get dressed, princess. There is plenty of time to ravage your body," he says with a smirk filled with promises of later.

I take a deep, cleansing breath and smile sweetly at him in gratitude. He bends and kisses my lips chastely and while there is definite sparks igniting, he pulls back before letting the kiss get out of hand. "How…" I breathe.

He gives me a knowing grin. "Believe me, it's not easy, but the last thing I want to do is hurt you."

I don't know what to say to that so I nod and he releases me from his gaze and I confess, "I didn't bring much." I honestly didn't know what to expect and I took his advice and packed lightly. I knew this was going to happen. In fact I wanted it and more than anything, I needed it to happen. As much as our first time together nearly killed me, I needed to find some way to replace the old with something new. I needed to finish wiping away the pain. At least this time, if I walk away, I'll know I got a much better version of Dyson than the one in my head.

He walks through a door, his closet, and returns a moment later with something in his hands and he hands it to me. It's the softest t-shirt I've ever held in my hands. It's a well-worn one and I smile as I unfold it to see the word Dartmouth on the front. I look from the shirt to him and back to the shirt again. "You went to Dartmouth?" I ask skeptically.

He snorts a laugh, "Hardly, but it's my favorite shirt." I try to hand it back to him. "No, I want you to wear it."

"But I'm going to leave boob marks in it," I tease him.

He laughs as he pulls on a pair of dark grey flannel pants. "That will be quite the improvement." He smirks at me and nods, indicating I should put the shirt on.

I pull it over my head, pull my hair from the neckline and it slides down my body, covering my stomach and my sex and lands just below the apex of my thighs. I still need pants, but I can solve that problem. I turn to my suitcase and pull out a pair of jersey knit shorts. They don't leave a lot to the imagination but at least I'm covered up.

Making conversation, I ask him, "So you didn't go to Dartmouth. I doubt you went to ASU. So where did you go to college?"

"I went, my freshman year, to Clemson." My jaw drops. "I'd gotten a partial football scholarship, but I blew my elbow out in the second game."

"Oh shit, Dyson, I'm sorry."

He gives me a humorless laugh. "It all worked out in the end." His voice turns bitter.

"I know that was all you wanted, and schools wanted you too." I raise an eyebrow, curious why the partial scholarship.

"They did and most of them wanted me despite me not playing much my senior year. That's why I got a partial." He pulls a t-shirt over his head; this one is just a plain black V-neck that looks ridiculously comfortable. Not that the Dartmouth one isn't or maybe it's because it's on him that I want it. He continues talking, "But after I blew out my elbow, I started thinking about a lot of stuff, about school, life, shit like that. I wanted something to send me a sign about what to do." He holds his hand out to me in invitation and leads me from the room.

"And what conclusion did you come to?"

He gives me a sad smile as we descend the steps. "I lost the scholarship and I couldn't afford to keep going to school. My elbow was having a hard time healing and I took that as my sign I wasn't meant to play

football anymore." He leads me down the hall toward the game room. He'd said we were gonna watch movies in the bedroom, so I'm a bit confused until he starts to open the first of three cabinets containing his movie collection. "Pick something," he coaxes.

I step up to the first cabinet and look over his collection. I'd snooped earlier so I know what is in here. I kind of figured out his order for stuff; year then title. I go for some of the older stuff, well, to start. "So then what happened?" I prompt him to continue with his story.

"I got a phone call that changed everything."

I turn my head away from his movies to look at him. "Oh?" I urge him.

"My father died."

I blink at him. Dyson never talked about his father. Neither did his mother. It was something unspoken between the two of them and it never got brought up. My father was long gone before I was born which was long before Dyson and his mom moved to Joplin. Our moms were just two single moms who got along and became friends. Their husbands were never talked about. My mother dated some as I had got older, but like me, she always seemed to find men lacking and I was okay with that. "I'm sorry, Dyson."

He's staring toward the window of his game room, but he's not really here with me and that's okay. "I was angry, at first," he finally continues and I look away, giving him the space to tell his story, but I'm listening more to him than I am reading the titles of the movies. "But I wasn't angry because he was dead. I was angry because I wasn't the one who did it."

"Dyson…" My head snaps around to look at him. "Why would you want to kill your father?"

His eyes meet mine and I can see the anger there, anger unlike anything I've ever seen before and it has me straightening up. "Because my father was a self-centered-son-of-a-bitch who didn't deserve to live."

I take an involuntary step back, bumping into the cabinet behind me.

I stop, locked in place as his eyes shift from anger to concern. "Dyson, I…I'm sorry." I sigh, "I had no idea you felt that way about-"

"No, it's alright. I shouldn't have reacted that way. It still makes me so angry." He flexes his hands at his sides. "My father used to beat the shit out of my mother," he adds, completely unsolicited. "When I got old enough to step in and protect her, he turned to beating both of us."

My hand goes to my mouth, and my eyes shimmer with unshed tears at what he went through as a child. He was only eleven when I met him and to have had to go through all that before that age, I can't fathom it. "I had no idea," I say slowly.

"No one did. It wasn't something we talked about. My mom and I had a pact when we moved to Joplin. We wouldn't talk about it, ever. We'd been placed under protection."

"Witness?" He quickly shakes his head.

"No, more of a protective order. Cole is my birth name. It's my father's name. Richards was the name they'd told my mother to use when it came to me."

"Oh," I squeak. "That's why she had a different last name." I don't know why in the hell I'm remembering this now, after all this time, but I have a memory of asking him once when we were kids why his mother's last name was different from his. He'd just said he didn't want to talk about it.

"Mom reverted back to her maiden name. Like I said, it wasn't witness protection or anything, but it was an attempt to hide the truth. That's why the house in Joplin still stands empty. My mother inherited the house a few years ago. It was a family home – belonging to her mother's side. When we moved out, no one ever wanted to move in."

The memory of the day I threw the rock at the front door comes back to me and I wonder if, by some strange miracle, the rock is actually still there.

"So, your father died while you were in college." I try and change the subject back to college. "You said something about making a decision."

He softens a little at my distraction, his anger lightens. "You still need to pick a movie," he tells me.

"Maybe, but I want to hear the rest of your story."

He smirks. "I was the only living next of kin when my father died so his entire estate was left to me."

"That sounds like a lot." I meant it as a question but it doesn't come out right.

He gives me another humorless laugh. "That's an understatement. I finished up my freshman year, debating on what to do next. I hated school with a passion."

"You never seemed to mind high school."

He gives me a knowing smile. "That's because I wasn't a pariah there. I was popular, the girls dug me, I played football and it killed the time. But I sucked at school. My grades were only ever average at best and had I not had the scholarship, I doubt I would have gotten into college at all. Then I suddenly found myself with a lot of money."

"What kind of money are we talking about?" I ask, regretting the question as soon as it leaves my mouth. Something tells me it's not just a few thousand dollars.

"The kind of money that makes my first million look like chump change."

"Fuck me," I breathe

"Later," he smirks. "But I didn't want his money. That was the problem. Mom and I'd gotten by without him and his bullshit for years. She refused it then too but there wasn't much I could do. The IRS frowns on donating that much money to charity in a year unless you have marketable assets...anyway." I smile at his rambling. It's the first time he's rambled and I think it's sweet. "That's when I started thinking about a way to give it all back. A way to give it back to the community in some strange way, so I started Home Together."

I need to sit down.

"Ireland…what's wrong?" His voice is panicked and he comes over to me, but I ignore him and go to the couch to sit down.

I have to find my voice. I have to explain this to him. "Talk about six degrees," I mumble.

"What are you talking about? What's wrong?" The panic rises in his voice a little higher and he sits next to me. "Please, VeeVee, what's wrong?"

I hold my hand up and pull in a few deep breaths, hoping not to hyperventilate before I can explain this to him. He's growing more and more nervous. "I'm alright, I just…Do your remember what Home Together did in oh-nine?"

I watch as he racks his brain looking for a memory, looking for something, trying to search through it. "I'm drawing a blank. I'm sorry, I don't."

"Do you remember the contest Home Together did that year?"

"Oh, the branding contest. The one where we went to colleges across the country and asked them to come up with a business and marketing plan. The colleges filtered them to the students, they created their own plans and brand, then the colleges narrowed them down. They were only able to submit one entry into the official contest per school."

He's on the right track. Okay. I pull a deep breath in and let it out. "How many colleges?"

"There were fifty total, one from each state."

"So you know that ASU was one of those schools?"

"It wasn't one of the schools, it was *the* school. They won the contest. Someone named Ivy M. Kidd."

I smirk. "Not Ivy, Dyson. I. Vy., as in Ireland Vyolet. The school screwed up and my submission got fucked up."

He stands up; obvious shock is written across his features. He doesn't say anything as he starts to pace back and forth. His silence is uncomfortable and I don't know what to say to him. I don't know what

he's thinking. "Jesus, Dyson, say something."

"That fucking close...I was that fucking close to you seven years ago," he mumbles. "Did you know it was me? My company?" he asks, turning to me.

I shake my head vehemently. "No, I had no idea. It was incorporated under Tiger's Eye..." my words trail off and I just stare at him. My mind goes completely blank and he raises an eyebrow at me. "D. Cole," I mouth.

"You turned down a meeting with me then. Why?"

I shake my head. "The contest was meant to be anonymous, if I remember correctly."

"Fuck that, I was going to offer you a job. I was so impressed, in fact..." he leaves the room and I'm left sitting there dumbfounded. I want to follow him but my legs won't work. It's all too fucking weird, too damn crazy. *Fate.*

Don't you start, I scold my subconscious.

Just as fast as he was gone, he returns, breezing back into the room and he hands me a portfolio. I take it from him and open it.

"You found this really fast."

He snorts. "It sits on top of everything in my drawer." I flip through the well-worn pages, and I see a few notes in the margins in a script I'm assuming is Dyson's. "That business model was adopted into what is now the Tiger's Eye blanket plan and it's the foundation of Tigress's business plan," he breathes. "I need to go make a phone call. Will you excuse me a minute?"

I stare up at him and blink. "Uh, sure," I tell him and he leaves the room. I don't know until I hear the beep and click of what I'm assuming is his office door where he's going exactly. I try and shrug it off, but something is very wrong.

DYSON
Remedy - Adele

I look at my watch; it's just before eight and on a Friday night, he'd better answer his damn phone.

"Barker."

"Charlie, it's Dyson."

"Well, hello there. I was wondering if you were gonna call while you were in town."

I snort into the phone. "This isn't a social call."

"Well, that's disappointing. What can I do for you?"

"Do you remember back in oh-nine when we ran that contest for Home Together?" I ask. I know he remembers because we talk about it once in a while.

"Oh-nine…no."

I roll my eyes. "Yes, you do. You keep pestering me about that damn account."

"Oh, that account. What about it?"

"We need to change the name on it."

"You're going to have to give me a lot more than that, Dyson."

"The school screwed it up. Do you remember we tried to send out the compensation?"

He laughs, "Yeah, it got returned six times before we finally gave up."

"That's because we had the wrong name," I tell him.

"I'm pretty sure it was Ivy's way of telling you she didn't want your money."

"She doesn't have much of a choice now. That business plan was incorporated into Tiger's Eye and rules over Tigress."

227

He laughs, "That's why there's so much fucking money in there. It's a royalty pay out?"

"Exactly."

"I told you not to bother with all that. Considering the check kept getting sent back and it was only for what, twenty-five grand? How in the hell do you expect her to accept a portfolio worth nearly thirty million dollars?"

"Not give her a choice," I tell him.

"It's your funeral, my friend." He sighs, "So, what's the name?"

"Ireland Vyolet McKidd."

"Send me her details, address, etcetera. I'll get the guys looking into it. See if there is some way we can find out from the school that she was actually the winning submission. Does she have a lawyer?"

"Doubtful, but I'm sure I can set something up for her," I tell him and we end the call shortly after that.

I find another number in my phone and call it. Mick, my ever trusted financial god is quick to answer. He's back in Arizona, so it's earlier for him. "To what do I owe the pleasure?" he greets.

"We have a situation."

"Stick your dick in something you shouldn't have?"

I growl into the phone. "Yes, but it's not what you think."

He laughs into the phone, "Am I bailing you out? It's kind of early in New York to get your ass thrown in jail."

"I love how highly you think of me there, Mick."

"Well, if this is what I expect, then there can be no surprises."

"This one's gonna knock you on your ass."

I launch into the details, reminding him of the contract and trust agreements in place. Inform him Charlie is working on the legal end of things, and I will be getting the details to him as well as Charlie. When we finish the call, he's set to task and he thinks he can have

everything wrapped up and ready by Thursday. I learn from Mick that the money owed to one Ivy M. Kidd is about nine million in liquid cash, the remaining twenty million or so is in the form of company shares and stocks. Ivy M. Kidd is a five percent shareholder in Tiger's Eye, Incorporated and a ten percent holder in Tigress.

I send an email to Charlie, giving him what I know of Ireland, which is just about everything compliments of Shelly's human resources file and let him know he will need to be in Arizona on Thursday. I pace my office, trying to gather my wits about me while I figure out how to return to Ireland after leaving her so abruptly.

Deciding that I need a drink, and that Ireland and I need to talk, I leave my office and pull the door closed behind me. I've only been gone about fifteen minutes and when I return to the game room, she's curled up on the couch with her proposal in her lap and she's reading through it like it's the most interesting book in the world.

"If I'd known half of what I do today, this would have been a thousand times better," she tells me without even looking up from the folio in her lap.

"Oh yeah, what exactly would you change?" I ask. She makes the transition for me and I smile.

"You might want to get a notebook for this." She smirks and starts pacing the room. There's a desk near the door that has some pens and pads in there. A phone used to sit on the desk. The phone is gone, but the goods remain.

I get comfortable on the coffee table and watch her pace back and forth as she launches into a deeper, more detailed account of the portfolio she just read through.

We carry on a discussion that has a few arguments in it, but they aren't really that, more discussion like. At one point we carry the discussion into the kitchen where I pour us both some wine and continue listening to her talk on and on. She never loses my attention and it is nearly midnight before she runs out of steam and makes it through the entire portfolio.

I end up with more notes in the margin and nearly a whole letter sized legal pad full of notes.

"I don't care what Wellington is paying you, I will triple it if you come work for me." My voice is serious but yet she manages to laugh.

"I'd like to say something sarcastic, like you're insane or that you can't afford it, but I'm pretty sure you can."

"I can. How much are they paying you?" I ask her.

"Isn't that private information?"

No need to tell her I can get the information. I want her to tell me. "We've been discussing money all night. Why not tell me this now?"

"Because compared to what you make, it's embarrassing."

I give her a playful smirk and raise of my eyebrow. "You don't know what I make," I tease her.

"No, but I would wager a guess it would take me no less than twenty years, saving every single penny I make and not spending a single dime on anything for me to even come close to making a million dollars."

"Well, when you factor in cost of living increases, raises, things like that, I'd imagine it might take-"

"Okay, eighteen years," She laughs. "Seventy-five."

"Thousand?" I ask, joking aside.

"No, hundred."

"What?" I scoff.

She bursts out laughing, "Yes, seventy-five thousand."

"I was gonna fucking say I realize you're fresh out of college and all, but that's a bit low."

She laughs, "I made twelve thousand interning."

"A summer?"

She shakes her head. "Three summers," she clarifies.

"Well, that's just…" I don't even know what to say. "You're right, I won't triple it."

She gapes at me, "Then I won't work for you!"

"You mean you'd really consider it?"

"For two-hundred and twenty-five thou a year, fucking right I would."

"I love your mouth," I tell her. "Say yes, right here, on the spot."

"You just said you wouldn't triple it. So why, Mr. Big Shot, Three-Thousand Dollar Suit Wearing CEO, would I come and work for you?"

"Because I'll pay you five-hundred thou a year, plus a ten million dollar sign on bonus." The words fly out of my mouth before I stop them. I cringe, waiting for her reaction.

She bursts out laughing, "You're fucking funny."

"Can't fault a man for trying," I smirk. No need to tell her there is nearly thirty million coming to her whether or not she wants it or the job.

Chapter Twenty-Two

IRELAND
Say It - Flume ft. Tove Lo

"What are you looking at?" I tease as he stares at his phone. Looking for a distraction from his outrageous and unbelievable job offer.

"Oh, just this picture this gorgeous girl sent me today." He smirks at me and for some strange reason, my vision turns green. "I was in this meeting and she sent me this picture. It got my dick so fucking hard I couldn't concentrate on what I was doing." His hooded eyes meet my all too bright green ones. "Then I realized she was standing in my bathroom looking like sin on legs."

He drops his phone on the bed and staring back at me is the shot I'd sent him earlier. The green in my vision fades fast, and he wraps his arms around me. "It's all your fault, you know?"

He smirks, but the desire is still in his eyes as he looks at me. "Oh really? Why is that?" He's pretending to play the innocent but I know better.

"Because you make me fucking crazy, you insatiable fool."

He captures my lips in his, taking me for a soul sucking kiss that leaves me squirming. When he pulls back, our breathing is ragged and uneven. "Say my name." His voice has turned husky. His erection presses against me.

"Eccentric-suit-wearing-horn dog."

He bursts out laughing. "One of these days, princess, I will get you to say my name without an ounce of hesitation."

I smile at him, accepting his challenge. "Good luck with that."

He kisses my forehead, and the gesture is not new, but the meaning isn't entirely lost on me. He's accepting of whatever I'm willing to throw at him, no matter what.

Tonight took a turn for the crazy. I was expecting to pick a movie, to lie in bed and watch it snuggled in his arms, but instead, a simple conversation turned into an entire business discussion and a completely

unrealistic job proposal. Half a million dollars a year? No fucking way. I am not worth anywhere near that much money. Hell, I've barely finished college and while I worked three summers interning, I have no real world experience in marketing. But, I'll be, he fucking took notes like he needed my words as a lifeline. I wanted to ask him if Tigress was in trouble, but by the end of our discussion, I honestly felt like he was truly engaged in making Tigress better than what it currently is. Though I'm not entirely sure that's possible.

"You never did tell me if you went back to school after your freshman year," I state, attempting to change the subject. After our little pow-wow business discussion, I'm buzzing and not very tired.

"No, I didn't. I could have, easily, but I didn't have the drive and while I wasn't fully intent on spending my father's fortune on myself, I found a new purpose with the charity. It started small. I put up the cost to build a small complex of houses that would house single mothers who'd lost everything or were victims of abuse." My heart sinks with sadness at what he put his time into. I remember the organization well, I wrote a business plan for it after all. At the same time as my heart sinks, it starts to soar. The seventeen-year old asshole who left me cold and naked on the ground in a barn has grown up. "The building was a success. By the end of the first year, we'd filled all the apartments with families. Sponsorships started pouring in and while we were set pretty good, we wanted to expand further and in order to do that, we needed a business plan."

I smile at him. "I remember, I was there."

He gives me a slow smile as he sits on the bed. Moving his now dark phone to the nightstand, he gently pats the bed and I climb up, but rather than sitting with him hip to hip, I turn, crossing my legs so I can look at him. Without any prompting he continues. I can tell by the light in his eyes he thrives on this. "We expanded Home Together. Not only adding additional shelters but branching out into some of the rougher parts of Atlanta. For the first time in my life, I felt like I was really making a difference. Not just in the shelters, but in the communities. It gave me a sense of hope I hadn't felt in a long time." He gently lays his hand in my lap and I wrap my fingers with his, holding it tightly. "Hope I hadn't felt since that night."

His eyes are warm, sincere and raw with honesty. "I'd always said," he continues, "that I needed to make something of myself before I could consider going back for you. I mean that. But until tonight, I had no idea you helped me get there."

He hangs his head, his hair falls into his eyes and I use my free hand to push it back and he turns toward me, into my hand and I cup his cheek. "Some things, no matter how big, or how small they may seem, end up meaning so much more to us than we realized at the time." I had another snarky, Ireland style reply on the tip of my tongue, but his gentleness forces it to die on my lips.

"I had no choice when it came to leaving." His voice is but a whisper and his eyes are still closed. "But I wish I'd done it differently."

"I don't."

His eyes fly open. He's stares at me with fear in his eyes, and I need to find my voice before I lose the nerve. I swallow hard. "Think about it. If we'd parted on more amicable terms, where would we be now?" I ask him, giving him a moment to ponder my question.

"We'd be in Joplin."

"Doing what?" I pull my hand away and he shrugs.

"I don't know, VeeVee, I really can't answer that."

I smile. "Neither can I, but what I do know is this moment might not have ever happened. If you'd come back to Joplin after you graduated, we would have had to sneak around, or if we didn't, if mom accepted us being together, because I was only sixteen at that time, then maybe not. But still, things would have been so different between us. And right now, I don't know what tomorrow brings for us, but I'm not ready to give up trying to find out. I'm ready to put our past behind us. I want to move forward, see where this is going because thinking about how things might have been if you'd never moved away hurts too much. It hurts because I can't honestly say that at fifteen and seventeen we were right for each other."

"What about twenty-five and twenty-seven?"

I smile at him and release his hand. There is a twinge of disappointment that disappears the moment I climb on his lap to straddle him and look him square in the eye. I press my body to his, toss my hair over my right shoulder and grab the back of his neck with my left hand. "I think at twenty-five and twenty-seven," I pause, kissing his forehead, "that I haven't," I kiss the tip of his nose, "quite figured it out," I brush my lips against his, "but I'm not going to give up trying to."

I press my lips firmly to his, his arms wrap tightly around me, holding me to him like a lifeline he didn't know he needed. My sex heats, my desire for him evident between my thighs. I moan into our kiss and he growls at me.

His hands slide down my back to grip my ass cheeks as he stands up from the bed. I wrap my legs around him. His cock presses between us and I pull back, gasping for air.

His lips don't stop; they move down to my jaw, my neck and then onto what little of my shoulder is exposed to him. I tilt my head, finding more room for him to kiss and lick and suck as he turns me around, sitting me down on the bed. He reaches for the hem of his t-shirt that I'm wearing and pulls it up quickly. I'd never put on a bra, so he's greeted with my rose colored, taut nipples and his eyes flicker with some unnamed emotion. "So fucking perfect," he mutters as he reaches for the button of his pants. "I was going out of my fucking mind while you paced downstairs." He smirks, "I could see your soft nipples pressing into my shirt, then when you'd get really excited about something, they'd grow longer, and thicker as they hardened. Staring at me, daring me to take them in my mouth."

He pushes his pants down his legs and kneels before me, taking one of my nipples into his mouth. He sucks hard. The pleasure and twinge of pain cause my breathing to stop momentarily before picking back up in labored breaths. His tongue flicks along the sensitive bud as it hardens further in his mouth. He moans. The vibrations reach straight to my fucking core and all conscious thought evaporates.

His hand slides its way to my other nipple and he pinches it, hard. The

softness of his mouth on my other nipple makes it a sensation cocktail; soft and gentle mixed with a twinge of pain. It's like hot and cold, two different extremes, and they collide like fire and ice between my legs.

"Please," I cry out.

He releases the nipple in his mouth. The pop and surge of blood is heady and my eyes roll up. "Please what, princess?"

"I need you."

A sexy, mischievous grin slides across his lips. "How, princess?"

"Inside me," I groan. "Please."

Begging isn't something I'm accustomed to, but it's something I like, a lot. Especially when it comes to begging Dyson to do things to my body with his own.

His hand moves off my nipple to between my breasts. "One day, gorgeous, I will watch my cock disappear between these gorgeous tits of yours." His hand presses against my chest, urging me onto my back. "But for now…" His hands slide achingly slow down my body. The feather light touch leaves goosebumps in their wake and I shiver. My nipples harden painfully as he reaches the waistband of my shorts. He teases the skin just above it, causing me to jump with the tickling sensation.

His hands disappear altogether until I feel one of them press against my sex and I writhe under his touch. "So wet already, tigress." He pulls his hand back then presses it against me again and I feel the coolness against my sex briefly as I realize my arousal is visible on my shorts.

Embarrassment floods through me, but he eradicates my unease quickly when he slides his fingers into the waistband again, this time, tugging it down. I find some leverage with my legs hanging over the side of the bed and I lift my hips, allowing him the space to remove my shorts.

"Say it." His hot breath caresses over my sex.

I shiver. "What?" I breathe.

"Say." His breath hits me again. "My." His tongue darts out, pushing

only slightly into my entrance and my body begins to quake. His tongue disappears. A release is imminent if he gives me any more torture. "Name," he growls, then slides his hot, wet, fat tongue from my entrance up to my clit. His teeth nip into the overly sensitized bud and I explode.

"Dyson," I scream as my orgasm completely consumes me, mind, body and soul.

I hear him growl before I feel him. His mouth is on me with a fervor I've never felt before. He licks, sucks and teases the rest of my orgasm from my body and I'm shaking with each swipe of his tongue across my clit. He doesn't let up and the pleasure rolls from one into another building inside me. On the brink and near the edge again, he slows.

My body quakes under his expert tongue and I slide my hand into his hair, holding him to me. He moans. The vibrations are a whole new sensation and I shudder again. "Jesus," I breathe.

He releases my clit from his mouth, but doesn't move away from my sex. "I told you I'd make you scream my name," he says and I look at him. His eyes are wide and excited and I melt into the storminess I see within him.

"You don't play fair," I quip.

"Never said I would, princess." He sits up straighter, and then stands. His cock is hard and on full display. I lick my lips. "What do you want, VeeVee?" His voice is soft and I sit up, reaching for him. He doesn't move or flinch when I take his cock in my hand, stroking it gently. My hands tremble with the nerves I'm feeling. I've never done this before and my cheeks flush.

He steps closer to me. "

I look up at him through my eyelashes and he has a warm smile that makes my body ignite again. How the hell does one little look do this to me? "Do what your body is telling you," he says softly. "Don't think about it, feel it."

And feel it, I do.

DYSON
Let Me Love You - DJ Snake ft. Justin Bieber

Ireland slowly comes closer to me. Then her pink tongue darts out to lick along the underside of my cock and my eyes flutter closed briefly before finding hers again. My breathing changes, my mouth falls slack when she licks me again. Her hand is still wrapped around the base, holding me still as she slowly strokes up and then back down. Her tongue on my cock quickly turns to her entire mouth. Her eyes flutter, giving me a small break to close my eyes and enjoy the sensation of her perfect, hot mouth on my cock.

She's nervous, it's obvious, but she's doing as I told her. She's letting her body consume her desire to do what she's doing and when her tongue dances along my shaft, I shudder. Opening my eyes, I find her looking up at me. "Don't stop," I whisper and I see her lips form a smile around me and it makes me tremble. "God, please don't stop."

She releases my cock from her mouth and whispers, "Say my name." She smirks before slipping me back inside of her mouth.

"Tigress," I say and I feel her teeth clamp down slightly and I chuckle. "Princess," I tell her and she flicks her tongue along the underside and my skin erupts in a wave of goosebumps. "Baby girl." This time she nips a little harder and I laugh. "Not a favorite?" I ask and she shakes her head before she pulls back and pushes back down on me with her mouth and the tip of my cock touches the back of her throat. "What about tigress?" She blushes, but I feel the tiny nip of her teeth and it sends a shot straight to my balls. "That feels fucking amazing, so if you don't like that name, you're screwed."

She chuckles and releases me again. "My favorite," she admits and I hiss through my teeth when she sucks me back into her mouth and she hollows her cheeks, sucking me hard and furiously as she starts to really bob her head up and down. I can't stop sliding my hands into her hair, helping her, guiding her.

She's got me right on the edge. I'm almost there when she takes my balls into her free hand. She tickles them gently before playing with them. She flushes again, but doesn't stop when I let out a low rumbling groan. "Ireland?" I breathe and she looks at me with such devotion it makes my heart skip a beat and my balls tighten up. "I'm going to come. If you don't want…" Her pace picks up, telling me she doesn't care and I tighten my hands in her hair as I pour myself down her throat. Calling her name as I topple over the edge.

Chapter Twenty-Three

IRELAND
Latch - Sam Smith

Dyson did what I can only describe as 'make love' to me after I gave him my first blowjob. Then two more times in the night. Each time I awoke, he was doing something sweet to me, whether it was kissing along my shoulder or his hands roaming over my body. Every time I woke up, it was sweeter than the time before.

Eventually we both fell into a peaceful sleep wrapped in each other's arms.

When I wake in the morning, he isn't in bed with me and I am disappointed, but after pulling his Dartmouth t-shirt over my head, and nothing else, I go in search of him. I find him down in the living room with paperwork piled in front of him, spread out across the coffee table and his nose buried in his laptop. He looks up when he catches me watching him and gives me a gorgeous, panty melting smile that, had I been wearing them, might have caused them to combust. "Hi," he breathes.

"Hi you."

"I didn't wake you, did I?" he asks with genuine concern and that beautiful smile fades.

"No, you not being in bed woke me." I look around, looking for a clock and don't find one. "What time is it?" The windows are tinted compared to yesterday, but not darkened completely.

He checks his watch. "Just before one."

"Well crap." I walk to him and sit down on the couch next to his prone position on the floor. "I didn't mean to sleep that long."

He chuckles, "I kept you up all night."

I give him a sweet smile. "Oh, I'm not complaining." But then my stomach rumbles and he notices.

"Hungry?"

"Famished," I tell him and he smiles.

"Want to eat in or go out?"

"Erm… I didn't bring much for clothes," I remind him. Sure, I have jeans and a couple t-shirts, but that's about it.

"You have jeans, don't you?" I nod. "Then you don't need anything else. There's a great place around the corner that has some of the best burgers in the world."

I am so hungry I could eat a cow, but I don't tell him that. "I'll go get dressed." I move to stand but he stops me, pulling me down onto his lap and wrapping his arms around me as he buries his face in my neck. "What's this for?" I ask, more playful than anything. I like this side of him.

"Nothing, just wanted you in my arms," he tells me before squeezing me again and I wrap my arms around his neck and snake my fingers into his hair. I pull his head back and I press my lips to his. He groans and I smile. "Don't start something you can't finish," he teases back.

"Who said I wouldn't finish it?" I ask.

"Me. You're sore."

I take stock of my body and he's not wrong. I am deliciously sore in all the right places for all the right reasons. "You're an animal," I Retort.

"Only for you."

Only for you… Wow, he's got it bad. Like really bad. I capture his lips for a chaste kiss. I'm pretty sure no amount of begging, teasing or torturing him will get him to go back on his decision to give my body a break and I don't want to push him. "You're impossible to resist, you realize that, right?" I ask him.

"And you're undeniable. So go, before I change my mind and bend you over the coffee table." I squirm in his lap. He growls and grabs hold of my ass cheeks and squeezes hard. "Go," he groans.

"Crazy fool," I smirk and he helps me stand up.

"You look too fucking good in my t-shirt."

"Maybe I should wear it to lunch?" I joke.

He shrugs. "Then they really will be looking at you, smart and sexy as fuck."

I shake my head and scurry up the stairs to his room. I hear his laughter from the living room as I go to my suitcase. Finding a pair of jeans and socks, I grab my Chucks then search for something warmer than a t-shirt.

I move back to the door. "How cold is it outside?" I shout down to him.

"It's kind of mild outside right now." I hear the humor in his voice.

"Your idea of mild or mine?"

"Mine, it's about forty-eight right now."

"Fuck," I breathe out. "Mild, my ass!" I shout down at him.

A new roar of laughter comes up the stairs, and it takes a beat before I see his head, then the rest of him comes into view as he enters the room. He's wearing a plain black V-neck, like last night, and a pair of artfully faded, straight leg jeans and when his feet come into view, and they're bare. Fuck me, even his feet are sexy. God damn.

He ignores the lick of my lips as he comes closer to me. "I have a couple things that might help. I should have warned you it would be cold."

He leads me toward his closet, "I figured it would be, but warning me wouldn't have done anything. I don't own overly warm clothes." I sigh, remembering being in Joplin, but even there, I wore a hoodie and I was okay. I'm pretty sure the coldness that consumed me had nothing to do with the temperature outside.

He pulls back a few different things on the rack in his closet that's nearly full to the brim, by the way. He pulls a beautiful light green colored V-neck sweater from a hanger and hands it to me.

"Good god, that's soft," I practically moan as my hand grabs it from him and he smirks.

"It's small on me, so maybe it will fit you okay."

"I don't care, I'm wearing it anyway." I wink at him and head for the bathroom. I'd pulled a t-shirt from my suitcase and I decide I'm going to put the tank, t-shirt and finally the sweater over it. I'm going to need all the help I can get. Even on Phoenix's coldest nights, we rarely get this cold and I'm going to freeze.

I ditch the t-shirt, it looked awful under the sweater, but I look hot as hell in his clothes, not gonna lie on that one.

My own assessment is matched by the vacant expression on Dyson's face as he stares at me when I come down the stairs. Because the sweater is big on me, the V dips a little lower, and the girls look fucking hot. "Earth to Dyson," I tease and he snaps out of his little trance.

"I think I'm going to have to find you a few more of those." He winks and wraps his arms around me.

The sweater is so soft against my skin it gives Dyson's touch a run for its money, okay, not really, but I thought the t-shirt was soft.

I laugh and hug him back. "I'm starving."

"Good." He gives me a chaste kiss and releases me before he grabs my jacket off the back of the couch and holds it open for me. "I found this for you." He hands me a green and white striped scarf. "Thought it might help keep you warm."

I smile at his thoughtfulness and I wrap it around my neck, leaving my jacket open. He slings his jacket over his arm and takes my hand. It all seems so real, so normal and it's not easy to wrap my head around it. A part of me starts to wonder if the dream is going to end and I'm going to wake up alone.

I'm reminded of the dull ache that hasn't left my chest since my mother's passing and I can't imagine a dream that would be so sweet and potent and then be that cruel at the same time.

As we descend into the lobby, Dyson releases my hand and pulls his jacket on. His is much thicker and sexier than mine. It's one of those wool, hooded, double button jackets you see on models all the time and

Dyson does it justice. He's sexy as hell, and it doesn't matter whether he's naked, in jeans or in one of his expensive suits. And he's all mine.

Wait, is he?

Jesus, I've had sex what, five times, with someone and I don't even know what kind of relationship we've got going on. The thoughts cause me to stiffen and Dyson notices. "What's rolling around in that pretty little brain of yours, princess?"

I don't know if I really want to bring it up, but the elevator stops and someone joins us. Thankful for the distraction, I step back, but Dyson's right next to me. His warmth surrounds me and his scent is like the eraser to a whiteboard. I don't remember much of what I was thinking before his close proximity short circuited my brain.

When the elevator stops, we step off behind the other female passenger and we're headed toward the lobby when my cell phone rings. It hasn't made a sound in over twenty-four hours and it startles me. I debate on answering it. Dyson pauses, looking at me. "That's you, love."

There is that term again. What in the hell am I supposed to make of that?

I pull my phone from my back pocket and see Reese's face. I click the side of it, darkening and ignoring the call. "It's not important," I tell him and he takes my hand in his as we walk through the manned door of his building and into the Saturday morning foot traffic of New York City.

Stepping onto the sidewalk and looking around, I'm actually glad to get out of the apartment. I didn't think I'd want to leave, but I'll be dammed if this city isn't calling to me for some unknown reason.

With our hands joined, Dyson leads me casually down the street. When we turn the corner I am struck with a sense of déjà vu that has me slowing in my tracks. I feel like I've been here before, but I can't for the life of me figure out why. It's not a remarkable street. Not the type you'd see in a magazine or anything like that, but it's oddly familiar. "What's wrong?" Dyson asks me when our hands reach their limit and he rubber bands back to me. I keep staring down the street, trying to find where this street belongs in my memory but nothing is coming to mind. I try

and shake it off, but it's going to rattle my nerves until I can figure it out for myself.

"Nothing, I just…" I pull my eyes away from the street and find his. "I feel like I've been here before and I don't have any idea where or why."

"Maybe you were a New York debutante in a previous life?" He cocks an eyebrow in disbelief.

I chuckle, shaking off the odd feeling I'm missing something. "Hardly," I state simply. "Because if that were the case, the fact that you're a loaded CEO would do more than scare the hell out of me. I was probably a hippie," I tease.

"My money doesn't bother you at all, does it?"

"In the sense of 'I want you for your money', no. In the sense of 'I can't even begin to wrap my mind around more than three zeros in my bank account – to the left of the decimal', yes. But that's not your fault, Dyson. It's an accomplishment and one you should be proud of, I know I am." I wink at him and he kind of stares at me. I grin and ask, "What?"

He shakes his head, releases my hand wraps his arm around my shoulders, kissing my forehead. "I'm pretty sure I don't deserve you," he breathes. His voice is so low that if I wasn't expecting him to say something, I wouldn't have heard him.

I shiver, his warmth reminding me that I'm cold, and when I look back down the street, the déjà vu has disappeared altogether.

We walk a little ways before Dyson leads me between a couple parked cars. Looking both directions, he releases my shoulders and goes for my hand. As we cross the street, I notice a restaurant on the corner. The corner of the building has a red and white awning that wraps around the building with tables under it. There are actually people sitting at them. "They're crazy," I mutter.

He brings his arm back around my shoulders, holding me close and keeping me warm. I tighten my jacket around me. "This is normal for New Yorkers. You're the only one turning into a popsicle," he chuckles and I shoulder check him.

"I can't help what I'm used to. Then again, when it's a hundred and twenty in Phoenix, I can remember this and remember why I love winters in the Valley of the Sun."

"There is no argument from me." He leads me to an unimposing door around the corner from where we crossed and I'm immediately assaulted with the delicious scent of grilled onions, mushrooms and so much mouthwatering promise. Literally.

My phone rings again. I pull it from my back pocket and see it's Reese again. I look at Dyson. Something in my eyes tells him I need to take it and he shrugs. "Do your thing, baby girl." I scowl at him. He chuckles.

I press the green button and put the phone to my ear. "What's up Reese?"

"Hey, baby girl." And now you know why Dyson calling me that makes me twitchy. "It's really loud, where are you?"

Hmm, it's not that loud. "Hang on." I gesture toward the door and Dyson nods as I step back out into the cold. "I'm out to lunch…"

"It's not even eleven in the morning."

"I, erm…" I didn't really want to tell him where I was, but I know he's not gonna let it go. "I'm in New York."

"So you're not coming tonight?" he says dejected.

"Coming for what?"

"Blu – the concert." His voice is sad and I immediately remember what he's talking about. Fuck, he just reminded me earlier this week too. We were going to have some drinks and talk. Guilt slices through me.

"Shit, Reese, I'm sorry, I forgot. I, uh…"

"Just spill it, baby girl. What's going on?" He's not angry, which is just how Reese is. I'm not one to back out of our plans at the last minute, so he knows something's going on.

"I didn't plan on coming here. I got here yesterday morning," I explain, hoping to remain as vague as possible with Reese. We haven't talked much since before my mom passed, so I haven't told him hardly

anything other than I got the job.

"Is it for Wellington?"

"No, it was personal, last minute."

"Now I know you can't afford that." I picture him leaning against his kitchen counter, crossing his arms and tucking his phone to his shoulder.

I roll my eyes at no one. "I'll explain when I get home. Dinner, Tuesday night? I start on Monday."

"Oh, baby girl, that's awesome. And yes, Tuesday, dinner. Don't get dead."

I laugh, "I don't plan on it."

"Love ya."

"Reese?" I know he's gonna hang up.

"Yeah?"

"Thanks," I say.

"For what?"

"Not prying too far."

He snorts into the phone. "You know damn well I ain't gonna let you get away with not telling me, so the point is moot."

I laugh softly at his words, "I won't, promise. Dinner, Tuesday."

"You got it. Have fun."

"Love ya."

"Back at ya."

By the end of our convoluted conversation, Reese is fine. I know he'll be mad at me for missing the Lee Brice show at Blu tonight, but I didn't even think about it before hopping on a plane to fly out here. I shiver and decide I need to get back inside to Dyson and lunch.

I step inside the door and I look around for him.

That's when my heart freezes in my chest and my appetite dies.

DYSON
Crazy In Love - Beyonce
(From Fifty Shades of Grey)

"Jill, what the fuck?"

Jill walked up after Ireland walked outside to talk to her friend and I've been trying to get her away from me ever since. "I saw you come in, so I thought I'd say hi. We didn't leave things on very good terms yesterday."

"No, Jill, we left them on perfectly fine terms. Now what do you want? I know damn well if you're in this neighborhood, you only came for one reason." Thank god we weren't in the apartment when she decided to show up. God only knows how that would have gone over. Jill is the only woman I've ever allowed in my penthouse, and it was during a rare moment of weakness and an attempt to do the right thing. That's when I look up and see Ireland staring at me talking to Jill and my eyes widen. Fuck.

I lean in close to Jill and growl menacingly, "If you come near me again, I will call the cops and have you arrested for harassment. I mean it, Jill, no more."

Jill laughs, fuck. Ireland bolts out the door.

"Go to hell, Jill." She's still laughing as I follow Ireland. She turned right, back toward the apartment. Where the fuck is she gonna go?

I see her red hair disappear around the corner and I start jogging after her. I turn the corner and she's already half a block ahead of me. "Ireland!" I shout.

She doesn't stop. I knew she wouldn't. I pick up my pace. She's not exactly running and I have no problem catching up to her and grabbing her by the arm, spinning her around.

"Let. Go," she snaps.

"Stop it, right now," I bite back.

"Who is she?" She narrows her eyes at me.

Fuck. "Nobody, she's an old acquaintance."

"Looked a little cozier than just an acquaintance, Dyson."

She's still saying my name, this is good. "Will you retract the claws, tigress, and let me explain."

Wrong choice of words. Ireland's face turns red, literally, in anger. "You have exactly thirty seconds."

I sigh. "It's going to take much longer than that."

"Well, then start talking." She pulls her arm from my hand and crosses them over her chest. A jealous Ireland is a new sight to see, though not necessarily one I want to see, but the tiger that comes out is phenomenal to watch. I shouldn't want to laugh but I do because she's a damn tiger trapped in a human's body with a temper to match her hair.

"I met Jill…" I run my hand through my hair in frustration. "I don't even know. It was a long time ago."

"Did you sleep with her?"

"Fuck, VeeVee, yes, okay, I did. It was a mistake. A fucking mistake she's still trying to make me pay for. A mistake that…" Her features soften a little bit, and I lose my train of thought and the steam I thought I had going into this. "She played me. Played me for a fucking fool."

"How?" she asks.

"She tracked me down a few weeks after we'd…well, forget that, but she tracked me down and told me she was pregnant."

Her features harden again and I have to finish the rest of the story before she really runs away from me. That would be a valid reason to do so and if what Jill had tried to pull over came to fruition; Ireland and I might not be having this discussion or any others for that matter. "It didn't make any sense to me. I'd used a condom. Hell, I even pulled out. That's how I always fucking did it." My anger is getting the better of me. "But I wasn't going to be *that* guy. If it really was mine, then I

wasn't going to be that deadbeat asshole. Then things started not making sense. We'd only been together about a month before she came to me. I caught her coming out of the shower in my office and I noticed she was already showing a little bit. I knew that wasn't realistic and I started to question her about it. She kept insisting I didn't know what I was talking about. It was a fucking mess. I tried to force her to go to the doctor, do things, so on and so forth and she kept putting me off and I kept pushing her. Another couple weeks went by and she called me, said she was at the hospital." I sigh, letting my anger deflate completely. I'm not mad at Ireland, I'm fucking pissed at Jill and telling Ireland this story is making me crazy. "When I got there, I talked to the doctor, got some more information and discovered she miscarried, but at the same time, my suspicions were confirmed. The doctor had called it a late miscarriage because she was riding close to twelve weeks."

I watch as Ireland's features completely soften and her anger disappears.

I continue, "She did everything she could to try and convince me the doctors were wrong. She played a guilt trip on me and suckered me into feeling sorry for her. At the end of the day, she'd lost a child, whether it was mine or not, and I'm not a total heartless asshole. Anyway, I took care of her for a few days afterward and I haven't been able to get rid of her since. She came here, well, to the neighborhood, with the intention of coming to my apartment. She just happened to stop in here first."

"What did you say to her that made her laugh?" she asks me. She's still angry, but I get the impression she's not angry at me.

I give her a humorless snort. "She saw us come in together. She was playing you. I told her if she ever came near me again, I was going to call the cops and file harassment charges against her."

"Truly?" she asks.

"Always," I breathe.

She wraps her arms around me and mumbles, "I'm sorry."

I return her hug and kiss her forehead. "You've got nothing to be sorry about," I tell her as I rub her back. "Come on. Let's go back to the apartment."

"I'm still hungry."

I laugh and reach for my phone in my pocket and pull up Byron's number. He answers on the first ring, "Mr. Cole?"

"I need a favor."

"Yes, sir."

I relay to him the order from the restaurant and ask him to call it in and deliver it to the condo. He complies and Ireland and I walk back toward the apartment. She snakes her hand in mine as we walk and I can't help smiling at her.

"I'm sorry I ran."

"You should be. But next time," I wink at her, "run faster."

She shoulder checks me and I laugh. "What are we doing, Dyson?"

"What do you mean?"

"Us. What are we exactly?" she asks, her voice soft and curious.

"First off, what did your friend want?"

"Dodging questions now?"

"Nope, just curious," I tell her with a smirk.

"He wanted to remind me about tonight," she answers softly.

"What about it?" I ask. What could Reese want with her tonight?

"In my haste to come to New York, I completely forgot we had plans tonight."

I stop walking. "Why didn't you tell me?"

She shrugs. "I didn't think about it, honestly. I'd completely forgotten. So to make up for it, I promised him dinner on Tuesday."

"He's okay with it?"

"Well, I wasn't exactly forthcoming on why I wasn't in Phoenix. He's going to do his best to grill it out of me." She laughs, "It's what he's good at and he knows I'll tell him because he's Reese and nothing gets by him."

"So that's why you're asking what we are?"

"That's part of it," she says as we reach the doorway to my building and I open it for her.

"And the other part?" I reply as we enter the building and head for the elevator.

"It's what was on my mind in the elevator," She confesses, and I remember her stiffening up on me when that woman got on and ruined my chance to discuss it with her. I should have used my key to bypass the floors but I didn't think I'd need to. "The call with Reese and then my reaction to what happened in the restaurant, it just solidified that I need an answer to the question so I found the courage to ask," she states as we step into the elevator back up to my apartment. This time, I use my key and we're whisked upward without stops.

"What do you want us to be?" I ask her once we're inside my place The truth is I know what we are, or at least what I want and need us to be, but I can't possibly force that on her if that's not how she feels.

"I want us to finish what we started ten years ago."

My heart soars.

Chapter Twenty-four

IRELAND
Leave Your Lover - Sam Smith

I stormed out of that restaurant in a fit of jealousy I'm not even sure I have a right to feel. I just know seeing her with him made me see green and red like never before. Even compared to back in high school and the bevy of girls that surrounded him then. I don't know why I suddenly felt that way. I ran out so fast, I had no idea what I was doing. The minute I turned the corner I nearly stopped. Where was I going to go, how was I going to get there? I don't have enough money to fly my ass home, no way of getting into his apartment without him and certainly no one in New York to turn to.

When Dyson caught up to me, I wanted to be mad at him, but his brutal honesty floored me. I know we've been pushing it, and I've been completely honest with him, but I didn't expect him to tell me all that, especially not there on the street. Sure, we promised to be honest with each other, but sometimes that honesty comes with secrets we don't wish to reveal. When he wrapped his arms around me in our hug, then around my shoulders as we left, I secretly hoped she was watching. Just to show her I'm the better person in all of this.

Instead of being mad at Dyson for the woman he was talking to, I was pissed at her and until I wrapped my arms around him, I'd been fighting my anger for the woman who'd done that to him. Who does that to someone? I can't even wrap my head around it. But what I do manage to take hold of is the fact I have to find it, somewhere in me, to understand and accept the fact Dyson has a past. Unlike me, who only has Dyson.

When we were walking back, I couldn't help but bring up what had caused me to stiffen up in the elevator and then ultimately what led to my fleeing from the restaurant. Sure, I was jealous, but more importantly, I was scared because I didn't even know where I stood with him.

The last twenty-four hours have been amazing, beyond amazing, but that could all come to an end tomorrow when I have to fly back to Phoenix. I'm here, and I'm right now, but what happens when I'm no longer in his apartment. I just confessed to him I want the chance to

finish what we started ten years ago and he enveloped me into a hug and he hasn't let go for a good couple minutes.

"Dyson?"

"I love it when you say my name."

I shake my head and look into his blue-violet eyes with his hair sweeping into them and chant, "Dyson, Dyson, Dyson." I snicker.

He rolls his eyes. "You make me sound like Beetlejuice." We both laugh as we move into the living area.

"What do you want from this?" I ask him, no bushes to beat around, no evasiveness. I need to know. I need to know if I need to protect my heart once again or if I can finally let the walls start to crumble.

"I want you anyway you'll give yourself to me. I've never stopped wanting you, Ireland." He takes a deep breath and steps back, separating us a little. "But I don't know how to do this. I've spent so much of my life bouncing around between what I thought I wanted, what I wanted and more importantly, what I needed, that I haven't had the time to figure it all out." He runs a hand through his hair, a little frustrated. "I hate what happened downstairs." I don't say anything because I want him to continue talking, I need him to. "But in the same token, I warred with myself about whether or not to tell you about it."

"You wanted to lie to me?" I ask.

He shakes his head. "No, I just didn't want to tell you because it's embarrassing, for one, and for two, the whole situation was entirely fucked up."

"Do you want kids?" I ask him, point blank.

There's a flash of fear that ignites in his eyes and then it settles. "I never thought about it, not until Jill happened." He sighs. "I'm trying to figure out how to say this without sounding like a complete and total jackass." His eyes harden, but it's not a mask he's trying to put on, it's a mask he's trying to take off. He wants to be honest with me, but he doesn't want to hurt me further.

"You don't want kids?" I breathe out. This is a deal breaker for me.

Kids are something I've always wanted.

"Yes, I do," he tells me softly. "But when she told me about being pregnant, I was pissed. Not at her, but because it wasn't how I'd envisioned having children."

"You're going to have to explain this," I tell him.

"If I couldn't have kids with you, I wasn't going to have kids with anyone. Ever." My knees go weak and I take a seat on the couch, but he continues, "When I realized what I was giving up when it came to you, I knew it was so much more than a girlfriend or wife. I was giving up my future. I couldn't imagine going on with my life unless it was with you. But I tried. I really did try to move on. I quickly realized it was looks that brought them to me, and it was my looks that spread their legs. Then it wasn't just my looks, but also my bank account. It's women, like Jill, who only see a payday because of the size of my bank account or the height of my credit limits. They like to think because I'm a successful businessman I can accommodate whatever lifestyle they think they need or want. The socialite housewife is not the kind of woman I want in my bed every night."

I lean forward, putting my head between my knees, trying to breathe, trying to find some center of balance. I'd known my obsession with Dyson was unhealthy, I accepted it. I had to. I tried to move on, tried to put him out of my mind because hope was a bitch to hold on to. I couldn't keep going where he was concerned and so I vowed, that day in front of his house, to let him go completely. I thought I'd done that. But the more he talks, the more my heart aches. Not because I can't have him. If I want him, I know he is mine and he is exactly what I need. And that's what it is; it's no longer a want, but a necessity. My heartache is because we've lost so much valuable time to be together.

My mother's death has taught me life is too short and precious and I need to seize the day, live for today and pray for tomorrow, but this... this hurts too much. The tiny pieces of my shattered heart start to rattle around in my chest, trying to mend themselves back together and I don't even know where to begin anymore. What do I say to him? How do I say it to him?

I've been quiet so long that Dyson comes to sit next to me. "Say something, please."

"I don't..." I take a deep breath. "I haven't a clue where to begin. This is all so," I sigh, "it's heavy, Dyson. I was okay accepting the fact I could never let you go. I managed to deal with it as best I could. I really tried. I tried to move on, tried to find someone who could make me feel like you made me feel, but in the end, it never happened. I'd resigned myself to being alone for a little while, finding a job, getting my career started, just being me, being who I'm meant to be." I pause and look up at him. "Then my mother," a stray tear slides down my cheek, "she...god, Dyson, she was so young, so...it was too soon, for her, for me, Dusty, Anna, all of us, and I realized if I don't live in this moment, live a life for today, I'm going to let life pass me by. She sent me flowers, the day of the interview. She'd already planned ahead, expecting I would get the job. She had cards in a box saved for birthdays and other important days for not just Dusty and me, but for other friends, family members. She even had one for your mom," I tell him, the tears flowing now. "But then everything stopped. She stopped and yet there are pieces of her everywhere for every one and..." I wipe the tears from my cheeks, "She thought she had time. I don't feel like I have time. I feel like everything is only here for today, and tomorrow it will be gone and I'm afraid that if I let the shattered pieces of my broken heart mend back together, you're going to shatter it again. I won't survive that, Dyson. I can't. Not again."

He sits next to me on the couch and there is sadness in his eyes as he brings his hands up to push my hair out of my face, wipe away my tears and take my face in between his palms. His face is serious and all Dyson. "Ireland Vyolet McKidd, I lost you once in my life because I was seventeen, and an idiot. I will never, ever let that happen again. I can't. I need you more than I think you realize. Even if it means I can't have you, I'd rather have you as a friend in my life than nothing at all. But I would much rather have you standing beside me, lying in my bed curled in my arms than to never be able to touch you again." His thumbs gently stroke away some new tears. "But where we go from here is completely up to you. I am not capable of letting you go, I know that now, but I will step

back if that's what you need me to do."

No, no no no, no no no. I shake my head. "I can't do that. I can't live with having you so close and yet so far away from me," I breathe.

"So what do you want, VeeVee."

"I don't want anything, Dyson. I *need* you. When I ran out of that restaurant, I felt like I couldn't breathe, like all the oxygen had left the earth because I was running away from you, and I can't do that, I won't survive."

"That's all I needed to hear."

His lips press against mine and the gentle slow motion of lips and tongues, life and death, water and air, love, devotion, pain and heart-ache all pour between us and the tiny pieces of my shattered heart start melting back together.

Overcome with emotion, I start to cry again, but this time there is an overwhelming emotion winning out among the tangled mess of everything I'm feeling. Love.

He pulls back from me and cocks his head, looking at me as if he is desperate to see if what he's feeling is the same as what I'm feeling. I know the moment he sees it because his hands come away from my face and he stands ups. Confusion washes over me until he wraps his arms under my legs and along my back, lifting me off the couch. "Where are you taking me?"

"To bed. I need to make love to the woman who's stolen my heart."

DYSON
One And Only - Adele

I never imagined having her back in my arms, in my bed, in my life, but I will do anything and everything to keep her here. I have to. I don't

have a choice. I will not survive without her. Hope kept me hanging on for ten years. Hope that one day I would find her and I'd have the chance to try this again. I never imagined she'd hand it over to me like it was the most precious thing in the world.

I kick my bedroom door closed, and take her to the bed, laying her down and standing over her. I don't say anything, I don't have to. She sits up, pulling my sweater over her head, then her tank-top, then finally unhooking her bra, exposing herself to me. She stands and I step back, giving her room as she pushes her jeans down her legs and pulls off her socks before climbing back on the bed, right in the center. Her hair is a mess of red curls surrounding her face and shoulders. Her breasts are on full display, her nipples hard peaks. My breathing goes ragged and my mouth falls slack as my eyes roam down her body like it's my last meal. She gives me a come hither motion. My cock is harder than steel beneath my jeans. My body is alive, hungry and ready to show this beautiful woman everything I feel for her.

I quickly undress and the stand before her naked, waiting for her to say something but she doesn't. She doesn't have to. I climb onto the bed and settle myself between her legs, pressing my erection into the apex of her thighs and her eyes roll up into her head and her breathing catches in her throat. I haven't entered her, but I can feel her slick heat ready and waiting for me. I lower my lips to hers and brush them gently.

Her hand snakes around my neck, pulling me closer to her and she presses her lips to mine and then the dance ensues. Her lips, my tongue, her tongue, breathing ragged, hearts igniting, and my body hums with a new desire for her. Something I thought I felt ten years ago resurfaces. I fell in love with my VeeVee the day she gave me the rock. I fell in love with Ireland the day I took away her innocence because I was a selfish prick, and now, I am claiming the woman she has become. She moans into my mouth when I flick my hips against hers again and I pull back, kissing along her jaw and down her neck.

I push my body down on hers as I lick and suck my way to one nipple then the other and she writhes under me. I keep kissing my way down her body until I find her belly button ring and I tug on it. Her belly jumps

beneath my touch and my eyes meet hers to see the most glorious smile on her face that speaks everything our words are not. "Dyson," she coos and a thrill runs through me as my name passes her lips again, but I reach up with my hand and place my finger over her lips, silencing her and she nods in understanding.

I kiss my way lower, finding the cute little smattering of curls right above my destination and I can't help inhaling her scent. It's amazing and so sweet, yet the spice is everything Ireland. Her arousal is what drives me further to find the tight bundle of nerves and I suck her clit into my mouth. Our eyes never break their contact. Our eyes find each other's souls and grab hold. The connection is undeniable.

I don't spend too much time ravishing her sex with my mouth. My cock is growing impatient, desperate to be in the place he wants most. Inside the hot, slick, perfect pussy belonging to the woman he can't seem to forget.

I feel her juices coating my lips and I lick them and savor the taste. She shivers and her eyes grow dark and hooded as I slide back up her body, not stopping until I am nose to nose with her. Her hands grab hold of my hair and pull me down to her mouth. The moan she cries out makes my cock jump when she tastes her sex on my lips and she's determined to take it all. My tongue slides into her mouth and she cries out when I press my cock to her entrance. Just the tip, just enough to let her know I'm here, I'm ready and I need her. I pull back, seeking her silent permission.

She senses my hesitation and she wraps her legs around my waist. Giving me the answer I need and I slide home.

We both let out a strangled cry of pleasure.

This is it, this is home, this is where I so desperately need to be.

Her arms wrap around my shoulders, holding me to her and I lower myself to my elbows, needing to feel her body against mine as I push in and out of her. Her legs guide me, begging me to go faster and I give in, giving her a little more speed. I push my thighs up under hers so that the angle changes, giving me deeper access to her.

I use my hands to move the hair from her face and coax her eyes open.

The pleasure burning in them is almost my undoing, but I manage to get her to keep her eyes open. Her body begins to quake and tremble, her legs lock up and I know she's right there. I claim her mouth, swallowing the cries she can no longer keep inside.

For the first time since the morning after I left her, tears flow gently down my cheeks.

This is home, this is where I've always belonged and I will do anything to keep her here with me, forever.

Chapter Twenty-five

IRELAND
Back To The Start - Mr. Little Jeans

Heaven.

Bliss.

Perfection.

That's what I felt that afternoon with Dyson in his penthouse apartment.

That's what kept me going through the five hour flight back to Phoenix.

And most importantly, it's what got me through Sunday night.

I called Dyson once I was home and settled in. We talked briefly and he apologized for being short, but he was trying to wrap things up in New York so he could get back to Phoenix. I joked with him about being too cold in the Big Apple, but he said he was cold because I wasn't there. Said he was going to sleep in the game room because he didn't want to be in his bed alone. I laughed and told him he was a crazy fool and we hung up.

We spent the rest of Saturday in bed. With the exception of the best burger on the planet and when we went downstairs to finally pick out a movie.

Watching a movie, curled up naked in Dyson's arms, going to have to be repeated at least once a week. Definitely.

When I got home, Becca was nowhere to be found. I tried calling her and texting her several times, letting her know I was coming home, but she never responded to me. I called Reese back, confirming our dinner plans for Tuesday, and he was glad I'd made it home safe and sound.

I called Dusty, just to check in on him and Anna. She's only got a few more weeks to go before the baby is born and Dusty swore up and down he would call me the minute it happened. By then I should have my first paycheck, so with any luck, I can get up there for the weekend after the

baby is born. Despite being in Phoenix and Dusty being in Chicago, I want to be able to go up and see them anytime I want. Dusty is the only family I have left and I'm determined to bring us back together as one.

By ten Sunday night, I was exhausted. The traveling finally caught up to me and I climbed into bed. Ready to start my new job at Wellington in just under ten hours. After making sure my alarm was set, I texted Dyson a good night kiss. To which he didn't reply before I passed out.

Monday morning arrives and I head off to my new job. I'd planned a pantsuit for my first day. It's a light grey in color with wide legged pants, heels and an emerald green camisole underneath it. It's actually the outfit I wore for graduation a few months ago. The heels go into my bag and my walking shoes are on my feet. I love wearing heels, but sometimes you have to run a little faster for the train, which I do.

I make my train with my new iPad tucked into my bag and my headphones in my ears. My hair is down today and if I had that kind of confidence in myself, I'd say I looked hot.

My phone chimes just before I get to the stop before mine and I smile like an idiot, hoping it's Dyson and my smile falls when I see it's not.

Becca: *So you're home?*

I roll my eyes. What the hell has gotten into her since we were at the club that night? I shake my head. Please, for the love of everything, don't let it be Dyson. Becca isn't exactly the type to ignore someone after she figures out she wants them. Dyson, no doubt, is no exception and I'm pretty sure there is petty jealousy going on and I haven't the first clue how to deal with her.

I finally reply.

Yup, got home around seven, cleaned up, washed some clothes and passed out. Where have you been?

Her reply is almost instant.

Around.

I sigh and type out a message to her that I have a feeling is going to start a fight and frankly, I don't care right now. This crap with her has to stop.

What the hell is going on with you lately? You're so distant and not telling me anything. I don't like it.

For as pushy as she can be, I can be equally as pushy when I want to be. The train announces my stop is next and I put my phone away, ready to get off the train and stop for a cup of coffee before heading into the office. As I walk into Starbucks, I pull the unbreakable, sealable cup. Yeah, it's dumb, he's still in New York, but I really don't need or want a repeat of what happened two weeks ago.

I order my drink and wait.

My phone chimes again. I'd already forgotten about Becca and that I was waiting for a reply, which is why I'm surprised when I see her message.

Becca: I'm jealous, alright. There, I said it. He came up to me in the bar, he was hot, I wanted him and he only had eyes for you.

Ireland: He saw us come in together. He was trying to get a rise out of me, I'm sorry that you got caught in that.

Becca: It doesn't matter.

Ireland: It does matter Becca, you're my best friend and I miss my best friend.

I wait until my coffee is ready before tossing my phone back into my bag after waiting for a reply that never comes. I grab my coffee off the counter and leave out the same door I came in. There's a second door that leads to the building across from mine. My office building is directly across the street and Starbucks is close to a crosswalk that was added with the light rail and I head for it, waiting for the lights to switch over. I hear my phone chime again and I'm sure it's Becca, but not wanting to get anymore worked up than I already am, I ignore it.

Once I'm across the street, I find a bench and set my bag down. I swap my walking shoes for my heels. They're black, pointed at the toes. My favorite, most comfortable pair and I usually wear them for special occasions, so a new job called for them. I slip my walking shoes into the little bag I keep in there to keep the grime off of everything else and I see my phone. Dyson's name is flashing on the screen and the ringing finally reaches my ears. I reach in, grabbing it, and I hit the green button and put it to my ear. "Morning," I practically moan into it. "Just the voice I wanted to hear."

"How about the face you wanted to see?" he chuckles.

"Oh my god, are you home?" I smile wide, despite being on the phone.

"No, I'm outside your apartment."

"Well, that sucks," I groan.

"Why?"

"Uh, I'm already standing outside the building, I take the train, remember?"

"Shit," he groans into the phone.

"Guess you're gonna have to be quicker next time," I tease.

"I should've told you I was flying back early."

"It's okay. I'll see you in the office, won't I?"

"Maybe. I've got a lot of stuff to do today. I need to catch up and finish a few things from New York."

"Then what about tonight? Dinner?" I ask, surprised by my own forwardness with him. I'm not usually so forward, but something about this last weekend makes me feel like it's truly my place to ask him things like this.

"I'd like that," he breathes into the phone and I hear the train horn through the phone. "What time will you be done?"

"Erm…that's a good question. I was told to be here at seven-thirty so security could get my badge for me. Then they told me to go up when I was done. So I'm assuming five. But can I text you when I know for sure?"

"You better," he tells me. "I miss you."

"Aw, I miss you too," I tell him sweetly. "But I'll see you tonight, okay?"

"Okay." His voice is a little happier than it was when I told him I wasn't home.

"Okay, I gotta go."

"Say it," he breathes into the phone. If I'd been standing in front of him, it would have sounded sexy as hell, but through the phone, it sounds awful.

"Okay, creepy breather dude."

He laughs on the other end of the phone and the line goes dead.

I look at my phone. Becca has sent a string of messages and I bypass them all in favor of Dyson's. Opening it, I type out one word.

Dyson

DYSON
Slip - Elliot Moss

My morning sucks.

I flew back to Phoenix early, wanting to drive Ireland to her first day of work because I wanted to see her and wish her good luck in person and I missed her. The train ride from her apartment downtown isn't all that long, but I should have known she would have left early. That's the kind of woman she is.

I'm buried up to my elbows in paperwork, emails, spreadsheets, all of it, but concentrating is impossible knowing she's right downstairs. I already have an excuse to go down there. Wellington and I need to talk. At least, we will.

I'm about to call out to my secretary to order some lunch when Charlie and Mick walk into my office. "Well, this is odd," I mutter. "What are you two doing here? I thought we were meeting Thursday?"

"There's a problem," Charlie states deadpan. A problem coming from my lawyer and advisor is hardly a good sign.

I close the door behind them and with the flip of the switch turn the glass opaque. "I'm all ears."

"What do you know about Ireland?"

I sit in a chair opposite them as they sit on the couch across from me. Charlie has a thick folder in his hand and Mick has brought his messenger bag. This is not good.

"I sort of grew up with her from when I was about eleven until I was seventeen. After that I moved to Atlanta and I didn't see her again until two weeks ago. Why, what is it the two of you are not telling me?"

"I can't tell you anything, really," Mick says.

"Well then, why the fuck are you here?" I snap, my irritation growing

at the two of them and I want to smash their heads together.

"Let's just say you're not the only one looking for Ireland McKidd." Mick's voice is hesitant.

"Fuck, Mick, what the ever loving hell?"

He puts his hands up. "I'm bound to secrecy until I speak with Ms. McKidd."

"He's right," Charlie cuts in. "It's a long standing contract and violation of it means more than you can even afford to pay."

"So then, why are you here?" My stare grows hard as I look at Mick. We have a mutual connection, though I can't fathom what the hell that connection has to do with this, but something tells me it does.

"What do you know about her father?" Mick asks me.

"Nothing," I say, exasperated. "He wasn't around when I met Ireland, her mother, and her brother. I just know he was gone. From the way they talked about him, he's dead."

I watch both men carefully as they look at each other. They more or less shrug and let it go. "Do I need to call her up here?" I ask. "She's right downstairs."

"She's working here?" Mick asks me. His tone tells me he's shocked by this new development.

"No, she's working for Wellington, today's her first day." I stand up and head toward my sideboard. I need a fucking drink. These two are seriously pissing me the fuck off. "Is there anything you can tell me since you came all the way here to fucking play games with me?"

"Her father isn't dead," Mick says and I nearly drop my glass as I turn around to glare at him.

"What does that mean, exactly?"

"It means exactly that. He's not dead, but I highly doubt she has any clue who he is."

"Yeah, because that clears shit up." I let my mind wander a moment and curiosity burns hot when I realize neither one of them have brought

up Dusty. "What about Dusty? Why don't you want to talk to him?"

"Because he is her half-brother."

"Fuck. Does she know this?"

They both shake their heads. "Not that we can tell. I don't think either one of them know anything. But her mother's death has opened a can of worms we need to work on closing up as soon as possible and I still have a mountain of investigating to do." Mick looks at me, pleading with me to let this go. Telling me, without actually saying anything, he regrets coming here to interrogate me.

"Well, if you don't want her up here now, when?"

"Give me 'til Thursday?" he asks. "I will already be here to handle your situation with her, so let me get my ducks in a row. I will be here Thursday and with her permission, we will fill you in as well."

"Mick, if you didn't know where all the bodies are buried, I'd fucking fire you for this," I tell him with a glare.

"Understood. But you don't have anywhere near the amount of bodies piling up that I do. So let's just let this go." I give him a hard stare. "For now," he tacks on.

I pull a deep breath into my lungs and let it out before closing my eyes and nodding. "I don't like being kept in the dark."

"We know," Charlie pipes up. "But you need to understand that the ramifications of this fuck up will cost all of us more than we're capable of giving."

"Tell me one thing; is she a mobster's daughter or something like that?"

"No, more legitimate and legal than that," Mick states sincerely.

"Fine," I huff. "Anything else, gentlemen?" My irritation with both of them is through the roof and I don't even know why I'm so fucking pissed off.

IRELAND
Still Falling For You - Elle Goulding

By one o'clock, I am famished and my first day is nearly over, but it's been an amazing first day. I spent a good portion of the morning with human resources going over things that couldn't be discussed until today and I have a mountain of shit to look at when I can find some free time out of the office.

I'd gotten around to looking at Becca's text messages, there were four of them. First, she started off pissed, blaming me for not being around for her since I ran into Dyson and that eventually led to an apology. She wants to get together for dinner and it's killing me to tell her I already have plans. But with Becca, she's usually happy with an alternative.

Ireland: I have plans tonight, sorry, made them over the weekend, but we can do lunch anytime this week (tho I only have an hour) or we can have dinner Wednesday night?

Becca: It's okay, I got called into work for tonight, Wed is fine.

Ireland: going out or staying in.

Becca: Will you make chili?

Ireland: Sure. I'll put it in before I leave for work.

I don't get a reply, so I text Dyson.

Off work at five.

His reply comes quickly:

Good, I will meet you in the lobby.

Ireland: Why don't I just come to your office? Apparently I have a very special elevator keycard.

Dyson: Don't know what you're talking about.

Ireland: Are you always this controlling?

Dyson: Always.

Ireland: Figures.

Dyson: I can't help it. I want you to be able to come up to my office anytime you wish.

Ireland: How about now?

Dyson: What are you wearing?

I laugh, but reply without thinking.

Pantsuit.

Dyson: Get up here, now.

Ireland: Okay, Mr. Crazy Control Freak.

Dyson: Say my name.

I step into the elevator and smile down at my phone as I'm pulled up a few floors to the penthouse level and the elevator opens. The office is very white, with black and silver accents everywhere. Tile floors with silver desks. The receptionist greets me, "Can I help you?"

"Ireland McKidd for Mr. Cole," I tell her smoothly.

"Go on back, follow the hallway." She points to my left, her right, and I nod a thanks. My heels click across the tile floor and the room is eerily quiet. The last thing I want to do is trip or slip because everyone will hear. Once I'm around the corner, I pick up my pace a little bit. As soon

as my feet hit dark grey carpet I come to another open area.

"Ms. McKidd, Mr. Cole is expecting you."

A tall, lanky, yet not at all unattractive man greets me. "Uh, thank you," I say, surprised by the fact he knows who I am. He comes around the desk and ushers me toward a solid black glass wall and the door opens. I expect Dyson to step out, but there is no one there. I step inside his office. It's the same décor as the rest of the office, only this one has more black in the furniture, giving it a very contemporary yet powerful feel.

My eyes roam around the room until they meet a pair of blue-violet eyes staring at me. His eyes roam up and down my body and just the fact that he has his eyes on me is making me wet and my skin heats. He's got his suit jacket off, the Dyson standard vest on and his sleeves are rolled up. His tie is still pristine and perfect. My mouth waters as I watch him talk on the phone.

"Fine, no, I have to go. I have more important matters in my office. Thank you." He hangs up and stares at me like I'm his last meal. There is a clicking behind me followed by a gentle whirling sound and I turn just enough to see the door closing. I look back at him as a click slides a lock home in the door. "How long do you have?"

I look down at my phone, it's one fifteen. "Forty-five minutes."

"Have you eaten?"

I shake my head. "I was gonna go across the street and grab a bite."

He stands up and I get the full Dyson effect when I can see, despite the rolled up sleeves, he's every bit the CEO I met downstairs a couple weeks ago – sans jacket. The only real difference is his eyes are no longer angry. They're full of hunger and desire and they are ravaging my body as he approaches me.

Chapter Twenty-Six

IRELAND
Fumbling Toward Ecstasy - Sarah McLachlin

"I have to go back to work," I remind him and I put my hand up, but he doesn't stop, and I don't want him too. The hunger in his eyes is setting my insides on fire.

"And?" He wiggles his eyebrows and I giggle.

"And, I don't need to look like I've just had sex in the boss's office."

He smirks, "But I'm not your boss."

"Technically. But I am assigned to a Tigress project."

"I'd rather you be assigned to me, personally." He takes my face in his hands and slides up close to me. Our bodies melt together. I breathe in through my nose and the scent that is all Dyson fogs up my brain and I know I'm going to give him whatever he's after. "You look amazing." His voice is soft, reverent and my heart skips a beat. "You should wear suits more often." His lips brush against mine.

"This is the only one I own," I mutter.

"We're going to have to fix that. You're all power and sex and more power. You wear them well."

"And you're buttering me up so you can buy me more clothes, aren't you?" I raise an eyebrow at him.

He chuckles softly before claiming my lips with his. My body turns liquid at his touch and presses tighter against him. My brain short circuits and the only thing I can think about is having him between my legs. I pull back and ask, "So you missed me?"

His soft, soundless laughter blows hot huffs of air across my face. "You have no idea and I can't wait until dinner. I need you now."

"We're at work, Dyson."

"No, I'm at work, you're on lunch. But you can keep saying my name."

His hands roam from my cheeks, down my neck to my shoulders where he hooks my jacket with his thumbs and he starts to slide it down

my shoulders. The gentle warmth of his fingers sends goosebumps across my flesh and my nipples harden. He presses his erection into me, reminding me he wants this as much as I obviously seem to. He frees my hands from the jacket and I wrap them around his neck and pull his lips back to mine. My body ignites to the point of no return. The world around us falls away and it's just him and me, alone, in a room, ready to tear each other's clothes off. He releases me, steps back and gently lays my jacket over the back of one of the chairs.

"As much as I want your perfect nipples in my mouth, I'm going to fuck you, bent over the couch, hard and fast."

My breathing hitches and my mouth falls slack. His eyes narrow, hooded and dangerous. My brain is on the fritz as I stare at his gorgeous face and watch him undo the fly of his slacks, pull his shirt out, and lowers his pants and boxer briefs to his knees. His cock is on full display and I lick my lips. The idea of Dyson fucking me while mostly dressed sends a new wave of desire straight to my core and my pussy clenches around nothing, desperate to feel him.

I go for the hook and zipper of my pants, pulling my camisole from inside and revealing the white lace panties that match the bra I'm wearing and his eyes darken further.

I step around the couch, so that I'm standing behind it, but then decide on something different entirely. Taking back a little control, I walk up to his desk and lower my pants as I lean over. My ass is on display for him, showing him my wet sex and he hisses. I smile and lower my head. The next thing I know, Dyson slams into me and I start to cry out, but stop.

"Oh no, this room is soundproof."

"Oh fuck," I groan when he slams back into me.

"I like it when you say that word." He pulls back and slams in again. My pussy clenches down and pleasure explodes in my body and I know this won't take long. Not in the slightest.

He grabs hold of my hips, holding tightly to my flesh as he guides me up and down his cock and my eyes roll up. My body starts to lock up,

each thrust draws me closer. Sensing I need a little more, he releases one hip and brings his hand around to my clit. His fingers stroke me. "I'm so fucking close," he breathes. "Come on, baby, give it to me."

Then he pinches my clit between his fingers and stars ignite behind my eyelids and my legs shake as my orgasm consumes me.

"Oh, god!" he cries out and I feel him empty himself inside me.

Dyson helped me off his desk and into the bathroom to clean up after our desktop tryst. But it doesn't matter how long I stand here, the redness in my cheeks won't go away. Giving up, I leave the bathroom with my camisole tucked in and my pants back where they belong. Opening the door, an aroma that makes my mouth water hits me. "That smells amazing." There's a spicy mix in the air that reminds me of Indian food. He's sitting at the bar in his office. There is a small fridge, sink and a microwave. It's hardly a kitchen but it's set off, out of the line of sight from the door.

"Come, eat."

"I'm not eating your lunch." I reach for my jacket.

"You don't have time to go get anything else. Come on, there is plenty and I already made you a plate." I roll my eyes but go sit next to him. It smells wonderful and I can't help myself.

I take a bite of the rice on my plate and my mouth explodes with wonderful flavors and a little spice. "Wow," I say as I grab for the glass of water in front of me. "That's amazing."

"Good." He smiles and we eat in silence. Though it's not awkward, considering we just had sex, on his desk, in his office. I blush at the thought and I can't stop my eyes from wandering over to it. It brings a smile to my face. He notices but doesn't say anything. He can't hide his little smirk when he realizes I keep looking at.

"I've always wanted to do that," he mumbles under his breath.

I look at him in surprise. "You mean to tell me you've never had sex on your desk before?"

"Or my office." He leans in closer. "Or my own bed." His voice is so full of promise the desire I'd suppressed in the bathroom comes roaring back and I want to take him back to his house and christen his bed.

I lean in and whisper, "Mine either."

"So whose bed do we break in first?"

"Yours," I answer. "I want to see your place."

"I'll take you after dinner."

I shiver rocks through me at the promise of tonight. Dinner and his place. Dinner, his place and Dyson between my legs.

I look at the clock on the microwave. "Is that accurate?" My eyes widen.

"It is," he says, looking at me. I have about five minutes to get back to work. "I have to go."

I stand and go to my jacket, pulling it on and pulling my hair out from underneath it and look at him. His eyes almost look sad. "What's wrong?"

He gives me a sad smile. "I don't want you to leave."

"I have to go back to work," I tell him and he comes up to me and wraps me in a hug. I wrap my arms around his neck. "Three hours, baby." I smile and press my lips to his. He tries to push the kiss deeper and I stop him. He pouts, literally. I kiss his pouty lip and leave him to his office as I go back to work.

The next three hours pass by surprisingly fast. I get a chance to meet the rest of my team I'll be working with. They all seem really nice and very welcoming. As the day draws to a close, I'm glad the first day is over and I'm surprised by how exhausted I feel.

At three minutes to five, my phone chimes with a text from Dyson:

Meet me downstairs. If you come to my office again, we'll never leave.

I smile at my phone a goofy, smitten smile.

"I know that look," Shelly says and my eyes snap up to hers.

"I'm sorry, I…"

"Oh, stop. We're not crazy phone Nazis around here," she laughs. "Besides, judging from the look on your face, that's got to be a new boyfriend or someone you're hopelessly in love with." She sits down in a chair across from my desk, yes, my own desk, but not my own office. I share the room with three other people, but they're early birds so they're out the door by four-thirty. I blush. "That's what I thought," she says and her smile is genuine as she sits up a little straighter. "So, how'd your first day go?" she asks. I smile wider.

"Really good. I'm really excited to be here. Everyone was really nice, friendly and welcoming. I think we're going to get along well."

"Good," she says and she stands to leave. "See you tomorrow. Eight, right?"

"Yup, I'll be here."

"Have a good night." She waves as she leaves my office, headed for hers. That was kind of odd, but I don't dwell on it too much as I grab my bag from the drawer. I debate on swapping out my heels for my walking shoes. I flex my toes, checking to see how sore they are and realize they're not that bad and I'm not walking home, so I grab my stuff, and throw my bag over my shoulder, lock up my desk and computer and head for the door.

"Finally." I hear a voice; it's distant but sounds a lot like Shelly.

"What are you talking about?" Fuck, I know that voice. It's Dyson.

"You've come to take me to dinner," Shelly says back to him and I want to roll my eyes. She sounds desperate.

"Uh, no. Not now, not ever." I smile at his rejection of her.

"Oh, I'll make you change your mind." I put my finger in my mouth like I'm going to make myself puke.

"Shelly, I'm with someone." My heart soars.

"No, you're not." She snorts a laugh. "Dyson Cole doesn't date." Her voice is high-pitched, like she's some debutante working her way up the chain of men. Dyson's words from this weekend come back to me- "*The socialite housewife is not the kind of woman I want in my bed every night.*" And that is exactly what she sounds like. I have no doubt Shelly has money, whether it's been earned or given to her, I don't know, but she reminds me of the type always looking for more.

"I do and I am. Now if you'll excuse me."

"No, don't go, I'm sorry, let me start over." I shake my head. I should walk away, but it's like a train wreck and I have to watch, or in this case, listen.

"No, end of discussion. Now knock this shit off or I'll get your boss involved. I'm pretty sure you don't want that to happen, do you?"

"You're an ass," Shelly snaps and I chuckle before ducking back into my office and hiding behind the door. The lights are off, so it's dark in here and Dyson won't be able to see me if he passes by my office.

"You have no idea," Dyson replies to her. His voice is hard, cold, and I understand exactly what he's trying to do. He's letting me stake my claim on him without being there to do so and it makes me smile.

A few moments later someone breezes past my office door, deeper into the office and away from the elevators. I catch a glimpse of a dark suit, but it's gone before I can even see who it is. Seeing my chance, I sneak around the door and toward the hallway.

"Did it work?" A voice I don't recognize asks.

"No." It's Shelly who replies, she almost sounds dejected.

"What the fuck, Shelly?"

"Don't yell…" A door clicks closed and I can no longer hear the conversation. It didn't sound like it was coming from Shelly's office, which is between my office and the elevators. Not knowing where they are exactly stops me from going in search of them. I don't want to get caught snooping around.

I wait another minute or two, at least this way I can pretend like I

forgot something if someone sees me. As I'm about to slip out of my office, my phone buzzes in my hand. It's Dyson:

On my way down.

Shit. I move quickly toward the elevator. Shelly's office door is open and her office is empty, it makes me wonder if Dyson was coming to get me when she accosted him with her unsuccessful proposal for dinner. I keep walking, quickly as to not get caught by Shelly and whoever else is still in the office. The receptionist is gone, most of the offices are shut up and dark. Five o'clock warriors – gone before the minute hand reaches twelve.

I press the down button and wait a moment before it dings. The doors slide open and the car is empty, except for one, lone, sexy as hell, dark suit wearing Dyson Cole, who is leaning his hand on the bar along the back wall. His other hand is in his pocket; his legs are crossed at the ankles. He looks like he's just crawled out of a GQ Magazine spread. I stop breathing and stare. My jaw falls slack. He smirks, cocking his head and his hair falls down into his eye as he does it. The cover model image is complete. My sex heats. "Sex on legs," I mutter under my breath without realizing I'm saying it out loud.

He shakes his head in disbelief before reaching out to stop the closing elevator doors. "Are you coming?" he asks.

"Not yet." I smirk back at him.

"Well, well, my tigress is alive and well." I smile at the nickname and his catching of my innuendo. "So, Ms. McKidd, shall we skip dinner?"

"Yes," I breathe as the doors close and Dyson pounces on me, pressing me against the wall. He pulls my arms above my head and holds them in one hand, while his other hand slides up my body, cupping my breast and finding my nipple and rolling it between his fingers. My jacket, bra and camisole make his touch hard to feel but impossible to ignore.

"My place or yours?" he breathes against my lips.

"Mine," I say hotly.

"Why yours? I thought you wanted to see my place."

"No tours necessary." I lean my head forward, trying to catch his lips. He hasn't kissed me and yet he has me trussed up against the wall, and I need his lips. I need his kiss.

"Oh, there will be a tour." He tilts his head, like he's positioning me for a kiss. "It will just be my tongue touring your body."

"Dyson," I moan and the elevator slows to a stop. He releases me quickly, stepping back as if he hadn't just had me pinned against the wall.

"Fuck." His voice is breathy, hot, and my insides quiver. I try to find my brain enough to straighten myself out before the doors open.

Completely and totally unaffected. Yup, that's me. *Not.*

Chapter Twenty-Seven

DYSON
A Beautiful Mess - Jason Mraz

"How many cars do you own?" she asks as she takes in the sleek black Nissan Murano in the parking garage.

"A few," I tell her. "This is more my everyday car."

"What happened to the Tesla?"

I smile at her. "Nothing, she's at home. I haven't gotten around to having a charging station installed here. Once I do, I'll drive her more. You just got lucky that I happened to be driving her before." I wink and open the door for her. She slides in, setting her bag between her legs and reaching for her seatbelt as I close the door.

My heart sank when the elevator came to a stop on Wellington's floor. I panicked that it was Shelly trying to accost me again. When will that fucking woman get it through her head? *Never.* I shake my head and climb into the SUV. "What's wrong?" she asks me.

"Nothing, I'm just irritated."

"Did I do something?" she asks, her voice full of concern and I shake my head before pressing the ignition and starting the car. "Does it have anything to do with what happened a few minutes ago?"

My eyes shoot to hers and narrow in suspicion. "Spying on me?"

She snorts. "Hardly. I was leaving my office when I heard her. I didn't think anything of it until I heard your voice and I froze. What were you doing there anyway?"

My mind races through the conversation. Shit. What did I say to Shelly? "I had a meeting with Wellington that ran over," I explain.

"I'm not mad at you," she clarifies for me. "In fact, I'm..." she pauses and I see the flush of her cheeks, "I feel championed, vindicated and like I actually have a claim on you, even if I couldn't do it myself. Regardless of whether or not she knows you're talking about me." She turns to me, shock on her face. "Wait, you were talking about me, weren't you?"

I watch as shock rounds out her eyes, then worry raises her eyebrows

and then a huge smile spreads across her face as I'm about to go ballistic. She knows damn well I was talking about her. "Gotcha," she teases and I relax. "She's a bitch."

"You can say that again. I'd had a meeting with Wellington, and when I was leaving she caught me on my way to the elevator." I finally pull my eyes away from her and put the car in reverse, backing out of the parking stall.

"No, I mean it. Something is seriously up with her."

"What do you mean?" I ask without looking over at her.

"After you left, someone else came down the hall before I could escape. They had on a dark suit. I thought I recognized the voice, but I wasn't sure."

"What did they say?" I ask her as I pull onto Central Avenue, headed north toward home.

"That's it, I don't really know. He asked her something about it working. 'Did it work?' I think. Then when she said no, she almost sounded disappointed. I wouldn't have thought anymore about it except the fact that the guy got pissed and said something to the effect of 'what the fuck, Shelly' and she got defensive, told him to stop yelling, but then the door closed and cut off whatever was said after that. I'm not really sure where the sound was coming from, so I didn't go looking for it."

"Huh," I say, but the wheels are turning in my head.

"You don't think she's trying to play you or something, do you?" she asks me, concern coloring her tone.

I bring my eyes to meet hers briefly before returning my focus to the busy road. "I don't know. Maybe. Though I'm not entirely sure what she'd be playing me for."

"Money? Sex? A leg up in the business world? You name it; she'd be able to find a motive."

"She has money and I'm not sure how much higher in the business world she's gonna get. She's about to make partner at Wellington."

"Oh," she says, surprised.

"As for sex, I don't know if I've ever met anyone who didn't want sex."

"That's because you're a walking sex god." She slaps her hand over her mouth and my lips twitch in a smile.

"Am I now?" I tease her right back.

"Yup," she says through her hand, muffling it.

I burst out laughing, "Well, it's good to know you think so."

"Oh, I know I'm not the only one," she tells me, then without prompting adds, "She's jealous."

"Who, Shelly?" I ask for clarification.

"No, Becca." She turns back toward the front of the car, staring out the windshield.

"Why makes you say that?" I ask.

"She told me. That's why she's been a bitch the last week or so and why I haven't seen her."

"What exactly does she have to be jealous of?" I raise an eyebrow in wonder as I pull up to a stoplight and look over at her.

"You," she says so matter of fact it makes me feel like I should know this already.

"What did I do?" I follow up, prompting her to talk a little more.

"In my opinion or in hers?"

"Why don't we start with yours?"

"Then nothing. Well, not intentionally. Becca is the clingy type. Well, until she gets what she wants. She took your dancing with her seriously and she's jealous because I captured your attention and not her."

"I never even had eyes for her."

She snorts a laugh, "I know that. I know you were just using her to rile me up. Which worked, by the way."

I smirk at her and the light changes. "I know. My balls still hurt," I

tease.

"Want me to kiss them all better?"

Her candor throws me off guard and I let out a rushed breath at the idea of Ireland kissing my balls better. She bursts out laughing, "I'm sorry, I don't even know where that came from."

We both end up laughing for a minute as we draw closer to a choice. "Left or right?"

"What?"

"Which way, Ireland? Left or right?"

She smiles at me, then without prompting puts her hand on my thigh and slides it up until her fingers tickle along my cock. "Left," she smirks and pulls her hand away.

"Fucking, tigress," I grumble and step on the gas. Turning left, away from her apartment and toward mine.

IRELAND
Like A Wrecking Ball - Eric Church

When we pull into Dyson's complex parking lot, he points out Cami and Tristan's house. "I knew they lived over here, just not exactly where," I tell him and he smiles. The mention of Cami and Tristan reminds me I still need to apologize to Cami for kissing Tristan at the bar that night.

Dyson pulls into the garage next to his gorgeous Tesla and I can't stop staring at it. If I had a car, I'd want one of those, though I'd never be able to afford it, so it's - to use Reese's favorite word - moot.

"You sure you want to be here?" Dyson asks me. "I don't want to interrupt your plans or anything." His wink is cute and full of promise.

"Too late, we're already here." I shrug. I can wait a few minutes to attack him, right?

"And we won't be leaving. I'm going to order dinner in."

I blush. "I like the sound of that."

"Good." He climbs out of the car and walks around to my side to help me out. I climb out then gesture for him to lead on. It's his house after all.

There are three doors on the backside of the garage opposite where we pulled in. He picks the one in the middle. Then points to the one on the right. "That one leads to a different floor," Is the explanation he offers me before he leads me down a flight of stairs and into a room that reminds me of the penthouse's game room. It's pretty much the full size of the townhouse. From the outside, these buildings look like apartments, but in our search to find someplace to live, Becca and I discovered these are not apartments but rather very expensive condos. "The party room," he tells me.

"It doesn't look any different than the penthouse game room."

He snorts. "No, except there aren't as many goodies down here as there are in New York." I look around the room some more and on the far side is a wide patio door that leads out into a courtyard of sorts. It looks like the perfect place for warm winter nights. "Come on." He takes my hand and leads me into a little hallway that turns back around and leads to a set of stairs. The stairs are longer than most, but shallow as they lead up to the next floor. The next floor is mostly doors. "This floor is mostly for house staff."

"Oh, is Kathy here?"

He smiles, "No, she should be back tomorrow or Wednesday. She stays in New York to clean up after me and then spends some time with her family. Then she comes here."

"Oh," What else am I supposed to say to that?

"Byron's here though." I smile at the thought of the burly man who works for Dyson.

"Why doesn't he drive you to work?"

"He usually does, but I gave him the day off."

"So you could pick me up this morning?" I'm reminded of what seems like ages ago, but was really only this morning.

"Exactly." He winks and leads me up another staircase like the first. The stairs seem to spread the entire length of the house, which I find to be an odd waste of space, but then again, I don't have millions of dollars to purchase a place to live.

The next floor is a little more formal, but still homey in a way. Dyson's tastes for white, black and silver from his office extend over to his house with black leather sofas, a black dining room high top table, and silver fixtures. The entire floor is done in a pearl white tile that is a bit iridescent showing off different colors as you move throughout the room. The kitchen is state of the art and drool worthy with an oversized chrome fridge, double oven and an eight burner cooktop set in an island in the middle. "Wow," I breathe.

"You like to cook?"

I smile a little secret smile. "I love to cook."

"You any good at it?"

I scoff playfully at him. "Men and their love of food." He snorts and shrugs his shoulders, "um, Becca refuses to cook because she says that compared to my food, hers tastes like cardboard." I scrunch up my nose, "she's right."

"Well then, you're going to have to cook me dinner sometime."

I raise both my eyebrows, "oh really?"

"Yup, but not tonight," he smirks and leads me toward another staircase that leads us up to another floor.

"How many floors are there?" I ask him.

"Five. The game room, which is technically below ground. The house staff area is actually the same floor the garage is on, that door you saw?" I nod. "Then the main floor has a stairwell that leads to the front door that's on the side of the garage." He points down a hallway. "But I don't use it much," he says by way of explanation as to why we didn't just come in that way. "The next floor is a bedroom floor. It has my office, plus two

other bedrooms, but the level is mostly unused. Then the top floor," he explains as he pulls me up the second set of stairs, away from his office level. "Is my room." he finishes as he lets me enter first.

I climb the stairs and slowly the light comes into view. It only takes me a moment to realize one whole wall of his bedroom is glass. Though the landscape isn't drop dead impressive, it affords a better view of the Central Avenue area of Phoenix. It's gorgeous nonetheless. "What is it with you and massive windows?" I tease him.

"I don't like feeling trapped inside," he shares and while I can tell he knows I was teasing, the honesty of his statement is not lost on me. I can understand not wanting to feel that way. I smile in understanding and take in the rest of the room.

"Not much of a decorator?" I smirk.

"Ha, no," he laughs. "I like things simple."

"Then what are you doing with me?"

He saunters toward me and I take a step back. The look in his eyes is predatory and he has me cornered. "I like you wild and crazy, a princess and a tigress all at the same time."

"Kiss ass," I quip and he envelopes me in his arms, burying his face in my neck and hair and I hear his deep inhale as he pulls me into his body much the same way I do with him.

"The only ass I will ever kiss, princess, is yours."

"I hope so," I laugh and he lifts his eyes to mine. "Kiss me," I breathe.

"Your wish is my command, princess."

With that he claims my mouth with his own and my desire explodes in my veins. The next thing I know, we're both naked and landing on the bed. Dyson is on top of me and I push on his shoulder, rolling him onto his back. Our eyes meet and my body ignites when I feel his cock between my legs and I flick my hips. His cock rubs along my clit and pleasure pools in my core. I need him, want him and he's not stopping me from taking him.

His hands slide up my body from my thighs, over my hips, up my sides leaving goosebumps in his wake and I shiver. My nipples harden into tight elongated peaks and he rears up. He snakes an arm around my waist, holding me to him and his mouth finds a nipple and he sucks it in, sucking and nibbling on it. He lets it go with an audible pop. "I fucking love everything about you, but these," his tongue flicks out, catching my nipple, "are my fucking favorite." His breath is cool against the wetness surrounding my nipple from his mouth and I shiver. "Right up there next to these." His lips slant over mine again, his movement causing his cock to move between us and I writhe against him. My arms going around his neck, holding him to me and his other hand slides down between us. He moves his cock out from between us and I feel it bounce back against my ass cheek and settling along my crack and the sensation against my second entrance sends a new wave of pleasure into my already heightened senses and I moan into his mouth. "One day, princess." He smiles against our lips and I raise myself up, allowing him to position himself against my entrance and I slide down on his cock.

His eyes roll up, his hand on my back tightens then slides up into my hair. With his hand splayed wide, he tugs, pulling my head back, exposing my neck and his lips find the exposed flesh and I cry out when he slides all the way home. The roughness of the smattering of pubic hair he has brushes against my clit adding yet a whole new sensation and another thing to make my head swim.

The sensations on my neck and being held in his grasp are nearly enough to make me come undone. He brings his other hand around my body and he cups my breast, squeezing it, finding my nipple and rolling it. The sensation is too much and I rock my hips. My pussy clamps down and I have to move. With my hands on his shoulders, he releases my hair and I steady myself. I lift myself up and slide back down his shaft while his mouth works over my chest, from shoulder to nipple and back again.

"Oh god," I cry out when the pleasure becomes too much and my legs start to lock up on me. I start bucking on him harder. Grinding out my orgasm, praying he joins me.

"Give it to me, Ireland."

My name on his lips is my undoing and my orgasm consumes me as he grunts out his own

Chapter Twenty-Eight

IRELAND

Fear - Sarah McLachlin

Dyson left me naked in his bed while he donned a pair of flannel pajama bottoms to go order dinner. After we'd cleaned up, he pulled the covers back, and I laid back down on my stomach and he covered me with the sheet. The sheet stops at my hip leaving the rest of me exposed. I don't know why I am so comfortable being naked around Dyson, considering I'm more coherent naked than when we're fully dressed. Then again, when we're naked, it usually means I've just be sated. Though that's a loose interpretation of the word because around him, I'm never fully satisfied. I always want more.

He has this amazing ability to make me feel complete and while I truly enjoyed our first time – not all girls can say that – I never knew it could be better than that and I'm thankful I saved myself for Dyson. Because no matter where or how, he never fails to make me feel amazing, even with quick, hot as hell fucking in his office.

The memory sends a shiver over me and my nipples harden. They're tender from all his attention to them and the tiny bite of pain makes them harden farther.

DYSON

I called out for dinner then called Byron and, asked if he could pick it up and he was all too eager. I know Byron well enough to know I've made him twitchy all day. He doesn't like being away from me and most importantly, he doesn't like not having anything to do. I did hear he and Tyson – Tristan's security guy – have become friends over the past few months. Byron owns an old Harley he's been working on fixing up, so I think that's what they do when I'm not keeping Byron busy or Tyson's not off with Cami and Tristan.

When I climb back up the stairs to my bedroom, my phone rings and Mick's name flashes on the screen. Shit. I reach the top of the steps and look over at the goddess lying in my bed. She really looks like one. Her red hair is splayed down her back, the sheet covers her gorgeous butt and hips, but she's lying on her side, so I can't really see her face. My phone stops ringing and I'm glad I missed it.

Ireland has one arm outstretched, the other wrapped around a pillow and she's looking at something on her phone as I approach. It takes me a minute to realize she's reading to pass the time and I smile, until my phone rings again. Mick's name flashes. "Sorry, baby, I apparently need to take this."

She gives me a salacious smile and chirps, "Go ahead, I'm good."

"Thanks," I tell her and run back down the stairs. "What?" I snap into the phone as I round the corner, headed for my office.

"Well, aren't we punchy tonight?"

"You didn't exactly leave me with a whole lot of warm fuzziness in my office today and now you've called me, twice. What's going on?" I step into my office and close the door.

"I think we need to meet before Thursday." My eyes shoot to the ceiling. I'm just about directly underneath her and my heart pounds a little harder in my chest.

"You called me twice to say this? Seriously? Charlie won't be ready until Thursday and I'm not…no, because you know what? Whatever the fuck it is you're hiding I get the impression is going to fuck with her head. If one happens before the other, then something isn't going to happen."

"I can work with Charlie, push it up to tomorrow."

"No," I snap. "She has plans tomorrow night and I'm not going to ruin them for her."

"Wednesday?"

"Why are you in such a hurry to shatter this woman's world, Mick? I mean, seriously?"

"Because I've been holding on to this secret for twenty-five fucking years, I'm tired of it," he bellows. "My wife is about to leave me because I haven't been able to tell her a fucking thing and that's not fair. I'm tired."

"I hate to break it to you, Mick, she looks nothing like you."

He sighs. "She's not mine."

"Well, someone must trust you a whole lot to keep this kind of a secret that you would beat around the bush when it comes to me, but yet you're eager to tell her."

He sighs, "She's not the only person I have to tell this secret to. So please, don't push this, for me."

"What the fuck, Mick? You do realize I'm perfectly capable of shouldering this burden too."

"I know, but…" For a second I think he's going to give in, going to tell me everything. "I can't," he says instead.

"Alright, I won't push it. I don't like it, but I'm not going to push it anymore. I just need you to be a little more open with me, got it?"

"Yeah, listen, I'm sorry I snapped. It's been a hell of a few weeks."

I get it, despite the fact I don't know what the hell is going on. "Couple more days, and then you can be free of it."

"Thanks," he says and hangs up.

In an effort to calm down a little, I pace my office floor. Something that usually does the trick, but not tonight. I know I'm missing something. Somewhere in the back of my mind I'm reminded of Mick's background check. I go to my filing safe and punch in the code. *032491.*

It beeps and I pull it up, fingering through the folders until I come across the B's and Bass, Mick Bass.

Mick has worked for me for a few years, since shortly after the inception of Tigress, though he doesn't work for Tigress, he works for me. Which means I had his background check done when he was originally hired and then updated annually. The man is dealing with my finances. I need to make sure he's squeaky fucking clean. He's always come up that way.

His income has grown over the years, but everything I could tie to his bank account, I could tie to his taxes. He is a legitimate business man who easily made seven figures a year. Though his client list is small.

I look back over that list, hoping to see something that might stick out. There are two names I recognize on this list, and they're the mutual connection Mick and I have. Cameron (Cami) and Tristan Michaels.

A couple other names I recognize through business dealings, and then the last name on the list causes me to narrow my eyes- Robert Enders Estate.

That name sounds familiar, but I haven't a clue where or why. I rack my brain trying to figure it out but decide it's not worth the headache it's going to cause me and my girl is upstairs waiting for me. I put the file back and move to close up the drawer, but I stop when my eyes land on another file in the drawer. I don't pull it out, but instead I slam the draw closed and lock it up. That files been updated annually since I had the means to update it, but I've never actually looked in the file. I couldn't bring myself to look. I was afraid to find something I didn't want to see, like she got married, had children, or something else, something worse. It was sitting on my desk the day I ran into her. It was sitting there waiting for me to grow a pair of balls and look at it. Byron had recently updated it for me. As in, three days before.

I shake off the file folder, the one with Ireland Vyolet McKidd stamped across the tab, and leave my office in favor of my bedroom and the gorgeous redhead occupying my bed.

IRELAND
Stay With Me - Sam Smith

"Where are you going?" Dyson asks when I crawl out of bed. He had Byron bring us Fajitas for dinner since we never got to actually eat our food there last week. It was fun to sit around and bullshit with Byron,

who joined us for dinner. The man is a beast, but he's as sweet as a teddy bear. He and Dyson have been a team for the last six years after someone had sent Dyson death threats. It turned out to be bogus in the end, but Dyson hired him on full time.

"I need to go home. I have to work tomorrow." I wink at him.

"But I want you to stay here," he whines.

"Oh my god, are you actually whining?" I tease him.

"Yes, stay here."

"I have no clothes to wear for work tomorrow."

"So, we can leave here early, stop by your house, you can change and I'll take you to work."

"I'm pretty sure that cuts into the 'no fraternization' rules at work, doesn't it?"

"Fuck the rules. I'll give you a job." He rolls over, wraps his arms around my waist and holds me in the bed. I'd laugh if I didn't think his whining was so cute.

"So you say. But I get the impression that if I go to work for you that you'll be paying me for my body and not my mind," I tease and place my hand over his arm. "What time do you have to be in tomorrow?" I ask. "Never mind, you're the boss."

He chuckles behind me. "I am, so a better question is, what time do you have to be in?" He ignores the comment about paying me for my body. I haven't made it through an entire work day without being bent over his desk. The memory sends a shiver up my spine despite the fact we came back to bed after dinner and he ravished my body with his mouth and cock. It was delicious and I'm sore all over, but in the most delectable ways.

"Eight," I tell him, answering his question and tramping down thoughts of having Dyson inside me again. "And it's nearly midnight, you fiend." I laugh and he lets me go, but he makes no move to get up to take me home. "You're really going to make me walk home?"

ZOEY DERRICK

"Nope, you're staying."

"Oh really?" I raise an eyebrow at him. "And what makes you think you can convince me to stay?"

"Oh, not me." His eyes meet mine and they're alight with humor. He throws the covers off himself and his cock is standing at attention ready for another round. "But I'm sure he can."

My eyes travel down his body, taking in the sight of his hard length, ready and willing for more. "You insatiable fiend."

"Only for you, princess." He winks and I lick my lips as his cock jumps with his movement. He gets off the bed. "I'm going to take a shower. You can either join me and my cock or you can lay here and sulk that my cock is in the shower without you."

I snort, "I'm pretty sure he's the one that will be sulking."

"Touché," he chuckles as he walks into his enormous bathroom. I bite my lip, mulling over my options. Stay here, sleep with him and go home in the morning, or go home alone.

Without a second thought, I follow him into the shower.

His alarm starts blaring and I groan, rolling over and wrapping my arms around him as he reaches for the snooze. "It's too early," I groan, looking at the clock as it flashes five fifteen in the morning.

Warm lips press against my forehead and I stretch. My body is sore and it's starting to go beyond the point of pleasurable. I groan.

"Good thing you're going to dinner with your friend tonight," he says and I look at him in the dim light of dawn, his features are darkened and unreadable.

"What's the matter? Can't handle me?"

"I think it's the other way around, princess."

"Touché." I throw his word back at him and he chuckles.

"I'm always up this early. I'm usually in the office by six-thirty."

"Then I'll get dressed and you can take me home. I don't mind taking the train in." I bring my head up, resting my chin on the back of my hand so I can get a better look at him.

"Nope, not today. Whatever I have in the office can wait."

I shake my head. "You're too much," I tease and slide out of bed.

"Where are you going?"

I look at him, "To pee, Mister bossy pants boss man."

He laughs, "Say it?"

"Say what?"

"You know what?"

"Nope, sorry, no clue what you're talking about," I joke and disappear into the bathroom.

"You're impossible," he groans and I laugh to myself as I take care of business.

When I step out of the bathroom, there is a soft light on in the corner of the room and Dyson is spread out on the bed, taking up as much space as he can. With his six foot, three inch frame, it doesn't take much, even in his big bed. His head is buried under a pillow, his feet are tucked in under the covers, but the rest of his gorgeous body is on display for me, including his steely erection. Standing strong and pointed to the sky. I lick my lips.

"So are you going to just stand there and stare at me?" he mumbles through the pillow.

"Yup," I tease him back and he moves the pillow to look straight at me. I cross my arms under my tits, putting them up and on display for him. He groans, throwing his head back.

"Tease."

An idea comes to mind and before I can let it over ride whatever confidence I think I have to do this, I climb up on the bed between his

legs. He lifts his head and an eyebrow at me, wondering what I'm doing.

I lean back on one arm and throw my legs over the tops of his thighs. With my free hand, I tweak a nipple and watch as his mouth falls slack and his chest freezes. I slide my hand over my chest to my other breast and this time I pull up on my nipple. The shot of pain quickly melts into the most delicious pleasure as I roll it between my fingers.

He props himself up on an elbow and watches me intently. I slide my hand slowly down my body until my fingers brush along the triangle of hair at the junction of my thighs and he groans. I bypass my clit and slide my hand over and down my thigh. I throw my head back, watching him is almost too much.

"Look at me, princess. I want to look into your eyes as you pleasure yourself."

Oh, fuck. That's hot.

I lift my head up, meeting his eyes and his hand wraps around his cock and my pussy pulses with the need to be filled by him. The ache I felt when I woke up is still there, but it turns to pleasure as I slide my fingers into my slit. Finding my clit, I circle it gently at the same time he strokes up on his cock. The pleasure he's giving himself is enough to make his eyes flutter, but he keeps them open, holding mine. They're encouraging and enabling all at the same time and I can't stop myself from circling my clit again and again.

"Don't come," he tells me in a way that suggests I shouldn't argue with him, but I let out a whine in protest. "I want to make you come, princess, only me."

I moan, "Then you better fucking get over here." I barely recognize the wanton voice that comes from my lips but just like that, Dyson moves, pulling his legs out from underneath mine and then he's hovering over me.

"Say my name," he orders as the head of his cock teases my entrance.

"Fiend." Two can play at this game.

He shakes his head. "Try again, tigress."

The nickname sends a new thrill trough me and on instinct I start circling my clit faster. He notices and wraps his fingers around my wrist, pulling my hand from my clit. I cry out in frustration. "Say it," he commands.

"Sadist."

His eyes narrow. "Oh darling, you haven't seen anything yet." He pulls my fingers to his mouth and he kisses the pads of my middle and forefinger, and then licks them. When my juices meet his mouth, his eyes flutter before he wraps his entire mouth over my fingers, sucking them in and his tongue works them clean. I fall into the pillows watching him.

His cock shifts, pressing into me a little more and I clamp down involuntarily and I push him from my body. "You're close, aren't you?" I shake my head at him. "Liar. All you have to do is say my name."

"Self-assured cocky fiend." He narrows his eyes at me. Then his cock is back at my entrance. "Fuck. Dammit, Dyson, fuck me," I cry out and he slams into me and I explode all over his cock. My orgasm shatters me as he works his cock in and out of me until he is consumed with his own release.

Chapter Twenty-Nine

DYSON
Good Morning Beautiful - Steve Holy

Waking up to the feisty tigress that is *my* Ireland has become my new goal in life. I want to have her in my bed every night and wake up to her every morning. God, she never ceases to surprise and amaze me.

Her little stunt this morning was something I would have never imagined from her and her fucking mouth. God, she's going to keep me on my toes.

I'm standing in her kitchen, drinking coffee while she gets dressed and ready for her day. I'm already ready, but we need to make some wardrobe adjustments so she has a change or three of clothes at my house when we stay there. Hmm, wonder what she would think about me keeping clothes here too.

I ignore the thought as I scroll through emails on my phone.

There are too many to count and far too many to answer while I'm standing here. Business is booming and my life is finally getting to where I've always wanted it to be, thanks to Ireland. But more importantly, I finally feel like work isn't the most important thing in my life. Yeah, I'm a workaholic, but I think Ireland is starting to help me see there are more important things than working fourteen hours a day.

I look at my watch, it's nearly seven-thirty.

"You about ready, princess?"

"Just a minute," she shouts back. Her roommate Becca wasn't home when we got here and I could see Ireland is bothered by her absence. I tried to convince her that maybe she has a new boyfriend or something, but she's not buying it. I have this horrible feeling tonight is the last night I'm going to see Ireland before Thursday. She's a strong girl, but I haven't begun to process how she is going to react. I have a feeling there are going to be some choice words said.

"I'm ready," she says as she comes into the kitchen.

My eyes bug out of my head. "That's it, the next time we have sex,

you're keeping those on," I tell her as I stare down at her knee high, stiletto heeled boots. She laughs. My eyes roam up the rest of her body. She looks simply beautiful in a long sleeved emerald green wrap dress that's both professional and comfortable looking. Her hair's pulled back in a messy bun. "I thought you liked your hair down?" I ask also noting she's wearing a hint of makeup on her eyes. It looks good and unpainted. This is how I like her.

"I do, but I was moving around a lot yesterday and I realized I was a little warmer, so I wanted it up."

I wrap my arm around her, pulling her to my side. "Well, you look beautiful."

She blushes, but smiles. "Thank you."

"You ready?"

"Yup, just need to grab my bag." She walks over to the table where she put it when we got back her and she's looking for something. "Okay, I'm good."

"Find everything?" I raise an eyebrow in question.

"Yup, just wanted to make sure my other shoes were in here."

"What for?"

"In case I can't take the boots anymore, and I'm taking the train after work."

"Why?"

"Because I'm meeting Reese for dinner, remember?" She looks at me as if I could have forgotten the fact I won't be able to see her tonight.

"I remember, but I can take you."

She shakes her head. "No, that's okay. I'm sure you've got work to catch up on."

"Then let me have Byron take you? He's quite fond of you, you know?"

She gives me a warm smile. "And I him, but I'm not his responsibility."

"On the contrary, you're my responsibility, therefore you're his."

"Are we going to argue about it?" she asks me.

"Nope, it's all set."

She narrows her eyes at me and I don't blame her, I'm being a dick. "I just want to make sure you're safe."

"Dyson." There's my name again, but not in a way I enjoy. "I've been taking the train for as long as it has been up and running, I carry mace in my bag, easily accessible, and I've taken more than enough self-defense classes to be able to defend myself. Please don't argue with me on this. I will let you have your way more than you probably want, but if you try forcing me to do shit all the time you're going to make me crazy."

She has a point and I no valid argument for it. "Okay, but will you do something for me?"

"What?" She's not angry, just curious.

"Text me when you're leaving and when you get home so I know you're safe?"

"That is a reasonable request." She smiles and comes over, slinging her bag over her shoulder and kissing me on the cheek. "But remember, I've been independent for a long time, so don't go flipping your shit on me if I forget."

I chuckle, but it's really not funny. "I will try," I tell her, because in truth, I can't promise I won't. Having her out of my sight makes me crazy, having her riding the train, alone, at night, makes me mad with worry.

"Good, now let's go or I'm going to be late for my second day of work."

She grabs her to-go coffee cup off the counter and tosses it in her bag and leads me to the door and out into the chilly morning air.

IRELAND
9 to 5 - Emily Ann Roberts

Day two at Wellington goes much better than yesterday. I hate meeting new people, especially people I will be working with, for the first time. There is always those moments of awkward we can never seem to get past until we've been around people for a few days.

Shelly put me to task on a new marketing plan surrounding the slogan I'd come up with in my interview. Now that I know the business plan behind Tigress, making these changes is a whole lot easier. I wrote the damn thing.

Infinite possibilities, today.

That's what I'd come up with, that's what I was working with. The product line is a new cellphone. Sure, it's a cell phone but even I'm impressed with the features on this thing. There are a lot of similarities to what is already on the market today, so people won't be overwhelmed, but at the end of the day, this one is much better.

By lunch time, I am starving and in an attempt to keep good on my word to Dyson about communicating with him, I let him know I'm leaving the office and head across the street. Downtown Phoenix has a plethora of restaurants but most of them are reservations or seating only. Except in the City Center, which has more of my speed of food.

Dyson paying for all those clothes at the store has allowed me a little more leeway in my budget for things like coffee and lunch. But I should really plan on bringing my own lunch from now on. If Dyson ever lets me sleep in my own bed again.

I have to admit, last night was nicer than I'd expected it to be. After having worked all day, I didn't think I would want to hang around anyone, but in this case, it was nice. It was normal. Almost.

Jesus, the sex.

Fucking. Amazing.

But if this keeps up, this man is going to kill me with pleasure.

Then again, that might not be a bad way to go.

I'm standing in line at Chipotle, waiting my turn when my phone buzzes. I pull it out.

Dyson: Where'd you go?

Ireland: Chipotle, want something?

Dyson: Yes please. Burrito bowl, white rice, chicken, corn salsa, cheese and sour cream.

Ireland: next time just say what you're having minus the guac.

Dyson: Guac sounds awesome.

I smile at my phone and I'm up next when I text him back.

Ireland: most people would consider that creepy.

Dyson: I think it's cute. :-*

I roll my eyes and stow my phone before placing the order and making my way down the line to check out. I also order side guac and chips for each of us. If he doesn't want 'em, I'll save it for lunch tomorrow.

I walk back to the office, checking my phone again for the time. I have about thirty minutes left before my lunch is up and I head straight for the elevator, swiping my ultra-special, nearly all-access badge that I'm pretty sure doesn't come with a Wellington job and I push for the top floor and the elevator whisks me up.

When I step off the elevator, the receptionist from yesterday is there. She smiles at me and says, "Go on back, Ms. McKidd."

"Oh, thank you." I shake my head and smile. Obviously Dyson told them to let me through.

When I round the corner, I'm met with the same man from yesterday, but Dyson's door is closed. The glass is clear, and there are two men inside with Dyson. His assistant stops me. "Just a moment, Ms. McKidd."

"Vy, please," I tell him and extend my hand.

"Andy, it's a pleasure to meet you. Vy."

"Likewise. Is he going to be long?" I pull my phone out and notice I'm down to about twenty-five minutes. Just as I ask the question, Dyson's eyes meet mine through the glass and he's ushering the two men from his office.

"Nope," Andy laughs and takes his seat behind his desk.

"Thanks, Andy," Dyson says as he follows the two men out.

"You busy today?"

Dyson smiles at me. "Swamped, but I have a few minutes."

"I should get downstairs, so I can eat."

"Come inside, we can eat together. I have a meeting at two." He turns to Andy. "Hold my calls, please."

"No problem, sir." Andy winks at me as Dyson ushers me into his office. He leaves the door open and the glass clear as we sit down at the bar. I pull his food out for him and he laughs.

"Fiend, huh?"

I wink at him and pull mine from the bag, handing him a bag of chips and plastic cup of guac as I do. "Thank you," he says softly.

"Anytime," I tell him and pop the foil lid off my container revealing the same thing that's in his bowl and he chuckles.

"Is that really what you eat regularly?"

I smile around a bite of my dish, and swallow it before speaking. "Yes, though the guac is hit or miss. Depends on my mood."

He shakes his head, his smile spreads a little wider and he digs into his

food. We don't say anything during the meal, but there is this completely comfortable silence between us, it's normal.

When we finish, I have about ten minutes to get back downstairs. "How's your day been?" he asks.

"Good. Shelly has tasked me with your marketing project, though I think it's going to be more like a contest than anything."

"Why do you say that?"

"Because everyone seems to be talking about it. Though I have a rather unfair advantage," I say as I stand up to clean up our trays. Neither one of us touched our chips and guac. "You want this for later?" I ask. He nods and I turn around, putting it into the little fridge and setting the chips next to it.

"You were saying about unfair advantages?" he prompts.

I snort. "I know your business plan inside and out." I wink at him.

"That you do, Ms. McKidd. Speaking of which, I will be meeting with my lawyers and some of my top advisors to discuss some of the changes you mentioned over the weekend."

"Really?" I ask, shocked.

"Really," he states as fact. "They're brilliant ideas and I think Tigress can really benefit from them."

"Huh," I say. "I should really stop giving free advice," I mutter and he gives me a smile that says he knows something I don't, but Andy comes in.

"Five minutes, sir."

"Thank you, Andy," Dyson says but his eyes never leave mine. "What makes you say that?" he asks.

I shake my head. "Nothing,"

"Ireland?" he says in a way that makes me feel like I've just been busted with my hand in the candy jar.

I look at him. "We don't have time to discuss this right now. I have to

go back to work," I tell him, and it's true. Plus, I need some time to get over whatever it was that just washed over me before I say something I'll regret.

"Later, promise me?" he says as he puts his hand in mine, leading me toward the door.

"Promise." I smile and he kisses my forehead before I walk out past Andy.

I pause and go back to Andy. "Can I ask you something?"

"Anything, Ms.…." he stops himself. "Vy."

"Are you seeing anyone?"

I watch as he blushes, confirming my initial suspicion about his sexual orientation. I lean in closer, "Not for me." I wink.

"No, I'm not."

I smile wide. "Good. I'll be in touch," I tell him and walk back toward reception and the elevator.

"What was that all about?" I hear Dyson ask as I round the corner.

DYSON

"I'm not sure, sir. She asked me if I was seeing anyone."

I chuckle. "And what did you tell her?" He blushes again, same as I saw when she was talking to him.

"She winked at me and told me that it wasn't for her."

Reese, "well I would hope not."

"No, sir." He stiffens behind the desk.

"I'm not blind, or dumb, and I don't care." I tell Andy and he relaxes. "So are you?"

"Am I what, sir?"

"Seeing anyone?"

"No, sir."

"Good," I tell him and walk away shaking my head at the idea of Ireland setting up her friend Reese with my assistant.

As I walk toward my meeting, Ireland's comment plays in my head over and over again. *I should really stop giving free advice.* That comment brings new hope to our Thursday night discussion that will take place with Charlie and Mick, who were just in my office discussing Thursday. Mick is setting everything up for her. Her accounts, etcetera so he can hand her everything she needs in order to access her funds. When I tried to press for more information from yesterday, they both shot me down. It pissed me off, but then I saw Ireland standing there talking to Andy and I kicked them out.

So in other words, the money might not spook her as much, but apparently whatever else Mick has up his sleeve just might.

Chapter Thirty

IRELAND
The Only Exception - Paramore

Walking into Kobult – a trendy Central Phoenix restaurant, I see Reese sitting at our usual table. He jumps up and wraps his arms around me. "God, look at you. Are you getting laid?"

"Reese, seriously?" I playfully sock him in the arm.

"Oh my god, you are, aren't you?" he laughs. "Bitch." His lip curls up in a playful sneer.

"Well, if we're going to start off like this, I'm giving your number to a hottie I met at my new job." I sway side to side in my chair. The music is a little more upbeat than normal, but I like dangling boy carrots in front of Reese.

"Oh really? Do tell."

I launch into the details about Andy and Reese is all too excited for me to hand over his number. I promise Reese I would the next time I saw him with explicit instructions that they should at least text first. I roll my eyes. "What happened to meeting people the old-fashioned way?" I laugh.

Dinner with Reese is effortless. We talk about my new job, how things are going at his job. Then he prattles on about the concert I missed and the hotties that were there that night.

Then he brings up a subject I'm not sure I'm ready to talk about. "What the hell is wrong with Becca?" he asks me. I should have expected the question. Becca and Reese are friends, though not close like Reese and I are, or Becca and me for that matter. I think I'm the mutual glue of that project, but they are friends and they do talk outside of our mutual get togethers. It's no wonder he knows. He probably tried reaching out to her when I bailed on him Saturday night, which is more than likely how he knows she's being a bitch.

"Not you too?"

"What do you mean, not me too?" He gives me a 'what the fuck' kind

of look that is a signature Reese facial expression.

"She's being a royal bitch to me and I'm her damn roommate." I tell him as the waitress sets down our food and I ask for another drink. I don't know why, but I ordered coke tonight instead of my usual Cosmo. Reese looked at me funny and I just brushed him off. Something about Dyson's confession about keeping me safe rolls around in my brain and I realize that drinking isn't the best idea.

"She said that something happened a couple weeks ago?" he quirks an eyebrow at me, "something to do with why you were in New York?"

"Well, I guess the cat's out of the bag now. I might as well spill the beans." I smile and the waitress returns with my coke. Reese and I dive into our food. I'm eating a margarita pizza and Reese is working his way through his customary seven cheese macaroni and cheese while I tell him about what happened the night at Blu.

"So she figured since you kneed him in the nads, he was fair game."

"I guess so," I shrug. "But he went running after me which probably pissed her off even more."

"That girl has some real issues."

"Honestly," I tell him. "I think it has more to do with some type of abandonment issues."

"Oh, baby girl, do tell." He props his elbows up on the table, interlocks his fingers and rests his chin on them before batting his eyes.

I shake my head, but tell him my theory. "I don't know, but it's starting to make sense now. Sure, one night stands are easy for her. She can walk away on her terms. But when they leave on their own terms, she's pissed too. Or if they won't leave, she's pissed. I just think she has to find a way to control her surroundings. She wasn't ready to walk away from Dyson and he walked away from her and now she's pissed."

"Why would she still be pissed? She gets rejected by guys all the time."

"Erm..."

"Oh no, baby girl, spill this shit."

"Because Dyson and I are together."

"No shit," Reese squeals.

"Shhh, jeez, the whole restaurant is going to hear this conversation if you keep that up."

"Oh honey," he smirks. His eyes carry that mischievous look he wears so well, and I know I'm in trouble. "If you think nobody up in here ain't listenin', they always listenin'." He rolls his fingers closed before pressing his fist to the side of his face.

I laugh, "Because you are quite possibly the loudest person I know."

"So, do tell about this Mr. Dyson man who's finally got you spreading your legs."

"Reese, Jesus." My eyes go wide in shock and my face explodes in redness. I feel the flush of my cheeks and realize I've been busted.

"So, sweetheart, tell me he has a magic cock or something because-"

I blush even redder and he erupts into laughter. "Will you quit?" I scold him.

"Oh no, darling, spill it."

And spill it, I did.

I spilled everything to him. It was effortless and easy and I didn't realize until I was telling him everything, just how much I needed someone to talk to about everything going on in my brain about Dyson.

Reese listened like a champ and offered advice where it was needed, and by the end of my story, I think he was just as in love with Dyson as I am.

The reality of being in love with Dyson is something I didn't think I would let happen again, but in truth, I can't imagine a day without him. Without his banter, his affection, caring, and the most enjoyable, amazing sex.

I look at my phone to see it's nearly eleven when Reese and I are leaving the restaurant. I text Dyson.

Ireland: Reese is driving me home.

His reply is quick and sweet.

Dyson: Good, tell him to drop you off at my house.

I smile at my phone.

Ireland: aw, you miss me.
Dyson: of course I do. Please?
Ireland: are you begging?
Dyson: yes.
Ireland: no clothes with me. Too tired.

I don't get a reply before Reese is dropping me off in front of my apartment. Our assigned space is empty which means Becca's not home, again.

"Why does she feel like she can't even stay in her own house?" I mumble as Reese pulls to a stop.

"Let her go, baby girl. Eventually she'll come crawling back."

"I hope so," I tell him and then wrap my arms around his neck. "Miss your face." I kiss his cheek.

He laughs, "Miss yours more. Now go, you look exhausted."

I snort, "You have no idea."

"Get 'er done, girlfriend." I love Reese. There are no filters, no boundaries between us. He says the first thing that comes to his mind and he doesn't care who he pisses off. "Oh, and give that boy my number."

I smile and wink at him. "Oh, I will." He squeezes my hand.

"Vy?"

I stop exiting the car and look at him. "Yeah?"

"Be careful, okay?"

I cock my head at him. His expression is somber in a way I don't normally see from him. "Always."

"I mean it. Don't let this guy railroad you like he did before." His eyes are filled with concern. "I didn't realize, until tonight, how much pain you must have really been in. This is a side of you I've never seen in nearly six years and I like it."

I smile. "I'm being cautious, Reese, I promise."

"Good, because that cranky bitch you once were can stay far, far away," he laughs and I scoff.

"Call me this weekend?" I ask.

"Oh, you know I will, unless of course, Andy calls me." He winks, gives me a knowing smirk and I climb out of the car. As is customary for Reese, he waits until I'm inside the apartment before I give him one final wave and close the door.

I toss my purse on the island and take a look around the apartment, looking for a note or something from Becca and I don't see anything. Then there's a knock on the door. "Reese, what'd you forget?" I shout and open the door without looking.

"Well, hello there, hot stuff," I breathe as I take in the sexy, casual version of Dyson standing in my doorway. "What are you doing here?"

He holds up a garment bag. "I brought clothes."

"Oh really? And just what do you plan on doing with those clothes, Mister Sex on legs?"

He quirks an eyebrow at my name for him. "Wearing them to work tomorrow."

"Oh really, you had to pack your clothes for tomorrow. You couldn't

just pull them out of your closet?"

He knows I'm going to let him in, so he plays me, plucking the strings of any attempt I would have made to shoo him back to his own house. "I could, but I don't plan on seeing my closet in the morning."

"Oh, got a girlfriend you're running off to go see?" I tease.

"No, just this fiery redheaded tigress who likes to push my buttons. I'm hoping she'll let me snuggle her tonight. My bed and my condo are awfully lonely without her."

I smile wide and open the door. "You certainly know how to butter a girl up."

"Kisses were next," he snickers.

"Oh, those are still required."

"Good."

The next thing I know, Dyson's stuff is laid out on the island next to my purse and he has me pressed against the entryway closet door. My hands are above my head and his lips hover just above mine. "I missed you too much to wait for morning," he breathes before claiming my lips and turning every nerve in my body into a live wire of sensation.

Chapter Thirty-One

DYSON
It's Over - Civil Twilight

Waking up in Ireland's bed is almost better than my own.

We woke up and repeated the process from the day before, only this time, no one had to go home first and I am liking this new kind of 'normal' we have going on.

She'd gotten up early and put together a slow cooker full of chili for her and Becca tonight. When I asked why she was making chili, she just shrugged and said it was her and Becca's thing and for whatever reason, chili makes Becca a little more forthcoming. She's hoping like hell to finally get to the bottom of all this bullshit with her. I hope she does. I'd truly hate to come between Ireland and her best friend, but I have no qualms about making sure Becca drops the attitude toward Ireland. Ireland has done nothing wrong and she doesn't deserve Becca's ire. If I have to come between them on that matter, I will.

Driving to work with Ireland in my car is even better. The normalcy of the whole thing is just…comforting.

Our conversations about anything and nothing come easily. Much the way they did when we were kids. I didn't give her much chance to tell me about dinner with Reese, but she passed his number to me to give to Andy. I gave her shit for ten minutes about delivering it to him herself. She said today would be hard. She had a couple meetings and even brought her own lunch with her. I scrunched up my nose at the frozen meal she pulled out. Not because I can afford so much better, but because, eww. Those things are gross. She didn't seem to mind and I vowed to myself to have lunch delivered to her.

The day flew by. I don't know if it was a good thing or a bad thing. Either way, it was all kinds of suck because tonight, seeing Ireland isn't going to happen and it's killing me. Though she did let me drive her home.

"If anything changes, call me," I tell her as I pull away from her delectable body. My cock is hard, compliments of being in close

proximity to my gorgeous tigress, but I reined him in. No point in getting all worked up and there's nothing I can do about it.

"I will, promise."

"Pick you up tomorrow for work?"

She smiles. "I'd like that."

"Seven-thirty?"

She nods and kisses me again. Becca pulled into her spot but waited until I was leaving to get out of the car. Apparently Becca has it out for me because she was throwing daggers at me with her eyes as I pulled away. This is going to be an interesting evening.

Around ten, I get a text from Ireland.

Becca is moving out.

My heart breaks for her. I want to call her, but I don't want to force her into a conversation she doesn't want to have.

Dyson: Are you ok?

Ireland: I will be. I guess moving in with me wasn't something she wanted to do. She wanted to move out on her own and since you and I are together, she doesn't feel guilty about leaving me alone.

I frown at my phone. Why do people do shit like that?

Dyson: Can you afford the apartment on your own?

I ask the question because I don't want to give her any indication of what's coming in the next twenty-four hours. I don't know why, but I feel

the need to be on her level right now and let her be her.

Ireland: I think so. I'm going to have to look over everything to be sure. But I should be alright. And no, Dyson, you're not going to help me.

Hey, at least she said my name. Though it seems to flow out of her fingers when she's pissed or warning me about something. I chuckle as I reply.

Dyson: No promises, tigress. You know the rules, if I can fix it, I will. But I have a better solution.

Ireland: What's that?

Dyson: Move in with me.

Ireland: DYSON COLE!! You cannot be serious.

Oh shit, I got the full name. I laugh.

Dyson: as a heart attack.

She doesn't reply right away and I don't know if she's actually considering it or if she's just trying not to freak out on me.

My phone rings and her gorgeous face pops up.

"Hello, princess."

"Are you serious?" she asks, and her voice has no real emotion shining through so I can't read her.

"I am." But I decide I need to give her a little bit here. She needs to know there is an alternative. "If it would be easier for you to consider, I've got two rooms that are unoccupied, one completely empty. You could move in to my house, if moving into my bed scares you."

"I'm not afraid of you," she states matter of fact. "Or your bed," she adds in a softer tone.

"Good." I smile into the phone. "Want to come over?" I ask. I already know the answer.

"No, I just need some time to process everything from tonight." She sounds hurt.

"What's wrong, princess?"

She sighs into the phone. "I'm just surprised. I mean she was reluctant when we got this place, but I knew she couldn't afford a place on her own. But because I don't have a car, I kind of forced her into this neighborhood. It's expensive and…" she pauses, taking a deep breath, "she would rather live someplace else for the amount of money she has to pay. It's really childish. But now we're in a lease and she wants out."

"Then she should pay her way out of the lease."

She snorts into the phone. "Becca isn't exactly the type with savings or the ability to pay for two places."

"Not that I want to steer you away from the idea of moving in with me, but is there someone else, Reese maybe, who you could get as a roommate?"

"Reese owns his house. So again, I'm the one needing to move into something more affordable. We haven't even been here a month, so I don't know if there's some way I can get out of the lease under those circumstances. Or if I could transfer to a one bedroom or studio."

"Not likely," I tell her. "Unfortunately those contracts are pretty iron clad."

I hear her sniffle on the other end of the phone. "I don't know what to do," she says and I get up, grabbing a suit for tomorrow and throw it in my garment bag. "I'm just so…I don't need this right now, Dyson, I really don't. It's all just too much for me to handle anymore."

"Is Becca still there?" I ask.

"No, she ran off somewhere, said not to wait up for her. The problem I

have with all of this is she didn't apologize for last week. She doesn't even seem to care that what she said hurt me. I just…I feel betrayed."

I grab my keys off the hook and head down to the garage and I pass Byron's room. "Hang on, princess."

"Okay." Her voice is cracking with the emotion she's feeling and my heart breaks for her pain.

I put my phone to my chest. "I'm going to Ireland's," I whisper and he nods.

"Be careful," he says quietly back.

"I'm taking the Tesla." He nods. I'm taking the Tesla because I can start the car and she won't know. "Okay, baby, I'm back."

"I should go," she sniffs again.

"No, stay on the phone with me, please, I'm worried about you," I tell her as I toss the garment bag on the passenger seat, close the door and then open the garage and start the car. Its quiet purr tells me that she's running and I back out of the garage.

"I'll be alright. I just, I don't know what to do."

"Well, we will figure it out, baby, I promise."

"I know, I just, with everything, I feel so…" There is a long pause, but I don't say anything. She needs to find it in herself. "Lost," she finally says and her voice is barely a whisper.

"You're not lost, love. Not in the slightest."

"But I've lost my best friend, and I don't even know what I did to deserve it. That's the part that's eating at me the most. She didn't even tell me why, didn't even tell me if we were going to stay friends after this and I don't know if I want to. She's putting me in such an awful position and she doesn't even care. Can I afford it here, sure I can, but I won't be able to afford much else, not that I need much besides food." She's rambling and I let her go on as I pull into her parking lot. There is definitely a perk to being kitty-corner from her, makes getting here quick and easy. "What are you doing?" she asks.

"Walking up to your door. Will you please come open it?"

"Dyson…" She's shocked, but I know she's going to relent because she needs someone right now and I'm all she's got.

The next thing I know, the phone goes dead and the door lock disengages and the door opens. She's obviously been crying judging by the redness in her eyes. I walk in, drop my bag and wrap her in my arms and she falls apart. Her legs give out, her body weakens with sobs. I hold her to me for a moment before I scoop her up in my arms and carry her toward her bedroom. I sit her down on the bed. "I'll be right back," I tell her. "I'm just going to lock the door and get my stuff, okay?"

She nods and tries to wipe her tears away.

I lock the front door, grab my bag and then go to the kitchen for a glass of something, anything. I search her cabinets and find nothing, and then I notice wine glasses in the sink and I find a bottle of wine in the fridge. I pull it out and find two clean wine glasses, pouring one for each of us before returning to her room. I hand her a glass. "Here, might help," I tell her and she takes it with a sad smile but she swallows half of it before setting it on her bedside table. I add my glass before hanging my bag in her walk-in closet. I come out and she's still sitting there. She's wearing pajama pants and an old ASU t-shirt. "I'm going to crawl in bed with you," I tell her and she stands, pulls back her covers and she slides into bed and slides over. She lies on her side, facing me. "Roll over, princess, I want to hold you."

A weak smile spreads across her face and she does as I've asked. I pull my shirt over my head and slide in behind her. I wrap my arms around her, holding her to me and her silent tears continue. I reach over and turn out her light and that's how we fall asleep, wrapped in each other arms. It takes her a while but eventually her breathing settles into a slow and rhythmic pattern. Mine follows shortly after.

Chapter Thirty-Two

IRELAND

Gasoline - Halsey
Bad Blood - Taylor Swift
Pay Dearly - Johnnyswim

Last night, I realized that I am falling wholly and completely in love with Dyson.

Wrapped in his arms, I cried silent tears of pity for myself, letting the emotions of my mom, the whole 'my mother's will' debacle, Becca's decision, her being an asshole, and finally, having someone to hold me when I needed them most pour out of me. It was a pretty heady thing.

I wake up and stretch. My bed is cold and empty and my clock says it's just after six. Remembering that Dyson wakes up early, I wonder if he's already left. Then I see his bag hanging in the closet and I know he's here somewhere and I get up in search of him.

I find him sitting on the couch, bent over his laptop and staring intently at something on the screen I can't see. "It sucks waking up alone," I tell him and he jumps. "Sorry, I didn't mean to startle you."

His eyes meet mine and they're full of everything I realized I was feeling last night. "I didn't wake you, did I?" he asks.

I shake my head. "I woke up and you weren't there."

He comes over to me and runs his knuckles gently down my cheek. "I was going to come wake you in a few minutes."

"Then I'll go back to bed." I smile.

"There's my tigress." He smiles back at me.

"I need to take a shower." I put my hands on his hips and pull him toward me. "Care to join me?"

"You only have to ask, princess." I smile and turn toward the bathroom, pulling my t-shirt over my head as I go. He's hot on my heels and he wraps his arms around me, holding my back to his front. His erection presses into the small of my back and I shiver. His hands roam up my body as he guides me in front of my mirror. His eyes are hooded

as his hands roam up my stomach to cup my breasts and his fingers roll my nipples between them. I lift my head, putting it against his shoulder, giving him better access. He releases one of my nipples and moves my hair out of his way before returning his hand to my breast and planting gentle, full open mouth kisses along my neck and shoulder.

My sex heats. Pleasure pools in my core desperate to feel him inside of me. Watching Dyson torture my body is probably the hottest thing I've ever seen. He releases my breast and his hand slides down my stomach, into the waist of my pajama pants until his fingers find my slick sex. "So wet, so needy." His breath caresses my shoulder as he talks and I moan as his fingers circle around the sensitive bundle of nerves. My body trembles in time with his gentle strokes and my orgasm rises to the surface. Watching Dyson is a new experience I want to have more often. The tenderness he treats my body with is something else entirely and now I can see it firsthand with the help of the mirror.

He releases my nipple and slides his hand down to join the other, only he's using it to push my pants down my legs, exposing my sex for him to see in the mirror. His hand is cupped against my pubic bone and my trembling picks up a notch. "If I didn't know better, Ms. McKidd, I'd think you like watching me play with your body."

I shudder and give him a wicked smile as we make eye contact through the mirror. His smile sends a new fire through my veins and his hand comes away from my pussy. I'm disappointed, but he pulls my pants down to my ankles and I brace myself against the sink. My breasts are on full display as they hang between my arms.

I barely recognize the wanton woman in the mirror. Her mouth is hanging open, her eyes are hooded and full of orgasmic promise as Dyson stands behind me. He grabs hold of my hips and pulls them back. The angle changes and I see him naked behind me as he strokes his cock. "Watch, princess," he tells me as he presses his cock along my slit and my eyes roll up but I bring them back, focusing, finding his eyes to focus on.

As he slips inside of me, his eyes flutter, the color disappearing briefly as the pleasure my body is bringing him registers. His body shakes gently

as he slides all the way inside me. I cry out. "Oh god, Dyson, harder," I breathe.

I need him hard, fast. I need him to take control of my body the way he always does and he doesn't hesitate. His fingers grip onto my hips, holding on as if his life depends on it.

I watch as the most beautiful expression crosses his face as he looks at me in the mirror. It's gentle compared to his pounding into me. I can't describe it, but I know now that he loves me as much as I love him and that newfound knowledge pushes me over the edge as I explode around his cock. His own orgasm consumes him.

Like any other morning this week, we showered, together. He cleaned my body from head to toe and it was the most delicious torture I've ever felt in my entire life.

Just wanted to remind you of me today, he'd said as he brought me near orgasm again with his gentle washing of my body. He was right. I haven't been able to get him out of my mind all morning, or afternoon for that matter. Like yesterday, Dyson had lunch delivered for me and I need to remember to thank him for that. Despite the distraction of the gentle reminder of Dyson between my legs, I felt fully confident in the work I accomplish today.

Between Dyson holding me last night, then him giving me a few moments to forget, I haven't thought much about what I'm going to do in regards to Becca wanting to abandon me and the apartment we're sharing together. What can I do? I've asked her repeatedly if there was something we could do. I told her over and over again that we've hardly seen each other in a week and we could continue to live that way. But she didn't seem to care. I really think I've lost my best friend.

I text Reese during lunch to ask him if Andy had been in touch and he was all too eager to tell me he had and they were meeting for drinks after work tomorrow. That made me smile. At least one of my friends is happy.

At ten to five, my phone buzzes with a text and I pick it up.

Dyson: Can you come up when you're done? I have some things to finish up.

Ireland: No problem. I got my laptop today. I can work too.

Dyson: See you soon.

Shelly comes into my office. I've been avoiding her like the plague after what happened earlier this week. I don't know what her game is, but whatever it is I don't like it, or her. "How are you getting along?" she asks. The problem I have with Shelly is she seems genuine and maybe she is to me, because I don't think whatever is brewing for her has anything to do with me.

"Good, I got quite a bit done today and now that I have my laptop, I'll be getting some more work done outside of work."

"Don't work too hard." She smiles and sits down opposite me.

"It's impossible to work hard when the work is something you love," I tell her as I close up my laptop and grab for my bag on the floor. Something else to cart back and forth from work.

"This is very true. When do you think you'll have your first draft done?"

I think about it for a minute. "Probably early next week, depending on how the weekend goes. Am I missing a deadline?" I seem to remember the initial deadline as March fifteenth, but she obviously wants to see it sooner than that.

"Nope, just had a feeling you'd beat everyone else." Her tone is such that I feel like she's accusing me of being a brown noser. I shrug it off. She stands up and continues, "Just so you know, Wellington doesn't like over achievers." Her voice turns to a sneer and I stare at her.

"Excuse me?"

"Oh, don't play stupid with me. I've seen you going up to Tigress." Her accusation, while true, sends me leaning back in my chair. "Just so you know, Dyson is mine. There is nothing you can offer him he can't

get from me." Her lip curls. "Except business connections and a larger portfolio, something the likes of you will never understand."

My heart is pounding in my chest. I want to snap, to fight her on this, but that sneaking suspicion of maybe she's right slides over me. "I have no idea what you're talking about," I tell her, but my voice isn't as sure as I want it to be.

She leans in closer, placing her hands on my desk. "Watch yourself," she growls at me before flouncing from my office and I sit there struck stupid by everything she's just said to me. What a bitch.

Suddenly Dyson's idea of working for him starts to sound a little better and I wonder what Wellington would say if he knew what Shelly was up to.

I grab my stuff and start to head for the door when Mr. Wellington walks past my office toward Shelly's and I move to the door quickly, killing the lights as I listen. "Well?" the voice says. It's the same voice from the other night and suddenly my entire world comes crashing down on me. "Is she going to back off?"

I hear a catty laugh from Shelly's office. "Oh yeah, she'll back off alright."

My heart sinks as fear courses through me. Something tells me my days at Wellington are seriously numbered. I return to my desk, pulling a flash drive from my purse and open my laptop. I stick the drive in, and copy over the files I've saved in regards to my project and then copy a program that will cover my tracks after I delete all the files. I start up the program and set the laptop, open, in my bottom drawer so it will continue running. In about an hour, the entire laptop will be nothing more than a paperweight. Don't ask me where the program came from, but this isn't the first time it's been used, though not by me. Any tech guy will be able to figure out the hard drive has been wiped clean and is no longer viable, but by then, I will be long gone from here. Let them come after me for the cost of the laptop. What I did is not illegal, just a little unethical. Shortly after I lock my laptop in the drawer, I see shadows moving in the hallway and my breathing stops. "He's not going to have a

choice in the matter," Wellington states.

"Yes, but he can cut ties with us easier than you can with him."

"Don't worry about it, Shelly-belly." What the fuck? "We're going to have him where we need him and then we'll be able to move forward with our plan. The firm is going bust. If we don't tie our companies together with this project, we're screwed." The voices trail off as they move down the hallway. Fuck.

I wait about five minutes before I sneak out of my office again. I leave my laptop and the cell phone they'd given me, and take what little personal stuff I had here and toss it into my purse before heading upstairs.

When I get to reception, it's empty since it's after five. I walk back toward Dyson's office and find Andy still at his desk. "Why are you still here?" I ask him and he smiles at me.

"I'm usually here 'til six, but I've been told to take off."

I smile. "Good." I wonder if I should pry into his meeting with Reese on Friday, but before I can ask, he answers for me.

"I'm meeting your friend on Friday."

"Are you excited?"

"No, I'm nervous as hell."

I chuckle. "Reese is a very easy going guy. I think you guys will get along really well," I tell him and he smiles.

"I agree."

"Good."

Dyson's door opens and the two men who were here the other day step out and Dyson is right behind them with a somber expression on his face. I wink at Andy and walk to Dyson. The two men head down the hall to presumably the elevator.

"Hey, princess." His features soften, and I wrap my arms around him.

"Hi you," His arms wrap around me. "We need to talk," I tell him and he stiffens.

"Sure," he says with hesitation.

"What's wrong?"

"Nothing, love. Come on." He ushers me inside.

"Good night, Mr. Cole." Andy calls from the desk. I don't hear a reply from Dyson. I assume he waves before closing his office door. The glass is black because of the meeting he was just in.

"I need a drink." He says as way of greeting. "Want one?"

"Yes, please." I say breathlessly.

He goes to the sideboard and pours some amber liquid from a crystal canter into two crystal glasses. Bringing it over to me and I take it.

"We have a problem," I tell him, cutting to the meat of what I need to talk to him about. Something in his expression tells me something has happened and he's upset about it.

"What's going on?" he says and his voice is cold, calculated almost.

"Wellington is trying to fuck you over." His eyes dart to mine and flare briefly then they narrow at me.

"What are you talking about?"

I remind him about the other night, after I heard him talking to Shelly and what happened afterward. He nods in acknowledgement, but it's rather absentminded and it's starting to make me worry. I stay focused on the task at hand. I need to tell him, let him know, then we can deal with him. I tell him about tonight.

"That son of a bitch." His eyes are staring at me. "He was using you?"

"I think so. I think he saw something in me or between us that day and he figured he could use it to his advantage. I get the impression that's why I wasn't just a marketing assistant like I'd applied for. Then, they've had us working on this marketing plan with a deadline of the fifteenth of March for initial drafts and Shelly was in my face about when my first would be done. When I told her it would probably be done early

next week, depending on how much work I got done this weekend." I wink at him, but he's not really seeing me and I don't understand what could have happened before I got here that would put him on edge like this. I take a deep breath and continue about Shelly. "Then she got pissy with me about Wellington not liking 'over-achievers'. I chalked that up to jealousy but then she turned on me. She told me you were hers and I couldn't give you anything and she has wealth and business contacts that you need in order to succeed in business."

"That's not true, and she fucking knows it." He slams back his drink. "How'd she even know there was a connection?"

"She claims she's seen me going up to your office. Though I think she was just trying to bait me and I didn't bite. She's a bitch. But," I reach into my bag and pull out the thumb drive. "I saved my project after their initial conversation. If I'd been smarter I would have gone into the servers, but I didn't want to set off any alarm bells, and I left my laptop in the desk, along with the cell phone they'd given me and took my personal stuff. I'm no longer going to be their lapdog."

"They'll bury you."

I shrug. "I don't care. I know what I heard, and what I heard is unethical. Let them bury me. I seem to remember some super sexy, three-thousand dollar suit wearing CEO offering me a job." I wink.

"Today's suit is only fifteen hundred."

"Oh, well." I wiggle my eyebrows at him and for the first time I manage to make him smile. "Can you cut ties with them?"

He nods. "I have an easy out clause. Our business relationship hinged on whether or not they could come through on this project. In hindsight, that might be part of the reason I didn't want you working there in the first place. Somehow, I knew you'd come through for them. Have they seen any of your project?" he asks.

"Not to my knowledge, but if I quit now, will that cause you legal problems?"

"I doubt it. When you copied the file, did you delete it?"

I smirk. "I did more than that."

He raises an eyebrow at me. "They can recover deleted items."

I snort, "They can, but they can't recover them when the entire hard drive is being shredded by a nice little piece of computer software. That computer will be done for. They may be able to recover the hard drive, but the documents on it will be in tiny pieces throughout and by the time they can piece them all together, they'll already have a breach of contract lawsuit on their hands."

"My little fucking tigress," he says as he rounds his desk, coming for me.

His lips slant over mine in a greedy, hungry kiss but he pulls back too soon. "I'll have Charlie draw up an employment contract," he smiles.

"Good." I grin.

"Now, will you come with me?" The stony mask from before has returned and I don't understand it.

Reluctantly, I nod my head and he takes my hand, leading me from his office, down a hallway and deeper into the penthouse floor until we come across a conference room. Inside the room are the two men from earlier in his office tonight and earlier this week. They both stand as we enter.

"Ireland McKidd, I'd like you to meet my lawyer, Charlie Dupree and my financial advisor, Mick Bass."

"M. Bass?" I scrutinize the man standing before me. I've seen him before, but I can't quite place him. The name rings a bell from some crazy ass letter I opened last night in an effort to keep myself distracted as Becca packed up some of her stuff.

He clears his throat. "So I see you've gotten my letter?"

Dyson's eyes bounce between me to Mick and back again. "Can we discuss the other stuff first, before you get into all that?" Dyson snaps and I stare at him.

"What is going on here, Dyson?"

"Ms. McKidd?" Charlie says.

"Vy or Ireland, please."

"Ireland, I represent Dyson personally and all things pertaining to Tiger's Eye and Tigress and we've discovered you are the original author of the Home Together business plan from two thousand nine at ASU. Is this correct?"

"Yes," I say with hesitation.

"As Mr. Cole has already informed you, that business plan was then modified to accommodate a for profit company, correct?"

"Yes," I say, confusion rolling around in my.

"In oh nine," Mick cuts in, "Tigress's foundation was formed using a model you had proposed…"

"I already know that. How about you stop beating around the bush and tell me why you're hashing out old history?"

Dyson speaks up, "In 2009 when that business plan won the contest, ASU received a very large donation from me and the writer of the plan was supposed to receive a twenty-five thousand dollar scholarship but the school couldn't find Ivy M. Kidd so the money was returned repeatedly. The money was then placed into a trust fund and the hunt began to track down this person who wrote this business plan because it was going to be modified and incorporated into another business entirely."

I stare at him. He was looking for me without realizing he was looking for me. My heart hurts a little at the thought and I'm furious with the school for screwing with my submission. He would have found me years ago if they hadn't fucked up. Fucking fate, she's a bitch. And karma? Don't get me started on her. She was trying to punish Dyson and I got shafted too. *Fucker.*

Charlie moves back to the table and starts pulling things out of a file folder. "Here are the contracts that were drawn up in oh-nine, and a few in twenty-ten that outline the silent partnership with the absentee Ivy M. Kidd. We figured you'd want to see these, considering…" He doesn't need to finish the sentence; I finish it for him in my head. This is Dyson's way

of helping me. At least that is the first thought that comes to my mind.

"Remember, in my office the other day, you said something about offering up your advice for free?"

I nod absently at him. "Well, you weren't," Mick chimes in. "Dyson established a trust and with each year that has passed, Ivy M. Kidd was paid royalties according to her percentage of ownership in Tiger's Eye, the parent company, and a separate percentage for Tigress." Mick slides something else across the table. It appears to be a bank statement but there is a thumb drive attached to a clip at the corner. I hesitantly reach for it. Looking at the top part of it, I see Bank of California, followed by my name, a P.O. Box address I've never seen before, then some details of the bank account that make my knees go weak and Dyson catches me before I hit the floor. "Don't," I tell him and I pull out a chair and sit down. My head spins and Dyson's hurt expression makes my heart break.

"This can't be right." I look at Mick.

He smiles. "I assure you, it is. But part of the contract and alterations to the contracts over the years include when the company went public. There are stock shares in the company that are about three times that much money. This is what's liquid and available to you now."

I set the paperwork down, and I stand up. "I don't want it."

"Ireland, don't," Dyson urges.

I glare at him. "I signed an agreement when I did that contest that I was not held liable and that no further compensation would be given to me regarding my work. I will hold to that agreement."

"That agreement only applied to Home Together," Charlie cuts in. "When the plan was modified to meet Tiger's Eye's corporation standards, that contract no longer applied. There is no legal ramification for accepting this money."

"And ASU continues to receive huge grants from the Tigress name as a way of compensation for providing the business plan," Mick says.

"There's nine million dollars in that account." I point to the statement. "I have less than three thousand dollars in my savings account. You can't

expect me to just accept this kind of money when all I did was write a business plan for a college project. It's ridiculous."

Dyson's words in New York come flooding through me, *I'll offer you half a million plus a ten million dollar signing bonus.* I glare at him. "Is this why you want me to work for you? So you could have slid this under my nose without me thinking twice about it?"

"No, not at all. This meeting has been planned since this weekend. Since I found out you and Ivy M. Kidd are one in the same. No matter how hard we searched, Ivy M. Kidd did not exist. Charlie went to ASU, was able to pull the class records and the list of participants regarding the contest and we were able to confirm you were a part of it, it was in fact your plan that won and your plan I now use to run my business by. It is also your plan and your changes we discussed openly and freely in my penthouse in New York that will be rolled into a newer, better plan. One that accommodates the expansion and type of business I want Tigress to be. You said it the other day about giving away free advice. Well, you're not giving your advice away for free. This is what your advice from seven years ago is worth today." He takes a deep breath. "This is not my way of helping you. This has nothing to do with us, not in the slightest. This has everything to do with me honoring a contract and an agreement I made seven years ago. Whether this ended up being you or someone else, the payout would be the same, Ireland. It just so happens to be you."

His words knock me back and I stare at the statements in front of me. I shove them away and I fight the tears of frustration from boiling over. "Did your mother know about this? Would she have told my mother?"

"No, why would you think that?" His eyebrows knit together in confusion.

I take a deep breath. "She left me out of her will, Dyson. Gave all the money she had to my brother because of Anna and the baby on the way with a cryptic, private note to me that said all things would be taken care of. Is this," I flip the pages on the statement, "what she meant?"

I watch him look to Mick for help and my eyes follow over to Mick. "No, this," he gestures toward the table, "has nothing to do with what was in your mother's will."

I narrow my eyes at him. "But you know something about that, don't you?" Though I can't wrap my head around why. "That letter you sent me?" He nods. "You weren't very forthcoming in that letter."

"Because the discussion I need to have with you is one that needs to be done privately."

He very pointedly looks at Dyson. I look over at him and I see worry and fear in his eyes. He has a right to be worried because right now, I don't know what I think of him at this moment. "He can stay."

Everyone except me visibly relaxes in the room and I stare at Mick. "Spill it."

Charlie cleans up all the papers on the table, stacks them up and slides them all into an accordion file folder. Mick hands him another stack of information and he adds it to the file folder and Charlie slides it over to me. "Everything you need to access that account is inside that folder. Including debit cards, statements, account passwords, it's all there," Mick says. "If you'd like, I will continue doing with the money what I've been doing for the last seven years."

"Which is what?" I raise an eyebrow.

"Nothing really, just moving some investments when needed. Though nothing has been liquidated to date. It is all yours to do with as you please. However, as an advisor, I will advise you when I see fit, good or bad."

"And if I tell you to give it all to charity?" I ask.

Dyson stiffens and sadness washes through his eyes. He really wants me to keep this money, really wants me to help myself. I suddenly feel very exposed. He laid in bed with me last night and cuddled me, held me, was there for me and now I feel like it was all a lie.

I look back to Mick, desperate for a distraction from the betrayal I'm feeling at the moment. I will deal with all this shit later. "So, what exactly do you know about my mother?"

Dyson and Charlie take a seat. Mick begins to pace the room. "I'm about to tell you a secret I've held on to for nearly twenty-five years. It has

more to do with your father, than it does with your mother."

"My father's dead, I don't see how he's relevant."

"Oh, he's not dead, Ireland. He's very much alive."

"Fuck!" Dyson growls as the world dips and fades then starts spinning.

Mick continues, "You were born in New York City, March twenty-fourth, nineteen ninety one to one Lauren V. McKidd. Your birth certificate, it's blank under father, is it not?"

I nod, not really realizing what's going through my head as he talks. "But it also states Kansas City, Missouri as my place of birth, not New York." That moment, the day with Dyson, when we rounded the corner, the déjà vu I experienced.

"It was amended in nineteen ninety-three when your mother moved you and your brother to Joplin, Missouri to remove your biological father. It was an agreement he made with your mother that his name be removed from the certificate in exchange for financial compensation. Your mother reluctantly agreed to the exchange, but in the end, your father had convinced her it would be better that you not know who your father is. In the end, it was better that only he knew. Mick takes a drink of water from a glass on the table; disappointment flares in his eyes like he wishes it were something stronger. For me, time is standing still and my mind is racing a million miles an hour at the words Mick is telling me.

"My father is alive."

"Publicly, no" Mick states. "Publicly, your father died May thirty-first of two-thousand eleven. At which time he was forced to enter into the witness protection program in exchange for testifying against some seriously powerful people. At that time, myself, along with one other employee who works for him, were the only ones privy to the situation outside of the law enforcement individuals who were handling the situation. At the time of his 'death'," he uses air quotes, "His assets were divided equally among his three children. Most of that division was handled by myself and in an effort to keep your mother's and your name

out of it, the assets you acquired were locked away, per his will, until such a time as your mother's death, or until you turned twenty-five."

I gasp, fighting to put air in my lungs, fighting to wrap my head around everything this man is saying to me. "What about Dusty?" I breathe.

Mick simply shakes his head. "His father, your mother's husband, died before Dusty was born."

All the stories from my childhood start to click into place. We never talked about my father. Or Dusty's for that matter. We always just said he was gone. Neither one of us ever considering that we both had separate fathers. Why would we? We looked enough alike that it never even crossed my mind he wasn't a full blooded brother. When in fact, he's a half-brother, and I have two more siblings I never even knew about. "I have to get out of here." I stand up.

"We've thrown a lot at you tonight," Charlie chimes in as he hands me a card, his business card. "This is for me, and this," he slides another one over, "is Mick's. Inside of that file you will find everything related to Tigress."

I look to Mick. "Who is he?"

He looks pained by my voice and my expression. "Robert Enders."

Chapter Thirty-Three

DYSON

Pieces - Rob Thomas

Suddenly, Mick's client list makes perfect sense. *Robert Enders' Estate.*

She is so mad at me. I expected that. I expected her to accuse me of trying to rectify her horrible financial situation by throwing my money at her, which is not at all what I'm doing, and I can only hope she will see it that way.

"You say that name like it's someone I should know. I'm sorry, Mick. I have no idea who that is." Her tone is clipped, short. She's irritated and rightfully so. I would be too if I were in her shoes. At least I knew my father, as much of an asshole as he was, I still knew him.

"He is the owner of Bold International, Inc., a PR and Marketing firm based in Los Angeles and New York. His daughter, your half-sister, runs the company now. Your half-brother is…well, let's just say there is a good chance you'll never get to meet him. He and Bobby never got along and as far as I know, he doesn't know Bobby is alive."

"Where is he?" she asks him and I'm curious about this answer myself.

"I can't tell you that. Not that I don't want to, but there are only a handful of people who are aware of where he is. I can attempt to put you in touch with him, but I can tell you that it's not an immediate process. It took me more than a week to tell him your mother had passed away."

She closes her eyes and shakes her head back and forth, but reaches onto the table, grabbing the overstuffed accordion folder and Mick hands her another, not as thick, file folder, that has all the information pertaining to her father.

"Your father left you a large sum of money."

"How much?" she asks.

Mick hesitates. "I can say it aloud, or you can read it in there for yourself." He points to the folder in her arms.

"It can't possibly be any worse," she states and I watch Mick visibly

cringe, giving me and Ireland the impression that it is worse than what I've just handed to her. "What in the ever loving fuck?" she growls and storms out of the room taking everything with her in her arms as she goes. I run after her.

"VeeVee!"

"Don't call me that," she snaps and keeps walking. I freeze. I stand there and watch her walk away, and with each step she takes I feel my heart ripping to shreds as she goes. My life is walking out the door and I don't have any idea what to say to her. How can I fix this?

Once she disappears from view, Charlie and Mick come out of the conference room. "Give her some time, she'll come around. I know, her sister did the same thing when she found out her father was still alive."

I grab Mick around the throat and push him up against the wall. "That woman who just walked out of here has no one and she's just learned the only family she knows isn't entirely her family. Tell me how the fuck would you feel?"

I let him go. He straightens up. "Believe me, it's not easy and no, I didn't handle it very well, but this has been weighing on me for years. I can't even tell my wife about it and now I have to go tell my wife's best friend she has a sister she didn't know about. So forgive me if I'm not all sunshine and roses, Dyson."

"Fuck!"

I get the impression my night is not going to get any better.

That was the understatement of the century when my doorbell rings about an hour after I got home from the office around nine thirty. I'd stayed at the office, hoping to get Byron working on some things when it comes to Ireland and her long lost family. All I have is a name. Mick didn't even disclose to me who her sister is. I'm not sure what I'm more pissed off about? The fact that Ireland has a family she never knew about or the fact that I truly have no answers.

I bound down the stairs on the hope that it's Ireland standing on the other side of the door. I swing the door open and freeze. There is a

disheveled woman standing on the other side of my door. Her hair is in perfect order, but her makeup is a mess, like she's been crying. "Cami?"

"We need to talk?" she states. "Can I come in?"

"Uh, sure." I step aside, holding the door open for her. "Upstairs," I tell her and she climbs the stairs. "Is everything alright with Tristan?" I ask as a way of conversation, or a way of getting to the bottom of why she's knocking on my door.

"Tristan's fine. Well, freaking out, but he's fine."

We step into my living room. "Can I get you something to drink? Water, wine? Tequila?"

"Bourbon?"

I smile. "A woman after my own heart." I lead her to the dining room table. Best to keep this formal, I don't want Tristan getting the wrong idea about what's happening here.

I step into the wine cellar and pull out a bottle of Pappy Van Winkle's 15 year-old family reserve and open it. Letting it breathe before pouring it into two low ball glasses. Usually I throw down about two fingers, but she looks like she could use a little more.

I take the glasses back to the table and slide one over to her. She picks it up and I go to warn her but my words die on my tongue when she slams back a good portion of what I gave her.

"What's going on with you and Ireland?" she asks and I immediately raise an eyebrow.

"Up until a few hours ago, I would have thought everything was perfect, but now…"

"What did you do to her?" Her face is hard like she truly thinks I've done something to hurt her, "Sorry," she says before finishing off her glass.

I cock my head at her. "I've not done a single thing, well, that's not entirely true, but nothing to warrant her running out on me and turning off her phone."

"I went to her apartment. Her blonde bitch of a roommate answered and said she wasn't at home. I don't like that girl." She wrinkles her nose.

I snort, "That makes two of us."

"Back to my question." She gives me a pointed look of 'don't deflect'. The look she gives me reminds me of Ireland, it makes my chest ache.

"Are you going to be as evasive as Mick with me about whatever the hell is going on? I'm assuming you know something because you're asking the same questions he did and frankly, I need answers, not a thousand more questions."

"No, I'll answer your questions, but I need to know what it is with the two of you. The last time I saw either one of you, she was taking you out with her knee and kissing my husband." Though she smiles a little at that, she doesn't say anything further.

"Which version do you want? The full, long version or the short and sweet?"

"Long," she states matter of fact and I proceed to tell Cami how Ireland and I were friends as kids until I moved away, right around the time that I broke her heart. Then I move into the present when we ran into each other in the lobby of my building, then Blu, and up to now.

"Good," she says when I'm done. She polishes off the last little swallow of her bourbon. "She's going to need you."

"Now, will you please explain to me what in the hell is going on? And why are you here?"

Cami's eyes shoot to mine, searching for answers. I don't know if she's seeking out the truth or what exactly she's hoping to see in them, but those blue eyes are burrowing deep and calculating what to say next. "Do you know anything about her father?"

"Up until a few hours ago, I would have told you no, I know nothing about him, which I don't, beyond his name. That was as far as Ireland would let Mick get before she ran out of my office."

"She knows?" Her voice is full of shock.

"His name, yes, where he is or how to reach him, no."

"What do you know about her father?" She changes the direction of her questions, pointing at me.

"I know his name. I know he slept with Ireland's mother, knocked her up and paid her off to keep quiet, but now that Lauren is dead, secrets are crawling out of the woodwork and no one will give me a straight answer." I huff in frustration.

"Is she your girlfriend?" Cami asks. Avoiding the reason why she's here.

"Yes," I tell her.

"Do you love her?" she asks.

"Yes, I do," I answer honestly and without a second thought. If it wasn't for the fact I'm dying to know why in the hell Cami is sitting here at my dining room table with some big, bad secret to tell me, I'd be freaking out over that realization.

"She just turned twenty-five, didn't she?"

"Uh, no, next month, why?"

"Huh?" she says as if she's trying to figure something out, but she shrugs.

"Does this have anything to do with her mother dying?"

Cami's eyes widen. "What? When?"

"Uh, about three weeks ago, give or take. I don't remember exactly."

"That's why. Fuck, fuck, fuck."

"Why, what? I'm starting to lose my patience with this. Will someone please tell me what in the hell is going on?"

"Her father is not dead. Gone, but not dead."

"What are you talking about?" This evasiveness is going to piss me off and cause me to break something. "Why would you know all this about Ireland?"

"Because I've just found out from Mick that she's my sister." Cami's

words are so matter of fact, so cold and yet deliberate at the same time. I'm not sure how exactly to read this woman who's explaining this to me.

"Fuck me," I breathe and sit down in the chair across from her.

"Her mother and my father had an affair back in the early nineties. I was only about three or four at the time, but my mother was a cold hearted bitch. I don't blame my father for cheating on her. In fact, in hindsight it was probably a blessing. But while he was in New York, working, he met Lauren McKidd in his office. They worked together for some time and Bobby did what he does best. Until she turned up pregnant and Bobby did the second thing he's best at. Ran away and threw money at the 'problem'." She looks down at her glass, looking for more. I slam back mine as I take in what she's saying to me. Ireland is the product of a clandestine love affair between her mother and her mother's boss. Oh, the irony. I grab Cami's glass and go into the cellar again. This time I don't put quite as much in hers and much more in mine.

When I come back, Cami has a few tears streaking down her face. I slide her glass back to her, but she doesn't drink it. "I don't know about throwing money at Lauren. They weren't exactly rolling in it when we were kids."

"No?" She cocks her head. "Well, if you're anything like me, you have a file on her?" She raises an eyebrow.

I nod. "But I've never opened it. I couldn't bring myself to look because I was afraid of what I would find inside. You have to remember, she was everything to me, though I didn't know it at the time, I was a kid. It wasn't until I wasn't around her anymore that I realized what she meant to me. Once I did, and I had the means, I started looking for her, tracking her down so when I was ready to swoop in again, I would have everything I needed. But I was too afraid to find her married, having babies, or worse. So I never looked."

"You might want to look now," she tells me with a pointed look. "I'm sure you're going to find some more answers in there. But according to Mick, her mother paid a hundred percent of her tuition. She worked, but she received money from her mom every month while she was in college.

My understanding is that Lauren McKidd banked that money and then disbursed it. Ireland, being the kind of daughter I get the feeling she is, didn't say anything about it, other than knowing her mom wanted to do something, pay for her to go to school, or whatever the case was."

My mind is blank. I don't even know what to say, how to say it or where to even start with all this nonsense. I guess it's going to be good for Ireland, maybe, in the long run.

"You said something about gone, but not dead? Where is her father?"

"That's a little more complicated and something that I can't go into full detail about. If Ireland chooses to find out and tell you, that's her choice, but there are other factors at work behind why he's gone, and frankly, I'd rather him stay gone than go back to thinking he's dead, or him truly being dead."

"God," I grumble. "I can't even begin to imagine what's going through her head right now between the shit I threw at her, and then Mick opening up this big ass can of fucking worms on her too."

She raises an eyebrow at me and I explain the contest and what happened afterward. "Basically, she's been a silent partner in Tigress from day one. I knew one day I would find Ivy Kidd and tell her she was rich and then, if necessary, buy her out of the business."

"That's honorable of you," she tells me with a smile. "I know she was going to school for marketing, business management…"

"How'd you know that?"

"She hangs out at my bar, remember?" she says with a slightly playful tone in her voice. "We've talked over the years. I've grown quite fond of her, which isn't an easy feat when it comes to me, but I don't know, there was something special about her. Now, I understand why. I guess it was just my way of looking out for my kid sister." She lowers her head, shaking it. "That's going to take some getting used to."

"What do I do now?" I sit and put my head in my hands.

"That might be a better conversation for Tristan. If she's anything like me and what happened when I found out he was still alive," she shudders,

"then you need to find her and get to her fast because she's about to spiral into a place you may never get her back from."

I slap my hand down on the table. "God! Dammit!" I shout and stand up, pulling my phone from my pocket.

"Yeah, boss?" Byron answers.

"Track her, everything, all her movements, her credit cards, all of it."

"On it, boss." I press the red button.

Cami's eyes meet mine and I see what I saw in the bar that night. With the exception of the blue color of Cami's eyes, they are the same as Ireland's. "She's smarter than that. If she doesn't want to be found, you won't find her," Cami says and I nod. Not wanting to argue with her because she's right. Ireland's going to go off the grid and I just handed her everything she needs to do exactly that in the form of a bank account with more than nine million dollars and a means to disappear completely. Fuck.

"I'll put my crew on it too," Cami tells me. "They're pretty good about it. I'll have Mills reach out to you in the morning. He's the best I've got at tracking down people."

"I don't know what to say."

She gives me a sad smile. "I should hate her, Dyson, and I really should. But how can I? She's an innocent bystander in all of this. She was born into it and there is nothing I can do to fix what he did. But I can fix the fact she has family, she has a job if she wants it, and most importantly, she has you. Don't let her let you go."

"I will die before I let that happen again."

She squeezes my arm. "When you find her, will you let me know? I'd like to introduce myself to her, as her sister, not just her friend."

I give her a reassuring nod and she smiles at me before she leaves my condo.

Chapter Thirty-four

IRELAND
'Til Kingdom Come - Coldplay

With tears streaking down my face, I stand in front of Reese's house. The lights are on and his car is in the driveway. The cab is waiting for me to pay him, but I need Reese to answer the door. I pound on it again. "Reese," I scream.

"I'm coming, baby girl." I hear from the other side of the door and my heart starts pounding in my chest. I should have gone home. I should have gone to a hotel, anything, I shouldn't be here. Being here means I have to explain everything to him and I don't know if I can. The door swings open. "Jesus, what's wrong?"

His arms wrap awkwardly around me and all the shit in my hands. "I don't have any cash," I mumble through sobs. "The cab."

"I got it, go inside." I nod and he lets me in and goes down to the cab. I drop everything in my arms on the couch. I don't want to touch it anymore, and I don't want to look at it.

Reese comes back. I notice he's shirtless, wearing nothing but flannel pajama bottoms. His chest is toned and gorgeous. His dirty blonde, normally perfectly styled hair is disheveled, his brown eyes bright with concern. "I'm sorry, is someone here?" I try to back pedal, reaching for the shit on the couch. "I should go, I shouldn't have…"

"Shh, baby girl." He comes over and wraps his arms around me. "No one's here, okay? Just me and you." He pulls back and gives me a th9orough once-over. "You're a hot mess," he says with his typical flare.

"Thanks, Capitan jackass."

He laughs, "Talk first or drink?"

"Drink, lots of drinking."

"Is this one of those nights I should be calling in sick after?"

I nod my head and new tears form. "You got it, baby girl. Alcohol, here we come." He leaves the living room in favor of the kitchen and comes back with a bottle of something, vodka, maybe, and a whole half-gallon of orange juice.

"Screwdrivers?" I raise an eyebrow. "How apt," I tell him.

"It's all I got." He smiles and pulls the glasses out from under his arm. I take one, filling it halfway with vodka and then a splash of orange juice before downing the entire thing. "Oh shit, this is bad." He sobers.

"It's really bad." I refill the glass. This time with a lot less vodka and a whole lot of orange juice.

"Do you remember oh nine, twenty-ten?" I ask. He was two years ahead of me but he took part in the contest with me.

"I remember a lot of shit, sweetheart, but you're going to have to be more specific."

"The business plan contest for that charity out of Georgia?"

"Oh, that, the one you won?" He winks at me.

I try and fail to smile at him. "Well, did you know the school got a huge donation from that company for ASU having the student with the winning business plan?"

"I remember something along those lines. That it was a school thing, so the school would profit from any money given by the company. What was it called?"

"Home Together," I remind him.

"That's it, it was a non-profit helping abused women and kids, and they were expanding into rebuilding the projects in Atlanta. What does this have to do with why you're crying your eyes out on my front step?"

I swallow more alcohol, the burn of the orange juice is enough to keep me in check and I nod at him. "Well, Home Together is owned and operated by one Mr. Dyson Cole."

"No fucking way?" He leans back, giving me a look like I've lost my mind.

"One Mr. Dyson Cole took my business plan and incorporated it into his current business, also known as…"

"Tigress," he finishes for me.

I nod.

"Wait, can he do that? Wouldn't he owe you some type of payment for that? I mean, if he were a decent human being. Shit, is that why you're here, he's not willing to pay you…"

"Reese, shut up."

He claps his hand over his mouth and I explain. "Legally, no, he owes me nothing. He took an existing non-profit business plan and turned it into something that would work on a for-profit company. Morally, it's the right thing to do."

"So let me guess. You've now got some bank account stuffed full of cash and you're freaking out about it?"

I glare at him. "Not just some bank account, Reese, multiple accounts. Everything from liquid assets to stock market shares…"

"Fuck me, how much you talking, girlfriend?"

"Liquid?" I ask and he nods. "Nine million and some change."

Reese literally falls off the stool he's sitting on.

I laugh despite myself. "That's how I looked when I saw the figures."

"Shit, baby girl, that's a hell of a lot of fucking money." He rights himself and drinks the rest of his drink before going back for more. I polish off mine and hand him my cup. "Are we sure he didn't do this because you're his girlfriend?"

"Well, between Dyson, his lawyer and his financial advisor guy, no. There were contracts put in place back in oh nine and twenty-ten. So I don't think so. I think they honestly believed Ivy M Kidd was a real person and one day they would find her. What they didn't realize was the school fucked up the submission and my name got messed up. So Dyson made Ivy a silent partner in his company and Ivy has been receiving royalty payouts every year since then. When the company went public she received a percentage of shares. How many, I don't know, I haven't been able to see straight long enough to look." My eyes wander over to the accordion file folder on the couch that looks like it's about to explode.

"Well, if you came here for advice, sweetheart, I ain't got none for you because you'd be stupid as fuck not to take that money, you earned it."

I snort, "Hardly, I wrote a business plan, nothing more."

"But didn't Dyson say something about you going to work for him? What if you did that? Would it feel like a total cop out then? I mean, I know you're working for Wellington and all, but, hello? Nine million dollars."

"That is the nine-million dollar question," I tell him before downing my new glass of alcohol.

Reese and I drank into the night, discussing Dyson's antics and I even got into what happened earlier in the night between my boss and Wellington. When I told him what I did, Reese flipped his shit with laughter. I'm not sure if it was his reaction or the alcohol, but after that, things seemed to settle some. It was after two before I passed out, completely hammered. The only thing I didn't tell him about was the information Mick saw fit to put on me about my so-called father. That is something I won't be able to be talked down from. I don't even know where to begin when it comes to that. Most importantly, for the first time since her death, I'm truly angry at my mother.

I wake up to the smell of bacon cooking, my head pounding and my stomach rolling. I lurch off the couch and dash to the bathroom. What's left of my stomach contents comes roaring back. The acid burns the back of my throat and if I ever drink orange juice again, it will be too soon.

I clean myself up, throwing my hair up into a bad twist in search of my bag and my beanie. "Morning, baby girl," Reese hollers from the kitchen and I flinch. He laughs.

"You're an ass." Ugh, I grab my head. "It hurts," I groan.

"I've got drugs, come here." I throw my hair into my beanie and head into the kitchen where he has a huge glass of ice water, two Tylenol and a couple ibuprofens waiting for me and I give him a silent thanks, down the pills and finish off the glass of water.

"I haven't been this hungover since sophomore year," I groan as I sit down at the breakfast bar while he whips up some eggs and bacon. "What time is it?"

"Just before eleven."

"Oh shit," I say, panicked.

"What?"

Then I laugh, "You know what? Fuck it."

"Fuck what, baby girl?"

"I'm pretty sure I'm getting fired right about now for not calling in and it's only my fifth day of work," I tell him and he laughs.

"You can afford not to work, unlike some of us lowly people."

I roll my eyes. "Ouch," I groan. "Don't make me do that again," I tease him, feeling lighter today about yesterday, until I catch a glimpse of the folders on the coffee table and it all comes rushing back to me. "Wanna help me with some stuff?" I ask him.

"Sure, ain't got anything better to do today. Except my date tonight." He smiles wide. He's positively glowing at the prospect of his date with Andy and I'm happy for him.

"Good." I walk over and I grab both folders.

"What is all that stuff?"

"This," I hold up the biggest one, "is all about my silent partnership with Tigress."

"And the other one?"

I sigh. "I'm not ready to talk about that one just yet."

"Whatever, baby girl, but you're going to have to talk about it sometime." He points his spatula at me, and then sets out two plates, putting eggs on each plate then a handful of bacon for each of us.

"Toast?" I remind him.

"Yup." He turns around and finds what he's looking for before bringing the plate over to me, setting it down in front of me and I butter some up and start downing the toast. On my empty, rolling stomach, the toast is perfect. After three half slices, I dig into the eggs after pouring on the salt, and then finally the bacon. I scarf down the entire thing

realizing I drank all that alcohol on an empty stomach.

When I'm done, I have a stroke of conscious about my phone and I go back to my purse and power it on. I regret it instantly when I see missed calls, texts, but only one voicemail. I click on it and see that it's from Dyson. Am I ready to hear his voice just yet? No, I'm not. I power the phone back down and put it back in my bag and go back to Reese who's cleaning up our plates. While he wipes down the counter I go for the big file folder and unwind the clasp holding it together.

There's so much stuff stuck inside that it pretty much spills out on to the counter. Most of what's in there is paperwork, but despite how full it is, it's rather organized with paperclips and binder clips. I start pulling stuff out. On top is whatever Mick handed Charlie last night and I open it. There are three envelopes inside with some papers tacked to the back side of the file folder. All of the envelopes have my name on them, with the P.O. Box address. I can only assume this belongs to Mick.

I open the first one and it is a shiny black card that says Bank of California on it with my name emblazoned in gold. The card expires four years from now. So I know the card is new. It still has the activation sticker on it. "What the hell is Bank of California?" I ask Reese.

"Phewweeee," he fans himself, "Girl, that's *thee* bank. You have to have a ridiculous amount of assets in order to even open an account."

I raise an eyebrow in question at him. "How do you know that?"

"Because, honey, I work with celebs and their moronic-ness, I see where their money comes from. So I looked."

I shake my head at him and set the card aside. I move on to the next one and it's my pin number for the card. The final envelope has a note on it, but I bypass that to look inside and I see it's another card. I open it up and it's- "Holy fuck."

"What is it?" Reese says from the sink and I flip it around. "Damn, girlfriend, that's platinum power right there."

It's an American Express card. I flip over to the note. "Automatic payment established, whatever is spent on this card every month will be

paid off automatically by your checking account." My eyes go wide. "I've never had a credit card," I tack on.

"That's not a credit card, honey, that's a plastic party card."

I laugh and thumb through some of the other stuff in the folder, most of it has to do with terms of service for the credit card, then finally a full size envelope that says 'access information' on it. I flip the flap and look inside and I see websites, followed by user names and passwords. I make a mental note to change them all, immediately. But I get the impression that won't stop Mick. I can at least update my address so the statements come to me.

"So the guy, the financial dude that works for Dyson, he offered to continue handling my finances."

Reese whistles. "What's that going to cost you?" I shrug. "Well, I guess it doesn't matter, considering you're going to have to have someone do it. At least if he's been doing it already, he might as well keep doing it."

I go for the cards they gave me last night. They're still in my pocket and I find Mick's card. "Let me use your phone."

"You have your own," he tells me.

"Yes, but my phone is blowing up with all things Dyson and right now, I don't want to talk to him."

Reese sighs and pulls his phone from his back pocket and hands it to me. I dial Mick's number and put the phone to my ear, after a couple rings he answers, "Mick,"

"Mick, it's Ireland."

I hear him take a deep cleansing breath. "We've been looking for you."

"We, who?"

"Dyson, me, your sister."

"I don't want to talk about her right now. I called for another reason and I would very much appreciate it if you left this between me and you. Do not tell Dyson."

"I'm over keeping secrets, Ireland. I still can't tell my wife and it's

fucking killing me."

"Tell your wife, I don't care."

"You...you don't?" I can hear the hope in his voice.

"Mick, I don't know your wife, so what do I care about whether or not you tell her. If it will make you feel better and a little less paranoid around me, then tell her."

"Thank you, Ireland."

"No problem. Now, about all this shit I'm looking at. I don't understand three-fourths of it. Can you dumb this down for me?"

He chuckles softly and I hear a door click closed. "Where are you?" he asks me.

"Nice try," I tell him.

"Alright, I'm in my office."

"Where's that?" I ask him.

"Away from Tigress and everyone else. I work for Dyson, not Tigress."

"Good, now, layman's terms, please." I don't even ask, I command more or less.

"Liquid assets are obvious. You have just over nine-million in that account. It grows daily and monthly based on interest earned. Because of the amount, often times your interest is sufficient that you can live off of it without tapping the principle balance."

"Okay, that I understand, but Bank of California. Is there one here in Phoenix?"

"No, but you can go to a local credit union, like Arizona Federal, and withdrawal cash. Or use the debit card and pull cash. But you're subject to their limits. As far as everything else Tigress related, you're non-liquid assets, like stock shares, are valued at close to thirty million."

"Fuck me," I breathe.

"Have you opened the other envelope?"

"Nope," I snap. "I'm not ready to go there yet."

"Well, what I'm going to tell you will apply to both. Should you choose to liquidate anything, just let me know, but there is more than enough for you to do whatever you want. Buy a house, anything. If you need more, we can get you more."

"Don't hold your breath on that. What happens to all this money if something happens to me?"

"That's something you'll need to discuss with Charlie or another lawyer, but if you go with another one, please talk to me first. I have a few friends not associated with Tigress that will work just fine for you."

"How much is all of what you're doing going to cost me?"

"It's not. It's included in Robert Enders…"

"These are separate, are they not?" I cut him off.

"They are, but they don't have to be. If you want me too, I can combine them both and they will fall under your father's…"

"Don't say it," I snap.

"Under Robert's decree, the services I provide are paid for. You owe me nothing."

"But are you getting paid?" I ask for clarification.

"Yes, you need not worry about it."

"Alright, that's all I needed to know.

"You really need to look at the other folder, Ireland."

"I'm not ready, when I'm ready I will, but not before then."

"Alright, but know you're free to spend your money how you see fit. When the year is out, I will get you everything you need to file taxes," he tells me.

"Okay, that goes beyond the scope of what I'm prepared to discuss, so for right now, I will keep looking through everything."

"Don't let it intimidate you. I know this has to be so overwhelming for you. Your sister…"

"Stop, please. I can only deal with one thing at a time and this is all I

can handle right now," I plead with him to drop the family talk. I'm not ready to even consider it right now. I need to wrap my head around the business side of what I'm looking at before I even fathom dealing with the other side.

"Let me just say this. She's ready when you are."

"Really?" I say, surprised. "She's okay with all this? Because I'm sure as hell not."

"Surprisingly, yes, she is. I didn't expect her to be and I'm sure she can provide you some more insight into Bobby than even I can. I think you'll see in the long run what he did regarding you were a blessing."

I sigh into the phone. "Alright, I will let you know."

"I'll be here when you're ready."

"Oh, and Mick?"

"Yeah?" His voice sounds a little more confident, a little less hesitant.

"Tell your wife, please. I'm not a fan of secrets."

"Thank you, Ireland, I will."

"Thanks." I hang up the phone.

"What was that all about?" Reese asks me.

"That other packet," I state simply and let it go. "His services will cost me nothing."

"Well, that's a perk, not that you can't afford it, but still." He smiles. "So what did he say?"

"We might need more alcohol," I tell him and then I launch into what Mick told me about the investments and whatnot. By the time I'm done, Reese just stares at me.

"You're a millionaire overnight. It's like winning the lottery," He teases, and in a way, he's right.

After another thirty minutes of looking at the stuff in the biggest file, my eyes are going cross and my hangover headache isn't going away so I put it all back in the file folder and shove it aside. "I'm pretty sure

all that shit is just for my records. Mick said something about getting me everything I needed to file my taxes at the end of the year so, if he's handling it all, I guess the rest is really nothing for me to stress over."

My fingers tap on the other folder.

"What are you gonna do, baby girl?" His eyes land on the folder I'm tapping.

"Honestly? I have no clue. I'm at war with myself. On one hand, I'm angry at Dyson for what he did. But in the same token, I'm angrier that he didn't just explain this to me earlier. Then I'm mad at myself because after he discovered I was the author of his business plan, we sat there for over four hours discussing many of the changes I would make to modernize it. I just rattled it off without even thinking about the consequences of my actions in doing so. I never even considered my opinion would be worth something, let alone, this much money." I take a deep breath. "To make matters worse, I opened up the can of worms the other day in an unguarded moment of muttering something he caught on to about offering up free advice. He used that as a weapon against me to get me to accept the money, though I'm pretty sure I didn't have a choice."

Tears form in my eyes. "I'm also mad at my mother."

"Why?" he asks, his face somber.

"I want her here. I want her to tell me this is a good thing, to get over myself and go back to Dyson. But in the same vein, I'm angry because for the last few weeks, I've been upset. I spent so much money, everything I had almost, to get to Joplin, to help bury my mother so my brother and his wife weren't burdened with the debt of doing so." The tears flow more freely now. "Then we sat around that lawyer's conference room the day before I flew back home and that lawyer sat there going through my mother's wishes and my brother got everything. Except the house, that's both of ours, and I got a letter."

"A letter? You didn't tell me about this."

"I know, because I haven't opened it."

"Maybe now you should?" he asks.

"The note on the envelope was enough to put me off wanting to read it. It said something to the effect of, 'I know you're angry with me, but please understand that all the answers you seek will come soon' and that's how I opened up the doors to this." I tap the package again.

"What is that?" he states, and I can tell he's growing irritated with me.

"This is information pertaining to my father," I confess.

I watch Reese's expression go from warm to cold and then back to warm again. "Isn't he dead?"

I shrug. "I thought he was, or rather I assumed he was. I never asked my mother. I didn't think I had to. Dusty and I both talked about our dad like he was dead, only last night I discovered Dusty and I do not share the same father."

"Oh fuck." Reese straightens up from his leaning position at the counter.

"My thoughts exactly."

Chapter Thirty-five

DYSON
She Is Love - Parachute

It's been a week since Ireland stormed out of my office conference room.

It's been a week since I've let myself feel much of anything.

It's been five days since anyone saw activity anywhere and when we saw it; we knew what she was doing. She went off the grid with a hundred thousand in cash. The only irony behind it, she went to California to get it. I assume she did it to throw us off her trail. Or she figured it would take us longer to get to her. It was true, though Cami sent some of her security guys to the bank and it was her that claimed the cash. After that, nothing.

My heart is lying on a floor somewhere, unmoving and completely lifeless.

I've been working from home, refusing to go to the office. Andy and reception have explicit instructions to contact me if she shows up.

I fired Wellington, and told them Ireland was no longer their employee. I give them a week before they're filing for bankruptcy. Shelly, being the tenacious bitch she is, has tried more than a few times to get into my office to see me, but each time she gets shot down. New key swipes were added in the stairwells so her card doesn't have access to the doors belonging to Tigress and her elevator key was restricted to just a few floors, all belonging to Wellington. After my second rejection, security finally got the hint and they don't call me anymore.

I haven't slept but a few hours here and there. I miss my girl more than anything. This hurts worse than it did in high school. I need her back in my life.

Andy and Reese are working on kindling something and I finally met Reese. Though he obviously didn't have much like for me, he was cordial, but shot down any attempt I made at asking where Ireland is.

Yesterday, Byron finally handed me something I was looking for.

Something that shouldn't have been as hard to get, but it wasn't entirely easy. Dusty's phone number and address. I figure if she's gone anywhere, it would be Chicago. But I haven't found it in myself to call him. Our separation, while not as long as mine and Ireland's, has been long enough that this is going to seem awkward coming from me after all these years.

I saw Becca moving out of the apartment when I stopped by. She gave me her key, said to give it to Ireland when I saw her. I partially blame Becca for all this and I really shouldn't.

"Someone paid the rent through the end of the lease," She'd told me.

"It wasn't me," I tell her. It's true. I didn't do it, which means Ireland did.

"She told me to stay, that she wasn't planning on coming back."

Those words were like a hot knife to my heart.

My doorbell rings.

I don't jump up. I know it's not Ireland, though I want it to be. Byron will get it. It rings again, but then I hear the alarm chime for the door.

Then I hear voices, sounds like a female, but it's not Ireland. They're talking about something and I finally find my feet and get up from my desk, moving down the hallway toward the stairs and I climb down them slowly. "This was in the door," the female says as I round the corner.

Cami is standing there talking to Byron. She's got her son on her hip. "You look like shit," she tells me.

"Thanks so much." Byron hands me an envelope. It's dirty, like it's been there for a while.

"Don't use your front door much?" she asks. I shake my head. "Well, that was stuck in there, and I have some news."

"Oh?" I ask her, and the hope in her voice is enough to ignite a spark of hope within me.

"Her passport was tagged at LAX last week. Leaving."

"That's not entirely good news," I mutter.

"Ah, but it was tagged coming back, this morning."

"Where?" I ask.

"Chicago." Dusty. "She have someone up there?"

"Her brother, Dusty," I share and I look at Byron.

"On it, boss."

"You really need to let her come to you."

"What makes you so certain she will?" I'm spinning the letter in my hand as I look at Cami and her son. He's nearly two and a little turd of a kid. Cami's small frame is nearly toppled by his. It's quite cute actually. If I were in a better mood, I'd smile.

"Because if you go chasing after her, you'll put her back into hiding. She's already off the grid. But eventually she will slip up. That money won't last forever and she'll end up using a card or something and you'll have a tag on her. She can't move in and out of this country without a flag. I just don't think she knows we're capable of tracking her through her passport."

"Honestly, I didn't think you had that kind of pull."

She winks. "I have a whole bag of tricks up my sleeve. You need to remember, I run Bold now. You'd be amazed at what kind of trouble celebrities get into." I shrug. "When and if she wants to come back to reality, and come back to work, she has a job waiting for her at Bold. She's earned it. I've seen her grades and her thesis. Trust me when I tell you, that girl has it going on when it comes to marketing."

"I'm very well aware; my business runs on her plans." Cami smiles at me and I do my best to return the smile.

"I'm aware. Listen, if you go to Chicago, just check on her, okay? Don't get in her face. Let her come to you. Who knows," she points to the letter in my hand, "that might be from her."

I nod and she excuses herself. "She'll come around," she says as she leaves. I tear into the letter as soon as the shuts behind her.

Dearest Dyson,

I came to tell you good-bye, but you weren't here.

I have to get away, find my head and most importantly, find out who I am. What happened last week was too much for me to handle, coupled with the betrayal of my own mother's trust, I just need some space.

I know you're capable of it, but please, don't track me down, don't follow me. When I'm ready, I will come back to you.

Please remember, I love you, always have, always will.

Yours,

Ireland

Byron cancelled our flight plans. I stayed in Phoenix, waiting, hoping.

IRELAND
Shut Up & Drive - Rihanna

"Oh my god, Dusty, look at her," I coo as I pick my niece up out of the bassinet in my sister-in-law's hospital suite. "She's absolutely perfect."

The smile on my face is the first real one I've worn in quite a while, and it's all thanks to Dusty, Anna and the newest addition to our family.

"What are you going to name her?" I ask them both.

They look at each other and Dusty nods before sharing, "Emma Lauren."

I smile at the mention of my mother's name and look back at little Emma. "She is totally an Emma."

I still haven't opened the other package. I can't bring myself to do it. I'm hoping after this trip to finally find the courage to do it. When Dusty emailed me, I had to come.

Anna is being discharged tomorrow and I don't want to intrude on them getting home and getting settled so I stopped by on my way to my hotel. I have some things to do tomorrow while I'm in town and tomorrow will be a good day to do it while they get settled, then I'll stop by before I finally take off.

I spend an hour with Emma, Anna and Dusty before I leave the hospital. I get nearly to the elevator when Dusty catches up to me. "What's going on with you?" he asks, his tone accusatory and I don't like it.

"Nothing, why?"

"You look like shit."

"Thanks, brother, I appreciate that."

"No, Vy, I mean it. You don't look so good. What's going on?"

"Honestly, Dusty, I'm fine. I just need some time to deal with things," I tell him by way of an explanation.

"Is this about mom? About the will?"

I glare at him. "No, Dusty, it's not. You and Anna need the money. I don't," I state simply.

"If you're here and you weren't in Phoenix when I got in touch with you, where were you?"

"I was in Vancouver."

"What were you doing up there? Didn't you start a new job a couple weeks ago?"

I pull in a deep breath. "It didn't work out."

"So what are you doing running to Canada?" The big brother is here, being a dick.

"I needed to get away," I tell him.

"This doesn't sound like you." His tone softens.

"I know, but I needed some space. I'm gonna hang around here for a couple days, let you and Anna get settled at home and then I'm going to

go home for a while."

"Back to Phoenix?"

I shake my head. "No, Joplin. I want to finish cleaning out the house."

"That's something we were going to do together," he says.

"When, Dusty? You've got Anna and the baby to take care of. Let me handle it. I'll get it cleaned out and then when it's done we'll both have a nice vacation spot to go to."

He smiles. "I like that idea, but you don't want to sell it? Get some of the money from it?"

I shake my head. "Not at all. It's mom's house, it's where we grew up. It needs to stay in the family."

He nods, the smile still on his face. "Go back to Anna. Keep me posted on what's going on tomorrow and let me know when you guys are home. I'll come over on Sunday and see you guys, give you guys a break and hang out with Emma, okay?"

"I'd like that." He wraps me in an awkward Dusty hug and he returns to his wife and baby girl. I get on the elevator and leave the hospital in a cab for my hotel room.

Three Weeks Later
Monster - Eminem ft. Rihanna
Broken - Seether ft. Amy Lee

Being back in Joplin has been weird.

Everyone seems to remember the fiery redhead who used to roam the streets of Joplin and I get recognized everywhere I go, but I try and ignore them all as best I can. Today I was in the grocery store and ran into two old friends from high school. Both of them pregnant, at least eight months. One with her first, the other – not surprisingly – with

her third. It was good to see them, but I like my happy little seclusion in my house on the outskirts of town. Especially considering most conversations start with, "Sorry to hear about your mom." I've heard enough sympathy to last me a lifetime. But it's to be expected in a town this small.

I'm back at the house, unpacking my groceries and about to step into mom's old room.

So far I've managed to clean up every room in the house, but hers. I even replaced some of the furniture, giving it a much more updated look than what we had before. After I've finished each room, I've been painting before putting things back where they belong. It's busy work, but it's good. Though each day I grow tired more quickly and I can't understand why.

I've been saving her room for last. I guess it is my way of putting off the inevitable. I know if I'm going to find anything out about my father, this is where it's going to be and I'm out of rooms to work on, so here goes.

I've been sleeping in my old room on my old full-size mattress and it brings back so many memories of life with my mom. I wake with a dull ache in my chest every day. The first day was the worst. It reminded me of when I stayed here during summer break between my sophomore and junior years in college. It was weird to be home for so long, but it was nice to reconnect with mom. We hadn't had that in a couple years because I'd chosen to stay in Phoenix during summer break, but I'd taken that one off and spent it here. Each day has gotten a little easier, but it still hurts.

Stepping into my mother's room is like déjà vu all over again. It hasn't changed much since I was a kid. I remember running in here on Saturday mornings and jumping up on the bed, snuggling with my mom. The memory brings a tear and a smile to my face. It's like watching it all on television. I can see her and I, snuggled on the bed until the inevitable tickle fest ensued. Remembering things like that reminds me I was really loved as a kid and no matter who my father is or was it shouldn't matter.

I became a payout to him and nothing more. That hurts, no matter how I try and slice it.

I start with the bed, stripping off the linens, then move to the curtains and pulling those down before I take them down to be washed. The house hasn't been empty for too long, but it's been long enough that some dust has piled up. It took two days and four cans of air freshener to get the musty smell out of the house. Despite being winter, it still smelled gross at first.

Once the soft stuff is in the laundry, I move on to her closet, grabbing a trash bag from the box, and bringing it with me. So far, I've donated all the clothes I've come across. My room was pretty barren because I took most everything to college with me. Dusty's was a mess that should never be touched again. I cleaned it up, took out his clothes, but I promised him I'd leave everything else for him to go through when he comes down.

In the closet, my mother had a wide variety of clothes that shouldn't have been worn in twenty-sixteen, but my mother was never a fashion trend setter. In the back of the closet, I come across a couple of garment bags hanging in the closet. I pull them out and lay them across the mattress before dusting them off and unzipping the first one.

Tears slide down my face when I see my mother's wedding dress. I've seen the pictures my whole life. Those pictures were never hidden and now that I know the truth, or at least some semblance of it, the pictures are clearer. There are pictures of my mom pregnant with her husband, but the dates are impossible to tell. There are no pictures of Dusty with his father.

"Hindsight is always twenty-twenty," I mutter and zip the bag back up and carry it into my room. This is going to come back with me to Phoenix. I may never wear it, but I want to keep it.

The other bag has a slinky black dress in it and I scold, "Mom. You little tease you."

The dress is hot and I hold it up to my body. It would totally fit if it weren't for the boobs. Then again, yup, keeping this one too.

Once both the bags are safely stowed in my room, I return to the closet and the items on the top shelf. Most of which are shoe boxes that

contain shoes. I don't even bother drooling because mom and I were not the same size what so ever. In the middle of the pile, I pull out a non-descript, shoe box that is significantly heavier than the rest of them and when I shake it, it doesn't sound like shoes.

I set all the boxes down on the table I set up and lift the lid on the heavy box. On top is a plain white envelope with one word written on it in her elegant script.

Ireland

This is it. This is what I've been searching for since coming back to the house. But can I bring myself to open it?

No, I can't. I walk the box downstairs to the coffee table and add it to the other stuff I have from her- the cards, the letter the attorney gave me after she died and a few things from my childhood that likely don't hold many clues, but it might hold something I've forgotten along the way. And old journals of mine.

I stare at the box for longer than I should before returning to her room to finish what I started.

Dinner time rolls around and my stomach rolls. I take one last look around mom's room. It's as clean as it's ever going to get. The curtains are rehung, the bed remade. I didn't repaint in here. I couldn't bring myself to do it and frankly, it doesn't need it. She'd just redone it a couple years ago. Satisfied with my work, I turn off the lights and close the door and head into the bathroom. I need to shower and clean myself up.

In all honesty, I'm avoiding what's sitting downstairs waiting for me.

After showering and eating an awful dinner of a sandwich, chips and a coke, I can't put it off any longer. I need to open this shit up. I need to stop running from my past and face the truth that has been laid out before me. Right? I can do this.

With a new bottle of wine, a glass and a little courage, I sit down and reach for the letter from the attorney.

I bypass the outside inscription and slide my finger under the flap.

I pull out a single sheet of paper, disappointed. I was hoping for more. I unfold it.

My Vyolet,

I know you're angry with me for making changes to the will and leaving you out. You have every right to be, but as the note on the outside says, you'll be taken care of, in time.

As you read this, people are scrambling to figure out how best to tell you all the words I never could. So please, when the time comes, listen to what they have to say. For the truth is all in there.

But first, go into my room, into my closet and find the brown box, in the middle of all the shoes. There you will find all the answers that you seek.

You're forever my beautiful Vyolet. I am sorry I hurt you and I hope you can find it in your heart to forgive me, one day. I love you, baby. Always have and I always will.

Mom

I have to read it twice because I keep getting blinded by the tears as they form in my eyes and drip down on to the letter as I read it.

I move the letter aside and go for the brown box sitting in the middle of the coffee table and I pull it into my lap, lifting the lid and pulling the letter on top from the box. Underneath it, there's a picture, it's faded and worn, but it's a sonogram picture.

In the upper right hand corner it says:

Baby Enders – Lauren McKidd.

I pull in a deep breath and open the letter that was on top. This one is many pages long, hand written by my mother.

Ireland,

If you're reading this, either you've turned twenty-five and I've given you the box, or I'm no longer with you. If the latter is true, baby, I am so sorry we never got to have this discussion. I promised some people that until you reached the age of twenty-five, I would keep this from you and it's a secret that has hurt me everyday since you were old enough to understand. But I knew, in time, you'd learn the truth and that I would be here to help you through it.

If I'm not, I hope this box will be enough to help you understand better.

When I was eighteen, I married Dusty's father. I was young, in love and wanted so bad to have the American dream of a white picket fence, two beautiful children and the life of a mom. When I was seven months pregnant with Dusty, his father was killed in a random robbery in New York City, which is where we're from.

When he died, I was left with a small child to raise on my own and I had to go back to work. I found a job at Bold International, Inc. as an assistant to the company's CEO and owner, Robert Enders. Bobby treated me like a queen. Gave me everything I needed and wanted without even having to ask for it. When Dusty was sick, I got the time off I needed. I was young, naïve and I thought I was falling in love with my boss.

After several months of working there, I approached Bobby and thus began an affair that would last for several months. I knew he was married, and I knew it was wrong, but I told myself I really truly loved this man and I needed to be with him. At the time, I didn't know Robert had a family back in California. I just knew he was married.

Our affair began and then a few months into it, you happened. I was pregnant with you and Bobby didn't handle it so well. Though our affair continued for some time after finding out I was pregnant, it didn't take Bobby long to return to California. It was at that time I learned of his other family, though I didn't have details, I just knew I would never have the great love of my life back. I was angry, I felt betrayed and I felt like the man owed me something for getting me pregnant, but when I felt you kick

for the first time, I no longer cared about any of that. I could have blown the lid on him, but I didn't. I kept quiet and went about my life until you were born.

When you were born, Bobby stepped up, though not as a father figure but as a source of financial stability for you, me and for Dusty. I hated that that was what he'd become, but I had what I always wanted. Two beautiful children and my life, with or without him, was complete. I just needed a little help getting there and he was all too willing to provide it to me without a second thought. I learned a little later on in life that he truly did care about you and about me, but at that time, I wasn't ready or willing to let him back into our lives. I don't think that's a path I could have or would have ever gone down. So in a way, it is my fault that you don't know your father like a woman should, but I did what I believed to be best for all of us.

When you were two, I moved you and your brother out of New York and to Joplin, Missouri to start over.

Here I started fresh with the two of you. I used money from Bobby to buy the house, and then proceeded to do what I should have done. I started working and taking care of our family. The money came in monthly like clockwork and every month, I banked that money, putting it away for when you would graduate high school. That money is how I was able to pay for you to go to college debt free. I know it's no consolation for not knowing the truth, but I want you to understand that I honestly believe the fiery spirit you have is because he wasn't a part of your life. I don't hate him, I should, but I don't and you shouldn't either. He gave me the best part of my life, you.

I know it won't be easy for you to accept this reality, but if it comes because I'm no longer with you, then please know I would support whatever decision you decide on. Whether your choice is to accept him or reject him.

If I am still here, please, forgive me. I only ever wanted what was best for you, and what I did was what I thought best. Talking about your father has never been a discussion point for us, so I hope I've given you a life

worth living with or without him in your life.

Remember, Ireland, I love you, with all my heart, and all my soul. I will always be with you, no matter how far away I may seem at times.

Inside this box you will find letters Bobby and I exchanged over the years when he would reach out to check on you. I always saved his letters and copied mine so that one day you would be able to have them to read for yourself. Trust me, this will be a lot to take in, so take baby steps, sweetheart.

Love you always & forever,

Mom

Every ounce of anger I felt for my mother washes away in the blink of my eyes, along with the tears streaming down my face.

Chapter Thirty-Six

IRELAND
It's Not Over - Daughtry

Life officially sucks ass.

Wake up, get dressed, work, come home, undress, shower, sleep. Rinse and repeat.

Ireland has been gone for six weeks without a trace. Without a word. My phone calls go unanswered, my emails go unanswered and I've put off calling Dusty as long as I can. I can't take it anymore.

I'd programmed his number in my phone and I find his name. After a moment of hesitation, I find it in me to press the phone button.

It rings, rings again, and by the third ring I'm about to hang up when I hear, "Hello?"

Finally. "If I were to call you Dirty-D, would you know who this is?"

There's a roar of laughter through the phone. "Fucking vacuum cleaner, how the hell are you?"

For the first time in six weeks, I smile. "I'm good man, could be better, but I'm surviving."

"Yeah? I hear you're some big shot in Phoenix."

"Where'd you hear that?"

He laughs. "I have ears, man, and I read the paper, though if I hadn't seen the picture of you to go along with it I would've never known it was you. You changed your name?"

I shake my head. "Nah, man, I just ditched Richards."

"Good, Cole works better for you anyway. So what's going on?"

"Forget about me, how are you?" I redirect him. I don't want to get into how miserable I am and how talking to my high school best friend isn't going to make that any better.

"I'm great. I'm running my own shop in Chicago, business is good. I got married about three years ago. We have a six week old baby girl named Emma." Six weeks, Chicago, she's been there.

"Wow, man, that's awesome. I'm really happy for you. I'll have to come up to Chicago and meet your family."

"Do me a favor though?" he asks.

"What's that?"

"Go home and cheer my sister up, will you? That girl's gonna kill me."

Go home? Joplin. "How long has she been there? Last I heard she was in Phoenix."

"Yeah, idiot, same city you're in. You know, I swear to god, Dyson, she never got over you. When she was here to see Emma, she looked like hell. I just came back from there a couple days ago and she's, yeah, she's in bad shape, but she won't tell me what the hell's wrong with her."

"Shit, man, I'm so sorry." Sorry doesn't cut it. This is my doing, and I know it.

"Nah, it's all good. I think mom…shit, did you hear about mom?"

I close my eyes. "Yeah, man, I saw it in the paper, my mom saw it too."

"My god, why didn't you guys come to the funeral?" His voice is soft, upset.

"Honestly, I didn't know until after it was over, about a week or so. My mom knew, and when I asked her about it, she said she'd have felt like she was intruding on you guys. She hadn't been around for so long, she didn't feel it was right."

"Ah man, I'm sorry. Would have loved to have both of you there." I hear him shuffle his phone then say something to someone. "Listen, man, I gotta run, is this your number?"

"It is." I confirm.

"Good, been wondering how to reach you for a while now. If you're serious about coming to Chi-town, holler, we'd love to have you. Anna would love to meet you."

I smile into the phone. "I'd like that."

"Good, later, man."

"Bye." I hang up with Dusty and my heart swells with hope. I know where she is and she's okay, other than being a basket case, and all things considered, I'd be one too. I just hope her pain is not all caused by me.

My doorbell rings and I look at the clock, it's eight, Cami's normal stop over time. At least today, I have news for her. I bound down the stairs and open the door. "I should just leave it open for you," I tell her and she gives me a sad smile. "Come in, I have some news."

"What?" Her shock is evident, both in her face and in her voice.

"I just talked to her brother."

"Oh my god, has he talked to her?"

I smile a little wider, hope blossoming inside of me. "He saw her a few days ago, said she looked like shit."

"That doesn't surprise me. Where is she?"

I snort. "She went home. The one place I didn't bother to look because I never expected her to go back there."

"Where's home?"

"Joplin, Missouri," I tell Cami.

"Will you let me go? Let me have some time with her?"

"If you promise to bring her home," I tell her sadly.

"I won't promise that, but I will do everything in my power to do just that." She smiles. "I'll leave tomorrow."

"How much time do you need?"

"I have no idea. One of two things is going to happen. She's either going to accept me into her home or shut me out. If she shuts me out, I'll keep trying. If she accepts me, I don't know. Why?"

"Because tomorrow is her birthday."

"Oh shit. That I didn't know."

"And next week is the anniversary of when I left her. I'd really like to have her back in my arms on the ten year anniversary, if that's okay with you." My voice is somber, but it's the truth and she sees it in my eyes.

"I will do everything I can to make that happen. One way or another."

"Good. I'm counting on you," I tell her and she smiles. "You have my number. Call me if you need anything. It's a small town, and I'd give you my mother's house but no one has been it in years. It's a mess."

"No worries, I'm hoping she'll let me stay with her, if not, I'll find a hotel or something."

With that, she leaves, headed for her home and to tell her husband the news we've been waiting for what feels like forever to hear. Now I just have to hope that Cami is the antidote to all things Ireland and bringing her home.

IRELAND
Everything - Lifehouse

"No fucking way…" I stare down at the row of sticks on my counter. I count them in my head. There are ten of them, and all ten of them say the same fucking thing over and over again.

"God, why does this feel like my mother all over again?" I groan as I look at the pink and blue plus signs, then the three different digital tests all flashing the same result over and over again. "Happy birthday to me," I groan as my doorbell rings. Panic surfaces quickly and before I think about it, I'm sweeping ten positive pregnancy tests into my trash can.

"Who the hell would be here?" You can freak out later. Right? You can get through this, huh? Yup, you'll survive this. The inner pep talk continues as I walk toward the door. I see an unfamiliar, unassuming car in the driveway. It has Missouri plates so I don't think much of it when I open the door.

I stand there, blinking like an idiot. "Did he send you here?"

She laughs, "No, I came on my own."

"It's a bit odd, don't you think?" I ask her.

She nods. "It is, but I assure you there is a reason for my visit. Can I come in?"

I hold the door open, letting the petite woman step inside my mother's home. The oddness of having her here is beyond strange, but I let it go. "What can I do for you, Cami?"

"Got anything to drink? We're gonna need it. We need to talk," she says, her voice soft, her eyes gentle. I nod and go to the kitchen.

"I just have wine, is that alright?"

"Perfect." She smiles and I realize I can't drink wine anymore. Fuck. This is going to suck ass. I have the feeling she's here to discuss Dyson with me and I'm not ready to talk about him, not yet, and not today. "Happy birthday, by the way," she says.

"Uh, thank you. How'd you know?"

She smirks and winks at me. "I have my sources."

I shake my head and grab a wine glass out of the dish rack and the bottle of wine from the counter and pour her a glass before pouring myself a glass of apple juice. I have a feeling I'm going to need a drink. "I love this house," she says from the living room.

"Thanks, it was my mother's. I've been cleaning and painting it since I came home," I tell her as I hand her a glass of wine.

"You're not drinking?" she asks and I shake my head.

"I've been drinking way too much these last few weeks," I tell her by way of an acceptable explanation. "You're a long way from home to wish me a happy birthday, Cami. What can I do for you?"

"Can we sit?" she asks.

"You're stalling."

"How long have we known each other?" she asks quickly.

"A while. We met in college, though you were nearly done, what fifth year, six? Then I started going to Blu and ran into you again, so, what,

five years maybe? Why?"

"I just want to make sure we're friends."

"Of course we're friends. Why wouldn't we be?" I pause a moment. "Did something happen with Tristan?"

"Oh no, we're good. Well, as good as he can be considering he's watching me like a hawk making sure I don't bolt again." I raise an eyebrow at her, encouraging her to continue. "I like to run away when shit gets too real."

"I can't imagine anything that would drive you away from Tristan, or your son, Cami. Is this something you want to talk about?" Because god knows I do not want to talk about Dyson, I add in my head.

"We have a mutual friend," she tells me.

"Dyson, I know. But I thought you weren't here because of him."

"I'm not and he's a mutual friend, but not the reason I'm here." She is being evasive and it's starting to piss me off. I don't want to play fucking games anymore.

"Spit it out, Cami. Seriously, all this brow beating is making me fucking bonkers."

I watch as her eyes darken, her body stiffens. "God, you're just like your father."

Her phrase sends me back and I land in one of the chairs in the living room. "What did you say?"

"I didn't want to be so fucking harsh about it, but damn, girl."

"How do you know my father?" I narrow my eyes at her. She repeats the same look and it looks just like me.

"Because you're my sister." Her voice softens. "Robert Enders is my father. My maiden name is Enders."

My stomach rolls. I swallow it back. What she's telling me has nothing to do with why my stomach is rolling around like someone set off a butterfly explosion and I don't want to go running to the toilet just this second.

"Are you alright?" Her voice is full of concern and I shake my head, throwing myself out of the chair and darting down the hallway until I get to the bathroom. "Ireland?" Cami calls.

She comes running after me as I lose my breakfast into the toilet.

She snickers. "I didn't realize having a sister could be so upsetting," she teases. "Or does it have something to do with the fact you kissed your brother-in-law like he was your next meal ticket."

The memory of that night in Blu, the night I kneed Dyson, comes racing back to me. I kissed Tristan in an effort to make Dyson jealous and failed miserably because I had no idea they knew each other. "I kissed my brother-in-law? Oh god." I retch again. She scoops up my hair and pulls it out of my way.

"You're forgiven, by the way. You're lucky I'm not the jealous type, otherwise, you know?" Her voice is a million times lighter than it was when she came in twenty minutes ago. I feel her stiffen behind me and my eyes happen to land on the trashcan I dumped all those tests into. They're hard to miss. "So, I don't make you sick?" I can't see it, but I can hear her smile.

"No, far from it actually. Though I guess I never expected my first sisterly bonding experience to come when I was puking into the toilet." I try to laugh and fail. "So..." I lean back and she releases my hair. I need a minute to recover so I sit down on the floor and flush the toilet. "You're my sister, huh?"

She shrugs like it's no big deal. "I guess so."

"How are you so calm about all this?" I ask her, unable to wrap my brain around it.

"Come on, let's get you cleaned up, then we can talk." She stands, holding out her hands to me and I take them as she helps me up. My head is still a little dizzy but it's getting better and I brush my teeth before leaving the bathroom. I find her in the kitchen dumping out her wine glass.

"Don't like it?" I ask.

She chuckles and turns. "I didn't try any. I was hoping you wouldn't notice I wasn't drinking it, and then you came back with apple juice and…"

I cock an eyebrow, questioning her. "Seriously? You too?"

She smiles a wide, gorgeous smile that reminds me of sunshine and happier days. "Shh, Tristan's the only one who knows. I'm only about eight weeks."

I count backward in my head. "Well, maybe we really are sisters. If all ten of those tests are accurate, I was only with Dyson for about a week, about seven weeks ago."

"So you haven't told him yet?"

I snort. "I haven't even processed it. Literally, my doorbell rang and I tossed them all in the trash. I was staring at them like a moron."

She laughs again, "I did the same thing. But then, I ran." She crosses her arms over her chest, staring at me. "You have to tell him."

"Gah." I throw my hands up in frustration. "I don't want to tell him anything. I just want to sit here in my own little piece of happy and be happy."

Cami bursts out laughing. "You look like shit. You have no food in your house, the house is immaculately spotless, and you're going fucking crazy sitting in this house day in and day out. You have millions of dollars in the bank and you want to start spending every fucking penny of it. You want to run around like a crazy woman but instead, you hole up here, wallowing in your self-pity while the reason for existing sits in Phoenix without you."

"I'm not sure how to take that statement," I scowl at her.

"It's fucking true and you know it."

"Well, aren't we just a big old anger-ball." I stick my tongue out at her and she explodes in laugher. It's infectious and I can't help laughing too.

I throw my hands up. "What do I do?"

She smiles. "You go home. You walk up to his door and you grovel at

his feet. Kiss them if you have to."

"I hurt him so bad."

"I think he understands you more than you realize. See, Dyson is a lot like Tristan. He understands that women need their space. This is why I'm here and not him," she tells me. "He's the one who told me where you were."

"How'd he find out?" I ask, honestly curious.

"Apparently he called an old friend," she says sweetly.

"Dusty."

"He's your brother?" I nod. "Well, sometimes siblings know best," she winks.

"I still don't understand how you're so cool with all this."

"Sit down and let me tell you a story."

Cami ushers me to the couch and she starts talking about Bobby and what it was like to grow up with him. It wasn't sunshine and roses for her either. But she talks about it freely and openly, like she's processed all the pain it's caused her and we talk until the early morning hours.

Talking to Cami was like talking to my best friend. She listened, was attentive, didn't interrupt unless she thought I was being an idiot, which she pointed out I was when it came to the package Mick had given me. She said the only thing in there that was going to scare me was the amount of money in my inheritance. She said she didn't know how much it was, but if it was anything like hers then it was a lot more than the nine-million I received from Dyson.

The next morning I am making coffee when she comes into the kitchen. She slept in my mom's room, after some arguing, but I convinced her it was okay and that's true, it was. When I got up, I grabbed the big bad bundle of avoidance and set it on the breakfast bar with the intention of opening it up when coffee was done.

"You're finally going to do it, aren't you?" she asks when she takes a seat next to the file.

"Morning to you too. Coffee?"

She yawns, "Yes, please."

"I don't do the half and half thing. I'm a creamer kind of girl."

She smiles wide. "Me too."

I slide her a cup and follow it up with the creamer, then I pour the remaining pot into an insulated decanter and start another pot. I have a feeling we're going to need it. "You're lucky," she says as I sit down.

"Why is that?" I ask.

"My package was full of disks and a ton of other shit and I had to sit and watch them all. I was quite the masochist when it came to all my drama, but the issue I had was I was discovering he was still alive." She pauses, takes a sip of her coffee. "Well, I guess it's not much different, only I lived through the funeral."

"I found a letter, in my box of shit, from him. He was telling my mother he had to go away for a while and he didn't know when or if he'd be back. It was dated in twenty-eleven."

She nods. "That would be when it happened."

"Why though? That's what I don't understand."

"Do you know anything about Bold International?" she asks me.

"A little. I'd done some research on it before I graduated, when I was looking for jobs. I wasn't sure I wanted to dive into celebrities, so I stuck with business management and marketing."

She winks. "Wise choice. Celebrities are a breed all their own. Tristan is no exception, though maybe a little. Being famous is not his ideal lifestyle and he does all he can to avoid it. This is why we live in Phoenix most of the time. But aside from that, they're different animals. The long and the short of it is Bobby walked in on something he was never meant to see. What he saw was something that put him in pretty deep with a Mexican cartel. The feds stepped in and helped clean it up in exchange for his testimony. I understand now why Bobby did a lot of the things he did when it came to me, you, our brother. He was determined to protect

us all, but in reality, he was hurting us more. He saw that with me, I was hoping he'd learned his lesson, but apparently not."

"I get the feeling, from the letters, my mom wouldn't let him back in. It was a few years ago, something shifted in his letters, I was still pretty young."

"That would be when my mother died."

"Oh Cami, I'm sorry."

She chokes on her coffee. "Don't be. My mother was a bitch, literally. No one cried when she died."

"Ouch, that had to hurt."

"In hindsight, my father did what he did to protect me. He did the same for you, just for different reasons. Just remember that. It doesn't mean you have to like him or know him, it just means that while he threw money at your mom, he didn't know any other way to handle the situation. He wasn't going to let his child grow up in poverty when he could fix the problem."

"He reminds me of Dyson." I smile at the name for the first time in weeks. Maybe Cami is right. It's time to go home.

"I can see that. You know, they say we marry our fathers." She laughs. "No, I take that back, Tristan is the exact opposite of my father, but maybe that's why I'm married to him." She winks.

"You're a lucky bitch," I tease her.

"So are you." She shoulder checks me. "Come on, let's do this together?"

I nod in agreement. "Together."

With that, the package was opened and my past spilled out onto the breakfast bar.

Inside the envelope were all the letters my mother had sent him. Though she never reached out to him first, he always seemed to reach out, at least a few times a year, to check in on me and my mother.

Beyond those letters was a DVD. It just said 'Ireland' on it. Cami stopped me from watching it. She said she had a feeling it was shot recently, or around the same time as hers was. Regardless, it would tear me down in a way she couldn't help me with. She suggested I save it for Dyson. Let him be the rock. When I asked her why, she just smiled and didn't explain. I get the impression maybe she didn't do that with Tristan. I don't know their whole story, but the more we talk as we go through this stuff, the more I'm starting to better understand Cami.

There was always a connection between the two of us but we could never put our finger on it. I can't wrap my head around the irony of small worlds. We both went to ASU, despite growing up in two different states. We live in the same neighborhood and she's neighbors with the man I'm truly starting to miss.

Mick wasn't kidding when he said my inheritance would make what Dyson gave me look like chump change. Though this money doesn't come with a mountain of investments like Dyson's did, it does come with a very large bank account. Between the money from Dyson and my inheritances, I am now pushing close to seventy-five million dollars in assets. Considering I didn't have seventy-five hundred dollars to my name two months ago, it's a huge pill to swallow. I can't even begin to imagine what I'm going to do with all this money. But for now, until I can fully accept the fact I have a father after twenty-five years, the money is staying untouched.

Cami's been in Joplin for three full days when I ask her to help me with something. "Anything." She smiled.

"Will you help me get my heart back?"

She chuckles, "Of course, whenever you're ready."

I think she thought I meant going back to Phoenix. I meant walking around the corner. As we walk she asks me what we were doing so I tell her about the day Dyson finally seemed to really notice me and the events that followed. I tell her how I stood in front of his old house and talked myself into letting him go. How when I did that, I threw something at the house that was very important to me.

She laughs, "You don't expect it to still be there do you?"

"No, but if it is, then I'll have my answer."

"Then let's find it."

We approach the house and so many memories come flooding back to me about when we were kids, including running up and down the steps until Dyson's mother would yell at us and we'd run off laughing. It was stupid, but we were kids.

"Is this it?" she asks and I turn around, looking at what she has in her hand.

"Oh my god, that's it."

"It's gorgeous. Like a tiger's eye."

I wink at her. "Why do you think he calls me tigress?"

"Isn't that…" Realization dawns on her when she puts his company and me together. "Well then, can we go home now?"

I nod enthusiastically.

Chapter Thirty-Seven

DYSON
Four Days Later
Closer - The Chainsmokers ft. Halsey
I Choose You - Sara Bareilles

March 31, 2016…

Ten years.

It's been ten years since the day I fell in love with the fiery fifteen year old and my life changed.

It's been seven weeks since she left me.

I deserved it. I pushed her too hard, too fast. I was talking about her moving in, then throwing money at her like she'd always had money in her life and the reality of that situation was too much. I should have let Mick have his way with her first. Let her process that, then eventually bring her around to the idea of accepting the money she's made through Tigress. Or vice versa. I never should have let her face both. I knew better. I knew everything I was telling her was going to drive her away.

I'm doing everything I can to respect her space, to respect her wishes by staying away from her, but each day it grows harder to concentrate on anything but going and getting her. And telling her she's being ridiculous and we can work through this together. That's what we're supposed to do. As a couple, as boyfriend and girlfriend, not her against me or me against her.

The bottom line is I fucked up and I'm waiting, impatiently for the woman I love to come back to me.

At eight p.m. on the nose, my doorbell rings, which means…I race down the stairs. If my doorbell is ringing at eight o'clock that means Cami is home. If Cami is home… I throw open the door and I blink like a fool. "Tristan, is everything alright?"

"Yeah, man, everything's good."

I raise an eyebrow at him. There's a sense of relief in his eyes I haven't seen in about a week. I would have gone over there to check on him and Jaden and ask how things were going in Joplin, but I got tied up the last

few days so I haven't gone over there. "Did you want to come in?"

"Nah, I gotta get back to the house."

"Is Cami home?" Hope blooms in my stomach. I don't know why, but I get the feeling he's here to deliver some bad news.

"She is, got home day before yesterday. She wanted me to come over, but she's loving on Jaden, she missed him." He smiles a genuine smile that I hadn't seen yet. I got the impression being away from Cami was just as hard on him as it's been on me being away from Ireland. "I came to let you know that we're having a big get together at Blu tomorrow." I scrunch my nose. Social events are not at the top of my list of things to do right now. "I know, trust me, I was you once, remember?" I nod. "But if you want to make things work with Ireland when she comes home, then getting together tomorrow is with our very closest friends, Cami's family. Would be good for Ireland if you're a part of that too."

"I don't know," I say with hesitation.

"Think about it. Oh, and I was told to deliver this to you," Tristan says as he hands me an envelope and I look at the writing of my name. It's the same script that was on the envelope left in my door when she left. I cringe, but take it from him. I don't need a kiss off letter. The least she can do is tell me to go to hell in person.

"The party starts at seven. The bar is closed to the public tomorrow. You don't have to stay all night, but I would love to have you there."

I nod. "Alright."

He smiles. "Good. Oh, and do me a favor?"

"Uh sure?" I say with hesitation.

"Clean yourself up. You look like hell," he says with a laugh.

I don't know why or where it comes from but I burst out laughing for the first time in weeks and he smiles as he walks away from my door. I close it and lean against it, holding the weight of the envelope in my hands before locking up and climbing all the way up to my bedroom. I sit on the bed before sliding my finger under the seal and opening up the folded pages.

Dearest Dyson,

I know a letter, on this day, is not what you want from me, but there are a few things I need to explain to you.

First of all, why I left.

I left because I couldn't handle everything being thrown at me at once. As you probably already know, I've come to accept the money you've given me for Tigress's business plan work I did all those years ago. It's too much, but I guess there really is no arguing with you on this matter and Mick won't let me donate it to charity. But I cannot accept this money if you cannot accept my terms. You see, I lost my job a few weeks ago and during the time of my self-imposed seclusion I've come to the realization I'm not going to be a very good housewife, then again, in an effort to hide my whereabouts, I've been living strictly on cash and it hasn't been much fun. So, I need a job.

But in my isolated state, I've learned more about myself than I could have ever learned without giving myself a chance away from everything. Including the fact that I was angry with my mother. You see, she left me out of her will. She handed over all her money, life insurance and the insurance payout from the accident to my brother because he needed it, and I couldn't understand why, until now. I went home, back to Joplin, back to my mother's house and back to her room because I had to find my answers and find them I did. At the end of a very long, trying day, I found it in my heart to forgive my mother for never telling me about my father. After countless days and years' worth of letters between my father and my mother, I realized that, in his own way, my father loved me too.

It wasn't until Cami showed up on my mother's door step that I learned a woman I considered a true friend, was really my sister and our connection was always there. We both knew, somewhere along the lines there was some type of deeper meaning for why we so easily became friends. Cami also told me about my father, about growing up with him. The reality of what he did to my mother and me is minor in comparison.

But at the end of the day and that discussion, I realized while it was a fucked up way of going about it, Bobby did what he had to do to protect me and Cami. I also learned Cami's brother isn't someone I will likely ever meet. He's pulled himself away from the family because Cami insisted on taking over Bold and he wants nothing to do with her or with the company. Apart from that, I also learned I have an even younger half-brother that was born after my father was forced into hiding. This news was surprising, but once Cami told me about his mother, I see things differently.

You see, his mother is his perfect half. There is so much love between the two of them that I think he may have finally found happiness with someone. And for that, I will accept my younger brother, just as I intend to accept the fact I have a father I've never known.

I've also learned that Bold International, Inc. is part mine. Though it's not exactly the profit kind of mine like Tigress is, I can choose to make it mine at any time. So maybe I don't need to work. I could stay at home, spend money while still making money, raise some babies and be with my one and only.

Speaking of my one and only. You see, there's this guy. He's complete and total sex on legs, with gorgeous light brown hair, blue-violet eyes that burrow deep into my soul and capture me wholly and completely. I think you'd really like him. He owns this company he named after a fiery redhead he met when he was a kid because he fell in love with her on the floor of a barn and he never let her go.

She fell in love with him the day she gave him her heart in the form of a tiger's eye rock. Then she fell in love with him again the same day he did, on the floor of that dingy barn. Somewhere along the line, she lost her heart, threw it at a door, hoping that doing so would push him away from her. But it only made her miss her heart that much more.

Then, in the middle of a lobby, nervous and a complete and total wreck, she spilled coffee all over him because he was in too much of a hurry to slow down. She apologized as best she could, but in the end, he was still mad at her. She thought her heart was gone forever until the

night, in a bar, when he made a move on her roommate and she realized, unequivocally, that no matter how hard she tried to ignore it, she was falling in love with him all over again.

He was a stuck-up three-thousand dollar suit wearing pencil dick, a cocky-bastard, a prickweed, asshat, manwhore, fuckwad, and all he begged for her to do was say his name.

Dyson!

P.S. If you look in the envelope, you will find my heart. I am giving it to you again to hold precious and dear until you can give it back to me, whole and complete.

P.P.S. I love you!

Always yours,

Your VeeVee

I flip the envelope over, spilling an identical rock to the one she gave me all those years ago, only this one is more weather worn where mine is more smooth and polished. Looking at the rocks in my hand, I see the difference.

I went on to be the polished, refined business man, with little in my past to harm me. My father's death wasn't a tragedy, it was a blessing. My choices in life were never really mine. Sure, I could have gone back to her in Joplin but if I had done I'd have never known what could have happened. Or whether or not I'd ever be able to have her as my own again. Because I'm selfish, I wanted to be sure that the woman I loved needed me as much as I needed her.

She lived a tougher life. Never knowing her father, having secrets held from her for years by the one person she was supposed to trust the most. Then going to college in an attempt to move on with her life, only to be brought back there when her mother died. Then, in a sick twist of fate, she runs into me, literally. And from that moment, she was pulled on a ride unlike anything she'd ever experienced only to be thrown into a brick wall and forced to face her past, face all the emotions she never

thought she was going to have to face. Those emotions threatened her spirit and she needed to find it in herself, somewhere, to process all of that.

She's finally done exactly that.

Chapter Thirty-Eight

IRELAND
This Love - Maroon 5

"Oh my god, you guys are fussing like I'm about to walk down the aisle."

"Dex is an ordained minister, you totally could."

"Oh my god, Raine, don't scare the poor girl," Cami scolds her friend.

My stomach rolls. "I've already thrown up like ten times today, don't push it," I tell them all.

Cami introduced me to an entire entourage of friends. Raine, Jolene, Naomi, and one I haven't stopped fangirling over, Addison Carver-Black. Raine is with Dex Harris, drummer for 69 Bottles, Beau is married to Mick; I've known Beau since I met Cami in college and compliments of going to Blu, but I didn't know she was married to Mick. Oh god, that meeting was awkward as all get out. But the woman is gorgeous with an amazing head on her shoulders. She holds no ill will toward me for what Mick went through, but Bobby is another story. Jolene is with Tyson, Tristan's wing man and head of security, and Naomi is with Travis Jackson. I mean, seriously? Next to Tristan, Travis is like the hottest fucking man in Hollywood right now and I envy her a little. Addison is married to two men, Talon Carver, lead singer of 69 Bottles and Kyle Black, the band's manager. I hear they have quite the story to tell when it comes to how they met, and I'm anxious to hear all about it. Best of all, I can't imagine having two men in my life and in my bed. Addison positively glows because of it.

All of us girls are holed up in Cami's house while we wait for our transport to the party. I feel like I've fallen into the kind of high society I can live with. Jolene and Naomi I've seen countless times at Blu. Apparently they, along with Beau, are all part owners of Blu Phoenix. They bought it when the owner decided to sell the old place after it sat empty for a long time. They've turned it into quite the hangout. It's always been my favorite place to be when I go out because you just never know who's going to show up.

Having owners like Cami and Tristan means their connections in the celebrity world run deep. Tonight, despite the club being closed to the public, is no exception.

"Are you ready?" Cami asks me. My stomach's doing flip-flops again and I'm pretty sure it has nothing to do with morning sickness.

I nod and look myself over in the mirror.

My hair is swept up into a high knot on top of my head with the length cascading down my back. I'm wearing an emerald green, strapless cocktail dress that has a lace overlay decorating the bodice and a little bit on the short, barely knee length skirt. It's capped off with matching peep-toe pumps, black and silver bangles on my wrists and large silver hoops in my ears. Cami's fault. She took me shopping today. The dress and the shoes, coupled with the jewelry, cost more than a single paycheck I would have received from Wellington.

It's April first.

Its ten years after the day Dyson left me in Joplin and tonight, I go back to him. Only this time, I tell him everything I wanted to say that day. But first, I have to get there and get through the rolling stomach.

"The car's here," someone calls, I think it's one of Addison's crew because she's pretty attached to her.

"You look fabulous," Addison tells me and I blush. She leans in close to my ear and says, "At the end of the day, I'm a friend. I know that's hard to see, but you'll understand, eventually." She winks at me. She totally gets me and I smile at her.

"I'm trying."

"Good, that's all I can ask for."

"Cotah, oh my god," Raine squeals. "I didn't think you were coming."

The blonde girl laughs. "We just landed a little while ago." She beams, looking around and saying hi to Cami, then the rest of the girls.

"Oh, shit," Cami says. "Dacotah, this is Ireland. Ireland, this is Cotah, she's married to Derek Hunter." Cami winks at me. "You two have more in common than you realize."

Cotah extends her hand to me. "Nice to meet you."

"Likewise, though I'm not sure what Cami is talking about," I say pointedly at Cami.

"Oh, Cotah fell in love with a millionaire too." She winks and runs off down the stairs, the rest of the girls follow behind her.

"Really?" I ask.

"Yeah, it's like a walking, talking romance novel." She beams.

I sigh, "Yes, yes, it is. Now it's time to get my happily ever after."

She smiles wide. "I heard. Let's go get him."

We all pile into a huge limo. I can't stop myself from looking over at Dyson's condo. There are lights on inside but the curtains are all drawn tight.

"He'll come," Cami whispers in my ear. "If not, I'll come and drag his ass out." I give her a soft laugh. "It will be alright. Look at it this way, he never stopped looking, he never stopped hoping and he said something before I went to Joplin that I think you need to hear."

"What's that?" I ask, my nerves shaking my voice.

"That he would do anything to hold you in his arms on this day. So if he has any inclination that you'll be at Blu tonight, he will be there." She winks and climbs in the limo. I reluctantly pull my eyes away from Dyson's windows and I follow her. Once the door is closed, we're off. As we drive past his place, the curtain on the top floor pulls back and he looks out the window at the limo as we drive through the parking lot.

"I'm here," I whisper.

The girls take all of two seconds to distract me. "Did the boys come?" Raine asks of someone.

Cotah is the one who answers with a chuckle. "They did. I have to tell you, those two, they've got it bad for each other."

Raine squeals and starts bouncing up and down.

"What are you two talking about?" Addison cuts in and now they

have everyone's undivided attention.

"You don't know?" Raine looks at her, obvious confusion in her eyes.

"Obviously not if I'm asking," she playfully scowls at Raine.

"If it makes you feel any better, we have no idea what their talking about either," Jolene cuts in.

Naomi laughs. "That's nothing new."

"Truth," Jolene says with a smirk. "So spill it already."

Raine looks nervous, even a little green. She looks at Cotah. "Will we get in trouble?"

Cotah snorts, "Yes."

"Okay, good." She is absolutely beaming with dreamy eyes.

"You're incorrigible. You know this, right, Raine? If I get my ass beat because you can't keep your mouth shut, I'll tell Dex."

"Back up the freight train. What the hell are you two talking about?" Cami interjects. "Why would you get your ass beat?" She turns to Cotah who turns as red as a damn cherry.

"Uh, Derek isn't just my husband." She smiles in a way that makes my insides melt. "He's my Master."

"As in," Addison chimes in, "he's a Dom?"

Cotah nods. "Dex is too."

Raine lights up with giddiness, as if it's the best news ever.

"Huh," Addison sits back, "and here I thought my sex life was kinky."

The entire limo erupts with laughter, including mine. "You have the kinkiest sex life, trust me, but Dex introduced Beck to the lifestyle," Raine says to Addison and Cami more than anyone else.

"Oh, shit," Cami says, "And?"

"Oh, he found what he was looking for without knowing he was looking for it," Cotah says gleefully.

"And that was?" Beau says, raising an eyebrow.

"His own Master."

"Beck's gay?" Addison squeals. "Jesus, I would have never…"

"Who's Beck?" Naomi pipes up.

"Jesus, I would have never…" Cami trails off.

"Okay, in Beck's defense, I'm not entirely sure he knew it either. It's more like, he found what he was looking for, but it wasn't between the legs of a woman," Raine says. "Though…" she stops herself.

"Oh no, spill it," Addison says, and it's obvious they're close – Raine and Addison.

"Erm…I kind of had a threesome with Beck and Dex." She blushes.

"What?" Everyone in the limo squeals. I sit back and watch the show.

Raine sighs. "Remember when I showed up in New York, after Cami sent me to help you?"

"Vaguely, that wasn't the happiest of times for me," she reminds Raine.

"No, it wasn't, but anyway Dex was putting the moves on me pretty hard and I made him work for it. Without thinking about it, I pulled Beck into the room with us. I…I needed buffer of sorts. But it all fell apart."

"That's disappointing," Cami chimes in. "That's a man sandwich I wouldn't mind being between."

"Cami," Beau, Jolene and Naomi scold her at the same time.

"What?" Cami says defensively. "They're fucking gorgeous and while I would never, ever sleep with anyone besides Tristan, I am a woman who isn't oblivious to sexy men." She blushes. "Besides, it would only be good for a night. Tristan is amazing for a lifetime." She gets dreamy dopey love eyes.

The rest of the car's occupants do too because they all seem to agree when it comes to their men. I won't lie, I had them too because Dyson was all I could think about.

The conversation dies down a little after that, but Addison is probing Raine for more information on Beck and his Master. She even seems to be asking questions about their relationship.

Cotah slides over to me, "you doing alright?"

I nod. "I'm freaking out a little."

"Why is that?" she asks, her voice soft, as we watch the rest of the girls.

"Because, it's not just me he has to take back," I tell her. I don't know why but I can talk to Cotah, she's easy and sweet to talk to. Maybe it's because we both have come from similar backgrounds and have both fallen in love with rich businessmen. "I'm pregnant," I whisper and despite my low tone, the entire limo seems to hear me and all eyes dart to me. "What?" I blush.

Cami gives me a reassuring smile. "Congrats," a couple of the girls say.

"Thanks, I just, I just need to get through tonight then go from there."

All the girls smile back at me. "It's all going to work out," Beau says. "Trust me. You're looking at a lot of women who've been in your shoes. Though Jo and Naomi had it a little easier. They just kind of fell in love. Right, Addison?" She turns her head to Addison.

"I met the guys at the end of January last year and I gave birth to twins in early November." She smiles wide. It's obvious by her expression those kids light up her life. I'd heard about it, but you know gossip magazines and their track record.

"I ran away from Tristan after finding out about our dad, because I was pregnant with Jaden and I didn't know how he would handle it."

"Wait a minute?" Jolene cuts in. "Our dad?" She points to me and then back to Cami.

Cami smiles at her, then at me. "You all know Bobby is a dick and has been for years. I found out recently Ireland is my half-sister."

There is a collective gasp.

Cotah chimes in to finish the story. "Derek and I started off as a one week arrangement. As bad as that may sound, I was in Vegas with my

girlfriends, he saw me, decided he had to have me, and he asked me to spend the week with him. That's how I met Cami and Tristan," she smiles at Cami, "and I made some new friends. By the end of the week, Derek wanted more. Afraid of what more meant, I ran away." She laughs. "Ironically, I think we all end up running to Cami in some way. I was here, in Phoenix, when Derek found me a week or so later. We've been together almost two years and have since gotten married and collared." She tacks on with a laugh.

"Some of us are a little less drama filled," Beau says. "But I met Mick because Cami was and is my best friend. We met in college and have been inseparable ever since."

"I was hired by Bobby," Raine adds, "as his assistant. When he died, I stayed on and became Addison's assistant. But she saw something more in me; I then became Addie's assistant for 69 Bottles."

"So you see we've all got a story. We've all got a history that seems to revolve around Cami," Naomi says.

"Naomi and I met Travis and Tyson because of Cami too."

"We're just one big happy family," Cami says. "They're my family and that means they're your family too."

The entire car nods in agreement and I start crying. "Dammit, you guys. You can't pull this shit on me. I'm pregnant and crazy hormonal." They laugh and I join them. Someone hands me a tissue and I clean up as best I can.

"That's how I know this will work out," Cotah says to me. "Because family sticks together. So one way or another, you'll have everything you need. Whether it's with him or with us or both."

"I'm praying for both," Beau chimes in. "I mean, come on, this is like the best romance novel in the world. They're getting their second chance. It has to be true love."

"I like your attitude. Can I borrow it for a while?" I ask Beau and she smiles.

"You already have it." She winks.

My head is spinning from all the talk and information I've learned from the fifteen-minute ride to the bar. These girls are as nuts as I am and for the first time in my life, I actually feel like I truly belong somewhere. Becca has completely ditched me. Not once has she called me since I left all those weeks ago. At least Reese and Dyson called, frequently. I guess that goes to show where I stand in her book. It hurts to think I gave so much of myself to someone who was too selfish to see what she had in front of her.

I shrug it off as we pull in front of Blu. There are dozens of cars in the lot and I'm not surprised I don't see the Tesla or the Nissan. He was still in his condo when we left. Outside, waiting by the doors are two very large men. One of them is the spitting image of Michael Clarke Duncan. The other is smaller, has slightly reddish hair, and a toned body. Not bad looking, if you ask me. The doors to the limo are opened by our driver.

"Let's party," Cami says and I slide out we step toward the entrance of Blu. I fall back with Dacotah and she walks in with me. Then a very tall, very handsome man with his hair tied at the nape of his neck comes over and wraps his arms around Cotah possessively and I smile at her obvious pleasure.

"Master," Cotah whispers. I see Derek stiffen and look at me, I blush. "Raine egged me on, I couldn't help myself," she says by way of explanation. "The entire car now knows you're my Master."

Derek smiles and shakes his head. "Well then." His voice is like melted chocolate, smooth and creamy in a way that makes my insides flutter.

"Master, this is Ireland, she's Cami's sister. Ireland, this is Derek."

"It's a pleasure to meet you, Derek."

"Likewise." His smile is warm, welcoming and inviting in a way I didn't expect when I found out he was Cotah's Master. He takes my hand.

"Dex," Derek says and my eyes follow Derek's to see Raine cringing in the corner, but there is a smirk on her face that tells me she's going to love this. "Kitten?"

"Yes, Master?" Cotah answers so naturally I look away.

"If they know about me, I'm assuming they know about Dex?"

"Yes, Master," she says sheepishly. "And Master Caden."

"Girl, you try my patience," he says, but there is a playful light in his eye that tells me she may get punished for her actions, but he's going to make sure she enjoys it.

"I'm sorry, Master. We were all talking about stuff and Raine asked if the boys came along and it…" she starts rambling, trying to explain things.

Dex joins us. "Our secrets out," Derek tells Dex.

"Oh thank god." Dex smirks then looks at me. "And who's this gorgeous drink of water?"

"Dex Harris," Raine snaps at him and Dex slinks back a little. "That's Cami's sister and you, Master, are with me. Don't you forget it."

"Your ass is mine," he groans and claims her mouth in a way that makes me look away again.

"Ireland," Cami calls for me and I excuse myself and join her. She's standing with Tristan and Mick.

"I knew I'd seen you somewhere before," I tell Mick, while narrowing my eyes. "I just couldn't place it."

He nods. "Are you doing okay?" he asks.

"I'm better, but I'll truly be better when everything settles back to normal and I have Dyson back." I tell him.

He nods. "I am sorry about everything."

"I'm not." I smile at him and wink at Cami. I watch as Mick visibly relaxes.

"Good," he smiles.

I turn to Tristan. "I owe you an apology," I tell him and he raises an eyebrow at me like I've lost my mind.

"For what, exactly?" he says. His voice is playful.

"For making out with my brother-in-law."

It takes a minute for him to remember and he bursts out laughing, bringing Cami, Mick and Beau into his laughter and he wraps his arms around me.

"You're welcome to use me anytime you need."

"Ewww," I breathe in his ear.

"Good point," he snorts. "Welcome home," he says and releases me. His voice is soft, tender and it's like a wave of calm washes over me. The words hold so much meaning, so much promise, and it makes my heart soar. He leans back in, whispering in my ear, "Have you told him?"

I shake my head. "I wanted to, in the letter you gave him last night, but I thought it might be better in person."

"Wise choice."

"I see Cami hasn't told anyone." I wink.

He shakes his head. "She won't for another month or so."

"Yeah, my beans got spilled in the car on the way over. Inadvertently, of course. He has to decide if he wants to take me back, but he also has to decide if he can take both of us back."

Tristan smiles at me. "Oh he will. You'd be amazed at what the idea of a baby can do to someone."

"I hope you're right."

It's true. Dyson and I are barely getting started and now this? Somehow I think I knew all along this was going to happen. It was inevitable. Then when I got to reading through mom's letters, I was wondering if I was going to become her. Alone with a paycheck. That's what scares me the most. So, if he decides he can't take both of us back, then I don't want anything from him. I'll move back into the house in Joplin. It was good to me growing up. It will be good for my child too.

I move around the room, meeting the rest of the people who are here tonight. I meet Beck, whose real name is Aryn, and his Master, Caden. They're quite sweet together and it's heartwarming. Then I move

on to Eric and Calvin, better known in 69 Bottles terms as Mouse and Peacock. They're together too and the way they look at each other tells me they've lived a thousand lives to get where they are today. Then I finally get to meet the infamous Talon Carver and good god, Addison is one lucky as hell woman. Because he's gorgeous in a rough, rocker kind of way, and then you have Kyle who is equally as beautiful, in a clean cut way that makes your insides tingle. The band was setting up the stage outside, intending to jam a little tonight and I'm excited because I get an exclusive, nearly private concert of one of my favorite bands.

After about an hour, everyone moves out back, and the drinks are flowing from the bar back there. I hadn't gotten around to meeting everyone, but I am determined at some point to do just that, and then 69 Bottles starts to play, and all else is lost. I'm enraptured watching them, then pulled onto the dance floor by nearly all the girls with the guys standing around watching us.

When the song ends, the guys kick over to one of my personal faves. I was at the concert in Phoenix when Addison joined them for what I think was the first time. Addison squeals and hops up on stage.

Over the last year or so, they've perfected it, from a single singer to an amazing duet. I'm watching them while most of the girls dance with their guys, and that's when I feel him before I see him.

The hair on the back of my neck stands on end and I slowly turn around.

DYSON
Storm Warning - Hunter Hayes

I'd come in to find the bar empty, but I could hear the music from the front of the building. I sat in the parking lot for a good twenty minutes trying to find the courage to come in here. I wasn't sure what I was going to find when I got inside.

Once I got to the door, there were two guys standing guard. From the car, I'd watched them turn away several people who tried to get in. Tristan had said it was a private party so I wasn't surprised.

When I approach, the shorter of the two at the door greet me, "You must be Dyson."

"I am."

"I'm Rusty, this is Leroy. We're part of Cami and 69 Bottles' security team."

"Ah, gotcha."

Rusty opens up the door for me. "Enjoy your night."

"Thanks."

"Oh, and wait by the door before you go out back, someone wants to talk to you."

"Uh, okay," I tell him and I do as he says. Cami joins me.

"I'm glad you came," she says.

I can't stop myself from asking the thing I need to know most. "Is she here?"

She smiles wide. "She is, she's expecting you. But the guys are gonna help you with that."

She leaves me to stand there alone as the band finishes their song. That's when I hear the familiar chords of a song I've always enjoyed. Everyone starts to shout with excitement and I step into the doorway as Cami joins her husband. The rest of their friends move in with them next and they all start dancing together. As they move, they part the seas of people and there, standing alone with one arm across her chest, the other arm resting on it, but her hand is playing with a stand of her hair.

God, she's so fucking gorgeous.

God, I fucking missed her.

I move into the courtyard, and stand there with my hands in my pockets, willing her to turn around. The guys slow the song, drawing it

out, giving me more time and I smile at Addison. She gives me a small smile back, not wanting to give me away. I stare at Ireland. Praying the connection to her I'm feeling is felt in her too.

I watch as she stiffens, her hand stills in her hair and she slowly starts to turn around. This is it. This is the moment I've been praying for these last several weeks. She's here, I'm here. Either she'll come to me, or she'll walk away. God, please don't let her walk away. I can't take that again.

I walked away ten years ago, and that's ten years we can't get back. I'll be damned if I'm going to let another ten years go by without her in my life. I can't, I won't. It will kill me.

Her eyes meet mine and the pieces all fall in place. The puzzle we've been building for sixteen years is complete. I rub both rocks in my pocket, reminded that she gave me her heart and I will never let it go.

IRELAND
Heartbeat - Carrie Underwood

My heart melts in my chest. He's wearing one of my favorite outfits of his. Black jeans, dress shirt tucked in with a vest and his sleeves rolled to his elbows. His blue-violet eyes are trained on me, his look is impassive. He's not happy or angry. He's just staring blankly and I unfurl my arms from my chest. I give him a wink and spin around, showing off my dress and my hair. When I'm done, I stand there, staring at him for a moment before I bring my hand up, bending my finger, beckoning him closer to me. It takes a beat before his feet start to move in my direction. The impassive face starts to turn into a smile the closer he gets to me.

Once he's standing right in front of me I realize for the first time in my life, I'm unafraid. I'm ready. I'm willing to accept everything he can throw at me and I'm going to do it with open arms.

"Say it," he breathes.

I give him a crooked smile. "Say what?" I play innocent.

"Say my name."

"Dyson," I breathe and his arms wrap tightly around me, holding me to him, lifting me off the ground, spinning me in a circle.

"Say it again."

"I love you, Dyson Cole."

His lips crash into mine. Our friends and my family erupt into cheers around us, but I don't care. I put my arms on his shoulders, clasping my hands behind his head, my eyes boring into his. "Say it," I breathe against his lips.

"I have no idea what you're talking about, tigress."

"Say my name."

"I fucking love you, Ireland Vyolet McKidd."

I slam my lips against his and that's all she wrote. My world spins as it rights itself on the axis it belongs on. Everything falls into place like it was never lost to begin with. Everything about this man is everything I have to have in my life.

"You're irresistible," he says against my lips.

"You're undeniable," I tell him back.

Chapter Thirty-Nine

IRELAND
Love Me Again - John Newman

We stayed at the party a little while longer. We danced, we laughed. Dyson got to meet everyone, and I grew nervous when he was talking to Dex, Derek, and Caden for a little too long.

"They won't convert him, will they?" I whisper to Cotah.

"Yes," she says.

"Oh shit," I giggle. "That could be fun."

Cotah winks at me with a huge smile. "So, happily ever after?"

"Almost." I smile and go up to him, wrapping my arms around his waist, my front to his back, hiding my face from the stare of the men he's talking to. No need to give them any ideas. Maybe one day, but for now, I want my Dyson just the way he is.

He turns in my arms, capturing my face between his hands and bringing my lips toward his. He plants a chaste, gentle kiss against my lips. "Can we go home?" I ask him.

He cocks his head at me, "hmm, where is home?"

"Your condo." I reply.

"Really? Is that so, Ms. McKidd?"

"Yes, it's the only place I want to be," I tell him. It's true, it's honest and it's raw. Exactly who I am. "I'm ready to start my life with you, Mr. Cole."

The most beautiful, gorgeous smile spreads across his lips and his eyes melt into the loving glow I've seen before and it makes my insides quiver. His lips press against mine again, then off, then back on, then back, I giggle and press up on my toes, getting closer to his ear. "I'm dripping wet, and not wearing any panties."

"Good night, guys," he says quickly, ushering me toward the door.

Cami is standing close by and I walk to her. Leaning over, I rest my chin on her shoulder and I wrap my hands around her, my fingers

brushing her stomach. "Thank you for everything."

"That's what sisters are for," she whispers and turns her head, kissing my cheek. Then her voice goes even lower so only I can hear. "Tell him, tonight."

I lower my voice to match, "I will."

"Promise?"

"Promise."

She kisses my cheek again. "Call me tomorrow."

"Ready?" Dyson's impatience gets the better of him.

I release Cami. "On second thought, call me on Sunday," she laughs and Dyson escorts me out of the bar toward his Tesla.

When we get there, he spins me around, pressing me up against it, pinning me with my back to the car and his hands roam up my body. "I don't think we're going to make it home."

His lips claim mine again and I moan into his mouth. I know what he's thinking about. I'm not wearing any panties and it would be so easy. I pull back and tell him, "Ten years ago, you left me in a puddle of tears because my heart was broken, shattered into a million tiny pieces after you took my virginity in a barn." I smile. "The least you can do is celebrate our anniversary in a bed, or up against a wall, or…"

He kisses me again, this time harder, more desperate than any kiss before this one. He rips himself away from me, and he opens the passenger door. "Get in before I bend you over the hood."

"Oh," I squeak and slide onto the leather seat and he walks around the car. Despite his attempts at hiding it, the bulge in his pants is real and I can see it. I lick my lips in anticipation of whatever he has in store for me when we get home.

He slides onto the seat next to me and he slides his fingers between mine. Holding my hand. I look at our joined hands; the current flying between us is unmistakable. God, I missed this. I sigh a happy contented sigh and his eyes meet mine as he starts the car. "When did you get home?" he asks me.

"Cami and I drove back to Phoenix and got here late on Tuesday."

"And you made me wait until tonight to see you?" He cocks an eyebrow before pulling out onto Highway Sixty, headed toward his house.

"I wanted to put us on neutral ground. I was afraid of what would happen if I came to your condo. I didn't want to feel like I was pressuring you," I tell him, and it's the truth.

"I only stayed away because you asked me to. It killed me a little everyday, but I knew if I could give you what you needed, without knowing what that was, someday you would come back. Though my ability to stay away was falling to pieces." His voice is so honest and sincere. "If you hadn't been there tonight, I would have been in Joplin by morning."

I smile at that. "I would have liked that," I tell him. "But, up until Cami showed up, I don't think I would have let you in. She opened my eyes to a lot of things, but most importantly, to what I wasn't seeing when it came to you and us." I sigh. "If she hadn't come to me, I wouldn't have come home yet."

I feel his hand tighten and the atmosphere shifts around us. "I hadn't figured out how to process everything. I was so mad at my mother for what she did, for keeping my father away, for holding out on me, never telling me, but it took a lot of tears, a lot of very trying days and a lot of reading of her old letters before I finally understood. She was never mad at my father for leaving her. She was only ever happy to have me. Dusty and I were all she ever wanted and she had that. She had her all, no matter what the price was and I wouldn't change it. Not for a second." I squeeze his fingers in mine and he relaxes. "The truth is, I honestly don't know how things would have been if I'd had Bobby in my life growing up. But I learned through Cami that everything he did, he did to protect his children. All of them." A tear slides down my face. "Someday I do hope to meet him."

"And what about everything else?" he asks.

"Did you read my letter?"

"I did," he tells me.

"Well, I meant what I said. I didn't run away from you because of Tigress. Please understand that, Dyson. I ran because of everything. Because I was forced to face the reality that my mother lied to me, or rather never admitted anything about my father to me and I had to hear it from someone I'd never even met. Coupled with the fact I'd already felt betrayed by her when she left me out of her will and then finding out that wasn't the only thing I was left out of. I never got to hear the words from her, instead, I had to read them, and I had to know. I'd gone to Vancouver because I wanted to just get away, face something different. Froze my ass off, then Dusty called and his daughter was born, so I ran to Chicago. I stayed there for three days and my brother was going out of his mind because I couldn't and wouldn't tell him what was going on. From there, I drove to Joplin intent on finding the answers I needed and little did I know, the letter the attorney had given me had told me where to find them. But after three weeks of cleaning, painting, doing some refurnishing of the entire house, I made it into my mother's room. It was there I found a box that contained all the answers. It still took me finishing her room before I could bring myself to open anything. I couldn't have done that with you. You would have pushed me to open it before I was ready and I didn't want that."

He gives me a sad smile as he pulls into his garage. "I'm sorry you felt I would have pushed you that way."

"Nothing to be sorry for, Dyson, it was just how I needed to handle things. On my own terms. Being here would have been a constant reminder of what I needed to do, and I couldn't do that to myself. I think it would have destroyed me beyond repair." I smile at him. "But I never stopped caring about you, loving you. God, I was so scared you weren't going to come tonight. I saw you, in your room, looking out the window as the limo drove off."

"You were in the limo?"

I laugh. "I was. I begged you to come tonight."

"Huh," he huffs as he turns off the car. "It wasn't until I saw that limo that I made my decision to go."

I smile at him. "I guess we have a knack for communicating with each other." I laugh again, "Like my other little hint?"

"What hint?" He asks.

I turn toward my left, looking back at the blue Nissan Rogue parked behind his Murano, "That's yours?" he asks with a little excitement.

I nod, the smile doesn't leave my face but I shrug. "Cami's driveway was full."

He snorts. "I figured someone told whoever to park over here. I didn't mind, but I didn't see it 'til I went to get in the Nissan and go to the bar only to realize it wasn't moving."

I snicker, "I know." I wink and move to climb out of the car. His hand still in mine stops me.

"That's my job," he winks and climbs out of the car, coming around to open my door and help me out.

He leads me into the house through the second floor. We pass by Byron's room and he calls, "Welcome back, Ms. McKidd."

I giggle. "Thank you, Byron," I say as Dyson ushers me quickly up the stairs to the living room.

"You want a drink?"

I shake my head, then pull out the clip and the rubber band holding my hair in place and let it fall down around my face. His eyes grow hooded as he watches me. I reach under my arm for the zipper of my dress and slowly slide it down. "Upstairs," he says in a tone I can't ignore, so I kick off my shoes and go running toward the stairs. When I get to the top, I finish with the zipper and my dress falls away from my body and I hear his intake of breath as he takes in my naked backside. "God, I fucking missed you," he breathes and I look at him over my shoulder and beckon him to me once again with the bend of my finger as I walk toward the bed and crawl on top of it, literally, like a cat, until I'm up at the pillows and I lay down on my side, hitching my leg up. Giving him a glimpse of my sex, and one of the tits he loves so much. His eyes darken and narrow. He's scrutinizing my body and this is how I knew I wasn't

going to be able to get away without telling him tonight.

"You're, Jesus, VeeVee, you're glowing." I smile wide at him. "There's something different about you."

I just nod, my voice on vacation as I watch him watching me, mindlessly shedding his clothes as he does, but I don't move, I just watch.

He slides down his jeans and boxer briefs, freeing his cock and my mouth waters. My sex heats and clenches around nothing and I writhe on the bed, begging him to come to me.

He does.

He climbs on the bed, straddling my straightened leg so I can feel his cock against my sex, I shiver. My nipples harden. There's a new kind of ache in them and I know why, but it's not entirely unpleasant, just different.

He brings his lips down to mine, kissing me senseless. It only takes a moment before my mind is swimming and my body is on fire for him. His hand comes to my bent leg, grabbing me behind the knee. He starts to lift it and pulls his kiss from my lips as he unfurls me on the bed. His eyes never leave mine.

His lips press against mine, his cock slides along my sex and he adjusts himself so both his legs are between mine before kissing down my jaw, down my neck, then across my shoulder until he finds a nipple and pulls it into his mouth. The sensation is an overwhelming mix of pain and pleasure and I cry out as his tongue flicks relentlessly against it.

He releases it with a pop before licking, kissing and sucking his way to the other one. The same spike of pain and pleasure ignites anew and my pussy clenches.

I want him inside of me, but I have to give him this chance, allow him the chance to worship my body. His mouth releases my breast and he starts kissing and licking his way down my body. I'm still wearing my belly button ring so he stops and flicks it, tugging on it. Then he starts kissing a perfectly straight line down my stomach, right over our baby and my eyes water, I can't help it. He doesn't know, but it... god, please let

him be okay with this. I will break apart forever if he doesn't.

"VeeVee," he says, his tone accusatory. I find strength to open my eyes and search for his, but they're not looking at mine, they're seeing the faint, yet notable brown line he was just kissing along. "What's this?" he questions. His voice is soft, gentle.

His eyes meet my tear filled ones and I unload. "I'm sorry, I'm so so sorry, I didn't, I was on birth control. I… I was on the shot, but… apparently I was at the end of my shot cycle and…" He comes up my body quickly and puts his face close to mine. Tears are flowing down my face. "I'm sorry. I know we talked about it, but…"

"You're pregnant?" he interrupts my babbling. That soft, velvet filled voice has me nodding instead of answering. "Truly?" I nod again then watch the proudest, smile spread across his face. "Really?" he breathes.

"Really." I find my voice.

"And you're okay with this?" he asks. I nod, then his arms slide under my shoulders and he's burying his head in my hair, in my neck, holding on to me for dear life. "It's too soon. It's… god, VeeVee, truly? This is really happening?"

"Yes, it is," I tell him.

That's when I feel it. The silent shaking of his chest and the gentle huffs of breath as he starts crying into my hair. I wrap my arms and legs around him, holding on to him for dear life. After a moment, he pulls back, his eyes red. "I'm going to make love to you now," he breathes, only releasing me a little so he can adjust himself, and line himself up with my entrance which clenches in anticipation of him sliding home, where I desperately need him.

When he does, my entire world rights itself further. He loves me, I love him. He's accepting our new path. He's making love to me.

He calls me irresistible, I call him undeniable. Together we are irresistibly undeniable. Everything I've ever wanted in my entire life is right here, right now, in my arms and inside my body.

Happy tears streak down my cheeks and he kisses each one of them

away, soaking up my sobs as he makes sweet love to me. My orgasm rushes to the surface faster than I could have ever imagined possible as he gently pushes in and out of me. "Oh god." I throw my head back as my orgasm consumes me. I scream out his name as I topple over the edge. His release follows mine.

As our breathing settles, his eyes stare into mine. "This is what I should have been doing ten years ago," he whispers. "Instead, I was a mess. I hurt you so bad and I realized I shouldn't have, that I was a complete and total dick for what I did. Now look at us."

"I wouldn't have it any other way," I tell him, my statement full of truth and the most brutal honesty I can muster. "Are you sure? Like really sure this is what you want?" He releases me and slides down my body, his face coming to rest below my belly button.

"I always knew I wanted kids, but I only ever wanted them with you. So yes, Ireland, this is what I want." He kisses me gently above my pelvic bone before climbing back over me. "I knew something was different about you." He flicks a tongue across my nipple. "My favorite toy is darker, fuller even."

"I knew the minute you got me naked, you'd know," I tease him.

"I did, but I didn't. I didn't know what to think. I kept thinking it couldn't be possible, but with you, anything is possible," he breathes before claiming my lips and then pulling back again.

"I love you, VeeVee."

"I love you, Dyson."

Chapter Forty

DYSON

Dancing In The Dark - Mat Kearney

Ireland I spent the next month in bed. Okay, not literally, well, maybe a little. I took a hiatus from work, though I still had to work some days, I kept it as short as possible. I couldn't stand to be away from her for more than a couple of hours.

She was always so sick every time she ate, it didn't matter what it was. But we somehow managed to get food in her, and slowly, over the course of the next month, more changes started happening. My favorite part, her tits, got bigger. Yup, I'm a complete and total boob man. I mean, come on, can you blame me?

The beginning of May brought more awesome things for us. I went back to work and so did Ireland, though she didn't come to work for me, well, not full time anyway. She started working for herself, really.

Bold International, Inc. was due for an overhaul of their business practices and who better to help them with that than my VeeVee. She and Cami spent their days discussing Bold business, and I spent my days handling Tigress business.

It was bliss, complete and total bliss, in a way I never pictured for my life.

Yesterday we had the first doctor's appointment where we got to hear the baby's heartbeat and next to Ireland saying my name, that is the most perfect sound in the world. Each day her morning sickness seemed to subside more. It was only about two weeks after I found out that I figured out Ireland wasn't the only pregnant one when Cami kept ignoring wine when we would have them over for dinner and vice versa. Finally, it slipped and I was in on the secret too. It was odd, and yet strangely exciting to have my fiancé and her sister pregnant at the same time.

Oh, did I leave that part out?

Somewhere, in the middle of rolling around in the sheets, I proposed to her and she said yes. Though she refuses to get married while pregnant, I'm still trying to convince her otherwise. She says she wants to be able to get drunk at her wedding, but I gently reminded her that no

matter what, our wedding night wouldn't be our own. We were going to have a little one somewhere to worry about.

By the end of May, we'd had our first ultrasound. Ireland decided she didn't want to know the gender of our baby, but then decided she wanted to have a gender reveal party. She and Cami are in the process of planning that one for some time in July. Tristan and I just let them have their fun. It's quite comical to watch Ireland and Cami together. You'd think they'd grown up together their whole lives because they are like two peas in a pod, constantly giggling and having a good time.

Tristan and I have gotten close, more friends than friendly and I guess it's that soon-to-be-brothers-by-marriage bond forming between us, but I think it goes beyond that.

Dusty, Anna and Emma have been to Phoenix since Ireland's return and Dusty and I slipped right back into our old ways of being dumb boys. I think if Ireland didn't love me as much, she would have left me based on sheer stupidity.

Ireland broke down and explained to Dusty about her father, about the secrets their mom kept and why it was Dusty got all her money. Ireland softened the blow by buying them a gorgeous new house in Chicago, and setting Emma up with her own little trust fund for when she graduated college. I kept telling her she didn't have to do that but she kept throwing my line back at me. If it is in her means to do it, she is going to do it.

She confessed to me one night that she would have never sued me over money from Tigress based on her business plan, but she was happy I had the sense of mind to think about the person who had written it. Even if it hadn't been her, she would have liked to see someone benefit from their hard work. I explained to her that if it had been someone else, I would have bought them out, probably with more money, just 'cause I couldn't imagine being working business partners with someone I don't know or trust. She'd scoffed and teased me about not being able to afford to buy her out and that she'd have taken me to the cleaners. Her ploy backfired when I told her she could have the business if it meant I could spend every day ravishing her body.

By late June, Ireland is feeling on top of the world. Her morning sickness seems to have vanished and she is eating just about everything in sight. I would be concerned, but her energy level rises with her appetite and she is exercising away most of her weight when she and Cami hit a maternity yoga class twice a week. Not only that, but she didn't seem to be gaining any weight, except her little pouch is now visible in most of her clothes, which brings us to now. Standing in the closet while she huffs and puffs over what to wear to Cami's birthday party tonight.

"I feel so bloated," she whines.

"But you look gorgeous." She glares at me.

"Are you going to remember that in about three months when I can barely move?"

I chuckle and wrap my arms around her, my hands resting on top of our little one. "I'll be here to pick you up." I kiss the hollow where her neck and shoulder meet.

"You keep that up and we'll never make it to the party." She spins around in my arms, wrapping her arms around my neck. "I'm okay with that. Then I can just stay naked."

"Mmm, tigress, that sounds amazing, but…" I kiss the tip of her nose. She pouts, I smirk. "But you will hate yourself tomorrow."

She sighs, kissing my jaw before releasing me. "Fine. What do you suggest I wear?" she asks me and I have the perfect outfit, but I was hoping she'd come to a conclusion on her own.

"On the bed," I tell her.

She glares at me. "What did you do?" she accuses.

I put my hands up in surrender. "I don't know what you're talking about."

"Ohh," she growls. "You, you're impossible." She stomps off toward the bedroom, her red hair bouncing, the point it comes to caresses the small of her back and the black boy short panties she's wearing. It's enough to make my already hard cock jump. "Oh my god, Dyson."

410

I still love it when she says my name.

"I can't wear that."

I walk out into the bedroom. "Says who?"

"Says me?" I look at the outfit on the bed. It's a new pair of artfully faded dark denim jeans that flare at the bottom, a new pair of lower, chunk heeled boots, to better help with her balance because I know how much she loves her heels, but even she's afraid to wear them. I paired the jeans with a white, sleeveless top with a deep V in the front. The jeans, though I won't tell her, are maternity, they have elastic in the waist. She's refusing maternity clothes, but the reality is she doesn't have a choice.

She throws her arms around my neck. "I love it." She pulls my lips down to hers and kisses me.

"Good, now get dressed or we're gonna be late," I tell her.

"Help me."

And help her I do.

IRELAND
Secrets - OneRepublic

The last time I walked into Blu, I was hopeful Dyson was going to show up. Tonight, I don't have to hope, I know, because he's walking in holding my hand. Everyone is here. Talon, Addison, Kyle, Dex, Raine, Eric, Calvin, Aryn, Caden, Derek, Cotah, Mick, Beau, Tyson, Jolene, Travis – yes, I drooled, hush, Naomi, Cami – obviously, Tristan, and quite a few other people I don't recognize and that's okay. If I know Cami, I'll know them by the end of the night.

Cotah and I have bonded quite a bit over the last month and a half. We've talked on the phone and become pretty good friends. Addison's even called me a time or two. It was odd at first, but now it's just kind of

normal. I walk over to Cotah and hug her. "My goodness, look at you," she coos.

I never bothered to look in the mirror before we left. I knew I would freak out. "Is it that obvious?"

She giggles, "Yes, but have you seen Cami? Poor girl." Sure enough, I look at Cami and the angle plus lighting is just all kinds of bad for her figure, but she is definitely showing more than I am and I take perverse comfort in that.

Dyson and Derek exchange handshakes and start talking. Cotah leans in and says, "So there's something in the Phoenix water."

I look at her, skeptical. "Are you serious?"

She beams at me and nods. "What are you two talking about?" Derek cuts in, but he's in an obvious playful mood.

"Just about the water in Phoenix, I hear it's pretty effective." I pointedly slide my hand along my belly and wink at Derek.

He gets the same dopey eyed expression Dyson gets every time we talk about the baby as he looks at Cotah. "Yeah, there is, but I like it." Derek kisses his wife who giggles.

I shake my head. "Remind me to keep you away from the water?" Dyson teases.

I lean up and whisper in his ear, "I like being pregnant He blushes a little.

"In that case, have at it." I playfully slap his shoulder.

"One at a time, please. Fiend."

"Only for you, tigress."

I growl at my nickname and his eyes darken. "Keep that up and we will find a dark corner to disappear too."

"Promise." I smirk.

"Fiend."

I laugh then I'm wrapped up in someone's arms. It takes a second before I realize it's Reese. "Hi baby girl."

"Oh my god, what are you doing here?" I narrow my eyes at him. He looks at Dyson, who is looking anywhere but at Reese. "Fiend," I say again and Dyson laughs. I hug Reese again. "Missed your face. How are you?"

He smiles wide. "I'm good." Someone joins us. "You remember Andy?"

"Eep," I squeal and bounce around like an idiot. "Really?" I ask Reese.

He nods. "It's still new but, it's all kinds of awesome." Andy blushes at Reese's words.

"Yay!" I hug both of them.

Cami comes over and asks, "Dyson, can I borrow Ireland for a moment?"

"Absolutely," Dyson says with a kiss to my temple and Cami leads me to where she was talking to some people before.

"Trinity, this is Ireland." I recognize the name from working on Bold plans with Cami.

"It's pleasure to meet you," I tell her, extending my hand to her. We chat for a little bit, about business mostly, before Cami whisks me away.

"I'm going to tell you something," Cami says. "I know you're all hormonal and shit, but promise me you won't freak out."

I blink at her. "I'm not that bad, am I?"

"No, but Trinity is going to flip the fuck out when I finally tell her." She turns to me. "Trinity is Carsen's mom."

I blink at Cami in wonder and confusion. I turn to look at Trinity who is talking to someone else now. God, she's barely ten years older than we are. "He really had a thing for office flings, didn't he?"

"Apparently," she snorts. "But Trinity is good people. She's got an amazing business sense, and despite everything, I can't help liking her. She got the shaft. Out of all of us, she got screwed because she was pregnant when Bobby disappeared. He didn't know until after he came back."

"Oh shit," I say.

"Don't worry, I'm taking care of them. Though she doesn't know that yet. Carsen is only five."

"Well, I'll help."

"Nonsense. It's Bold footing the bill, not me." She winks and off she goes. I'm only alone for a minute before Dyson is wrapping his arms around me and I rest my head on his shoulder.

"What's going on?" he asks.

"That woman, over there talking to Mick?"

"Yeah?"

"That's Carsen's mother," I tell him.

"Oh, oh…the baby brother?" I nod.

"She's also Cami's right hand at Bold. Bobby had a thing for office flings," I share.

Mick joins us and the night continues. I've been introduced to Vinnie and his wife. Vinnie is another one of Cami's people at Bold. At some point I've been told what they do, but it's moot at this point.

About an hour into the evening someone shows up I don't expect to see. "How'd you know about this?"

"Dyson called me," she says with a smile. "I've missed you."

I wrap my arms around Becca who carefully hugs me back. "I've missed you too."

"Come with me," Beau says, grabbing my arm.

"Uh, I'll be right back, I guess." Dyson is laughing but goes back to talking with Becca. I notice someone off in the corner looking at her, checking her out. I don't know who he is, except he's quite familiar is some strange way.

Cami and Cotah are whisked off to the back room with me. "Who's the guy, the one in the corner out there?" I ask Cami in the back room.

Cami looks over her shoulder then back at me. "You don't know who

that is?" She raises an eyebrow at me.

I shake my head. "He looks familiar, but...no."

"That's Bryan Hayes," she smirks.

"The country god?"

Cami laughs. "That's him. He and Addison did that duet and he's made friends with all of us. He's a really nice guy."

I smile. "So I shouldn't be worried about him making eyes at my old roommate?"

She snorts a laugh. "No, not unless you think it's a bad idea."

"For him, yes. For her..." I shrug. I guess that's something we'll have to see about. I turn the girls as Cotah joins Cami and I, "what is going on?" I ask.

"I have no idea," Cami says.

"Cotah?" She's giggling and then the next thing I know, all three of us are being blindfolded.

"How many fingers?" someone asks down the line, satisfied no one can see anything, we're all turned around and led out the door.

DYSON
Love Me Like You Do - Elle Goulding

Ireland disappeared on me, but when I look around, most of the girls, no, all of the girls are gone, including Addison, Beau, Jo and Naomi.

Finally, Jo and Naomi come out of the backroom, but they're carrying something. Cakes? I look a little closer as they set them down on a table and then Raine comes out carrying a third cake. They line them up and I step in closer.

They each have the same lettering on them.

'Baby Hunter, Baby Cole, Baby Michaels'

"Oh shit," I laugh. Tristan and Derek join me. "I guess the girls can't wait any longer," I tease.

"Cotah only found out a week ago, but she knows what's going on because they were all planning it, so hopefully she keeps her mouth shut and doesn't ruin it for the girls."

"Do you know?" Tristan asks Derek.

"No, she wanted to wait, but I slipped the envelope to Beau when we got here a couple days ago. She said she'd take care of it."

There are a bunch of girl squeals coming from the backroom as the three pregnant ones are lead out blindfolded and they line them up behind their cakes. "Come on, dads," Addison says, waving us forward and around the table.

"Take off the blindfolds," Beau orders.

The girls burst out laughing when they see the gender cakes on the table. They are covered in white frosting and the names are all done in green. There's no indication of what's inside. "If your filling is blue, you're having a boy. If your filling is pink, you're having a girl," Addison explains. "Dig in."

"Help me," Ireland says and we both take the knife in her hand and cut down the middle of the cake. "I can't look," she tells me, and I laugh, removing the slice of cake so the group can see it.

"It's a GIRL!" the crowd shouts and Ireland looks down at the cake then back up at me. She's beaming with pride and excitement as she wraps her arms around me to kiss me and my life feels complete.

"My two precious girls." I smile at her, capturing her mouth.

We're interrupted when someone else cuts their cake. "It's a Girl!" Ireland and I both look to see who has cut into their cake. It's Cotah. She looks as excited and shocked as Ireland did a moment ago.

Cami and Tristan are hesitating to give everyone else a chance to have a moment and then they finally cut into their cake. What are the odds

that all three of them would be pregnant with girls? Slim, but the proof is in the cake. Cami and Tristan's second child will be a girl.

"It's the damn water," Derek mutters before claiming Dacotah's lips with his own.

I do the same with Ireland and the group erupts into applause and cat calls.

IRELAND
Lost Stars – Adam Levine

I don't think I wanted to know, but now that I do, I'm glad because, hello, it's a girl.

Dyson and I are met with a bunch of congratulations and hugs from everyone, even the ones I don't know. It is like standing in a receiving line.

When the line draws to a close, Cami comes over and asks Dyson if he is ready for something and I didn't know what they were talking about. Cami looks at me. "There's someone here who wants to meet you," she says, and I'm assuming she's talking about one of her friends and she ushers me onto the back patio.

I turn to Dyson, who's leaving me alone. "Aren't you coming?"

"Not yet, you'll be alright." He gives me a reassuring smile and the door closes behind me and I take a look around. The stage is set up, no doubt we're about to have a party out here, but sitting at a table, the one Becca and I sat at when we were here the night I kneed Dyson, is a man. A rather large one at that. I turn back to the door then back to the man who is standing up and walking toward me. The light catches him just right and I step back against the wall.

"Bobby," I breathe.

"Hi, Ireland."

Tears well in my eyes as I stare at the man who looks a lot like I do. His hair, though short, is naturally curly, but not the red like mine. That I certainly got from my mother's side of the family. "I thought…" I don't finish.

"I'm not really here. At least, not to anyone else's knowledge. But I had to come. I've wanted to meet you for so long."

"I know," I say through tears. "I read the letters."

He smiles and steps a little closer to me, giving me a chance to really look at him in the lights closer to the building. "Good, I'm glad. I'm sorry," he says softly.

"I'm not mad at you," I tell him, and it's true. "I never really was. Well, Cami helped me deal with that part."

"She's a good kid, just like you. I heard you guys met in college?"

I smile and soften a little. "We did. Then I started hanging out here. We actually lived kitty corner from each other without realizing it."

"You guys have very similar tastes. I'm not surprised. She's quite…"

"Tenacious," I finish and he laughs.

"Yeah, she is." He takes a deep breath. "I'm glad you guys have each other."

"How long?"

"Before it's over?" he confirms and I nod.

He shrugs. "I don't know. It's been five years, I don't know if it will ever be over."

I walk toward him. "I hope it's over soon," I tell him before wrapping my arms around him and hugging him.

"Me too, baby girl, me too. I'd like to be a part of your life. Of my grandbaby's life too." His voice is soft and he kisses the top of my head.

"I'd like that."

"I'll try and come back again, soon. But I have to be careful."

"I understand," I tell him. "I don't like it, but I understand." I smile up at him and he kisses my forehead.

"Thank you for forgiving me."

I nod and just like that, he disappears, sliding out a back gate and I wrap my arms around myself, ready to collapse when warm arms wrap around me, holding me up. The scent that is all Dyson consumes me as he picks me up, leading me to a table to sit down with me in his lap. "Please don't cry, princess."

"I didn't realize I missed someone who's never been here before," I tell him, and it's true.

He sweeps the hair from my face. "That's what parents due to us. We miss them like crazy whether we want to or not."

"Do you miss your father?" I've never asked him that question before.

"Parts of him, yes. I miss the parts of him that were good. The parts that, despite his drinking and abusive nature, he couldn't let go of. I miss playing catch with him, things like that. No matter how angry I want to be at him for what he did to us, especially my mother, but the love I know he had for me in there somewhere wins out above all else."

I cry a few more tears then let them dry up. "I have no doubt one day he'll be back," Dyson says to me. "But until then, just remember him from today, remember him from the letters. Just because he wasn't there, doesn't mean he doesn't love you."

"That sounds like someone else I know," I tell him.

"Oh, who would that be?" His eyes light up.

"Oh, I don't know, this cocky-stuck up-expensive suit wearing-asshat who ran into me in the lobby of a building I was desperate to work in."

"Say it," he growls.

"Prickweed?"

He laughs, then sobers. "Say my name."

I grab his face in my hands, staring intently into his eyes. "Irresistibly undeniable."

"Say. My. Name."

"Dyson."

Epilogue

IRELAND
LOVE Song – Sara Bareilles

HARPER Lauren Cole was born October 28th, two days past my due date, and she weighed nine pounds, six ounces. She came out rocking a head of gorgeous red brown hair. Dyson swore up and down she looked just like me, but I think she looked just like Dyson.

She'll turn two tomorrow and we're getting ready for Halloween. All her buddies are coming, but that's a story for another day. She's super excited and doesn't want to sleep so Dyson has her curled on his lap reading Good Night, Moon to her and she's pointing out all the things on the pages and trying to say what they are. There's been one advantage to being a stay at home mom- I get to spend all my time with her, teaching her and helping her. I miss working, but once Harper was born, I couldn't imagine doing anything else with my days. Though Cami and I regularly work on Bold related business and Dyson and I are constantly working on Tigress together, I'm happy with it being just that.

Dyson and I married the following February, after Harper was born. It was the one year anniversary of the day I dumped coffee all over him and he sent me into the bathroom bawling my eyes out. Back then it had been overwhelming given the situation at the time, but now, I wouldn't trade that day for the world. It was the day that brought my long lost love back to me.

Watching him with Harper makes my heart swell impossibly bigger than it already is and he never fails to disappointment when it comes to taking care of her. He seems to have this unspoken rule about coming home from work and it being his time with Harper. I watch as he reads to her, absently playing with her red curls. Her hair is a darker red than my own, but the curl is just like mine.

Days like this, when he's all too eager to cuddle with her and play with her, I enjoy because I'll happily take the break. My hand rubs along my distended belly. Just a couple more weeks and Harper will be a big sister to a little brother. If his flipping and flopping inside of me is any indication, poor Harper is going to have her hands full of little brother before we know it.

"Billionaire business tycoon and founding owner of Bold International, Inc.…" The headline on the television captures my attention and I leave the doorway in favor of the TV in Dyson's office. "Robert Enders was seen walking down the streets of Hollywood today. This news comes after a joint task force between Mexico, ATF, FBI and CIA successfully apprehended and shut down the largest Mexican drug cartel Mexico has ever seen. There was rumored speculation that Robert Enders was involved in the case from twenty-eleven and he was believed to have died in May of that year. Now we're learning he is alive and well and back in Los Angeles."

My phone rings. I pull it from my back pocket. "Cami, is it true?" I ask her as a greeting.

She's crying into the phone. "It's over, Ireland, he's coming home." I put my hand over my mouth and the tears begin to stream down my cheeks. "He's safe, they've released him. He's supposed to be maintaining a low profile and he managed to board a plane before the news caught on. He's here in Phoenix. We're setting him up with someplace he can stay for a while, lay low. He came here because," she sniffles, "because he wants to be near us."

"My god, Cams, he's really coming home? It's really over?"

"It's over, baby sis. It's all over."

I sit down on Dyson's office couch and then I'm hit with a tightness in my abdomen and a hot rush of fluid streaming onto the floor. "Shit."

"What's wrong?" Cami says into the phone.

"Can you and Tristan come over and watch Harper?"

"Of course, but what's wrong?"

I'm cry laughing. "My water just broke."

"TRISTAN!" she shouts into the phone. "We'll be right there."

A new contraction strikes me and I groan, dropping my phone, breathing through it. I wait for it to subside, but I don't move. Not until I hear the door alarm chime and I find strength to stand up. I don't make it to the doorway before I'm hit with yet another contraction. "Shit, these are fast."

As it subsides, I start walking until I get to Harper's door. Harper is asleep on her daddy's chest, and I smile at him. "Please don't panic," I tell him. "Can you put Harper in her bed, please?"

He narrows his eyes, and then he takes in my horrible state of affairs and stands up quickly. "Cami, Tristan and the kids are here, they've got her," I tell him. "Just let her sleep."

His eyes are wild with fear, same as when Harper was born, so why he keeps getting me pregnant is beyond me. He's already talking about a third and fourth and I'm wholly and completely okay with that.

He lays Harper gently in her crib and comes to me just as another contraction hits. "Let's get you cleaned up," he tells me.

"We don't have time. They're not even two minutes apart," I huff.

"Well, okay then, let's get you downstairs."

"Good plan," I tease and he lifts me in his arms. "Dyson," I squeak.

"I got you, princess."

I shake my head and snuggle into him as he carries me downstairs. He sets me down on a dining room chair. Cami and Tristan are there, Jaden is playing on the floor and Sydney is asleep in Tristan's arms. "Harper's out. If you wanna go put her in bed with her." Tristan nods and goes upstairs with Sydney.

Cami looks at me in concern. "Are you alright?"

I give her a pained panicked look. "I'm about to push another one of these out of me. What the hell was I thinking?"

She laughs, "That makes two of us." Her hand slides over her much smaller, less obvious bump.

"We ready?" Dyson asks. He loaded the stuff in the car two days ago, hoping this would happen sooner rather than later, that and I was having Braxton Hicks pretty bad. I think he was a bit paranoid.

"As ready as I'll ever be, Hercules," I laugh and he scoops me up in his arms.

"I love you," he says as he kisses my cheek.

"Just remember that in about a week when I'm exhausted and biting your head off."

"I remember it, every day, every time I look at you."

"You're incorrigible, you know that?"

His lips slant over mine and despite everything going on around me, I know I'll always want him, that I will only ever want him because he is my forever.

"Say it," he teases.

"My forever, my irresistibly undeniable, my Dyson."

THE END

ACKNOWLEDGEMENTS

RACHEL - NO matter how many times I say Thank You in side the cover of a book, it will never be enough, you've been my rock even when I didn't think I needed one. P.S. Thanks for helping me hash out Ireland's History - She really needed to know.

Emily Kidman - GIRL!!! You are a goddess for which there are no better. You keep me sane and if you didn't do that, I'm pretty sure I have a purple padded room reserved for me somewhere. So, Thank You for keeping me out of it. Though purple is pretty.

Mandy and PJ (Rachel) - Thank you for sticking by me through all my crazy! The Editing is Amazing and the Cover is jaw dropping. I LURVE YOU BOTH!!

As always - my Mom and my Son, Thank you for putting up with left overs, pizza, and take-out while I found myself submerged in the world of Ireland and Dyson. Your patience is admirable and I cannot thank you enough for the love and support you show me every single day. Love You Both!

The Wicked Wenches - THANK YOU THANK YOU THANK YOU For showing me that my panic attacks were all worth it. You were the first to read Irresistibly Undeniable and the first to remind me that I haven't lost my touch. Thank You Ladies!!!

Readers - I hope you have enjoyed Ireland and Dyson's story. This one was an emotional roller coaster from start to finish and I'm honored to have you along for the ride!

Love You All!

Zoey

ABOUT THE AUTHOR

BEST SELLING Erotic, Paranormal and Contemporary Romance author Zoey Derrick comes from Glendale, Arizona. Zoey, was a mortgage underwriter by day and is now a romance and erotica novelist full-time. She writes stories as hot as the desert sun itself. It is this passion that drips off of her work, bringing excitement to anyone who enjoys a good and sensual love story.

Not only does she aim to take her readers on an erotic dance that lasts the night, it allows her to empty her mind of stories we all wish were true.

Her stories are hopeful yet true to life, skillfully avoiding melodrama and the unrealistic, bringing her gripping Erotica only closer to the heart of those that dare dipping into it.

The intimacy of her fantasies that she shares with her readers is thrilling and encouraging, climactic yet full of suspense. She is a loving mistress, up for anything, of which any reader is doomed to return to again and again

THIS PLAYLIST

CONSISTS of songs that inspired the specific scenes and chapters of Irresistibly Undeniable, including a few that inspired the story as a whole.

Enjoy!

The Sound of Silence - Disturbed
Fight Song (Acoustic) - Rachel Platten
Blue Ain't Your Color - Keith Urban
Titanium - David Guetta with Sia
Vice - Miranda Lambert
Never Say Never - Tristan Prettyman
Wish You Were Here - Pink Floyd
Wish You Were Here - Avril Lavigne
Go Ahead And Break My Heart - Blake Shelton & Gwen Stefani
I'm On Fire - AWOLNATION
Sweet Home Alabama - Lynyrd Skynyrd
So What - P!nk
I Know You - Skylar Grey
Peter Pan - Kelsea Ballerini
Damn, I Wish I Was Your Lover - Sophie B. Hawkins
Down - Jason Walker
Walk Into This Room - Edward Kowalczyk And Neneh Cherry
When We Were Young - Adele
Walk of Shame - P!nk
Kill A Word - Eric Church
Words - Skylar Grey
Say Something - A Great Big World
Little Did You Know - Alex & Sierra
Feel Again - Onerepublic
Sound of Your Heart (Workout Mix) - Shawn Hook
Don't You Remember - Adele
Leaving On A Jetplane - Caroline Pennell
Learning to Live Again - Garth Brooks
Lego House - Ed Sheeran
Kiss Me - Ed Sheeran
Dangerous Woman - Ariana Grande
Be Still - The Fray
Gonna Make You Love Me - Ryan Adams
First Love - Adele
Skinny Love - Birdy
Lover's Will - Bonnie Raitt
Ride – Chase Rice
I Want Crazy - Hunter Hayes
Already Home - A Great Big World
18th Floor Balcony - Blue October
Pillow Talk - Zayn
Beneath Your Beautiful - Labirinth
Lay Me Down - Sam Smith

I Think I'm In Love - Kat Dahlia
Setting The World On Fire - Kenny Chesney with P!nk
Remedy - Adele
Say It – Flume ft. Tove Lo
Let Me Love You – DJ Snake ft. Justin Bieber
Latch - Sam Smith
Crazy In Love - Beyonce (From Fifty Shades of Grey)
Leave Your Lover - Sam Smith
One and Only - Adele
Back To The Start - Mr. Little Jeans
Slip – Elliot Moss
Still Falling for You - Elle Goulding
Fumbling Toward Ecstasy - Sarah Mclachlan
A Beautiful Mess - Jason Mraz
Like A Wrecking Ball - Eric Church
Fear - Sarah Mclachlan
Stay With Me - Sam Smith
Good Morning Beautiful - Steve Holy
9 to 5 - Emily Ann Roberts
The Only Exception - Paramore
It's Over - Civil Twilight
Gasoline – Halsey
Bad Blood – Taylor Swift
Pay Dearly – Johnnyswim
Pieces – Rob Thomas
'Til Kingdom Come - Coldplay
She is Love – Parachute
Shut Up & Drive - Rihanna
Monster - Eminem
Broken - Seether w/ Amy Lee
It's Not Over – Daughtry
Everything – Lifehouse
Home - Daughtry
Closer - The Chainsmokers w/ Halsey
I Choose You - Sara Bareilles
This Love - Maroon 5
Storm Warning - Hunter Hayes
Heartbeat - Carrie Underwood
Love Me Again - John Newman
Dancing In The Dark - Mat Kearney
Secrets - OneRepublic
Small Bump - Ed Sheeran
Lost Stars - Adam Levine
Love Song - Sara Bareilles

DID YOU KNOW...

That several of the couples you've met in this book have their own stories...

CAMI & TRISTAN

With Cami and Tristan's story you will meet - Beau & Mick, Travis & Naomi and Jolene & Tyson

Finding Love's Wings
Chasing Love's Wings

DEREK & DACOTAH

One Week

ADDISON, TALON, & KYLE

Claiming Addison
Craving Talon
Redeeming Kyle

DEX & RAINE

Taming Dex
Devouring Raine

CALVIN & ERIC (MOUSE & PEACOCK)

Defining Us

ARYN & CADEN

Aryn's Desire
Caden's Command (Coming Soon)

Happy Reading!

www.ingramcontent.com/pod-product-compliance
Lightning Source LLC
Chambersburg PA
CBHW060137260626
47160CB00001B/14